THE SCOTSMAN'S BRIDE

Ballard slipped his arms around Clover's waist and lifted her onto his lap. "I do not believe this position will facilitate your reading," she said even as he draped her arms around his neck.

He started to unbutton the bodice of her gown. "I dinnae feel inclined to be tutored just now, leastwise not in reading and writing."

"Ballard, we are in the kitchen. Anyone could come in and see us."

"Then we had best go somewhere private," he said as he stood up, keeping her in his arms.

"Ballard, 'tis the middle of the day and we have work to do."

"Newlyweds are expected to be, er, distracted."

"Distracted, is it? I call this shirking."

"Well, lass, I intend to have a verra enjoyable shirk afore the noon meal . . ."

Books by Hannah Howell

ONLY FOR YOU
MY VALIANT KNIGHT
UNCONQUERED
WILD ROSES
A TASTE OF FIRE
HIGHLAND DESTINY
HIGHLAND HONOR
HIGHLAND PROMISE
A STOCKINGFUL OF JOY
HIGHLAND VOW
HIGHLAND KNIGHT
HIGHLAND HEARTS
HIGHLAND BRIDE
HIGHLAND ANGEL
HIGHLAND GROOM
HIGHLAND WARRIOR
RECKLESS
HIGHLAND CONQUEROR
HIGHLAND CHAMPION
HIGHLAND LOVER
HIGHLAND VAMPIRE
CONQUEROR'S KISS
HIGHLAND BARBARIAN
BEAUTY AND THE BEAST
HIGHLAND SAVAGE
HIGHLAND THIRST
HIGHLAND WEDDING
HIGHLAND WOLF
SILVER FLAME
HIGHLAND FIRE
NATURE OF THE BEAST
HIGHLAND CAPTIVE
HIGHLAND SINNER
MY LADY CAPTOR
IF HE'S WICKED
WILD CONQUEST
IF HE'S SINFUL
KENTUCKY BRIDE
IF HE'S WILD

Published by Zebra Books

HANNAH HOWELL

KENTUCKY BRIDE

ZEBRA BOOKS
KENSINGTON PUBLISHING CORP.
http://www.kensingtonbooks.com

ZEBRA BOOKS are published by

Kensington Publishing Corp.
119 West 40th Street
New York, NY 10018

All Kensington titles, imprints, and distributed lines are available at special quantity discounts for bulk purchases for sales promotion, premiums, fund-raising, educational, or institutional use.

Special book excerpts or customized printings can also be created to fit specific needs. For details, write or phone the office of the Kensington Special Sales Manager: Attn: Special Sales Department. Kensington Publishing Corp., 119 West 40th Street, New York, NY 10018, Phone: 1-800-221-2647.

Zebra and the Z logo Reg. U.S. Pat. & TM Off.

ISBN-13: 978-1-4201-2972-4
ISBN-10: 1-4201-2972-4

Kentucky Bride was previously published by Avon Books in March 1994.

10 9 8 7 6 5 4 3

Printed in the United States of America

Chapter One

Langleyville, Pennsylvania
April 1794

"You are not getting married?"

"No, Mama, I am not getting married. This is a letter from Thomas in which he ends our engagement. Very politely, of course."

Clover Sherwood sighed and glanced out the small parlor window of their brick town house. It was a beautiful morning, but she was unable to appreciate it. Spring was a time of renewal and hope, but she, her mother, and her young twin brothers were weighted down by scandal and poverty.

Her pale mother, Agnes, almost looked worse than Clover felt. Almost. It was an effort for Clover not to tear at her blond hair—the hair her fiancé had so often admired—but she had no wish to display such unseemly emotion. Her fiancé, Thomas Dillingsworth, a prominent man in Langleyville, had been the rock upon which they had built their hopes and that rock had just crumbled to dust. Clover knew her own personal hurt over being so rudely jilted was insignificant compared to the desperate uncertainty her family now faced, but that did not make it any easier to bear.

"Oh, heavens, what are we going to do?" whispered Agnes.

As her mother covered her face with her dimpled hands and began to weep, Clover bit back a stream of angry words and fought hard to restrain her own tears. The letter she clutched was indisputable proof that Thomas Dillingsworth was not worth even one tear. For all his flowery protestations of love and sweet poetic murmurings about her periwinkle-blue eyes, he had deserted her with no lack of speed the moment her family's troubles began. His love was a complete sham, a fleeting, shallow thing. Clover was determined that her pain would be no less fleeting.

Her mother continued to weep. Clover decided to get her a cup of herbal tea. Since the servants had abandoned them shortly after her father's suicide, she had to go to the kitchens herself, but she did not mind. It would give her a moment alone, and her poor mother time to compose herself. She knew her mother had every right to cry, but Clover was growing heartily sick of misery.

As she set the heavy iron kettle over the kitchen fire, she reflected that there would undoubtedly be a lot of misery yet to come. All the debts her late, desperate father had left behind were now paid off, but the family was totally impoverished. In just two weeks they would be forced to leave their fine brick home. As yet, they had no new place to live. Even finding food to put on the table was becoming a problem, one that was bound to worsen unless their fortunes suddenly improved. Now that Thomas had deserted her, she saw little chance of that.

That dismal picture of the future occupied her thoughts as she took the tea back to her mother. To her relief her mother looked more herself. Strength and calm were what they needed now. There simply had to be something they could do to halt their plummet into utter ruin and destitution, but they would only discover it if they refused to succumb to self-pity.

"Here, Mama, drink this. It will soothe you." After handing her mother the tea, Clover sat in a dainty chair facing the settee upon which Agnes was seated. "We must keep our heads if we are to overcome this trouble."

"Perhaps you should go and speak with Thomas," Agnes said after taking several sips of the aromatic tea.

Thinking that was a poor start to solving their problems, Clover struggled to keep the sharpness from her voice as she replied, "Why should I do that?" She took the letter from the pocket in her pale blue skirt and waved it at her mother. "Thomas's letter is most clear—our engagement is at an end."

"Yes, but there are many reasons why he might have acted so ungentlemanly. He may be regretting his behavior already."

"There is only one reason why he broke our engagement—I no longer possess an attractive dowry." Clover stuffed the letter back into her pocket.

"But he loved you."

"So he said, but 'tis clear that he did not. If he did, he would be here to help us. Instead, he has cut us adrift." She sighed when her mother continued to frown in confusion and disbelief. "Mama, one of the few things I still possess is my pride. I cannot—I will not—grovel before that man."

"Pride sets a poor table." Agnes grimaced, then took a quick drink of tea to still her trembling lips. "Oh, Clover, m'dear, I do not ask you to grovel or beg, just to go and speak with him."

For one solid hour Clover tried to convince her unusually stubborn mother that talking to Thomas was not a wise step, but it was no use. Her mother refused to believe that Thomas's love had been based solely upon the Sherwood wealth. Clover reluctantly agreed to go and talk to Thomas after midday. Nothing else would be accomplished until she did.

Something as simple as a walk through the small yet growing riverside town had become an ordeal, Clover realized before she was even halfway to Thomas's waterfront offices. She resisted the urge to huddle in the folds of her cloak and tip her head so that the brim of her bonnet would hide her face. The few people who did acknowledge her presence seemed embarrassed to do so. She wondered crossly if they feared she would hurl herself to the ground at their feet and plead for money.

It was not as if they had no money to spare either, she thought with a touch of bitterness. Langleyville was perfectly situated to profit from the trade from the young settlements along the Ohio River. Thomas was just one of several men who were making good livings buying trade goods from the frontiersmen and shipping them on to Pittsburgh, Philadelphia, and farther east. Many of the backwoodsmen did not wish to make the longer trips to the larger cities, which ensured Langleyville a steady source of profit. It seemed cruel to Clover that no one in town wished to share that prosperity with her family, who had lost everything.

Just as she was about to enter Thomas's warehouse offices, Clover glanced around her and frowned. The docks were extremely busy and crowded with frontiersmen. She had completely forgotten that spring was the time of year when the backwoodsmen showed up in town in large numbers to trade and to enjoy riotous evenings in the riverside taverns. It was one of the few times she made a point of avoiding the Dillingsworth docks.

She shrugged her slim shoulders and entered Thomas's offices, smiling at his startled clerk, John Thimble. He smiled back, but began to look extremely nervous. It was clear that Thomas's jilting of her was already becoming known.

"Is Thomas in?" she asked quietly, determined to be calm and dignified.

"Er, I am not sure. I will go and look." John hastily disappeared into the inner office, careful to give Clover no clear glimpse of the inside.

She tapped her foot in annoyance. She knew she was likely to receive a polite dismissal. She recognized the signs; they were becoming painfully familiar to her. She decided she was not going to be shunted aside like some beggar. After taking a deep breath, she straightened up to her full four feet, eleven inches and marched into Thomas's office— almost colliding with John, who was hurrying out. A crooked smile touched her lips as she looked around

John and saw Thomas struggling to open a begrimed window.

"Running away, darling?" she asked in a sweet voice. She heard John hurry from the room, firmly shutting the door after him.

"I do not understand why you feel a need to force this awkward confrontation," Thomas said, a hint of sulkiness in his voice.

As she watched him shut the window and move back to his desk, she acknowledged that he was a very handsome young man with his thick golden hair and hazel eyes. She supposed it was not surprising that such a fine-looking, well-to-do man would balk at taking on a poor wife and her dependents, especially since they were now tainted with scandal. It would severely curtail his continuous rise in the world. He could do so much better. Nevertheless, it hurt to think that his feelings for her had been so shallow.

"Actually, Thomas, I am here at my mother's insistence. She is a dear, romantic soul who finds it hard to believe that your avidly declared love for me could vanish so abruptly."

He flushed. "A man has to look to his future."

"And a poor wife with a mother and two young brothers depending on her will not help you at all."

"Well, I am glad that you understand."

"What I understand, Thomas, is that I have spent too many months of my life listening to your sweet lies. I tried to tell my mother that was the way of it, but, as I have said, she is of a romantic turn of mind."

"Are you quite finished?" he said testily as he stood up and grabbed his hat from a rack just behind his chair.

"Ah, you have an appointment, do you?"

"As a matter of fact, I do." He strode to the door and flung it open, then turned back and scowled at her.

"Well, do not let me keep you," she murmured as she walked through the door. "Sarah Marsten always insists upon promptness."

"What makes you think I am going to see Miss Marsten?"

"I read it in your appointment diary. It was open on your desk."

"Do you need a ride home?" he snapped.

"You always did have such nice manners, but, no, I think not. Good day," she said cheerfully and winced when he strode out of the building and slammed the door behind him.

"I am sorry, Miss Sherwood," John murmured, stepping forward.

The sincerity in his pleasant face made Clover smile. "Except for the fact that we had pinned our hopes on him, there is really no call to be sorry. In a way, 'tis best to find out before the wedding that his heartstrings are so firmly tied to his pursestrings."

"Perhaps it is better for you that you will not be his wife."

"What do you mean?"

"Oh, nothing. Just referring to his obvious fickleness," John stuttered, then blushed before he collected himself. "What will you do now, Miss Sherwood?"

"That is going to take a great deal of thought."

"What about your sister, Mrs. Lavington? Could she not help?"

"She could, but she will not. Family loyalty was never one of Alice's strong points."

"Well, if I hear of anything that could be of help, I will be sure to tell you."

"Thank you very much, John. I had best be making my way home."

"You be careful, Miss Sherwood. There is a rough group of men in town today."

Rough men was correct, Clover mused as she left Thomas's offices. Unfortunately, the men were spreading outward from the docks. She was going to have to walk past several knots of them on her way home. Straightening her shoulders and silently cursing her small stature, she started off. Just because the men looked rough did not mean that they were rough, she told herself firmly, not allowing them to frighten her.

She was just about to breathe a sigh of relief, certain that she had passed them all unscathed, when a large bearded man suddenly blocked her path. The three men with him chuckled softly as he grinned at her, revealing a mouthful of blackened and broken teeth. She wrinkled her nose as she caught the strong scent of rum, just one of the unpleasant aromas emanating from his bulk.

"Here now, little darlin', where are you going?" he asked.

"Home," she replied, "if you would be so kind as to remove yourself from my path."

"Feisty little thing, ain't she?" He laughed heartily, as did his three hairy companions.

Clover attempted to sidle around the huge man and suddenly found herself encircled by two burly buckskin-clad arms, then slammed up against a hard chest. The man was even more aromatic than she had first thought. Her concerns about his odor were overridden by the discovery that he was holding her so tight that she could not even attempt to wriggle free. In fact, she was beginning to have trouble breathing. She was able to kick her legs against his, but without any apparent effect on him.

She could not believe that fate could be so cruel. Her family had already been scarred by scandal, suicide, complete ostracization, and dire poverty. It now appeared that her rape was about to be added to that list of woes.

"C'mon, darlin'," her captor said. "You and Big Jim gots some fun to attend to."

"Put me down this minute, you foul-smelling heathen." Her last word ended on a screech as he abruptly tucked her under one massive arm.

After her first shock, Clover tried to pummel him, but the pounding of her small fists against his bulk only made him laugh. Just as she opened her mouth to scream, though she doubted anyone near at hand would come to her aid, he clamped a filthy hand over her mouth. He had barely taken two steps, however, when he suddenly stopped. Clover glanced up and her eyes widened. A hand was tangled in her captor's greasy black hair, pulling his head back, and a very impressive knife was pressed against his thick, dirt-encrusted throat.

"Put the wee lass down, Big Jim," drawled a deep voice.

An instant later Clover found herself sprawled face-down in the dusty road. She turned to sit up and stare at the man who was now holding Big Jim. Slowly the man released Jim. Her rescuer was a lot better dressed than Big Jim and his friends, but she did not need her assailant's recognition of the man to tell her that he too was from the frontier. He had a distinctly uncivilized air about him. Although he had come to her aid, she was not sure that his acquaintance with Big Jim boded well for her.

"Ain't no need to take a knife to me, MacGregor," said Big Jim.

"I am wearing my courting clothes, Big Jim. I wasnae of a mind to risk messing them up by 'discussing' things. Ye all right, little girl?" he asked Clover.

Again she cursed her diminutive size as she stared up at her rescuer. For a reason she could not even begin to understand, it deeply troubled her that this man called MacGregor thought she was a child. Another thing that puzzled her was the way his deep, smooth voice with its attractive Scottish burr made her feel decidedly warm. She hastily gathered the wit to nod. As she reached out to accept the helping hand he extended, she caught sight of a movement to his right.

"Look out, sir!" she warned, then realized the words were unnecessary, for even as she spoke, MacGregor swung, blocking Big Jim's stealthy attack and sending him sprawling in the dirt.

"Weel, I reckon this means that Big Jim wants to dicker," MacGregor said as he slipped out of his black dress coat and handed it to one of two companions that Clover noticed for the first time. "Hold this, Lambert. It seems our old friend Big Jim didnae learn nothing from the whupping I gave him back home."

One of the slender buckskin-clad youths took MacGregor's coat. The other one grinned at her, then neatly grasped her under the arms and set her on her feet next to them. Just like a little child, she thought a bit crossly, before her full attention was taken up by the ensuing fisticuffs. Mr. MacGregor looked too slender to best the hulking Big Jim, and she feared she would be the cause of some serious injury to him.

But Big Jim was quickly shown to be greatly outclassed. Even with her total lack of knowledge about the art of fist-fighting, Clover could see that. Mr. MacGregor was able to neatly avoid any damage to himself and his courting clothes while thoroughly beating Big Jim. The only part of Mr. MacGregor that came into contact with Big Jim was his swift and powerful fists. When Big Jim finally went down and stayed down, his friends hurriedly picked him up and scurried off, shouting curses as they left.

MacGregor returned to where Clover still stood and redonned his fine black coat. He had to be over six feet tall, Clover noticed, lean and possessing a wiry strength. She was a little disconcerted to discover that she only reached his broad chest. When he put one long finger beneath her chin, tilted her face up to his, and smiled at her, she became alarmingly short of breath. His rich green eyes seemed almost startling in his handsome, dark face. She noticed that the fight had not even disarranged the neat queue into which he had forced his thick ebony hair.

"Did he hurt ye, lassie?" he asked.

"No," she managed to reply, her voice barely a hoarse croak, then she frowned. "Unfortunately, I did him no harm either." He laughed, and it was such a rich, free sound that she was compelled to smile. "I thank you for your help, sir."

"Ballard MacGregor," he said as he took her by the elbow and started up the street. "The laddie on your right is my brother Shelton, and next to him is my cousin Lambert Aldritch."

"I am very pleased to make your acquaintance. I am Clover Sherwood."

"Now, I dinnae want ye to be thinking all Kentuckians are like Big Jim Wallis. He isnae much liked back in Pottersville."

She nodded. "Every town has a Big Jim, I fear." Curiosity got the better of her and she added, "You are clearly a Scot, yet Ballard, Shelton, and Lambert are not very Scottish names."

"Our mother was English, an Aldritch like Lambert. She told our father that since she was the one bearing us, she would be the one to name us. Our father gave us a second name to placate our Scottish ancestors. Mine is Alexander and Shelton's is Robert." He winked at her. "Made our names as grand as the rich folk carry."

She smiled fleetingly, then asked, "Where are you going, sir?"

"I am taking ye home, my bonnie wee lassie. Where do ye live?"

"Bolton Street. Do you know where that is?" She knew it was not an area of town the backwoodsmen usually frequented.

"Weel, hellfire, isnae that a quirk, eh? 'Tis exactly where I am headed."

"Do you know someone on Bolton Street?"

"Aye, a Miss Sarah Marsten. I am courting the lass."

"Dang fool," muttered his brother.

"That is enough out of ye, Shelton, my lad." Ballard only briefly glanced at his young brother as they headed up the street.

"Weel, hot damn, Ballard, she isnae the sort of lass to be taking back to Kentucky."

"Then what do ye think she is letting me court her for, eh?"

"How the hell should I ken what the lass is playing at?"

"Then ye can keep your yapping mouth shut."

"I do not know what you need a wife for anyhow," grumbled Lambert in a gentle, cultured English accent.

"I dinnae intend to spend another winter alone," snapped Ballard.

"Ye are nae alone. Ye have us," replied Shelton.

"My dear stupid brother, there are a few things a wife can give me that ye two cannae, and if ye dinnae ken what those things are, weel, I think 'tis time we had us a long talk. But not in front of the wee lassie here."

"Do ye ken this Miss Marsten?" Shelton asked Clover, ignoring his brother's sarcasm.

"Er, not very well. We are neighbors though," Clover replied.

"Of course she doesnae ken Sarah," said Ballard. "They are nae of an age, are they?"

He was right, but Clover decided it was not the time to tell Ballard MacGregor that she was a full year older than the much-sought-after Sarah. She wondered if her obscuring cloak was what kept him from seeing that she was not a child. She also wondered whether it was her place to tell him that Sarah was already entertaining a beau, then decided it was best if she kept quiet. It was not a triangle she wished to set herself in the middle of.

"Here is my home," she said quietly, even as they almost walked past it.

Ballard stopped and smiled at her. "Weel, now, ye best be more careful where ye go. And dinnae go out alone."

Clover found his scolding tone vastly irritating, but she smiled. "Yes, I will, sir. Thank you again." She hesitated, decided there was nothing more to be said, and dashed up the brick steps to the front door.

"A cute wee thing," Ballard murmured as the door shut behind Clover, then he scowled at his companions. "I dinnae need your help to do my courting."

"I was thinking we ought to get to ken this Sarah lass since ye are thinking of marrying her and all," Shelton said.

"Ye will have plenty of time to ken who she is on our way back to Kentucky. Now—git."

As soon as Shelton and Lambert had disappeared down the street, Ballard straightened his coat and headed to Sarah Marsten's house.

"Sarah Marsten," Clover grumbled as she hurried into the kitchen, pausing only to toss her cloak over a padded bench in the front hall. "That witch is just playing with that poor man."

She rushed to make up two glasses of lemonade. The drink was a luxury, but the plan she had suddenly concocted required such an extravagance. She was glad of the need to hurry for it kept her from thinking too hard about her wild scheme. It was so mad that it would undoubtedly crumble beneath any real scrutiny. If she paused, she knew she would grow cautious and hesitant, and she could afford neither.

"What are you going to do with that lemonade?" demanded a young voice. "Mama said we are not allowed to have it any more."

Clover started, whispered a curse, and turned to face her twin brothers, seven-year-old Clayton and Damien. Two more reasons that she could not swerve from her impulsive plan, she thought, then sighed and answered Clayton's question. "Yes, 'tis very precious, but I have a real need for it now. You see, I have a plan and this could help. It is the best hospitality we can offer just now and 'tis very important that I offer the best."

"Are you getting us a new house?" asked Damien.

"Just possibly, dear. Just possibly. I cannot say for certain yet. 'Tis still only a plan."

She picked up the glasses of lemonade and started back toward the front door, the twins following her. Damien opened the door for her, but as she was about to step outside, her mother entered the hallway. Clover groaned. She did not have time for all these interruptions. She was certain that Ballard MacGregor would not be staying at Sarah's very long, and she must be out on the steps when he left the Marsten house.

"Where are you going with that lemonade?" asked her mother.

"She had a plan, Mama," Clayton answered.

"Oh, wonderful." Agnes clapped her hands together. "Then I was right. Thomas did—"

"Thomas did nothing except get angry and rush off. You see, he was nearly late to court Sarah Marsten. Now, Mama, I cannot talk," she said in a gentler tone, for her news about Thomas had clearly shocked

her mother. "I must get back outside. Please, just
trust me. All right?"

"All right, dear," Agnes said. "You do what you feel
you must. Take your cloak." Agnes draped it over
Clover's shoulders.

Clover breathed a sigh of relief and hurried outside. She set down the lemonade, then took off the
cloak, spread it on the step, and she sat down. Considering what she was about to do, it would be best if
Mr. MacGregor could see her face and form clearly.
She felt fairly confident that Ballard Alexander Mac-
Gregor would not place undue importance on the
size of a woman's dowry in his search for a wife.

She looked down at her very slim curves and grimaced. Even there she did not have as much to offer
as Sarah Marsten. A man might easily think she was
too slim, too boyish or childish in form. It would be
mortifying if Mr. MacGregor took another look at
her and still did not realize she was a fully grown
woman. She quickly shook that thought aside. It
would only make her back down, and she could not
afford to do that. Mr. MacGregor might well be her
last hope to save herself and her family.

She prayed that her father could not see what she
had been brought to. He would be eaten up with
guilt. The elder Clayton Sherwood had been tragi-
cally naive, trusting people far too easily. In the end
it had cost him his fortune and then his life. Clover
regretted that he had lacked the strength to pull
himself out of his black despair. When he had put
the bullet into his head he had deserted his family,
left them alone to face whatever misery lay ahead.

For one brief moment she felt the sharpness of re-
newed grief over the loss of her father. He had been

a good man. Their home had been a happy one. She would miss that happiness more than she would ever miss the money and the comforts it had bought.

It made Clover feel somewhat guilty, but she wished her mother were stronger. She loved her mother, thought she was a dear, sweet woman, but Agnes Sherwood had no idea how to take care of herself. Unfortunately, that was exactly what they all so desperately needed to know now. Clover prayed she could solve their difficulties before she began to resent her mother for her dependence on Clover, as she had depended on her husband.

Cursing softly, Clover suddenly wondered if she was any more independent than her mother. After all, she was busily trying to find a man to solve their problems. No, she decided, that was not exactly what she was going to do. She was not looking for a man to take over all her responsibilities, just someone to share them with her. What she sought was a partner, not a master.

Suddenly the heavy, ornately carved door of the Marsten house was flung open. Clover tensed and nervously smoothed the skirt of her blue gown. She tensed even more when an easily recognizable tall, lean man strode out onto the street. Picking up the glasses of lemonade, she quickly stood up, ready to stop his angry retreat. She found herself thinking that Sarah Marsten was an utter fool, then wondered why, for she did not know Ballard MacGregor at all.

"Mr. MacGregor," she called as he marched past her house.

He stopped short and looked at her. "What are ye still doing outside, bonnie Clover?"

A little set back by his easy compliment, she heard

her voice wobble as she asked, "Would you like some lemonade?" She held out the glass.

He hesitated only a moment before stepping up to accept the drink. "Ye were waiting for me."

She sat down again as she nodded and patted the step next to her in a silent invitation. "I thought you might like some refreshment."

"Ye kenned I wouldnae be staying long at Miss Sarah's. Ye kenned that someone else was there, didnae ye," he said as he sat down.

"Yes, I did. I considered saying something earlier, but"—she shrugged—"I could not think how to say it."

He nodded in understanding and took a swallow even as his gaze ran down the length of her form, then quickly back up to her face. He nearly choked on the tart lemonade. Slowly, carefully, he looked her over again. He rested his gaze briefly on her high breasts. They were on the small side but not too small. She had a tiny waist and gently rounded hips. He narrowed his eyes slightly and carefully studied her dainty heart-shaped face. Wide periwinkle-blue eyes with long, dark lashes were set beneath delicately arched brows. A small straight nose led to a slightly full mouth that promised to be very kissable. He looked at her thick blond hair, which was in danger of escaping the neat style she had forced it into.

"Ye are no child," he finally said. "Ye couldnae think of a way to tell me that either, could you?"

"Ah, well, I did not see that it mattered, as ours was to be a momentary meeting."

She covertly watched him as he sipped his drink. He was a very handsome man, she decided. Some people might consider him too tall, too slim, or too dark, but she did not. It did not surprise her at all that Sarah Marsten had initially encouraged his attentions. His finely hewn features and deep, rich voice would attract many a woman. Clover had the feeling he was not fully aware of his good looks, however, or of how easily they could gain him, if not a wife, at least many a liaison. With a little education he could be quite the lothario, she mused.

His face fascinated her. Its lines were so cleanly drawn. A long straight nose cut its way between high-boned cheeks to point to a nicely shaped mouth, the lips not too thin. Gently arched black brows topped his thickly lashed green eyes. He had a strong chin and a wide, intelligent forehead. His thick ebony hair was slowly easing free of its tidy queue. His looks perfectly suited the finery he wore, but she could see that he already found the clothes confining.

There was no denying that his appearance alone was probably responsible for putting her wild idea in her head, that and her desperate need, but she knew that was not all of it. Although she did not know him, she had already seen evidence of several positive aspects of his character in their brief but tumultuous first meeting. Ballard MacGregor could be gallant, rushing to the rescue of a woman he did not know. He could also be violent, yet if Big Jim had not attacked him, he would have been willing to avoid a battle. He could be teasing, sarcastic, and, she thought with an inner smile, he could sulk when he did not get what he wanted.

"Just how old are ye?" he asked abruptly.

"Nineteen," she replied with a little smile.

"Ye certainly are a little bit of a thing, are nae ye?"

"Perhaps you are just oversized."

He grinned. "I am a tall drink of water, but it doesnae change the fact that ye are a wee lass. That fellow I just met, has he been courting Miss Sarah for verra long?"

"Well, he was engaged until this morning, but he could have been calling on her before he was free."

"What happened to the lass he was promised to?"

"She got poor, Mr. MacGregor," she replied, fighting to keep her lingering bitterness out of her voice.

"That's all?"

"Yes. That is all."

"Maybe I should have bounced him around a wee bit like I was feeling inclined to do."

His obvious outrage gave Clover some hope, but she tried not to let it grow too big. A lot of people mouthed admirable principles but balked when the time came to act on them. People were often sincere when they spoke, but reality could wreak havoc with sincerity. Since her family's troubles had begun she had seen that proven time and time again.

At that moment Thomas and Sarah emerged from the Marsten house. Clover watched Ballard's face harden and his eyes narrow as he watched the pair stroll by. She thought that Sarah and Thomas were being irritatingly audacious, even cruelly inconsiderate, to walk past their rejected lovers arm in arm. It was rather like rubbing salt in open wounds. The intensity of Ballard's reaction troubled her a little.

"Did you love her?" she asked with a soft abruptness, her own audacity making her blush.

"I dinnae ken. Did ye love him?" He smiled in response to her look of surprise. "There was a hint of something in your voice when ye spoke of him that told me ye were probably the one he had been promised to."

"I fear I was. I was jilted only this morning. He sent me a letter. I have not had time to get beyond being very angry."

"Aye, I reckon. I am a mite angry myself. I spent a fair bit of silver on these courting clothes."

"You look very fine in them."

"Thank ye, ma'am." His lips twitched as he suppressed a smile.

"You are quite welcome," she replied with extra-ordinary politeness.

He laughed softly, set down his now empty glass, and stood, his careful movements suggesting he was reluctant to leave. "I thank ye kindly for the lemonade, lass, but I really must be on my way."

Clover felt her heart clench with panic. Their meeting was ending far too soon. She had wanted gradually to present her proposition to him. It was her plan to ease slowly into the subject of a wife and matrimony, but he was not going to give her that luxury. She frantically tried to think of what to do next, but panic made her mind go blank.

"Mr. MacGregor," she cried when he started to move away. "Wait a moment, please."

"Ah, ye have finally decided to ask me that question, have ye?"

"How did you know I had something I wanted to ask you?" The shock of having him guess her intentions stole some of her resolution.

"Ah, weel, ye had that air about ye, lass," he replied as he resumed his seat by her side. "Ye are a wee bit tense, as if ye are steadying yourself for something, but when ye didnae say anything—" He shrugged. "I decided ye must have had a change of heart."

"No, I have not changed my mind. In truth, I *cannot* change my mind."

"Weel, then ask me what ye wish. 'Tis always best just to spit these things out."

She felt that he was probably right, but the words were stuck firmly in her throat. Despite the speeches she had hurriedly rehearsed, she could think of nothing to say. The way Ballard sat there watching her with an amiable expression was not making it any easier. There was little doubt in her mind that, unless she presented her plan with the utmost care, he was going to think she was utterly mad, yet no clever words or phrases presented themselves.

The harder she thought, the worse her confusion became, until, in sheer desperation, she blurted out, "Will you marry me, Mr. MacGregor?"

Chapter Two

Ballard blinked, then stared at her blankly for a moment. He noted a little dazedly that her soft ivory skin was now tinted a lovely rose. Finally he shook his head, but that did not dislodge the words he had just heard.

"Did ye just ask me to marry ye?" he asked cautiously, still afraid that he had misheard and would now embarrass himself.

"Yes, I did. Oh, I am dreadfully sorry," she said, her meager courage swiftly waning. "I am doing this all wrong, terribly wrong. I had it all planned out so that I would approach the matter slowly, asking a few questions, then explaining a few things, and only then putting forth my proposition, but you started to leave sooner than I had planned. That put me into such a state of confusion and—" She stared at him, wide-eyed, when he lightly placed one long finger over her full mouth.

"Ye are getting yourself into a dither, lassie. Why dinnae ye just start all over again, doing it just as ye planned to? Ask me your questions, make all your explanations, and we can see how it rides. Weel, what did ye want to ask me?" he prodded gently when she hesitated.

She sighed and nervously smoothed her skirts. "All right. Why did you want to marry Sarah Marsten, aside from the fact that she is very comely?"

"Weel, I did notice that first," he admitted.

"Ye-es, I am certain you did," she drawled.

"Also, she showed some interest and was willing to let me call on her. She is a lady and all, with learning and fine manners. I am a rough mon, I ken it, and I live a rough life, but Kentucky is getting settled. 'Tis a state now and 'tis becoming mighty civilized. I reckon I was looking to take some of that culture back home with me. How did ye feel about that Thomas fellow?" he asked in an abrupt change of subject.

"That can wait. I am not finished with my questions yet."

"Fine then, ye ask me a few more. Then I shall be wanting an answer."

Clover was about to tell him that it was none of his business how she felt about Thomas, but quickly bit back the tart words. It certainly *was* his business if he accepted her proposition. If he was to be her husband, he had every right to know all about her former beau.

"There is only one more question," she said. "Did you think of marriage only when you saw Sarah Marsten or was the thought of marriage already in your head and she just seemed suitable?"

"I was thinking of marriage when I set out from Kentucky. This summer I will see in eight and twenty years. I have got my house built, my land's all cleared and is producing nicely, and the horses I breed are fetching a fair price. So now I am able to set aside some coin and spend it on more than just staying alive. Decided it was past time I had me a family."

"Are there no women in Kentucky to choose from?"

"Few who are nae already married or are old enough. A mon comes out to Kentucky to make a start. He might bring his wife with him, but many come out alone, just as I did. They want to get settled some before they start a family. Aye, there are a few single lasses about my home, but I wasnae of a mind to put my name to them. What about Thomas?"

"Oh, all right, if you must know."

"I must."

"Thomas and I were engaged for three months. Before that we knew each other for nearly a year, and sometime during that year, he became a beau. Two weeks ago my family fell upon hard times rather abruptly. As a result Thomas sent me a letter this morning in which he formally ended our betrothal. I should have anticipated it, for he has assiduously avoided me since my family's troubles began."

"But how do ye feel about that?" He wondered if she was just trying to salvage her pride when she asked him to marry her, thus showing Thomas and the world how quickly she could replace the man.

"I told you—I have not really thought on it. When I begin my explanations, I believe you will understand why. I am angry, very angry. That much I do know." She frowned as she sought the right words. "I feel deeply betrayed, but that comes mostly from the fact that I counted on Thomas and he failed me. I suppose my heart ought to be breaking, yet it does not seem to be. However, the poor thing has suffered so many blows just lately that it may be beyond pain."

"What are these troubles ye keep talking about?" he asked gently, deciding that he would get no better idea of her feelings for Thomas. She seemed to be very confused on the matter.

"It would be best if I started from the beginning. Two weeks ago my father came home, went into his study, and put a pistol to his head."

Ballard cursed softly and took one of her tiny hands in his. "I am powerful sorry, lass."

"Thank you." She found herself briefly speechless, strongly affected by his touch, and nervously cleared her throat. "Well, to continue—we barely had time to see to Papa's burial when the reasons for his suicide became all too clear. My father was a naive, trusting man, and he had put his faith in the wrong people to invest his money. Once he began to lose money, he borrowed in a vain attempt to recoup through other schemes—all dismal failures. The debts he left behind were very large ones. They have been paid, but we have no money left and in two weeks we shall have no home. All that remains to us are our clothes and furniture. All lands, silver, jewelry, and such assets went to pay off those debts."

"And when Thomas heard that he jilted ye."

"That he did. Not only have I lost my dowry, but my brothers and my mother would have become his responsibility as well." She watched Ballard Mac-Gregor closely, for she knew it would be those dependents who would be the biggest impediment to their union.

"Ye have no kin to help ye?"

"Only one," Clover replied slowly as she fixed her

gaze upon a familiar carriage that was coincidentally just now drawing to a halt before the house. "But she will not help. In fact, this is she now. Hello, Alice," she said as her elder sister approached and Ballard stood to greet her.

For the thousandth time Clover wondered how someone as lovely as her sister could be so mean and small. As always, the voluptuous, blond Alice was adorned in the height of fashion, but Clover noticed that her sister's much admired rosebud mouth was beginning to look pinched. Alice's inner self was starting to alter her angelic features.

"Why are you sitting on the stoop like some servant?" Alice demanded.

"I *was* having a pleasant conversation in the afternoon sun with Mr. MacGregor. What are you doing here?"

"I was at Mrs. Langdon's hat shop and saw Thomas strolling through town with Sarah Marsten. Is your engagement to him at an end?"

"Yes. Did you come to commiserate with me?"

Alice ignored that. "I have been expecting it. Well, let me get by."

"Why?" Clover did not move out of the way, determined to find out the reason for her callous sister's visit before allowing her to take one more step.

"Since you obviously will not be moving in with Thomas Dillingsworth, you have no need for all that furniture."

"No? It could provide ample firewood for whatever hovel we may find." Clover dearly wanted to slap her sister's sulky face but held back, not wishing to make an even bigger scene in front of Ballard.

"Do not be so absurd. However, before you do

anything too foolish, I wish to rescue a few pieces. I am particularly interested in that little marble table in Mama's bedchamber. It would look lovely in my sitting room." When Alice tried to ascend the steps, Clover blocked her way. "Would you move?" Alice snapped.

"Take one step closer to that door and you certainly will get that little table—rammed right down your traitorous throat." Clover clenched her hands into tight fists as she continued to fight the nearly overwhelming urge to inflict bodily harm on her sister. "Get out of here, Alice."

"How dare you speak to me like that! I have every right to be here and to take anything I like after our father's miserable failure."

"I would burn every stick of furniture in that house before I would let you get your hands on it."

"Alice! Why have you come here?"

When she heard her mother's voice, Clover silently cursed. She allowed Alice to push past her, then turned to watch her sister greet their mother. There was no doubt in her mind that Alice was about to deliver yet another blow to their mother, and Clover dearly wished she could stop it.

"Really, Mama, you should have heard how Clover spoke to me," Alice complained. "I have come to take some of the furniture off your hands. Now that you will not be going to live with Thomas, you will have no need of so many fine pieces. Clover simply refuses to understand that I have as much right to what little Papa left as anyone else in the family. After all, I am your daughter."

"No." A pale Agnes choked out the word. "No, you are no daughter of mine." She shut the door in her eldest child's face, and the sound of the bolt being shot home echoed with stark clarity in the sudden silence.

"I see," Alice murmured as she turned to face Clover. "So none of you sees fit to understand my position."

"We understand that you want nothing to do with us," Clover answered. "We are simply paying that back in kind."

Alice started down the steps, carefully holding her skirts so they would not brush against Clover. "I suppose I am to get no thanks at all for what I did for Papa."

"You? What did you ever do for Papa?"

"If it was not for me, for my position in what meager society exists in this town, Papa would not have been buried in consecrated ground. I had a word with the preacher."

"Do not wear out your lily-white hand patting yourself on the back, sister dear. You had absolutely nothing to do with that."

"Nonsense. No one believed it was an accident. Why should the preacher go along with a lie unless he was prompted to it by me and my husband John's influence?"

"Because I told him that if he did not do it I would see that everyone in Langleyville learned about his frequent trysts with Mrs. Patterson on Harbor Road."

Alice gaped at Clover in utter horror. "You blackmailed a man of the cloth?"

"I did."

"Well, I am very glad that I shall have no further association with someone who would act so dastardly."

"Not nearly as *dastardly* as kin who turn their back on their own in their time of need."

"I cannot afford such charity. I have a position to uphold in this pathetic town."

"Fine. Go uphold it somewhere else, please. You have hurt Mama for the last time." Clover sighed as she watched Alice hurry into her carriage and ride away. She turned to Ballard and said in a quiet voice, "I am very sorry you had to witness that, Mr. Mac-Gregor."

"It was verra informative," he murmured.

"Perhaps. I apologize again, for I could see that you were uncomfortable."

"Ah, weel, it wasnae the squabble between ye and your sister that caused that. Seeing her ride up reminded me of a time back in Edinburgh."

"If Alice reminded you of something, it was probably not good."

Ballard briefly smiled at her tartness. "Nay, it wasnae. She reminded me of all the ladies I used to watch in Edinburgh. I used to stand for hours on the busiest streets in the city just to watch the people, specifically the wealthy people, and the ladies never failed to hold my attention."

"They can be quite colorful when all decked out in their finery," Clover agreed.

"Aye, that they can be. My family was tossed off our land in the Highlands so that the laird could raise sheep. 'Twas a common practice at that time. So we went to Edinburgh. In that city poverty was not simply a matter of lack of ready coin."

"What do you mean?"

"In the city poverty was a grinding way of life. Surrounded by filth and violence, we had to fight for every crumb of bread, for every one of the too-few jobs. Even as a wee lad I kenned that only a few were able to escape such a life and gain a better one."

"*You* did," she whispered, touched by the plight of that small boy.

"Aye, I was one of the fortunate ones. As a lad in the city, I began to watch those rich folk, envying their fine clothes and cleanliness. The women always looked so far above the squalor all around them, so beautifully untouched and so temptingly close. I had some verra wild, childish fancies about their origins and true natures."

"They did not live up to those fancies, did they?"

"Nay. Once, a carriage stopped near me. I was struck dumb, as if caught by a spell, when a lady stepped out, her silk skirts rustling and the air filled with her perfume. I reached out to her but barely brushed the soft silk of her gown before her escort noticed me. That man struck me so hard that I fell into the street, dazed. I suffered a great many kicks and blows as I scrambled out of the way of the vehicles, horses, and people. It was a rough lesson, but I am a fast learner. There are lines ye dinnae cross. Aye, even in this new land. Unlike in England, across the big pond in America ye can move up with the right amount of coin in your pocket. But until ye have it, ye had best not even try."

His tale made Clover uneasy, for she was of the class that had treated him so poorly. She wondered if he was preparing to tell her a match between them was impossible.

"And now that you have the coin, you mean to try?" she asked.

"I do, and ye will help me. Now, just how many of ye is Alice turning her back on?"

"Myself, my twin brothers Clayton and Damien—who are seven, almost eight—and my mother Agnes."

"I see. Sit back down here, lassie, and let me hear your plans. I have answered your questions and heard your explanations," he continued as they got comfortable on the steps. "I think I can see what your plan is, but it might be best if ye put it to me in your own words."

Clover took a deep breath to restore her calm, but it was only partly successful. "I thought that if you are very eager for a wife, you will be willing to take one even if she has no dowry and brings three dependents with her. I can offer you all that you sought in Sarah Marsten except for her unquestionable beauty."

"Ye are nae ugly, wee Clover," he drawled, and smiled when she blushed.

"Thank you kindly, Mr. MacGregor, but I know full well I am not Sarah Marsten's equal. I do, however, have the same level of learning that she does, perhaps even a bit more. I have had the same kind of upbringing." She frowned slightly. "It may be easier for me to defend my qualifications if you tell me exactly what you are seeking in a wife."

Ballard leaned a little closer, watching her intently as he answered, "I dinnae want a wife who sees me as no more than a means to a roof over her pretty head and food on the table."

"I understand. I know it sounds as if that is all I seek, but although those needs have prompted me to act in this rash manner, 'tis not the whole of it. I believe in marriage, Mr. MacGregor. I would not take such vows lightly. I intend to be as good a wife as I can and make as good a marriage as possible."

"And bairns—babies," he murmured, his gaze settling on her mouth.

"Yes." She swallowed hard. "Babies are a part of marriage, if God wills it so."

He traced the shape of her mouth with his finger and spoke in a soft but firm voice. "I want a woman in my bed, in my kitchen, and at my side in the fields if need be." Ballard watched how her quickening breath made her breasts move. "I dinnae want to be worrying that she will be squawking or sulking because I cannae buy her a new silk dress. I want bairns."

"I am willing to do all of that, Mr. MacGregor." Clover began to find his nearness unsettling, but was unable to pull away.

"Just how engaged were ye to this Thomas fellow?"

"What do you mean? Thomas and I were to be married. That is what *engaged* means."

"Ye said that Thomas stepped out with ye for a year and that ye were engaged to the mon for three months. Ye willnae be presenting me with another dependent in but a few months, will ye?" When she tried to leap to her feet in red-faced outrage, he swiftly grabbed her by the arms and held her still. "Steady on, lass. A lot of engaged couples anticipate their wedding night."

Clover gave up struggling against his firm hold and glared at him. "Thomas was a gentleman. He and I behaved with the utmost decorum. We were always chaperoned. My father was adamant about it. 'Tis most unkind of you to suggest that—"

"Not unkind at all," he interrupted. "'Tisnae often

that a mon gets himself engaged to a lass but does-nae wed her. Many folk consider a betrothal as good as a wedding. Now, if that lad had ye and left ye with a babe growing, I wouldnae be too inclined to slap my name on it. Nay, but I would help ye get the scoundrel to the altar to wed ye as he should." Even as he said the words, he was not sure he meant them, and wondered why.

"Well, Thomas has *not* left me with child." She wriggled in his hold, but it was clear that he was not going to release her. When he began to lower his mouth toward hers, she gasped. "We are out in public, Mr. MacGregor."

"Aye, so? Let these folks see how a Kentuckian does his courting."

Ballard gently pressed his mouth to hers. He teased her lips with his and found her taste very sweet. She clutched at his coat with her dainty hands and trembled slightly as he enfolded her in his arms. Her reaction was encouraging, but he sensed that something was missing. It was a moment before he realized what it was—skill. Clover Sherwood had the warmest, sweetest mouth he had ever had the privilege of tasting, but she had no idea how to use it. He halfway opened one eye and found her staring at him.

"I think that ye and young Thomas were verra weel-behaved indeed," he murmured. "Ye are supposed to close those bonnie blue eyes when ye kiss a mon, wee Clover."

"Oh. We should not be doing this," Clover whispered, but she closed her eyes and made no effort to escape his hold. She was finding his kiss delightful and exhilarating. "Someone might see us."

"A mon ought to be able to kiss the woman who proposes to him."

Before Clover could think of a response to that impertinence, Ballard was kissing her again. The soft heat of his mouth against hers clouded her mind and fired her blood. When he gently pushed his tongue against her lips, however, she came out of her passion-induced stupor enough to push weakly against his broad chest and open her eyes.

"What are you doing?" she asked in a voice so husky she barely recognized it as her own.

"I am trying to kiss ye, lassie. Doesnae old Thomas have any blood in his veins?"

"Of course he does. He is alive, is he not?"

"I reckon. Now, hush and part those bonnie lips."

She knew she ought to refuse, to push him away, but she dutifully parted her lips. A small voice in her head pointed out that if he liked kissing her, then he might well accept her proposal. She also decided that it would not hurt to know whether she liked kissing him. So far she had found it almost alarmingly delightful.

When he gently slipped his tongue between her parted lips and stroked the inside of her mouth, Clover decided that she might well like it far more than was good for her. She became so caught up in the rush of feeling his kiss invoked, it took her a moment to realize that he had ended the kiss. It took her a few more moments to sense that he was staring at her. She felt such a surge of embarrassment that she did not want to look at him.

Ballard studied her upturned face. There was a light flush decorating her ivory cheeks, and he savored the feel of her breasts moving against his chest in a quickened rhythm. Her lips glistened with the moisture of his kiss and were still faintly parted, tempting him. She had a very sweet mouth, and Ballard was convinced that he was the first man to taste that sweetness. That knowledge gave him a feeling he found difficult to describe except to say that it was good.

"Ye can open your eyes now, lassie," he said and caught his breath when she did, for the rich blue was smoky with a lingering passion. He swiftly released her before he answered the invitation he read there. "Weel? What did ye think of your first kiss, wee Clover?"

Clover decided that the man looked far too cocky and she struggled to appear stern and haughty. "My first kiss? Perhaps, Mr. MacGregor, 'tis not my first, but one of hundreds."

"Then ye have some powerful poor kissers in Pennsylvania, lass." He shrugged. "I was just curious."

"Oh, all right then. It was—well—all right."

"Only all right, hmmm? Tsk. That could prove to be a problem, kissing and all being such a big part of being married."

"Is it?"

"Oh, aye, a verra big part." He struggled to keep his amusement well-hidden.

She grimaced and forced herself to be completely honest, for she knew she could not afford to lose the chance to solve so many of her problems. "Well then, it was pleasant."

"Only pleasant?"

"I am developing a strong urge to box your ears, Mr. MacGregor."

He laughed, but his good humor swiftly fled when

he saw his brother and cousin striding toward them. "What are ye doing back here so soon?" he demanded of them.

Shelton ran his hand through his thick black hair and eyed Ballard warily. "We saw Sarah Marsten walking about with some fancy mon and got to puzzling over what had happened to ye."

When Clover saw Ballard glance down the road, then stare intently at his nails, clearly hesitant to reply to his brother's question, she blurted out, "'Tis all my fault. I wished to speak to your brother and delayed him so long that Miss Marsten decided to turn her attentions elsewhere."

"Why should she get herself in a tiff just because Ballard was talking to a little girl?" Shelton's last two words ended in a squeak as he looked Clover over more carefully.

The way Shelton's blue-green gaze was fixed upon her breasts, his eyes wide with shock, made Clover feel uncomfortable. The heat of a blush stung her cheeks, and it increased when Lambert aped Shelton's stare. Clover had the sudden sensation that she was completely exposed to their view, though she successfully quelled the urge to cover herself.

Abruptly noticing what his brother and cousin were doing, Ballard growled, "Do ye two fools want to stop ogling my fiancée?"

Shelton and Lambert both jumped in surprise, then blushed, only to gape suddenly at Ballard. "Your *what?*" they yelped in unison.

Ballard draped his arm around Clover's slim shoulders and said, "My bride."

"What is going on here, Ballard?" demanded Lambert. "You did not even know this girl an hour ago.

Hellfire, cousin, when we left you, you were talking about marrying Sarah Marsten."

"A mon has a perfect right to change his mind."

"Are you sure about this?" Clover whispered to Ballard. "You *do* fully understand all the things I explained to you?"

"Aye, lass," he replied in an equally soft voice, giving his relatives a look that stopped them from edging closer and listening. "Ye have no dowry, no money at all, and ye have two brothers and a mother to care for. Even as ye were telling me all about it, I was pondering your proposal. Now, I got to thinking that ye so badly needing a husband could be a good thing for me. It means ye really want to get hitched and, even though I was willing to spend some time courting me a wife, I wouldnae mind getting right back to Kentucky either. There is also the fact that ye are nae in a position to be particular about where ye must go or what will be there."

"That is quite true, Mr. MacGregor," she admitted, somewhat reluctantly, for she regretted that circumstances had stolen all the romance from her life. "Are you able to take in all four of us?"

"Aye. I have a sizable house, although it isnae quite as grand as this one. When I built it I figured I might as weel build it big. I made the shell and we have been finishing it off slowly. It still needs some work. We can put your brothers in a room together and your ma can have a room to herself. Mind ye, Lambert and Shelton abide there with me."

"If you are willing to accept my three dependents, then I can certainly accept the added work your brother and cousin may cause me. I must be honest, however, Mr. MacGregor. Although I am very good at

sewing, needlepoint, and the like, my cooking skills
are but newly learned and leave much to be desired."

"If ye learned some cooking, then ye will be able to
learn even more. I have been doing the cooking for
the three of us for nearly a dozen years. Reckon even
I can lend ye a hand until ye can manage on your
own."

Even though it was a mutually beneficial arrangement, Clover knew that Ballard was being generous.
Her problems were now solved. She had found a
home and a provider for her family. She should be
happy, and she was in a small way, but she also felt a
sharp pang of sadness over all she was missing because of the need to arrange her future in such a
practical way.

Ballard frowned when he saw a hint of sadness
cloud her expression, despite her lingering smile. In
a quiet, solemn voice, he said, "Now, lassie, just because we are doing this in a commonsense way and
getting married quick doesnae mean I cannae practice a wee bit of courting with ye. We will still be
needing to learn about each other."

"Oh, that is so very nice of you," she whispered,
her voice thin as she fought a sudden urge to cry.

"Here now." He frowned even more at the telltale
glitter of tears in her eyes. "Are ye sure about this
plan?"

"Yes, Mr. MacGregor, I am very sure."

"Weel, there may be other ways to see to the care
of your family." Ballard was surprised to find himself
fervently hoping that Clover did not know of any
other ways.

She shook her head. "I have spent two long weeks
considering all those other ways, even though I

thought Thomas was still the answer to my difficulties. There is very little work to be had, and what there is would never pay enough to keep a roof over our heads. Of course, the barkeep at the Sly Dog Tavern indicated that there were ways for a woman to enhance the meager pay he offered, but I decided against that." She grimaced at the note of bitterness in her voice.

"Of course ye did." Ballard wondered if he had time to go to the Sly Dog Tavern and instruct the proprietor in some good manners.

"Mr. MacGregor, I left that tavern declaring righteously that I would rather die a thousand deaths than sink to such a depth. I was only a few yards from the door, however, when I realized that 'twas not only my life at stake. I began to think about how I would feel if I saw the pinch of hunger in my family's faces. Suddenly I was no longer filled with outrage and no longer so sure that I would never debase myself so. That is the fear that prompts me to approach you so boldly now."

Ballard thought of his past, of the days when he was a callow youth of seventeen who had been left with the care of Shelton and Lambert, boys of only eight and ten. He tightened his arm around Clover's shoulders in sympathetic understanding. "Aye, I understand. When I was little more than a beardless lad myself, I was left with the care of those two." He nodded toward his companions standing a few feet away. "There are a few things I did to keep them fed that I dinnae feel too proud of."

"Are ye going to tell us what is going on here?" Shelton called.

"I am going to marry Miss Clover Sherwood," Ballard replied.

"I see. Now, I dinnae mean any offense to ye, lass, but, hellfire, Ballard, ye didnae even ken the girl until an hour ago. And *then* ye were talking on marrying Sarah Marsten, just like Lambert said."

"I came to this town to get wed. It seems Miss Marsten wasnae as interested as she allowed me to think she was, while Miss Sherwood is verra interested. There willnae be any time wasted either. Miss Sherwood's of a mind to set to it, and so am I. That means we can head back to Kentucky real soon."

Shelton grabbed his brother by the arm and paused to smile apologetically at Clover. "Miss, I am of a strong mind to have me a wee talk with my brother in private. It isnae because of ye personally, truly, but I—"

"That is quite all right," Clover said even as Ballard was tugged away from her side. "I do understand."

"Ye are going to make her feel real insulted," Ballard reprimanded when the three men stopped far enough away from Clover so that they could talk quietly without being overheard.

"I dinnae mean to do that and weel ye ken it," Shelton muttered, then snapped, "Hellfire and damnation, Ballard! Ye cannae expect us *not* to wonder what the devil is going on."

"Fair enough. What is going on is that I have found me a wife, just like I said I would."

"But you do not even know this girl," Lambert protested.

"I ken enough," answered Ballard. "I will have plenty of time to learn the rest later."

"And just how much can you possibly learn after only an hour?"

"Enough, I told ye. She is a lady, just like Sarah is. Clover has all the same learning and polish."

"I dinnae ken what ye want that for," grumbled Shelton.

"Then ye have nae been listening close, brother. We are nae going to be set firm where we are now for the rest of our lives. We are doing fine and we are going to do even better. Aye, until we are equal to the folks who buy our goods. I am *not* talking about turning our backs on where we sprung from, but of learning how to be a part of both worlds. I want us to be able to go to a barn dance with the Mahoneys one day and then to tea with Mr. Potsdam the next and to feel at ease in both places.

"Now, tell the truth, lads, didnae ye feel a might awkward when Mr. Potsdam had us in his fine rich house for a wee drink after we sold him those horses last month?" He smiled when they reluctantly nodded. "Aye, so did I. That was when I got to thinking that having a highborn, refined lady for a wife could help us. She can teach us some of them pretty manners."

"Weel, I reckon I can see the sense of that right enough, but it still isnae a good reason to marry the lass."

"It isnae the only reason, Shelton. Ye have to admit she is a bonnie wee lass. She also has a powerful need of a husband. It seems her pa made some bad investments, lost all their money, and shot himself a fortnight ago." Ballard nodded when Lambert's and Shelton's faces were briefly transformed by shock. "Then her beau up and jilted her because she has no more money. She is also responsible for her two wee brothers and her mother. The only kin she has willnae help and they all have to be out of this house in about two weeks. Aye, that wee lass is in sore need of help."

"I feel powerful sorry for her, Ballard, but are ye sure ye can take on the care of four more folk?"

"I am sure. Aye, it could mean that our progress slows a wee bit, but I will have me a wife and one who chose to wed me, who picked me out because she is in real need. That can only be a good thing."

"I reckon. Weel, she seems a nice enough lass and if ye are *verra* certain—"

"Verra certain, Shelton. I have a real need for a wife." He winked and the two youths laughed. "I also have a real hankering to start my family. Hellfire, most men my age have a bairn or two made already. Aye, the more I think on this, the better I like it."

"Weel, if ye are that sure, I reckon 'tis fine with me," Shelton said, and Lambert nodded.

Clover tensed slightly as the three men moved back toward her. The whole situation was a little mad and it would not surprise her at all if Ballard's kinsmen had been diligently talking him out of it. If they had been, she fervently prayed they had failed.

Ballard stopped in front of her, saw the hint of fear in her eyes, and smiled. "Do ye think I ought to meet your kinfolk before I go and speak to the preacher?"

"Are we still to be married then?" she asked, unable to conceal her relief.

"Aye, lass. Do ye have any objections to it being done quickly?"

"No, none at all. If that is what you wish, then it is all right with me."

"Weel then, do we meet with your kin now or later?"

"Now, I suppose," Clover murmured as she wondered how she was going to break the news to her mother. "Do you need any furniture, Mr. MacGregor?" she asked as she stood and picked up her cloak.

"We dinnae have verra much and that is a fact." He collected their glasses. "We have to be careful what we try to take with us though. It will have to be toted a fair long way, downriver and over some verra poor roads."

"Ah, of course. I had not given that any thought. Will I have time to sell off the pieces you do not want?"

"Ye willnae be giving them to your sister, eh?" He grinned in response to her look of mild disgust.

"I think not." Clover opened the door, silently giving thanks that someone had remembered to unbolt it after Alice had stomped off. "I suppose I will inform dear Alice that the furniture is up for sale if she feels inclined to buy some."

Ballard looked around as Clover led him into the front hall, then signaled that he and the others should follow her. The signs of past wealth were clear to see in the rich warm woods, the remaining pieces of elegant furniture, and even the heavy wallpaper. When the Sherwoods had fallen, they had fallen far. Ballard could not help but wonder how the family would adapt to the life he offered them in Kentucky.

Then he inwardly shrugged. The Sherwoods may have possessed a great deal, but now they had nothing, and he was sure Clover had fully accepted her fate. He was certain she was of a mind to be glad of what he could offer. What he could not even begin to guess, however, was how her mother and little brothers were going to react.

They had all stepped into the front parlor. Ballard studied Clover's family as she introduced everybody. Agnes Sherwood was still very attractive, although plumper than he liked, and her blond hair and smooth complexion showed few signs of age. The twins appeared to be a lively, bright pair of lads, and Ballard felt his qualms about them ease. Copper-haired and blue-eyed, the boys showed a hint of deviltry, but Ballard sensed that they were essentially good boys.

Clover was so filled with dread that she had to clear her throat before she could speak. "Mama, Mr. Mac-Gregor and I have been talking outside all this time."

Agnes frowned a little. "Does this have to do with the plan the boys said you had devised?"

"Yes, Mama." Clover decided it would be best to speak bluntly. "Mr. MacGregor came to Langleyville looking for a wife, and my plan was to get him to choose me. He has. We are to be married as soon as possible, and all of us will travel with him to his home in Kentucky."

Chapter Three

"I never expected her to faint," Clover muttered.

Ballard choked back a laugh as he helped Clover lift her prostrate mother onto the settee. "Ye were a mite blunt, lassie."

"I know, but I could not think of a subtle approach. I am sorry, Mr. MacGregor. It is not you, I am certain of it."

"Lass, since we are soon to be wed, 'twould be best if ye call me Ballard. And, dinnae fret, I dinnae take this personal-like."

Clover suddenly caught the glint of laughter in his eyes and frowned at him. "'Tis *not* funny either."

"Er, nay. Nay, of course it isnae." Ballard slanted a quelling glance at his brother and cousin, who were doing a poor job of concealing their hearty amusement, then looked down at Clover's mother. "Do ye think she will come 'round soon?"

"Yes." Clover stopped lightly patting her mother's cheeks. "She appears to be stirring already." She turned to one of the twins, who was standing at the end of the settee. "Damien, fetch me some brandy and a glass, please." Clover frowned when her brother handed her the crystal decanter, for the level of the amber liquid had gone down a great deal since she had last looked. "What has happened to this?"

Damien shrugged. "Mama says that Alice is turning her into a lush."

Out of the corner of her eye, Clover was sure she saw her mother peek at her. She glanced back at the depleted decanter in her hand and frowned. Undoubtedly her mother had seen her disapproval and decided to pretend she was still deep in the throes of a swoon. Lately there were too many times when her role and her mother's were reversed, when she could hear herself speaking to her mother as if the woman were an errant little girl. Clover suspected her mother noticed as well and was trying to avoid a confrontation on the matter. When her mother chanced a second peek and swiftly grimaced, Clover knew the swoon was about to end. She idly wondered what ploy her mother would use to try to keep her diverted from the matter of the disappearing brandy.

Agnes moaned softly and asked in a weak, unsteady voice, "Kentucky?"

"Yes, Mama," Clover replied. "Kentucky is what I said. Have a sip of brandy. It will restore you—as you know." Clover stressed the last three words and gave her mother a stern look intended to let Agnes know that her little ploy was not working.

As she sat up and took a sip of brandy, Agnes doggedly said, "That is the frontier."

"It has been a state for near to two years now, ma'am," Ballard said.

"There are wild, savage Indians out there," Agnes murmured.

"Weel now, we did have a wee spot of trouble with the Indians, who seemed to object to white folk taking all their land," Ballard drawled. "That business is mostly done with now. 'Tis a fair settled place where I come from."

"This is all so very confusing." Agnes looked at Clover. "You were engaged to Thomas this morning, dear."

"I was *jilted* by Thomas this morning, Mama," Clover corrected.

"Well, you certainly cannot have known this man, this Mr. MacGregor, for very long."

Ballard took his watch from his vest pocket and studied it. "I make it about two." He glanced at Clover, who nodded.

"Two weeks?" Agnes asked.

"No, Mama," Clover replied. "Two hours. Now, I should be very careful with that drink if you plan to swoon again, for that is the only one I intend to give you." She almost smiled when her mother immediately recovered.

"You cannot intend to wed a man you have known for only two hours." Agnes shook her head. "Why, you cannot possibly know anything about him."

"Now, Mama, did you forget that in two short weeks we shall be put out on the street? I have tried and tried to find employment, but I cannot find anything that will pay enough to house and feed all of us adequately. Mr. MacGregor can do both. He came here looking for a wife, and a husband is just what I need."

"But Kentucky is so far away."

"What is there for us here, Mama?" Clover asked in a gentle voice. "Think on this too—Kentucky is far away from all that has happened to us, from all those shadowed memories and hurts that have you reaching for that brandy decanter so often."

Agnes said nothing as she considered Clover's words, then she nodded. "You are quite right, dear. When will you wed?"

Both Clover and her mother looked expectantly at Ballard, who replied, "As soon as we can. I will go speak to the preacher now." He grasped Clover's arm and gently towed her along as he started to leave the room. "Shelton, ye and Lambert can have a wee chat with your new kin. I want a private word with my bride before we set out to find that preacher."

Clover was prepared to ask Ballard what he wanted the minute they reached the front hall, but when she opened her mouth to speak, Ballard pulled her into his arms and lifted her up until their faces were level. She flung her arms around his neck in an unthinking response as her feet left the floor. The closeness of the embrace made her breathless, and it annoyed her a little that Ballard did not appear to be equally affected. He leaned casually against the wall and smiled at her. Clover sent up a swift, silent prayer of thanks that he did not seem to realize the power of his smile. She took a deep breath and fruitlessly tried to stifle the wealth of feeling he was stirring within her.

"Would this discussion not go better if my feet were on the ground?" she asked in a sweet voice.

"I can see that ye are a wee bit pert, loving, but I like a touch of spice in a lass."

"Just what did you wish to speak to me about?" She struggled not to stare at his mouth and wondered why, when he had kissed her only once, she should have developed such a craving for it.

"Weel, now, I am headed out to find us a preacher, wee Clover." As he talked he brushed light, warm kisses over her upturned face. "I intend to have us wedded right as soon as I can. It might even be to-morrow."

"There seems to be no reason to hesitate." Clover barely recognized her own voice, which was oddly soft and throaty.

"None that I can see. However, I can see that ye are a mite innocent and maybe I ought to be giving ye some time to get to ken me as a mon afore we set down to the business of being mon and wife. Truth is, I am not of a mind to do that."

A little of the fog he was creating in her mind cleared away, and she blushed as she realized he was referring to the intimacies married people shared. "Oh. I see." She wondered why the thought of sharing those intimacies with this tall man did not frighten her. "We are to be wed, Ballard. 'Tis probably best to jump right in. We can sort it out as we go along." She hoped she sounded as brave and unconcerned as she was trying to be.

"Maybe ye ought to have a talk with your ma afore ye agree with me."

Although she was unable to subdue her blushes, she spoke calmly. "Mother has already spoken with me. She sat me down for a talk when I became engaged to Thomas."

"I thought that talk usually didnae come until after ye were wed or verra close to it."

"Mother felt I ought to know about such things. Although Thomas and I were never left alone, she wanted me to know if Thomas attempted to take any liberties with me." She tried to look stern, to let him know that she was well-aware that he was taking liberties and that she did not approve.

Ballard grinned and lightly kissed her down-turned mouth. "There is no harm in a wee bit of canoodling between a mon and his betrothed." He grew serious as he recalled what little he knew about what a mother told her daughter. "I am not talking about duty, bonnie Clover. That isnae what will keep me warm when winter's chill is in the air."

"My mother told me that duty is what puts a married couple into the same bed, but after that, 'tis up to them what they make of it." She inwardly cursed the color that kept heating her cheeks, for it clearly amused Ballard.

"Your mother sounds like a verra sensible woman."

"She can be, Ballard." Clover recalled the poor impression her mother had made so far and felt compelled to add, "'Tis just that she has had so very much go wrong these last few weeks. She does not—"

He stopped her words with another brief kiss. "There is no need to make excuses for the woman, punkin. She has had a hard row to hoe just lately. She isnae doing so badly. I reckon the blows have been coming too hard and fast for her to regain her feet. Now, there is just one more thing I must do afore I go and find us a preacher."

"And what is that?"

"This," he murmured, and covered her mouth with his.

Clover felt herself sink into that oddly invigorating fog Ballard so easily pulled her into. When he finally ended the kiss and set her back on her feet, she stared up at him in a daze. He said nothing, just took her by the hand and pulled her along behind him as he strode back into the parlor, where the others were waiting for them. Clover struggled to clear her head.

"Come on, lads," Ballard said to Shelton and Lambert. "We need to be setting out after that preacher, and we have to meet that man about selling our horses,"

"Who are you to meet?" asked Agnes.

"A Mr. Grendall."

"He is said to be a good man, fair and honest. Are you staying at the inn, Mr. MacGregor?" Agnes asked Ballard as he and the boys prepared to leave.

"Aye," Ballard replied.

"Then you must move yourselves out of there and come stay here—all of you. We are allowed to stay in this house for another two weeks. We might as well use the place to its fullest. There is no need for you to throw your money away."

"Thank you, ma'am. We will do just that."

"And Clover and I shall have a nice meal prepared for you when you return."

As soon as the men were gone, Agnes turned to Clover and with a brief, sad smile said, "I think it best if we get busy trying to find some food for that meal."

Ballard and his companions were several yards down the street, striding toward a tiny church near the docks, when Shelton asked, "Are ye still sure about this, Ballard?"

"Aye, and so is the lassie. She needs me, needs someone to help her provide for and protect her family. The lass would do her best on her own, but she cannae care for four. Trust me, Shelton, that need can only do me good. Now, there is one stop we must make afore I find me that preacher."

"What is that?" asked Lambert as he kept pace between Shelton and Ballard.

"Food, cousin," answered Ballard. "Good manners made Mrs. Sherwood offer us a meal, but I would wager my fine courting clothes that they have nae got much to offer us."

Clover stared at the meager collection of vegetables and tiny scraps of ham that lay scattered on the workworn kitchen table and sighed. There was not enough to fill the bellies of three grown men. Even a soup would end up being more water than substance.

Fifteen minutes later, she was still struggling to think of some way to feed seven with what was barely enough for four when there was a sharp rap at the kitchen door. Clover was both curious and wary as she opened the door, for no one had come to the house since her father's death. She stared in surprise at the plump young woman who was standing on the back stoop, and the two youths behind her with their arms full of parcels.

"Miss Clover Sherwood?" the woman asked in a brisk Irish brogue.

"Yes. May I help you?"

"Mr. MacGregor sent us to you." She turned to the two young men. "Put that food on the table there, lads."

Clover watched in confusion as the youths set their parcels down on her table and left. "Ma'am?" she asked as the woman entered the kitchen, hung her cloak and hat on the pegs near the door, and began to unpack the parcels, revealing a mouth-watering assortment of food.

"I am Mrs. O'Toole, a widow, but you can call me Molly. Your fine Mr. MacGregor hired me."

"Hired you?"

"Aye. He said you would be needing time to prepare to be wed and that I should be seeing to the meal." She faced Clover and clasped her hands in front of her crisp white apron. "He also said you might be wanting a few lessons in cooking. If you are of a mind to accept my help, he will even be taking me along with you when you leave for Kentucky." Molly tucked a stray strand of chestnut hair under her starched white mobcap. "Now, miss, afore you answer, I would like to be saying a word or two about that."

Clover was stunned by this gesture of Ballard's, but she fought to keep her full attention on Molly. "Of course. Go right ahead and speak your mind."

"Well, miss, I am of a strong inclination to go to this Kentucky. I have been working long, hard hours at the inn, with blessed little to show for it and no hope of finding meself a new man, even though I be but eight and twenty. I will be fair pleased to be teaching you all I can about kitchen and housekeeping arts, but you got no need to fear that I will be setting firm in your new home, for I will be keeping a keen eye out for a new husband."

"Fair enough, Molly." Clover smiled. "Do we start now, then?"

"That we do."

Until the meal was well under way, Clover stayed with Molly, watching and learning. Then she decided it was time to have her bath. As she and Molly dragged the heavy metal tub into the small pantry just off the kitchen, Agnes and the twins arrived, drawn by the rich aroma of food. Clover introduced everyone as she filled the tub with hot water and sprinkled a little dried lavender on top. She shut the door, shed her clothes, and was just climbing into the tub when her mother slipped into the room. Clover inwardly groaned. Her mother's expression told her that Agnes intended to have a serious talk with her. She was not confident that she was prepared to answer the questions her mother was sure to ask.

Agnes stood next to the tub, folding her hands in front of her, and began, "Dearest, I know you are marrying him to help us, but—"

"Wait, Mama. Yes, I *am* marrying Ballard Mac-Gregor for you and the boys, but I am also doing it for myself." She frowned at the sliver of lavender-scented soap, all that remained of her favorite, and then began to wash.

"For yourself? I fear I do not understand. You have known this Mr. MacGregor for only a few hours. How can you care for him so quickly?"

"Oh, I do not mean that. I am marrying him for my own good as well as for the good of the rest of you. When Papa died and Thomas did not come around, then continued to stay away, I began to doubt the wisdom of relying on him. I went and looked for work, Mama, any work at all. I searched for a new home for us. The more I looked, the more I realized it would be a struggle to provide you and the boys with even one shabby room and one meager meal a day. Even with the fine lace you can make and sell, and with the boys picking up some coin here and there, our prospects were frighteningly dismal."

"It was truly that bad?"

"Yes, it was truly that bad. To be blunt, Mama, the best offer I got was from the owner of the Sly Dog." She nodded when her mother gasped in shock. "It all became too much for me, Mama, as much as I hate to admit that. I felt crippled with the weight of responsibility. Then I met Ballard." She started to wash her hair.

"Just how did you meet him?"

"On my way home from Thomas's offices I was set upon by a brutish frontiersman. Ballard came to my rescue. As he escorted me home I discovered that he was looking for a wife, and courting Sarah Marsten."

"Yet another man courting Sarah? What is it about that woman that they all want?"

"Well, she *is* very pretty, fair and fulsome, and rich. Ballard believed that the interest she showed in him was more sincere than it was. I knew Thomas was there today so I waited for Ballard to leave Sarah's. Then I offered to be his wife. He will get a wife with all the learning and etiquette he thinks he wants, and we will get a home and a provider. It seems a fair deal to me." Clover reached for the bucket of rinse water for her hair.

Agnes stepped forward and picked up the bucket. "I will do that for you. Close your eyes and lean your head back."

Once Clover's hair was rinsed, she watched her thoughtful mother a little warily. Matters would go a great deal more smoothly if her mother accepted the marriage.

"He does appear to be a good man," Agnes murmured.

"He does," agreed Clover as she stepped out of the tub, picked up the large cloth draped over a stool, and began to dry herself. "The bathwater is still hot."

Agnes hesitated only a moment before undressing and stepping into the tub. "He is very good-looking too."

"Yes, and do you know, Mama, I have the strongest feeling he does not know just how handsome he is."

"That can only be for the best. His manner is definitely rough, but he has a lot of gentlemanly qualities."

Clover donned her robe and moved to help her mother wash her hair. "I know it is hard to say for certain, as I have known him for so short a time, but I have already formed a few opinions of his character. I believe he was being quite himself when he was with me, no airs at all. In truth, I do not think he knows how to be otherwise."

"Another good thing. So, what is your judgment of his character?"

"Well, he can fight, yet is willing to avoid it. He has a sense of honor and likes to tease. I know he was furious when he left Sarah's house, but he was able to set his anger aside quickly. He says what he thinks, and for all it makes me blush, I believe I like that. I often had the feeling with Thomas that he was not being fully honest with me. Ballard also made it very clear what he seeks in a wife."

"And what is that?"

"Someone to keep his house, work beside him if need be, not whine if he cannot afford certain fineries, have his babies, and keep his bed warm."

"Blunt, indeed," Agnes murmured as she stepped out of the tub and began to dry off. "No wonder you blush." She sighed. "Well, I suppose he will give you some time to know him before you are truly man and wife."

"No, Mama, he will not." Clover shrugged. "He admits that he ought to, but he is not of a mind to do so."

"Oh dear, oh dear. All those things I told you when you became betrothed to Thomas—well—I mean, I thought you were to be married for love." Agnes continued to frown and shake her head as she took her robe from a hook on the door and put it on. "I simply have no idea what to tell you now."

"I should not worry about it, Mama."

"But, dear, without love—" Agnes faltered, at a loss for words.

"Mama," Clover began, blushing as she confessed, "he has already kissed me."

"Such a bold man."

"Well, he said a man ought to be able to kiss the woman who has proposed to him." Clover could not repress a smile as she recalled his teasing remark.

"Oh, my saints, do you think he means to remember that?"

"I suspect it is not a thing a man easily forgets."

Agnes smiled faintly, then grew serious again. "I do not speak of mere kisses, Clover."

"I know, Mama. I will be honest, for I wish to ease your mind." Clover started to fuss about, tidying up the room, so that she did not have to look her mother in the eye and embarrass them both. "I like his kisses, Mama. Very much. Truth to tell, I find it hard to think when he puts his arms around me and smiles at me. I want to keep on kissing him. I know it is not love. How can it be after so short an acquaintance? Yet I feel no fear of becoming his wife in all ways. In fact, I have the strongest feeling that I shall enjoy it." She shook her head. "I am explaining myself badly." She gave a start of surprise when she felt her mother's hand on her arm.

"I know exactly what you mean, Clover. Of course, I felt it for your father." A brief spasm of grief darkened Agnes's face. "That was love. But I am speaking of another man." Agnes blushed and gave a nervous giggle. "When your papa was courting me, I met this other man—Colin—and, oh, such a man he was. His voice, his smile, each and every aspect of his character and form sent me into a veritable swoon."

"What happened?"

"Well, your mother is not as flighty as she often appears to be. I knew it was his beauty and the often careless desires of youth that had my feckless heart pounding. Fortunately, Colin was a good man and not one to force a girl to change her mind." Agnes blushed again. "I knew then, and still do, that it would have been a glorious experience to have him as my lover, but I truly loved your father. I could not risk the future I knew I could have with him for something that might not last, that might be a fleeting if heady thing."

"Do you think that is all I suffer from now? A fleeting infatuation? Simply youth and hot blood?"

"At this moment—quite probably. But, unlike myself and Colin, you and Mr. MacGregor are planning a future. You will soon be married and are prepared to make a home and a family. This feeling he stirs inside you can only be good."

"I am glad you think so."

"You do not?"

"It is just that I begin to wonder if I am not merely selling myself, if I am little better than a whore."

"No, child. You are marrying the man for the same reasons that many a woman takes a husband. Your needs are simply more pressing. I am sorry that I cannot be of more help to you. I was one of a very fortunate few because there was love between your father and me, but I would have been married sooner or later in any case, with or without love. No, marrying Ballard MacGregor does not make you a whore."

"I should have liked to have found what you and Papa shared. I thought I had it with Thomas."

"You may yet find love, dear."

"Do you truly think so?"

"Of course. You and Mr. MacGregor will be man and wife, and if he speaks true, he is most serious about marriage. He seems to want all that marriage and family can give a man. Since you will both be working hard toward the same goal, there is good reason to hope for something good. If not a deep, true love, then comfort, security, and compatibility. Do not frown, child. Those things are very valuable, as valuable as love. I was fortunate to get most of them as well as love from your father."

"Yes, I see how fortunate you were."

"And you may yet find that you have the same good luck. I too feel that Mr. MacGregor is an honorable man. Now, let us go and have some tea."

Agnes made no further comment about Ballard and the upcoming marriage until she and Clover were comfortably seated in the sitting room of the master suite and Molly had served them tea. Molly also brought word that Ballard had sent a message—he had found a preacher, and their marriage was arranged to take place at four the next afternoon. As she sipped the strong, fragrant tea and savored a freshly baked scone smothered in butter, Clover sensed that her mother had more to say. She realized that she did not mind discussing the matter. It was helping her clear up a few of her own doubts and concerns.

"There is one small thing that still troubles me," Agnes finally said, a hint of reluctance in her voice.

"And what is that, Mama?" Clover wiped her fingers on a fine linen napkin and wondered if it too would have to be sold.

"You and Mr. MacGregor are from two very different worlds."

"Do you really think that matters?"

"It can, Clover. Differences in taste, in learning, even in manners can prove to be a trial in marriage."

"Ballard claims that that is the very difference he seeks."

"Does he?"

"Yes. He told me that his circumstances are improving and he believes they will continue to do so. He spoke of how Kentucky is becoming more settled and civilized every day, that it is no longer the haven of trappers and rough backwoodsmen. Since he intends to continue to prosper, he wants what I can bring to him and to our family. He wants the learning and etiquette that we are taught from the cradle. Ballard sees it all as part of the advancement he is seeking."

"It is a wise man who recognizes such a thing and seeks it out. Well, there is another worry laid to rest."

"Did you have a lot, Mama?" Clover asked helping herself to another scone.

"What mother would not when her daughter

announces that she is to marry a man she has known for only a few hours?" Agnes buttered another scone, hesitated, then spread a thin layer of apple preserves on it.

Clover smiled crookedly. "I have a few qualms myself."

"As you should at such a time. Marriage is forever, or it should be. That thought, even when love burns strongly, can be frightening. To commit oneself to a situation, to another person, for a lifetime is not easy."

The mere thought of it had Clover taking a bracing sip of tea. *Forever* and *lifetime* were two words that had been echoing intermittently in her head since she had first proposed to Ballard. As she left her mother's room and went to her own to dress, she wondered if Ballard was also wrestling with those weighty words.

Ballard grimaced as he hurried out of the small riverside church, his brother and cousin right behind him. The aging Reverend Denning had been inclined to pontificate on the dangers of a hasty marriage, which Ballard had found increasingly irritating. The way Shelton and Lambert had nodded their agreement to a lot of what the reverend said had only further soured Ballard's mood.

"Ballard," Shelton began.

"Not now, brother. That reverend droned on so long I am late for my meeting with Mr. Grendall."

"We ought to talk."

"Right now I have been talked near to death." Ballard pointed at a neat, white inn that stood just beyond the less reputable dock area. "I am going in there to try and convince Mr. Grendall he wants to pay good money for our horses. I will pay our room bill while I am there. Ye can come with me or find something else to do."

Shelton grimaced. "I think we will go have us an ale at a less proper tavern. Do ye want us to take our belongings over to the Sherwoods?"

"Nay. I will have the innkeeper's lads do that."

"Fine. We will meet ye back at the Sherwoods come mealtime," Shelton called as he and Lambert turned and headed toward the waterfront.

As Ballard entered the inn, he met the plump, graying Grendall preparing to leave. He heartily apologized to the man, explained his tardiness, and soon had the man seated at a table sharing some ale. Across the way, Ballard noticed Thomas Dillingsworth deep in conversation with a man at a small table near the massive fireplace, but when the man paid him no heed, Ballard turned his full attention back to Grendall. They discussed prices as they drank, Ballard praising the quality of the stallion and two mares he had to offer, and Mr. Grendall playing the part of a man of severely limited funds.

Once they had finished their drinks, Ballard escorted Mr. Grendall out to the inn's stables where he had quartered his horses. He left Grendall standing there and went to get his stallion. As he led the horse out, Ballard saw the look on Mr. Grendall's round face and knew he would get his full asking price after the appropriate amount of haggling.

Just as he and Mr. Grendall neared an agreement, Ballard saw Thomas approaching. He tensed. Thomas stared at the black stallion for a long moment before coming closer. He greeted Mr. Grendall with cool politeness but just nodded at Ballard. The gesture was so short as to be rude, and Ballard felt his insides knot with anger over the insult.

Thomas ran his hand over the stallion's taut, strong flank. "Grendall, my man, I had no idea you had such fine horseflesh in your stables."

"He is not in my stables yet. Mr. MacGregor and I are just now discussing my purchasing the beast."

Ballard gave Thomas a cold smile when the man finally looked at him. He realized he neither liked nor trusted Thomas Dillingsworth, and not simply because of the way the man had treated Clover. Something about Thomas made him uneasy, put him immediately on his guard.

"So this stallion is for sale, is he?" Thomas abruptly offered a price twice what Mr. Grendall had offered. "I can have the coin for you within the hour."

It was easy to see from the look on Grendall's face that he could not meet such a price. Although the money was tempting, Ballard had no intention of accepting, partly out of perversity and partly because his instincts told him it would be an ill-advised move. The stallion kept shifting away from Thomas's touch, and Ballard knew he should not ignore the animal's instincts any more than he should ignore his own.

"I cannae accept, Dillingsworth," Ballard said, carefully noting the fury that hardened Thomas's features. "Me and Mr. Grendall have as good as shaken on the deal."

"He cannot match my offer."

"True. And I willnae ask him to. I posted my intention to sell these beasts when I came to town three days ago. Ye should have approached me sooner."

"I see." Thomas stepped away from the stallion, which immediately ceased its restless movements. "This is not to my liking. I must advise you that it is not good business to refuse my generous offer."

"'Tisnae good business to back out of a deal just because another mon waves a wee bit more coin in my face."

"You may soon change your mind."

Thomas turned and disappeared into the stables. Before Ballard could remark on the brief but tense confrontation, Thomas emerged driving his carriage. Ballard and Grendall had to scramble out of the way or be run down as Thomas slapped his team into a gallop and sped toward them.

"Are ye all right, sir?" Ballard asked Grendall as the older man brushed off the dust kicked up by Thomas's carriage. "The mon is mad," he grumbled as he soothed the agitated stallion.

"There is a chance that he is," murmured Grendall.

Ballard frowned. "I thought he was one of the leading citizens of the town."

Mr. Grendall smiled faintly. "He is. His father helped build this town and Thomas inherited a goodly part of the waterfront. Such power makes most people overlook his, er, quirks. When Thomas says he is displeased, one should take note. It has been that way since he was a small boy."

"Yet ye do nothing?"

"As I said, he still has power, although his wealth is somewhat in doubt now. Bad investments, you see. 'Tis why he is ready to wed Sarah Marsten, despite the fact that everyone save her doting if neglectful parents knows she is little better than a whore. The man has a vicious streak in him, Mr. MacGregor. Perhaps you should rethink his offer."

"Nay. I was ready to accept yours and I willnae change my mind. I dinnae intend to linger in this town long. I doubt Dillingsworth can do me much harm."

The look on Grendall's face told Ballard he was being naive, but the older man said no more. Ballard accepted Grendall's offer for the stallion and the two mares. They arranged for Ballard to bring the horses to Grendall's home on the west side of town in the morning, when he would collect his money. As Ballard returned his animals to the stables, he wondered just how much he should worry about Thomas's veiled threats.

Clover started toward the kitchen, intending to tell Molly that she should serve the meal now and not wait any longer for the men. She was only a few steps from the kitchen door when the front door slammed open. Shelton and Lambert stumbled in and, as she neared them, she caught the strong scent of ale. Right behind them came Ballard, who appeared to be sober but was covered in dust and mud, his fine courting clothes badly disarranged.

"Sorry we are a wee bit late, lass," Ballard said as he tossed his hat on a hall table, "but I had to go and collect these two fools. Ye can serve up the food now."

He started to usher his unsteady companions toward the dining room, but Clover quickly blocked him. "Oh no, you cannot." She almost smiled at the startled looks on their faces. "You will go and clean up first. Your things arrived from the inn a short while ago."

"Weel, I reckon we can wash our hands."

"You need to wash a great deal more than your hands, Mr. MacGregor, if you intend to sit at my table."

"But the food will be cold," protested Shelton as he ineptly tried to straighten his disordered clothes.

"If Molly has managed to keep it edible this long, she can do so for a little while longer." Clover saw her brothers peeking out between the parlor doors. "Boys, you can show the gentlemen their rooms and where they can wash." She shook her head as the boys led the men away, then she hurried to the kitchen to speak to Molly.

"Why didnae ye stand your ground, Ballard?" grumbled Shelton as he made his unsteady way up the stairs.

"Why? Ye stink like a dockside tavern and I smell like horses. I wouldnae want to sit to table with us either. A little water willnae kill us. This is one of them lessons in manners we need to learn."

"I think I prefer ignorance and a full belly."

Ballard laughed. "Hurry up, lads. From what I can smell, there is a fine meal awaiting us."

Clover was just helping Molly set the last dishes on the table when Ballard, Shelton, and Lambert entered the dining room. She hid a smile as she noted their clean homespun shirts and breeches, and their still damp hair. For a brief moment after she had ordered them to wash and change, she had worried that she had overstepped herself, but it had been a fleeting concern. Ballard said he wanted to learn good manners and the way of the gentry. There was no need to wait until they were married to start those lessons.

As they ate Clover took careful note of their table manners. They were not as unschooled as she had feared, but there was certainly a lot of room for improvement. Ballard, Shelton, and Lambert clearly had only one concern at mealtime, and that was to get as much food as possible into their mouths as fast as they could. When Ballard glanced up at her, she just smiled, however. Their first meal together was not the time to start their lessons in genteel dining.

A little hesitantly Ballard returned Clover's smile. It took only one glance around at Clover and her family to make him uncomfortably aware that his table manners were all wrong. He watched Clover more carefully, imitating her actions, but knew he looked awkward. It pinched at his vanity and he fought his wounded pride. All he needed was a little education, which Clover would provide.

After the meal was over, as they gathered in the parlor for an after-dinner drink, Ballard felt his wavering confidence return. Their sobriety restored, it was not long before Shelton and Lambert slipped away to tour the waterfront for drinks and excitement. Soon afterward, Agnes ushered the twins off to bed, her intention of giving him some time alone with Clover so clear that Ballard had to smile. He finished off his brandy and moved to sit next to Clover on the settee, grinning at the nervous glance she gave him as he draped his arm around her shoulders.

"Weel, lass, ye still have time to change your mind." He nuzzled her thick, sweet-smelling hair and felt a light tremor pass through her slim frame.

"I do not want to change my mind." She turned to look at him. "I *cannot*."

He lightly traced the shape of her face with his fingertips. "I willnae argue with ye, lass, for I am getting what I want. Now, your mother left us alone to learn to ken each other a wee bit better."

"I do not believe she intended you to try and *ken* me this well, sir." Clover made what even she recognized as a weak attempt to wriggle out of his hold.

"A kiss between betrothed folk isnae such a bad thing."

"It is not very proper either."

"Ah, wee Clover, there are times when ye are *too* proper. I shall have to break ye of that."

Before Clover could respond, Ballard kissed her. Clover gave only one fleeting thought to pushing him away before she wrapped her arms around his neck. She savored the taste of him as he stroked the inside of her mouth with his tongue. For a while she immersed herself in the pleasure his kiss inspired. Then she felt his hands slide up the sides of her breasts. The way he moved his thumbs against the swells made her shiver with desire, but it also shocked her back to sensibility. She abruptly moved out of his hold and stumbled to her feet.

"I believe we have been alone long enough, Mr. MacGregor," she said, inwardly cursing her breathlessness.

Ballard reached for her, laughing when she jumped back. "*I* was thinking we had just begun."

"You can think again. Now, although it has been a very pleasant evening," she said as she backed toward the door, "I believe I must retire for the night. 'Twill be a very busy day tomorrow. Good night, Mr. Mac-Gregor."

"Sleep weel, lassie," he called after her as she hurried out the door. "Ye willnae be able to run away on the morrow."

She shut the door on his soft chuckles and muttered what few curses she knew as she went up the stairs. The man had a disturbing ability to turn her mind to mush. Clover sighed as she entered her room. Marriage to Mr. Ballard MacGregor might prove to be an even mix of delight and aggravation.

Chapter Four

"Are ye sure ye are doing the right thing, Ballard?" Shelton asked as he, Lambert, and Ballard stepped out of a carriage in front of the Sherwood home.

Ballard cursed, then muttered an apology to the Reverend Denning as he helped the elderly preacher out of the carriage. He had been so busy all morning delivering his horses to Mr. Grendall that he had barely had time to prepare for his own wedding. It had been advantageous in that he had had little time to ponder the big step he was about to take. Now he wished he had set aside a few moments to have a serious talk with his young relatives.

"Shelton, ye have been asking me that almost continuously since I announced my marriage plans," he answered.

"Needs to be asked," muttered Lambert.

"Marriage is a serious step," Reverend Denning intoned as he brushed off his black frock coat.

"It is forever," grumbled Shelton.

"For a lifetime," added Lambert.

"I reckon I ken that weel enough," Ballard snapped

as he lifted the heavy brass knocker on the Sherwoods' front door.

Agnes opened the door, greeted Reverend Denning, and led them all into the parlor. Molly served a light refreshment as Agnes left to fetch the rest of the Sherwoods. Ballard grimaced when his family cornered him by the window overlooking the side garden. He wished they would just quietly accept the arrangement as they had said they would, for he had a qualm or two of his own. A sigh of resignation and exasperation escaped him when he saw that Shelton and Lambert intended to prod at those qualms yet again.

"Leave off it, laddies," he said.

Shelton shook his head, then hastily finger-combed his thick dark hair. "I ken that we are being pests about this, but ye dinnae leave us much choice."

"Quite right," agreed Lambert. "In but a few minutes the deed will be done and there will be no turning back."

"Dinnae ye like the lass, Lambert?" Ballard studied his young cousin closely as he sipped his tea.

"Oh, that is not the problem. I do not know her, do I? Fact is, she does not trouble me like that Sarah Marsten did."

As he nodded his agreement, Shelton continued, "This lass does seem to be a nicer sort. 'Tis just that this is all happening so cursed quick. *Too* quick."

"I explained about the lass's troubles—" Ballard began.

"Aye, aye." Shelton sighed. "Ye could still wait a mite longer, couldnae ye? She and her kin are nae being tossed out on the street today."

"There is no point in waiting."

"How can ye be so sure of that?"

Ballard did not have a good answer for Shelton. He was not sure why he felt so confident of what he was about to do. After his first surprise over Clover's proposal, he had never considered refusing. Each word he had since exchanged with her, each look, had made him even more certain. He had considered everything that could go wrong and was not at all deterred. It was just as easy to think about everything that could go right. And there was the lingering memory of her sweet kisses.

"I am sure," Ballard finally said, "but I ken there isnae much I can say to make ye feel the same. Ye will just have to set back and see that I have made the right choice. Ye willnae be letting the lass see your doubts either."

"She sees them already," Shelton said.

"Aye, she is a clever lass, but as soon as the wedding vows are said, the two of ye are to act like those doubts have disappeared. I will need help to make this work. Clover will be my wife and ye are to treat her as such, with all due respect, kindness, and assistance. If ye let her ken that ye still have doubts, or get stroppy with her, then ye could make a fine mess of something that could turn out to be verra good."

"Ye dinnae need to fret about us," Shelton assured him. "We will gladly do all of that. Once ye and the lass are wed, there isnae any turning back and we want it to work out well as much as ye do."

"True," agreed Lambert. "We are just trying to stop or delay it."

"Weel, ye cannae," said Ballard. "So let that be an end to it."

"Aye, let that be an end to it, for here she comes," Shelton murmured. Even though his eyes reflected admiration as he looked at Clover, he sighed. "Ye sure as Hades cannae turn around and walk out on the lass now."

"Nay, I cannae and I willnae," Ballard said in a hushed voice as he set his teacup down on a small table and went to meet Clover.

As he neared her, Ballard was glad he had stopped by the inn to bathe and had had a boy fetch his cleaned and pressed courting clothes so that he could change out of his homespuns.

Clover grew lovelier each time he looked at her. She was tiny, but her slim figure was perfection in his eyes. He stopped directly in front of her and met her wide-eyed gaze. It was obvious that she was nervous and a little bit afraid. Ballard was determined to eradicate both of those emotions.

Clover had forgotten how big Ballard MacGregor was. Even though his kisses had shown her how easily passion could flare between them, she was suddenly a little afraid of what she would face tonight, on her wedding night. It was hard to believe that a woman of her diminutive stature would be able to accommodate a man of Ballard's impressive size. She recalled her mother's words about lovemaking and was only slightly calmed, for she also recalled that her father had not been a very large man. Clover jumped nervously when Ballard suddenly took her small, trembling hand between his two big, callused ones.

"Are ye thinking of bolting, wee Clover?" he asked in a soft voice.

"The thought is lurking in the back of my mind," she admitted.

"Weel, ye just keep a tight rein on it until this spindly old preacher has done his business."

She stiffened her resolve, squared her shoulders, and nodded. "I will do that Mr. MacGregor."

"That is a good lass. Weel, let us go and make ye Mrs. MacGregor."

It was done. They were married.

Clover sipped from a glass of sweet red wine and struggled to quell yet another attack of nerves. She heartily cursed the fact that she could not stop thinking about the wedding night ahead. It did not help that, ever since the preacher had left, there had been a distinct gleam in Ballard's eyes. Clearly the wedding night was just about all he was thinking of.

"And is that not just like a man," she mused to herself with an inward grimace. Ballard had made it abundantly clear why he wanted a wife. She had no right to be cross. In truth, she suspected a lot of men got married just to bed their wives. Liaisons could be dangerous, causing scandal or worse, and she suspected there were men who were not fond of using the whores who seemed to proliferate wherever there was coin and the men to spend it.

A sudden commotion in the front hall yanked Clover from her musings. Someone had just slammed open the front door and was approaching the parlor with loud, angry strides. She gasped when Thomas burst into the room. He was the very last person she had expected to see at her wedding.

"Just what the hell are you doing, Clover?" he demanded as he strode over to the settee where she sat with Ballard.

Stunned, Clover could only stare up at the furious man before her. "What did you say?"

"I heard all about it in town and simply could not believe it. Clover Sherwood would never wed some ruffian from the backwoods, I said, but I now see that I was wrong to trust in your good judgment, young lady. Why have you done it?"

"I needed a husband," she replied in a soft voice, wondering why he was so upset.

"So you grabbed the first stranger who passed by? I know things are bad for you right now, Clover, but to hurl yourself at some ruffian like a common doxy?" He shook his head. "To sell yourself like some *whore*—"

Thomas's words ended in a squeak and Clover found herself gasping yet again. Her new husband was suddenly on his feet. Ballard grabbed Thomas by his crisp white shirtfront and lifted the startled man off the ground.

"I think ye have said more than enough, laddie," Ballard said through clenched teeth.

"Unhand me, you barbarian! Do you know who you are dealing with?"

Clover leaped to her feet and placed a hand on Ballard's arm. She was alarmed at the pure rage twisting Thomas's handsome features and the fury brightening Ballard's eyes. She quickly composed herself, for clearly a calming influence was needed. She sent Ballard a silent plea for peace. Her family had suffered enough scandal. She did not want a brawl in her front parlor on her wedding day.

Ballard read the plea in Clover's wide eyes and fought to control his anger. He had a strong urge to beat the fair-haired young man he held to within an inch of his life. The ferocity of his anger surprised him. With a murmur of regret he did not mean, he set the flushed Thomas back on his feet, though he did not leave Clover's side. He disliked allowing the man to get away with his insults and did not intend to let him deliver any more.

"I should like to speak to Clover alone," Thomas said in a haughty voice as he readjusted his clothes. "Come along, Clover."

When Thomas took her by the arm, Ballard tensed. "Just a moment cannot hurt," she murmured.

She could see by the taut set of Ballard's features that he did not like it at all, but he made no move to halt them as Thomas tugged her out into the hallway. Despite his extraordinarily insulting outburst, Clover wanted to hear what Thomas had to say. She was curious to know why he was in such an agitated state over her marriage to Ballard. Thomas was so enraged that he was shaking. She could feel his hand tremble. Since the man had jilted her and had begun to court Sarah, his fury made no sense at all.

Once they were in the hall and the parlor door was shut, Thomas turned to face her. She briefly felt she was confronting a stranger. This coldly infuriated man was a Thomas she had never seen before. He looked dangerous, and she inwardly shivered.

Clover wondered if he was about to renew his promise to marry her, but she knew that no matter what Thomas said, she would stay with Ballard.

"What are you doing here, Thomas?" she demanded.

"I am trying to save you from plunging headlong into the greatest of follies."

"I got married, Thomas. A great many people do so. It can hardly be termed a great folly."

"You just got married to some man you do not even know."

"He wants a wife and I need a husband. There seemed to be a sudden dearth of prospective husbands in the area." She was not surprised that Thomas was not embarrassed by her reference to his shabby treatment of her.

"You know why I had to end our engagement, Clover, but that was hardly reason to leap into the arms of the first man who ambled by. And one who has just been cast off by Sarah Marsten!" He grasped her gently by the shoulders. "I had no intention of putting you aside completely. You must have known that."

"You jilted me, Thomas. I cannot see what else that could have meant." His abrupt shift from fury to cajolery unsettled her, especially when she noticed how the hard, cold look in his eyes differed so dramatically from the soothing tone of his voice.

"I had to do that, Clover." Thomas winced and briefly rubbed at his temples. "I have my future to consider. It did not, however, mean that I had stopped caring about you. I am truly sorry if my actions led you to believe that."

Clover began to get the sinking feeling that Thomas was leading up to something that not only would be very insulting, but would make her furious as well. "I misunderstood, did I?" she said.

"Yes, love, you did. I felt you needed some time to understand fully why I had to end our engagement, but I was not idle during that time. I have been arranging for us to be together. As soon as you are evicted from this house, you can move into a cottage I have secured just outside of town. Of course, it would be best if you did not take your family with you, but I can understand your sense of loyalty."

"How kind." She could see that her sarcasm eluded him.

Thomas nodded and briefly smiled at her. "It will not be very fancy in the beginning, and I regret that. When I am wed to Sarah and much plumper in the pocket, however, I will be able to do very well by you. So you see, Clover, you must put an end to this farce immediately. You were not meant to be shackled to some rough backwoodsman. Given some time, I can provide you with a very comfortable life. Do you understand?"

"Very well, Thomas." She wondered how she could sound so calm when she was shaking with fury.

He gave her a brief kiss. "Then it is all settled. Now go and talk to that ruffian. The marriage can be annulled. Would you like me to talk to him with you?"

"Oh no, Thomas. I can say what must be said quite easily without your kind assistance. In truth, we do not need to trouble Ballard at all." She took a deep breath to hold on to her facade of calm. "I do not believe I have ever been so thoroughly insulted. This makes your dishonorable jilting of me pale in comparison."

"What are you saying?"

"Was some part of what I just said unclear?" Clover knew her anger was sharpening her voice but did not care. "You call me a whore for marrying Ballard so quickly, yet you have no qualms about treating me like one. I might grasp at some scrap of understanding if this nefarious offer was made because you thought I had acted shamefully, but 'tis clear you have been planning this arrangement for quite a while."

"I but tried to think of a way to help you in your time of need."

"Oh, do not pretend that any sense of nobility prompted you. You played the genteel beau so well, I was kept blissfully ignorant of your true despicable nature. I begin to understand why Papa was so adamant that we never be left alone together. He must have suspected what a cad you really are, but being a fair man, he dared not act against you without proof. I am glad he is not alive to see your true colors now."

"Now wait just a blasted minute," Thomas snapped, raising the riding crop he clutched tightly in his right hand. "You forget to whom you are speaking, Clover Sherwood."

"No, I do not. I should probably thank you for curing me of my incredible naivete. I now know exactly what sort of low, lying cur you are." Clover cried out as Thomas suddenly grasped her arm tightly and raised the riding crop as if to strike her.

"You are a very stupid girl," hissed Thomas. "You would choose that illiterate backwoods fool over *me?*"

"I would choose honorable marriage over being your whore."

"You little bitch!"

Clover cried out as Thomas struck her with his riding crop. She ducked in time to avoid the worst of the blow, but the rawhide tore through the sleeve of her dress, stinging her arm. Thomas jerked her back toward him and was about to strike again when the parlor door was flung open and Ballard was there, tearing the riding crop from Thomas's hand.

Clover slumped against the wall, stunned by Thomas's violence.

"Are ye all right, lass?" Ballard asked her.

Before Clover could reply, Thomas lunged at Ballard. She pressed herself hard against the wall to get out of the way of the ensuing fight. Horrified by a nasty fight in her front hall on her wedding day, Clover required a moment to find her voice.

"Stop this immediately!" she cried.

After throwing Thomas off, Ballard prepared for another attack from the man. "I would like to oblige ye, wee Clover, but it appears your old beau is of a different turn of mind," he said as he hastily removed his coat and tossed it at her. "Get in the parlor, lass, and shut the door."

She was about to argue when Thomas charged Ballard again. As both men slammed up against the stair rails, she ducked into the parlor and shut the door. Clutching Ballard's coat to her chest, she faced the others in the room, who all gaped at her. Clover sighed and moved shakily to sit on the settee.

"My dear, what is going on out there?" Agnes asked, her wide gaze fixed upon the parlor door as she twisted a lacy white handkerchief in her hands.

"Ballard is thumping Thomas," Clover replied.

"Good heavens—why?"

"I really do not wish to talk about it now, Mama."

Clover shut her eyes and tried to get her anger under control. She frowned when, after a brief moment of silence, the slamming of the front door echoed through the house. When Ballard did not immediately enter the parlor, Clover opened her eyes and started to rise. She could not believe that Thomas had won the battle, yet she could not be sure. The wild-eyed Thomas in the hall was not the man she had thought she knew. Before she could move, Shelton and Lambert dashed out into the hallway, only to return a moment later looking totally confused.

"There isnae anyone out there," Shelton announced.

"Perhaps they decided to continue the fight outside," Clover said.

"Nay. We looked out there too."

A moment later Ballard strode into the parlor, looking only slightly ruffled and quite pleased with himself. He sat down next to her, took his coat to which she still clung, and draped it over the back of the settee. Shelton served him a large tankard of ale and Clover waited a little impatiently as he took a long drink.

"Well?" Clover finally asked, certain that Ballard was dawdling over every tiny drop of ale just to irritate her. "What happened and where is Thomas?"

"I took the mon over to Miss Sarah's house. I reckoned that she could doctor him since she has been stepping out with him," Ballard replied.

"Oh. Thomas needed some doctoring, did he?"

"Aye, a wee bit. Now, lassie . . ." He cocked one finely drawn brow at her. "Dinnae ye think ye ought to tell your husband why the mon was set to beat ye?"

"I believe I may have irritated him," she replied hesitantly, not wanting to repeat what Thomas had said to her.

Ballard stared at her with one dark brow raised. "Is this the face of a fool? I heard your voices growing louder and angrier. You were arguing about something."

"Oh, I am sure you are not really interested," she mumbled, and took a long sip of wine.

"Aye, I am—verra interested. Did he ask ye to marry him again? Did he change his mind and decide that money didnae really matter?"

Now that Thomas was gone, Ballard felt relatively at ease. He had actually felt afraid when Thomas had burst into the room and made it clear that he was opposed to the wedding. His jealousy puzzled him, but Ballard knew he could not ignore it or shrug it away. He had seen Thomas as a threat and had ached to get rid of the man, swiftly and violently. It had taken every ounce of his willpower to do as Clover had asked, to stand back and allow her to talk to the man first, on her own. He had considered it a big risk, had feared that Clover would leave him for Thomas. Now, as Clover took a deep breath and gave him a look of reluctance and exasperation, he centered all his attention on her.

"Money still matters a great deal to Thomas and he did not ask me to marry him."

Ballard knew she was reluctant to tell him the truth, but he was as determined to hear it as she was to hide it. "That wasnae enough to put him in such a lather. He also wouldnae come here to tell ye something ye already kenned. *Why* did he storm in here and try to end our marriage?"

Clover sighed. "He did have plans for me. They concerned a cottage just outside of town."

A soft curse escaped Ballard and he muttered an apology. He could see by the darkening looks on Shelton's and Lambert's faces that they also understood what Clover was saying. Agnes just looked confused and Ballard was a little surprised at the woman's naivete.

"Do you mean that Thomas has actually been planning to help us?" Agnes asked.

"In a way, Mama," Clover replied.

"But the price was bloody high, wasnae it?" Ballard snapped, clenching his hands into tight fists as he was swamped with an urge to go next door and bounce Thomas around some more.

"I fear I do not understand," Agnes said.

"Old Thomas didnae want to marry Clover, but he didnae want to let her go either, if ye catch my meaning, ma'am," Ballard answered, his fury at Thomas roughening his voice. "He was planning to make Clover the little plaything the wife doesnae ken about."

Agnes frowned, then blushed a deep red. "Oh dear. Thomas planned such a thing? Are you certain?"

Clover nodded. "Quite certain, Mama. And he was enraged near to madness that I would have the temerity to refuse him." She touched the ripped sleeve of her gown.

It was easy to see in her mother's face how abruptly the woman's faith in Thomas had crumbled. There were no explanations Agnes could dredge up to excuse such an insult. Thomas had become finally, irrevocably tarnished in Agnes's eyes. This sordid offer was a far worse crime than the act of jilting her. Clover felt a little sorry for her mother, for she knew the woman had already suffered too many disappointments in people.

When no one had any more to say, Clover quietly suggested that they retire to the dining room to enjoy the hearty meal Molly had prepared. Clover began to feel tense the moment she took her seat next to Ballard at the linen-draped table. As she ate the smoked ham, hot buttered vegetables, and plump rolls, she drank a lot more wine than she ever had before. She knew it was not particularly wise, but she could not seem to maintain any control over her actions. The thought of the wedding night to come made her increasingly nervous, which made her mouth dry, which made her drink more. By the time they all returned to the parlor she was feeling decidedly light-headed. She wondered if her mother had guessed at her inebriated state, for Agnes quickly bustled her out of the room for bed, before she had a chance to get settled in her seat.

"Mama?" she asked in what she hoped was a whisper. "Is it not a little early yet?"

"I begin to fear that it may be too late," Agnes muttered as she urged her slightly unsteady daughter up the stairs to the room she would be sharing with Ballard.

"Too late for what?" Clover asked as she stumbled into the bedroom.

"Too late to keep you awake for your wedding night."

As her mother started to help her undress, Clover said, "No, not too late for that. I will not fall into a drunken stupor."

"Are you sure?" Agnes put Clover's gown away in the big oak wardrobe. "I wish we had not lost your fine wedding dress because we could not pay the dress shop bill."

"This blue gown was pretty enough, Mama. Now, do not worry. I am not so tipsy that I will fall asleep any earlier than usual. I but sought to calm my sudden attack of nerves."

"Well, be sure to splash a lot of cold water on your

face. That man is expecting a wedding night and you have promised him one. Now, here is something frilly and romantic for you to wear." Agnes tugged a new nightdress out of the wardrobe.

Clover breathed a sigh of appreciation as she smoothed her hand over the white silk and lace nightgown her mother held out to her. "'Tis lovely, Mama. So rich and delicate. Where did you get it?"

"I bought it for your wedding day before our fortunes soured. The groom may have changed but 'tis still a wedding." Agnes helped Clover slip into the thin nightgown. "Truth to tell, I think it may be important for you to wear something that will make you feel pretty and well . . ." Agnes blushed. "Perhaps even a bit naughty."

The wine Clover had consumed had succeeded in easing her fears and she giggled. "I believe that Mr. Ballard MacGregor is one of those men who *would* like his wife to be naughty in the bedchamber."

Agnes laughed. "Yes, I suspect so." She grew serious and gently grasped Clover by the shoulders. "There is no fault in liking the intimate side of marriage. 'Tis an important thing to a man. The passion is, I mean. Even a husband who loves his wife might stray if their bed is cold or holds naught but duty and tolerance. Feel no shame, m'dear, if you like lying with the man, for there is where the foundation of a firm marriage will be built. Are you ready now?"

"Yes, Mama. Send the groom up to me."

A little of Clover's bravado faded as soon as her mother left the room. She was about to do something very intimate with a man she barely knew. It was a frightening thought, and no amount of wine could fully banish that fear. She began to feel nervous again and hoped that Ballard would understand.

"I think your wee bride was a wee bit tipsy, Ballard," Shelton murmured, grinning.

"Aye, a wee bit." Ballard could not keep his amusement from his voice.

"A bit eager, are you, cousin?" Lambert teased, nodding at the way Ballard was seated on the very edge of his chair.

"Now, lads, I am powerful sorry to be depriving ye of the right to tease me without mercy, but let us have no rough talking in front of the children." Ballard sent a pointed glance toward the twins who sat nearby, watching him, Lambert, and Shelton with wide eyes and attentive faces.

"Are you our brother now, sir?" Clayton asked Ballard in a quiet, shy voice.

"Aye," Ballard replied. "I am now your kin by marriage, so ye may call me Ballard."

"Ballard?" Damien asked. "Are you gonna share Clover's bed like Mama shared Papa's?"

Ballard was taken aback by the bluntness of the question. "Ah, weel, aye. That is how it should be when folks are wedded."

"Oh. So that means we cannot be putting things in Clover's bed anymore," Clayton said.

"Ye put things in her bed? What things?"

"Damien put a frog in her bed once. And a lizard. I like putting snakes in. Not poisonous ones, just plain old snakes."

"Ah, and then Clover screams and hollers, does she?"

"We-ell, she screeches our names, then curses as she chases us. Then Mama starts chasing Clover and telling her she ought not to be cursing," Clayton revealed just as his mother entered the parlor.

"Clayton, I think it is time for you to go to bed, young man," Agnes said in a stern voice as she faced her son.

"But, Mama, Shelton and Lambert said they would play draughts with us."

"Aye, we did that ma'am," Shelton agreed as he fought an urge to laugh.

"Oh." Agnes sighed. "All right then, Clayton, you and Damien can play for a while, but there will be no more telling tales." After they nodded with obvious reluctance, Agnes looked at Ballard. "Your room is ready," she mumbled, and blushed slightly.

Ballard smiled gently and headed out of the room, trying not to reveal his eagerness too blatantly. He was just about to climb the stairs when he felt someone lightly grasp his arm. He looked down at an obviously nervous Agnes. It occurred to him that she might try to get him to wait before asserting his husbandly rights. He hurriedly tried to think of a gentle, polite way to tell her that there was no chance of that.

"Sir, I just wished to, well, to remind you that my daughter is very innocent," Agnes said.

"I had noticed that, ma'am. It wasnae hard to see."

Agnes bit her lip and pressed on. "Are you certain you cannot give her more time?"

"Oh, aye, verra certain, and it isnae just because I am feeling a need to have me a woman. I think it is best if Clover and I start as we mean to go on. If we wait, that could bring on its own problems. I mean, who will decide when she is ready? There is also the fact that when I am busy at my work, and she at hers, this time at night, this sharing of a bed, will be about the only time we will have together in private."

"Of course. And if you have little private time, then you cannot grow to really know each other. I do understand. Just please remember that she has not even been properly kissed. Well, leastwise not until you arrived."

"Dinnae ye fret, ma'am. If nothing else, I am bound to be careful tonight for it could determine how all the other nights of my married life are spent."

Agnes nodded, then murmured, "I shall see you in the morning then. Good night, Ballard."

"Good night, ma'am."

Clover heard the steady tread of Ballard's booted feet and scrambled into the big four-poster bed. She tried very hard not to look as nervous and afraid as she was beginning to feel. Unfortunately, the only thought pounding in her head was that an awful lot of man was about to climb into her bed.

When Ballard stepped into the room, she could not manage even a tiny welcoming smile.

Ballard snuffed out all the candles in the room except the one on a table by the bed. Clover struggled to calm herself, but it was futile. He began to undress, being very careful to put his courting clothes away properly. Each piece of clothing he removed made her heart pound harder. He hesitated a moment before shedding his drawers, then shrugged. For one brief moment Clover had the urge to bolt as he took off his drawers, strode to the bed, and climbed in beside her.

She had never seen a naked man. Ballard was so tall, lean, and taut with muscles. He was dark all over, with a neat vee of black curls on his broad chest which tapered into a thin line, blossomed around his loins, and lightly coated his long, well-formed legs. As he turned on his side next to her and propped himself up on one elbow, Clover tried not to cringe away from him.

He gently caressed her cheek with the back of his fingers, feeling her tremble, and asked in a soft voice, "Are ye afraid of me, wee Clover? Ye look a wee bit like a startled rabbit."

"No," she answered, but when he brushed soft kisses over her face, she whispered, "Yes."

"Dinnae be, lass. I willnae hurt ye."

He slowly stroked his hand down her side from her shoulder to her thigh, and she felt her fears begin to recede. "I am not afraid of—well—that," she admitted with wine-induced honesty.

"Then what are ye afraid of, sweeting?"

"Of doing something I have never done before. I am afraid to be looked upon as no man has ever looked upon me, and touched as I have never been touched before. Even though I know it will hurt only the first time, I am a little afraid of being hurt, for no one likes to be, do they, and I cannot be certain that it will only be a little hurt. Lord, you are so big, and that frightens me some, for I feel so very small just now, and 'tis not a particularly pleasant feeling. And—" Her nervous rambling ceased the moment she felt him begin to undo her nightgown.

"And what, little one?" He gently removed her nightgown and tossed it aside.

"And I am afraid that I will not like it," she whispered in a tremulous voice. "Or that you will not."

"Ye just give me a smattering of the warmth I have felt in ye each time we kissed and I am going to like it just fine." He pulled her faintly trembling body close to his and echoed the tremor that went through her, although he suspected hers was prompted by a more confusing jumble of emotion. "I will admit that I am a wee bit afraid myself."

It was almost impossible for Clover to talk, for she was caught up in a tangled morass of strong feeling. As he held her so close, she became more and more aware of the size and strength of him. She was also a little surprised at how good it felt to be skin to skin against him. The nudity required to consummate their marriage had been one of the things that had worried her. She was amazed that something that should shock her felt so enticing instead.

"What could *you* possibly be afraid of?" she finally managed to ask.

"That ye willnae like it. I have never bedded down with an innocent before. The sheltered daughters of the wealthy were ne'er within my reach."

"I believe that when it comes to lovemaking, the sheltered daughters of the wealthy are no different than any other women."

"True enough, lass, but 'tis verra important that I do this well now. A lass's first time can determine how she will feel about the business every time after that. I dinnae want to hurt ye, but for His own reasons, God decided that to make ye my wife I shall have to inflict some pain. I am a wee bit afeared that I willnae be able to lessen the hurt. Aye, and I also can feel how small ye are and worry about my size. But I will never use my size and strength against ye, Clover. I swear to that."

All the time he spoke, he stroked her slim body with his hands. Clover felt herself relaxing, her thoughts growing decidedly foggy. He touched every part of her face with feathery kisses, teased her ears with his warm breath and caressed her neck with his lips and tongue. She felt an unknown craving growing within her and realized with a start that it was a craving for a little less gentleness, a little less circumspection. When he touched his mouth to hers again, she twined her arms around his neck and held his lips against hers. With a soft growl, Ballard was quick to grant her silent request.

Clover quickly became drugged by his kisses, hardly aware of how much bolder his caresses grew. Then, suddenly, he cupped her breast with his big, lightly callused hand. She gave a start as the heat that raced through her was heightened by a shaft of fire as he began to toy with her aching nipple. With a soft cry, she arched into the curve of his hand. Just as she decided that nothing had ever felt so good, he flicked his tongue over the taut tip of her breast and produced an even more exquisite sensation.

She clung to him, tentatively stroking his broad, strong back with her hands. Beneath her hands she felt a fine tremor rippling through Ballard. She realized that he was controlling his own passion even as he tried to fire hers past control. He clearly felt far more than he was revealing to her. That knowledge added to the desire already swamping her. Clover became a little bolder with her caresses.

A shock went through her and she froze for a minute when Ballard slid his hand upward along her inner thigh. She could not believe that he would touch her so intimately. Her shock eased as she realized that she did not find it distasteful. In fact, she began to arch to his touch, desiring the intense feelings that were flooding her body. For a moment she wondered about the rightness of accepting his touch so wantonly. Then she heard him release a soft groan. He kissed her with an almost fierce hunger, and she knew she was doing exactly what he wanted.

Suddenly, Ballard lost his tightly held control. His kisses and caresses became feverish. He stroked her until she felt the same. A tiny flicker of sanity edged into her mind when she felt him probe for entry into her body. Something inside her tensed, but not from fear. Clover knew she was taut with anticipation. She then realized that Ballard was hesitant. Gripping his broad shoulders, she looked up at him. There was such heat in his eyes, she could feel it burn through her.

"Ballard?" she whispered.

"Ah, lass, I want to do this right. I dinnae want to hurt ye."

"Do it quickly," she advised in a soft voice.

He nodded, and with one hard thrust pushed inside her. Clover gasped and shuddered as a flash of pain tore through the desire that had warmed her. She clutched Ballard tightly as he went still. After a moment the pain began to fade and her anticipation returned, a sharp, demanding anticipation. But Clover was not quite sure what she wanted, or how to ask for it. She concentrated on how it felt to be one with the big, strong man she held, and her passion rose again. The renewal of her desire was aided by his touch and soft kisses. She could feel him trembling and knew he fought to control his passion until she was over the shock and pain of losing her maidenhead. Instinct suddenly told her how to let him know that she was more than ready to continue.

She released a soft sigh and arched toward him, encircling him with her limbs. He gave a hoarse cry and began to move. There was a barely leashed wildness in Ballard; Clover savored it. She eagerly sought the culmination of her passion. Even as he pulled her into a blinding maelstrom of fulfillment, she heard him cry out and tense as his seed poured into her. Her last clear thought was to wonder what it would be like if Ballard ever lost all control over himself.

Heavy-limbed and somnolent, Clover barely blinked as Ballard rose from her arms and cleansed them both with a cool, damp cloth. She readily curled up against him when he returned to bed and took her into his arms. The way he felt, the warmth that still lingered within her veins, and even the scent of him began to revive her desire. She smiled faintly, amused by how quickly she had gone from timidity to greediness.

Grinning, Ballard held Clover's slim form as close as he could while still being gentle. All his instincts had proven correct. Even though it had been Clover's first time, he had been able to pleasure her. He had sensed the passion in her, sensed from the very beginning how they would respond to each other. It was one of the reasons he had suffered so few qualms about their hasty marriage. Now that the painful part had passed, he knew the lovemaking would only get better.

He looked down at Clover as he lightly combed his fingers through her thick golden hair. Ballard wondered if she knew the value of the passion they had found together. He had often heard that well-bred ladies considered lovemaking something one should not mention or enjoy. Despite the wisdom of what her mother had said to her, he wondered if Clover had accepted such teachings or if she would now try to deny what they had shared. The only way their marriage could have a chance was if Clover's mind and heart agreed with her body, if she recognized, accepted, and enjoyed the passion that flowed between them.

"'Tis a powerful shame that God decided to mark a woman's chastity in such a way," he murmured.

"It was not so bad, and now it is over."

"True, but it would be better still if, weel, if your hair changed color or ye got a wee beauty mark or the like. I never could figure out why it had to hurt."

"I believe it is so women will be hesitant," Clover said, watching her fingers as she idly toyed with the black curls on Ballard's chest. "All those other things could be disguised or hidden away. I think God balanced the scales by allowing us to feel pleasure too."

He tightened his hold on her. "And did ye feel pleasure?"

Clover felt herself blush, but softly answered, "Yes. I rather liked it. Did you?" She smiled when he laughed.

"Oh, aye, my wee bonnie wife, ye could say that. Do ye think ye liked it enough to want a bit more?"

With a daring that surprised her, Clover slid her hand over his trim hip in a slow caress as she replied, "Possibly, but I am too new at this to be sure how to let you know that." She realized she really did want more even though she still suffered a little stinging.

"Weel, lass, ye could just start getting frisky."

"Frisky, hmmm?"

"Aye. Of course, if ye are too shy to do that, ye could just ask for more."

The slight tension Clover felt in Ballard told her that she was not the only one who wanted another taste of passion. He clearly shared her inclination to enjoy a time when timidity and fear did not intervene to possibly dull what they could feel. She also knew that, at least this once, Ballard would not do anything unless she made her wants very clear.

Taking a deep breath to quell a lingering flicker of shyness, she touched her lips to his, met his steady, passion-warmed gaze, and whispered, "More."

Chapter Five

A wayward lock of hair tickled Clover's nose and she absently pushed it off her face as she studied the lists spread out on the bedcovers in front of her. She had carefully itemized and priced everything in the house they had decided to sell, even though she knew the prices would be negotiable. It had kept her very busy in the week since her wedding. Because not every potential buyer would have cash to spare, she had also made up a list of items they would accept in barter. Except for tidily copying each list over five times so that there would be enough for buyers to peruse and the sellers to refer to, she felt she was ready for the sale they would hold today.

She glanced at her new husband and decided she would not pester him to look over her lists. He deserved a good sleep. For the last three days he, Shelton, and Lambert had worked very hard. In addition to the horse trading and buying of supplies they needed to complete before they began the trip back to Kentucky, they had helped her get everything that needed to be sold arranged in the downstairs rooms. She resisted the urge to smooth her hand over Ballard's broad back or burrow her fingers in his thick raven hair, and turned her attention back to her lists. A moment later a long dark hand appeared on her nightshift-clad thigh, which was exposed by her cross-legged position on the bed.

"I thought you were asleep," she murmured, glancing at him again.

"I just thought I would wait until ye were done ogling me," Ballard drawled.

"I was not ogling you," she said haughtily as he rose, naked, and disappeared into the small privy chamber.

"Admiring me then," he called back, and shut the door.

"What vanity," she scolded, but smiled.

Clover shook her head and chuckled. So far their hasty marriage was working out well. She knew it was far too soon to tell whether it would be a success, but she did not think it was foolish to see their good beginning as an encouraging sign. A great deal of the awkwardness which might have come between them, simply because they were comparative strangers, did not seem to exist.

Several things about Ballard were already apparent despite their short acquaintance. He was a very clean man, and although rough in his manner, he was far more of a gentleman than many who had been born and bred to be one.

When Ballard returned to the room and walked to their bed, Clover stared blindly at her lists. It occurred to her that Ballard could do with a touch more modesty. She was not sure she would ever get used to seeing so much man stride around unclothed.

Ballard smiled and Clover blushed as he sat down behind her. He draped his arms around her and stretched out his long legs, trapping her between them. As he nuzzled her neck, she felt both contented and aroused.

"What do ye have there, love?" he asked.

She found it difficult to think clearly when he was gently caressing her bare arms and kissing her nape, but managed to reply in a faintly unsteady voice, "I have been making up some lists. One is what we have to sell and one is what we might take in trade if a buyer does not have the necessary coin. Sadly, that is the situation for many people."

"Have ye got things such as sugar and flour on that barter list?"

"Yes, right here," she said with a touch of confusion, for he could see the lists for himself. She looked over her shoulder at him. "Ballard, can you read?"

"A wee bit. I ken enough to see what jar holds the poison."

"Well, I can teach you." She turned to face him, unable to hide her eagerness.

"Can ye now?"

"Yes. It will be something *I* can give *you*. I mean, you have given me so much, I should like to repay that somehow."

Ballard flopped back onto the pillows and tugged her down so that she was sprawled atop him. "Ye are already giving me plenty, lass."

"Well, I was not, er, counting that sort of thing," she murmured as he took away the lists she still held and placed them on a small table by the bed.

"That sort of thing counts very high with a mon." He slid his hands up under her shift to cup her slender backside.

"Ballard, 'tis morning!" she whispered in shock.

"What a clever wee darlin' ye are." He laughed softly as he kissed her throat.

"Ballard, I am going to hit you." She smiled faintly, for her husky voice, thickened with the desire he was stirring inside her, completely undermined her threat.

"Mmm. Later, sweeting. Ah, lass, ye are a fine mix of lady and wanton. There ye are, blushing and looking so prettily innocent. Yet I ken that if I do this"— he slid his hands over her backside and pressed her body against his—"it starts your blood running hot and then ye meet my passion with all the fire any mon could ask for."

Clover knew she was blushing even redder. She wanted to scold him for speaking so plainly, but then he slid his big callused hands up her sides and covered her breasts. As he kissed her, she decided to reprimand him later.

When Ballard rose from their bed once again, he stretched with pure male satisfaction. Clover roused herself from her sated lethargy enough to give his taut backside a sharp slap. She giggled when he yelped, more from surprise than from pain. He whirled to look at her and she smiled sweetly.

"I told you I would hit you."

He tugged on his drawers and regarded her with mock sternness. "If I didnae have work to do, ye would pay for that impudence, lass." He continued to dress as he asked, "Ye didnae put the mattresses and pillows on that list, did ye?"

Clover bit back a smile and shook her head. Ballard, Shelton, and Lambert had been possessive of the bedding from the very beginning. The feather mattress and pillows, fine linen sheets, and warm coverlets were a great luxury, and worth paying extra to ship them down the Ohio River. Ballard was determined to take every piece of bedding, having stated firmly that there would undoubtedly be a need for spare bedding. It was an attitude that contrasted sharply with the extreme care he had taken in selecting the other things they would take with them to Kentucky.

As soon as Ballard left the room, Clover hurried to get dressed. Her thoughts were fixed on what her husband was allowing them to take to Kentucky. Although he had been relatively lenient, he had made it clear that usefulness and necessity were the criteria for any choice. He took all the bedding, but not all the beds, for he felt something just as good could be bought or made in Kentucky. Clover shared some of her mother's sorrow at parting with so many of their possessions, but she believed Ballard was being not only practical but also fair.

She pushed aside her musings as she finished pinning up her hair and quickly went downstairs. Despite Molly's dire warnings that she would get stomach pains, Clover rushed through her breakfast. She was not sure how she could have moved any faster, but she had only just finished making copies of her lists when people began to arrive to see what was being offered for sale.

The morning sped by and was already over before Clover found a moment simply to stand back and take a few relaxing breaths. She thought briefly of her sister Alice, who had marched in at the very start of the sale. Alice had picked up the little table she had coveted, slapped the money for it into Clover's hand, and left. Clover had pocketed the money and sworn that she would not allow her sister's pettiness to ruin the day. The pleasure she felt over the success of the sale faded abruptly when she finally located her husband. Sarah Marsten was standing much too close to Ballard as far as Clover was concerned and the woman did not seem especially interested in the oak sideboard beside which they stood. Clover told herself not to be jealous, but little good that did.

Ballard frowned down at the fulsome Sarah pressing embarrassingly close to him. He had the distinct feeling that she was playing some sort of game, but he was not sure what it was. Clearly, despite her claims, she was not really interested in buying any of the goods Clover was offering for sale.

"We are willing to take something in trade," he said, stepping back from her. "Ye dinnae have to pay in coin."

Sarah stepped closer and stroked his arm with one gloved hand. "Now, what could I possibly have that you might want?"

When she subtly rubbed her breasts against his arm, Ballard lost all doubt about what she was up to. For just a moment he was flattered, then he grew angry. The woman had not wanted him when he had been available. Now that he was married and could never be more than a lover, she was eager to have him. He might not be good enough for marriage, but he would suffice for stud service. Sarah felt safe in playing her games with him now, for she knew he would not trouble her with expectations of permanence.

He stepped away from her again. "'Tis clear that ye have nae quite made up your mind, Miss Sarah. Ye just give me a holler when ye do decide."

He walked away, shaking his head. Did Sarah really think he was that dumb? Even if he was stupid enough to want to indulge in an affair with her, he certainly would not start one with his wife, her kin, and half the town of Langleyville watching!

Clover breathed a sigh of relief as she watched Ballard leave Sarah. She admitted she had been both worried and frightened by what had appeared to be happening between the pair. The way Ballard had marched away, a deep scowl on his face, eased her concern.

She decided she would puzzle over her feelings later and turned all her attention back to the sale. By the time the last customer had left in the late afternoon, Clover heartily wished she had made some attempt to keep an eye on Ballard and Sarah. Both were gone. As she asked the others if they had seen her husband, it became painfully clear that the last anyone had seen of him, he had been helping Sarah Marsten's groom carry the sideboard outside, with Sarah following close behind.

* * *

With a muttered curse, Ballard helped set the sideboard down and watched Sarah's groom nearly run out of her dining room. Sarah then ordered her timid aunt to leave and Ballard wondered how Sarah's parents could have thought the old woman a proper chaperone while they jaunted all around Europe. He then looked at Sarah, who smiled sweetly and urged him to come into the parlor for a cool drink before he returned home. It was on the tip of his tongue to refuse, but he nodded curtly. It was about time he set Miss Sarah Marsten straight about a few things. There was only a little time remaining before he left for Kentucky and he did not want the woman stirring up trouble.

Once Sarah had served tall glasses of chilled lemonade, she insisted on sitting as close to him as possible on her ornate settee.

"There, is this not just like before?" Sarah asked, pressing her side against his.

"Nay, it isnae, Miss Sarah. I am a wedded mon now," Ballard replied.

"Oh, Ballard dearest, whyever did you do it? Surely you did not take that insignificant little episode with Thomas to heart? 'Twas just a little flirtation."

"I have never been partial to games. I am not partial to the one ye are playing now either. I am not a free mon." He set his empty glass aside and turned toward her to say good-bye.

All at once Sarah flung herself into his arms. "How can you prefer that scrawny child to me? I can give you all a man needs."

Ballard suddenly realized that Sarah was probably not boasting, that this fine lady he had seriously considered marrying was well-versed in the bedroom arts. The way she moved her hands over his body was proof of that. Sarah's parents had obviously left the woman alone far too often. To his shame, when she rubbed her hand over the front of his breeches, desire hardened him. Ballard shoved her away and stood up.

"I am not interested, lass," he snapped.

"Not interested? You prefer that fleshless Sherwood girl to me?"

"I do, for all my fool body perks up in interest at a skilled touch. Ye cannae be giving me anything I cannae get at home. I dinnae lie in a bed so cold I have to look elsewhere for some loving." He gave her a brief smile. "I willnae deny that ye could probably give me one fine roll in the heather, but it isnae worth losing what I have now. Ye just are nae worth that much."

"You bastard!" screeched Sarah as she leaped to her feet and swung at him.

Ballard easily caught her wrist. "I wouldnae do that, miss. I am not one of your fine gents who will just stand here and take it. Ye hit me and I just might hit ye back." He tossed her hand aside. "Now, I believe I will amble back to my wife."

"Go ahead. Enjoy what little time you will have with her."

"We are wed. We have a lifetime ahead of us," Ballard said as he paused in the doorway to look back at her.

"You are from two different worlds. Clover is desperate now and will grasp at any chance she can to save herself and her pathetic little family from utter destitution. But you cannot give her the life she is accustomed to. One day she will wake up, look at you, and wonder why, in God's sweet name, she is with you."

Sarah's words aroused all the fears Ballard thought he had subdued, and he glared at her. "Nay. Clover Sherwood isnae like that."

She laughed. "Fool. Clover comes from people who would barely consider you suitable to clean out their stables. You have reached far above yourself, Scotsman, and your fall will be hard."

There was nothing Ballard could think to say. Her words cut too close to the bone. He gave her a curt bow and walked from the room.

Sarah's words pounded in his head as he left her house. He struggled to banish them as he walked down her front steps. He was so deep in thought that he bumped into Mr. Grendall. As he muttered an apology, he noticed how agitated the man was and frowned.

"Is something wrong, Mr. Grendall?" he asked.

"The stallion you sold me has fallen ill. I do not believe it will survive the afternoon." Grendall took a large white handkerchief from his coat pocket and wiped the sweat from his round face.

"I didnae sell ye a sick horse," Ballard protested, yet he did not believe the man was questioning his integrity.

"Of course not. I beg your forgiveness if I led you to believe that. I sought you out because I hoped you might have some knowledge of what ails the beast. You raise such fine animals, I thought you must have some skill with them."

"A horse doctor might be better."

"We have none. Never have, really. Can you come with me and have a look at the animal?"

"Aye."

As Ballard followed Grendall, he briefly considered stopping to tell Clover where he was going, but the frantic man waved him along. He shrugged and climbed into Grendall's carriage. The sale would continue for a few more hours and he would be back before Clover noticed he was missing.

By the time they reached Grendall's large farm, Ballard had a strong suspicion about what ailed the stallion he had sold to Grendall. It had been poisoned. Yet that made no sense to Ballard. Grendall knew enough about horses not to have done it accidentally and would never have done it intentionally. Although Ballard had not been in the area long, he had not noticed any plants that might be dangerous to a grazing horse. If he was right and the horse had been poisoned, they had to find out who had done it, and why.

Once Ballard saw the horse, he stripped to his breeches and set to work trying to save the animal. He covered the animal with blankets and led it out into the paddock. It was necessary to keep the animal on its feet and moving so that it could sweat out the poisons. Ballard and Grendall also dosed the animal with diuretics and laxatives to purge its system. It took a long time and was hot, messy work. With Grendall's help the stallion began to show signs of improvement by late afternoon. Confident the animal would continue to recover, Ballard joined Grendall in washing up and partook of a strong drink of brandy in his elegant parlor. Although Ballard felt out of place on the delicately carved settee and feared he might break the expensive brandy snifter he held, the stallion's illness was his overriding concern.

"I have nae seen anything, but mayhap there be a disagreeable plant about that he ate. Everything growing out of the ground doesnae suit the animals," Ballard said as he gingerly set the brandy snifter down on a small table.

"If so, I would have had trouble with my other horses, and I have had none." Grendall stopped pacing the room to lean against the marble fireplace. "I have a sick feeling I know what happened." He sighed, shook his head, and took a long sip of his brandy.

"What do ye suspect?" Ballard pressed when the man said no more.

"Dillingsworth was not pleased that I got the horse he wanted."

"Ye think Dillingsworth tried to kill the animal?" Ballard exclaimed, then realized he was not really surprised. He too had wondered if Dillingsworth would stoop to such an act.

Grendall nodded and shrugged. "Someone gave the animal whatever made him ill, and Dillingsworth did threaten us."

"True, but killing the beast doesnae make any sense."

"No? He wanted it but could not have it. He tried to make sure I could not have it either. That has often been Dillingsworth's way. He can be dangerously spiteful. You should keep that in mind. After all, you now have something he wanted—little Clover Sherwood."

"But he ended their engagement." Ballard's agitation made him want to pace the room, but he forced himself to remain still, for he feared accidentally breaking some of the delicate furniture cluttering Grendall's front parlor.

"He did end their engagement, but he still planned to keep her. A lot of us figured that out when he got his greedy hands on Miller's old cottage just outside of town."

"Yet none of ye thought to warn Clover."

"We had no proof, only a strong suspicion. Dillingsworth is a power to be reckoned with around here. No one dares make idle accusations. Hellfire, a lot of us owe Dillingsworth money. He could break many a family in Langleyville just by demanding payment of all debts."

Ballard stood up. "I understand, yet sitting back and doing naught only gives the man more power. Such hesitation is why he continues to do as he pleases. The man kens that ye are all too afraid to stop him."

"I know. Well, he failed to get me this time. Perhaps that will be the end of it."

"I hope ye are right," Ballard said, and shook the man's hand. "I will be here one or two more days. Call on me if ye need to. I best get back to my wife."

Grendall stood upright and stared at Ballard. "You did not tell her where you were going?"

"Nay. Ye were in a wee bit of a hurry if ye recall."

"Of course. I am sorry. Let us hope Clover is understanding. If you need to smooth some troubled waters, call on me."

"Clover will understand."

"Ah, the bliss of the newlywed."

Grendall chuckled as he led Ballard to the door and ordered the carriage brought around for him. Ballard was tempted to ask what the man found so amusing, but hesitated. He did not want to appear ignorant about married life. Still resisting the urge to question Grendall, Ballard said good-bye and got into the carriage.

He forgot all about Grendall's remarks when he spotted Aaron Spaulding outside the Sly Dog. The man had indicated a strong interest in horse dealing after seeing the stallion Grendall had bought. Ballard stopped the carriage, tipped the driver, and hurried after Spaulding, hoping to get some stronger commitment from the man.

It was dark before Ballard left the Sly Dog with several ales under his belt and a promise from Spaulding to buy another stallion and three mares if Ballard could provide them within a year. He paused near a shadowed alley to try and put some order to his clothes. A grunt of surprise escaped him when he was suddenly grabbed from behind and dragged into the alley.

Caught completely off-guard, his head a little clouded by drink, Ballard was unable to recover from his surprise in time to win the fight. He got in a few good blows to his two attackers, however, before he was brought down. As he lay in the filthy alley, one man kicked him in the ribs and the head. Ballard clung desperately to consciousness. He knew that without it, he would be ready prey for any ruffian who happened along. When the other man found only a few coins in his pocket and kicked him again, Ballard tried fruitlessly to grab the man by the boot and trip him.

"He ain't dead, Jake," grumbled the heavier of the two men. "Dillingsworth said he wanted him dead."

"I ain't risking my neck for that fop," grumbled Jake as he pocketed Ballard's money.

"Maybe you oughta worry about what Dillingsworth'll do if'n he finds out we didn't kill this feller."

"Ain't worried about that neither, 'cause we ain't gonna be here."

"We ain't?"

"No, Tim, me boy, we ain't. Dillingsworth was fool enough to pay us after we done as he wanted. He was just so mad that horse didn't die, I reckon he weren't thinking too straight. Fine by me. I'm taking my share of the money and getting outta here. Maybe to one of them big cities. Oughta be lots of work there. You'd be smart to come with me."

"Yeh, think I will at that. What about this feller?"

"Leave him. I will sorely miss seeing Dillingsworth's face when this rogue comes back from the dead. The fool's in for a powerful surprise when he trots over to comfort the grieving widow on the morrow."

Both men laughed, delivered one more kick to Ballard's ribs, and hurried away. Ballard cursed as he fought the waves of pain washing over him and waited to be sure both men were gone. Then he tried to stagger to his feet. It took several tries before he had the strength to make his way home.

As he stumbled along the street to Clover's house, he wondered what to do about Dillingsworth—if there was anything he *could* do. He knew from Grendall that no one stood against Dillingsworth. There was little chance a rough backwoodsman would be heeded if he accused the man. All Ballard knew was that he had to get back to Clover, had to get himself patched up and ready to face Thomas Dillingsworth in the morning. It was going to be a pleasure to thwart the man once again. He also planned to get Clover out of Langleyville before Dillingsworth could try anything else. A man who would poison a horse and pay to have him murdered was capable of anything.

Ballard realized he was deeply afraid for Clover.

Clover sprawled on her bed and stared up at the ceiling. The last thing she felt like doing was sleeping. She had come to her room to escape all the sympathetic looks of her kin, old and new, and their weak excuses for Ballard's continued absence. Now only her own thoughts and feelings tormented her. She decided that was enough for anyone.

She was a little surprised to discover that Ballard's defection hurt far more than being jilted by Thomas had. The explanation she gave herself, that she had been intimate with Ballard, did not really satisfy her. She did not really want to look much deeper for an answer, however, especially not since he had chosen Sarah Marsten over her. There could be no other explanation for Ballard's long disappearance with Sarah.

As Clover clenched her hands into fists where they lay on top of the coverlet, she fought the urge to cry. She refused to let this betrayal break her. If this chance for security for her family was gone, she would find another one. She would have to be strong to do that. It would be a great folly to allow self-pity and hurt pride to rule her.

"Oh, Ballard, you great oaf of a Scotsman, where the hell are you? Please, please, do not do this to me."

She turned onto her side and clutched the pillow.

The deep breath she took to steady herself filled her nose with the clean, male scent of him, and tears blurred her eyes. She quickly reached for the anger inside her and used it to push the other feelings aside. When and if Ballard returned, she preferred to meet him with righteous fury rather than weak tears.

Ballard slumped against one of the short pillars that framed the stairs leading to Clover's home and gathered the strength to climb them. He was pleased to see that no one appeared to be visiting the family. That meant that his absence was probably not public yet and that Thomas had not already come to claim the prize he thought he had won. *I will be waiting for the bastard when he does show*, Ballard thought grimly as he made his painful way up the steps and into the house.

"Where the bloody hell have ye been?" demanded Shelton the minute Ballard entered the parlor.

Stopping inches inside the room, Ballard stared at his young brother in some surprise. Shelton and Lambert stood glaring at him in a way that made him feel like an errant youth. If the situation were not so serious, he would have found the reversal of roles highly amusing.

"Where is Clover?" Ballard asked after a quick look around the room revealed that she was not present.

"'Tis a fine time to be worrying about her now. Ye should have given a thought or two to her before ye ran off with that slut Sarah Marsten. Curse it, Ballard, aside from it being all wrong, how could ye put me and Lambert into such an awkward position? What did ye expect us to tell Clover?"

At that moment Agnes rose from her chair and walked over to him. Ballard eyed her a bit warily, then began to relax. The expression of disappointment and disgust she had worn when he had first entered the room had been replaced by one of confusion and concern.

"You are bleeding, Ballard." She gingerly touched the drying streak of blood by his ear.

Shelton, with Lambert close on his heels, edged closer to Ballard. "Have ye been in a fight?"

"Ye could say that." He gave them a succinct summary of what had happened to him and watched their expressions of disbelief change to outrage.

"Lord Almighty and His mother," muttered Shelton. "Is Dillingsworth all right in his head?"

"I dinnae think he is too sane and, Shelton, ye shouldnae be swearing in front of Mrs. Sherwood."

Agnes smiled briefly at a blushing Shelton. "In such a situation cursing is easily forgiven. Come, Ballard, let me tend to your injuries."

"Nay, but thank ye, ma'am. It occurred to me as I stumbled here that no one has seen or heard from me since I left with Miss Marsten. I reckon I can guess what folk began to think. I have a wild tale to tell Clover, and these wounds may help to make her believe it. Where is she?"

"She went to bed." Agnes sighed and shook her head. "We all tried to reassure her, but I think we only made matters worse. I am sorry, Ballard, but when you did not return, we all began to believe the worst."

"There is no need to apologize, ma'am. Ye all ken that I was sniffing 'round Miss Marsten and ye only thought what anyone would think. I should have stopped to tell ye I was going with Grendall, but I reckon I am not used to having to answer to anyone. Now Dillingsworth thinks his men have killed me, so I suspect that cur will be here bright and early in the morning, wanting to soothe my poor grieving widow. If I am not here to greet him, dinnae let him ken that I have returned. Just come and tell me he is here."

"Ye dinnae think he will discover ye have escaped before then?" asked Shelton.

"Nay, I doubt it. Those two men were nae eager to have Dillingsworth discover that they didnae do what he had paid them to do. They are probably halfway to Philadelphia by now. Nay, Dillingsworth will be here to try and take advantage of Clover."

"Perhaps Shelton and I ought to keep an eye out, just in case Dillingsworth cannot wait until morning or discovers you are not dead and decides to hire someone to do the job right this time," suggested Lambert.

"It cannae hurt. Aye. Just be sure he doesnae see ye, as that could warn him that we ken his games. If Dillingsworth thinks that, he may turn on the two of ye. I have enough to fret o'er. He may also take it into his head to flee and hide away until I have returned to Kentucky, and I dinnae want him slipping out of my reach. I want a chance to confront that slinking dog."

"Dinnae worry, Ballard," Shelton assured him.

"We will do our best to make sure you have that chance," Lambert said.

"I just find this all so very hard to understand," Agnes said as Shelton and Lambert left.

"Dillingsworth wants it all, ma'am. 'Tis that simple. And he doesnae much like that it was a mon like me who got Clover. He also didnae like being beaten by me. That means he has lost to me twice. There are some men who just cannae abide losing. In truth, I suspect Dillingsworth wasnae too stable before I came on the scene. Grendall implied a lot of people know what Dillingsworth is like but are too afraid to stand against him. Dillingsworth has stepped right o'er the edge now, though."

"Yes, he must be mad. Well, you go and speak to Clover, and I wish you luck."

"Thank ye, ma'am. I will need it."

Ballard started on his way to their bedchamber. He ached all over, but it was not that pain which slowed his pace as he drew nearer. Convincing Clover to believe him was not going to be easy.

As Ballard closed his hand around the door latch, he prayed that she would at least hear him out.

Chapter Six

The sound of someone approaching the door pulled Clover out of her depressing thoughts. It was a man's tread, and she tensed as she sat up. She could not believe Ballard would have the gall to return to her after spending a long, undoubtedly lusty afternoon with Sarah Marsten. Suddenly, her anger took over. She grabbed a heavy candlestick from the bedside table and stood up on the bed. If Ballard stepped through that doorway, she had every intention of doing him some harm. It would never make up for the injury he had inflicted upon her, but it sure would make her feel better.

She watched the door latch move and steadied her aim. The minute the door opened to reveal Ballard standing there, Clover hurled the candlestick at him. A curse hissed through her teeth when he quickly dodged the candlestick, which thumped uselessly against the door he had just closed.

"Now, lass," Ballard began as he moved warily toward her.

"Do not '*now, lass*' me, you randy Scot!"

Clover looked around for another weapon, wishing she had had the foresight to stockpile a few within easy reach. On the other side of the bed, she saw the mate to the candlestick she had just thrown. She moved to grab it, but Ballard was quicker. A screech of frustration and anger escaped her when he tackled her onto the bed. Clover tried to hit and kick him, but after a brief, undignified struggle, Ballard succeeded in pinning her to the mattress.

"I suppose I shouldnae be surprised that a lass with a touch of red in her hair should have a temper," Ballard muttered with a catch of his breath, as if he were in pain.

"My hair does not have red in it. 'Tis blond. Now get off me, you lecherous barbarian. Sarah is probably eagerly awaiting your return."

"Clover, look at me," Ballard demanded.

She continued to glare at the tip of his long straight nose. The very last thing she wished to do was to look into his eyes. They had been married only a week, but she had already learned how dangerously alluring his rich green eyes could be. He could probably make her believe that he and Sarah had done no more than discuss the merits of the sideboard she had purchased.

"Did you expect me to smile and welcome you after you have been dallying with Sarah Marsten for hours?"

"I have nae been dallying with Sarah!"

"There is no need to shout."

"Look at me, Clover."

It occurred to her that if she kept avoiding his gaze, he might guess her weakness. Somehow she was going to have to look into his eyes yet not be lulled by his lies. At the same time she dared not let hurt pride endanger her future with this man, and her family's security.

Inwardly bracing herself, she finally looked fully at his face and gasped. There was blood on the side and a bruise or two beneath the dirt smudges. She quickly looked over what she could see of the rest of him and her confusion grew. His homespun breeches were quite dirty and torn at the knee. His shirt was half untucked and his buckskin coat was covered in dust. If he and Sarah had been misbehaving, they had indulged in some very rough play and, by the looks of it, done so in the middle of the road. He also smelled as if he had been wallowing in a trash heap.

Still, meeting his gaze, she remained wary. "Did you and Sarah decide to roll about in the fields?" she asked. It would take a lot of explaining from Ballard before she would relinquish her skepticism.

"Nay, we didnae roll about anywhere." He took a deep breath, knowing that letting her snide remarks provoke him into anger would only make a bad situation worse. "I am about to tell ye a tale ye may find hard to believe."

"What a surprise!"

Ballard ignored her sarcasm. "I took that hulking piece of furniture to Sarah's house. Now, I had already figured out that she was trying to, er, pull me into her web. For a fact, I didnae believe it at first, her behavior was so brazen. I thought 'twas just my vanity. But she got so forward I couldnae ignore it."

"Neither could anyone else."

"Once we got to her house, she continued her little game." Ballard could see that despite her tart remarks, Clover would hear him out, so he released her arms and sat up a little. "She offered me a cool drink and I accepted. I felt she had some wrong ideas about me and I wanted to set her straight. I didnae want her fluttering about and causing trouble atween us."

"Sarah must be a great deal more witless than I thought if it took you all afternoon to do that."

He held her gaze and hoped that his sincerity showed in his face. "I willnae swear that I will never stray, lass, for a mon's actions are nae always ruled by his brain, but I dinnae treat lightly the vows I spoke afore God. Fact is, I told her I wasnae interested, and I left her house hours ago. I met Grendall as I came here and he dragged me away. He thought the stallion I sold him was dying."

"And was it?"

"Aye, but we managed to save it. Someone had poisoned the beast. Grendall is sure it was Dillingsworth."

"Thomas? Why should he do something like that?"

"Because if he cannae have the beast, he doesnae want anyone else to have it. I left to return here, but at the tavern I saw Aaron Spaulding, a mon who is interested in my horses. He and I shared a few wee ales and made a bargain or two. 'Twas as I left the tavern that I was set upon by two men. They caught me by surprise, grabbing me from behind. I lost the fight and they played a wee bit of kick the ball with my head and ribs."

It all sounded a little too pat to Clover, but she reminded herself not to judge him too quickly. Ballard was looking very intense and sincere. She decided it would not be fair to assume immediately that it was all an act. She reached out to touch the back of his head and found a sizable swelling still sticky with blood just behind his right ear. It was not complete proof that he was telling the truth, but she almost believed him.

"Fell off the bed, did you?" she murmured, and met his annoyed glance with a calm look.

"Nay, the men tried to crack my skull. It was all part of Thomas's plan."

"Thomas was there too?"

"Nay, but he paid some low hirelings to do his dirty work. One of them cleaned out my pockets while the other revealed that Dillingsworth wanted me dead. 'Tis my good fortune that they had their money already and were nae inclined to bloody their hands. Thomas's plan is to come 'round here in the morning to comfort ye, the grieving widow."

"How kind of him." She frowned. "You were right to say that this tale is hard to believe. Why on earth would Thomas want to kill you? What could it possibly gain him?"

"Thomas believed he could get ye back, that ye would agree to be his mistress if ye believed I was dead and ye were alone and destitute again." Ballard was encouraged by the arrested look on Clover's face. "I signed my death warrant when I cured the stallion. The man must have learned of it immediately and felt I had thwarted him once too often. In the morning, Thomas is going to come after ye. He figures that, after everything else that has happened to ye—the loss of your new husband, the scandal of my being murdered in a filthy alley outside the Sly Dog—ye will be ready and willing to do all he says."

"And he will make me accept his nefarious offer." It all made chilling, horrible sense to Clover, and she grew so agitated she could not stay still. "Let me up, Ballard."

"Nay, I have nae finished with my story."

She swatted his arm. "I will not go anywhere and I *will* listen to you. I just cannot lie here like a lump any longer. Let me up."

Ballard cautiously moved off her, then watched as she slid from the bed and started to pace the room. After a moment or two she stopped by the washbowl, filled it with water, and brought it to the bedside table. When she retrieved washing and drying cloths, he realized that she intended to tend his wounds. His hopes rose.

Clover rolled up the long sleeves of her nightdress and soaked the washcloth in the cool water. "What else do you have to say? 'Tis clear that the plan to murder you failed, for here you are."

"Aye." He winced when she placed the cloth on the bump on his head. "Thomas didnae like ye marrying me, a mon he believes is far beneath him. I didnae help matters by thumping him or by selling the stallion to Grendall instead of him. He considers himself twice beaten and humiliated by a backwoods illiterate. That the whole town kens about his defeat, or so he believes, only makes him more enraged."

"If he wanted me so badly, why did he put an end to our betrothal?" Clover began gently to wash off Ballard's face and was pleased to see that, under all the dirt and smeared blood, his bruises were not severe.

"Money, lass. Ye kenned that before. Thomas wants and needs Sarah's money. He also wants ye to share his bed. He thought he could have both, but I mucked up his grand plan. Do ye ken, when I refused to sell him the stallion, he nearly ran me and Grendall down with his carriage as he left."

"He certainly sounds like a madman, yet why did I not see it in him before?"

"Ye were nae alone with him. There was always someone with ye, and he kens to behave weel before others. The airs and games one indulges in during courtship can hide a lot of ills. Lass, can ye check that other knot on my head? Just to the left. I dinnae think the skin was split, but it willnae hurt to be sure."

"They hit you twice?" Clover eased her fingers through his thick hair until she found another swelling. "It appears all right, with no blood or excessive swelling."

"When the rogues got me down, they gave me a hearty kick in the head to keep me down." He ran a hand over his rib cage and winced. "The cowards kicked me a few times."

"Take off your shirt and let me have a look." She hastily swallowed a gasp when he tossed his shirt aside, for the bruising along his ribs was startlingly livid. "That will have to be seen by a doctor and he might as well look at those head wounds to see if a stitch or two is required."

When she started walking away, Ballard grasped her arm. "We are nae done talking."

"You can talk until he arrives and, if that is not enough, after he leaves."

Clover tugged free of his hold and went to ask her mother to send for the doctor. She kept her conversation with her mother brief, although clearly Agnes could hardly contain her curiosity. Clover wanted to judge Ballard's truthfulness without other opinions influencing her, so she hurried back to her room.

"Mother has sent Molly after the doctor," she announced as she found Ballard still sitting tensely on the bed. "There is no telling when he will get here, though." She sat on the edge of the mattress and faced him. "Now you can finish this wild tale of yours."

"'Tis the truth."

"I am still undecided about that."

He described how the men had left him in the alley and he had staggered home. The look on her face told him she was seriously considering the truth of his tale. When even Lambert and Shelton suspected he had been trysting with Sarah, he had realized how bad his absence had looked. It was understandable that Clover was reluctant to believe his farfetched tale. He was not pleased when the doctor arrived just as he finished, for he was not sure such an interruption was in his best interest.

Clover left Ballard with the doctor and stepped out into the hall. She found herself smiling faintly when she heard Ballard's muttered curses at the old doctor. She prayed she was not being a fool, swayed by passion and fine green eyes, but she did believe her husband's story.

The moment the doctor left, Clover went back into the room. She winced in sympathy when she saw Ballard. He had been stripped to his drawers, a white bandage was wrapped around his head, and another bandage covered his bruised ribs. He looked a little pale.

"The doctor says your ribs are only bruised, not broken," she said, settling herself on the end of the bed.

"That old coot was so rough, he practically finished the job Thomas started."

Clover ignored that muttered complaint. "He also said you are to rest for the next few days and that I can remove the stitches from your head wound in ten days."

"I will take it easy after tomorrow. I mean to greet that bastard Thomas when he comes to the door tomorrow morning."

"Surely he will stay away now. He must know you have escaped."

"I cannae believe those two rogues will tell him they failed to do what he paid them for. I have Shelton and Lambert watching for Thomas. If anyone warns him I am still alive, we will ken it. I just hope the doctor's presence willnae make Dillingsworth suspicious."

"You mean to thrash Thomas again."

"Aye, I do."

"Well, I do not believe the doctor would approve."

"I dinnae give a tinker's damn what the doctor thinks. I do care what *ye* think. Ye have nae said ye believe me."

She sighed and shook her head. "I am torn. 'Tis such a wild tale, yet I cannot believe you would concoct it out of thin air. But it raises so many questions."

"What sort of questions?"

"How carefully could Thomas have thought this out? There are a great many holes in his plan."

"Enough to sail a clipper through," Ballard agreed. "I believe he or one of his hirelings was spying on Grendall, for he kenned I saved the horse. The rogues who set upon me thought it odd that they were paid ere they had done their work."

"What did Thomas plan to do when questions were asked about your death?"

"I suspect he thinks no one will care. I would be just another backwoodsmon killed outside a dock-side tavern."

"And, at the moment the fact that you are my husband would make little difference."

"Those who suspected something wouldnae speak out. Grendall made that plain enough. Thomas has a tight grip on this town."

"But he is short of funds."

"Probably because he lent out so much to tighten his hold on the people here. Grendall said a lot of people could be ruined if Thomas called in the debts owed him. Now, I ask ye again—do ye believe me?"

"Yes, I do. When he arrived on our wedding day, Thomas revealed how low he can sink. He thought he was offering me such a treat, that being his whore would be so much better than being your wife." Clover shook her head. "It is hard to understand how I could have been so blind to his true character."

Ballard started to reach out for her in sympathy, then cursed as pain gripped his ribs, echoing the throbbing in his head. As he sagged back against the pillow, Clover scrambled over to his side. He gave her a weak smile.

"I was going to give ye a wee bit of sympathy," he said.

"'Tis not I who need sympathy. And you plan to thrash Thomas tomorrow? In your bruised state?"

"After a good night's rest I can manage Thomas Dillingsworth."

She could see by the stubborn set of his jaw that he was not going to be convinced otherwise. Ballard would confront Thomas tomorrow even if someone had to hold him up. Clover sighed and lay down beside Ballard. Men were strange creatures.

"I was afeared ye wouldnae believe me," Ballard murmured as he slipped an arm around Clover and sighed when she cuddled up to him.

"It took some convincing," she admitted. "I will be glad to leave this town. Everything I believed about it and the people here has been turned on its head. And the way Thomas has acted makes it clear that it would be best to get as far away from him as possible."

"Aye, ye can soon leave it all behind ye."

Clover stood at the parlor window staring out at the road. She had not slept as well as Ballard had. He had the peace of mind that came from knowing exactly what he faced and how he would confront it, but that calm had eluded her.

When Thomas's carriage pulled up outside, she sighed with regret. She had hoped Ballard was wrong about Thomas's plans. She felt the worst of fools, blind and naive, for having seriously misjudged her former fiancé.

The rap on the front door made her wince. It was difficult to stay where she was and let Molly answer the door, but she had promised Ballard. Molly would come and get her. As she talked to Thomas, Molly would fetch Ballard from the kitchen. Clover suspected that Ballard wanted her to talk to Thomas so that she could see the final truth of his tale for herself. She dreaded the revelation.

"Miss," Molly called from the parlor doorway, "that man is here."

"I know." Clover started slowly toward the door, reluctance weighting her every step. "I just hope I can play the game and not give in to the urge to punch him right in the nose."

"Best to leave that to Mr. MacGregor."

Clover nodded and stepped out into the hall. She spared one brief glance toward Molly, who hurried off to the kitchen. She hoped Ballard would not leave her alone long with Thomas. It would be impossible to hide her anger for any considerable length of time. Besides, Thomas's arrival had given her all the proof of his perfidy that she needed.

Thomas was pacing the front hall and lightly slapping his gloves against his breeches. The bruises from Ballard's last beating were still faintly visible on his face. For reasons she could not grasp, the sight inspired her to remember things about Thomas she had chosen to ignore and forget—things she had shrugged away as mere rumor and unfounded gossip. The one that came to mind most clearly was the tale of John Reardon.

John had trounced Thomas at cards and had been found beaten nearly to death the next morning. Clover doubted that Thomas had done it himself, but she now strongly suspected he had ordered it done.

She took a deep breath, set her face in an expression of forlorn hurt, and cleared her throat, drawing Thomas's attention. "Good morning, Thomas. I am surprised you would show your face here after your behavior on my wedding day."

He took her hands in his. "I had to come, Clover. Once I heard the news—"

"What news?" Clover briefly feared that Ballard's plan to fool Thomas had also fooled the town, and now a new scandal was brewing around her.

"Come, Clover, there is no need to maintain this dignified facade. When I heard that that backwoods oaf had gotten himself killed in a drunken brawl, I had to come."

"Why?"

"Why? My dear girl, since that callow dog has been murdered, you are again in dire straits."

"Ah, and you are here to rescue me." Clover felt a strong unladylike urge to spit.

"My offer is still open. I realize it is not what a finely bred girl like you deserves, but my hands are tied. I assure you, however, that I will be a husband to you in all but name. This will not be some passing fancy where, in a year or two, you will again find yourself alone. Even if we no longer wish to reside together, I will see that you are well taken care of."

"She already has someone to take care of her," drawled Ballard as he stepped up behind Clover.

Clover was startled by Ballard's sudden arrival. She had not heard a sound until he spoke and slipped his arm around her shoulders. Despite her curiosity about how Ballard could come out of the kitchen and move along the hall like a wraith, unseen and unheard, she turned her full attention back to Thomas.

He looked as if he had seen a ghost. His fair skin had turned a sickly gray. It took only a moment for him to collect himself, however, and his abrupt mood change made her uneasy. He glared at her.

Still, she thought she saw fear lurking behind his anger.

"You might have told me that he had not died, Clover," Thomas snapped.

She shrugged. "You gave me little chance to speak. You were too intent upon your own plans." She shook her head. "I do not know which makes me sadder—that I misjudged your character and actually contemplated marrying you, or that after we have known each other so well, you would plot to hurt me so badly. In my time of need and grief you have thought only of yourself."

"How can you accuse me of selfishness? I did it all for you, to help you."

"Help me? Depriving me of my lawful husband, making me the laughingstock of the town, and setting me up to be your whore—all that was intended to help me? God save me from such help."

"You ungrateful bitch!" Oblivious of Ballard's presence, Thomas took a threatening step toward Clover.

"Ye are a little too free with your insults, laddie," said Ballard as he moved to put himself between Thomas and Clover. "Molly has some tea waiting for ye, Clover. I will join ye in a moment."

"Yes, send the child away," Thomas hissed. "Those two fools failed to end your wretched life, but I will not."

"Let us see if ye have the backbone to live up to your threats."

"Please," Clover began, afraid for Ballard.

"Go to the kitchen, Clover," he ordered.

After briefly hesitating while she debated the wisdom of meekly obeying Ballard's command, Clover went to the kitchen. Thomas was eager for a fight. In truth, he was eager to kill her husband. There was nothing she could do. Ballard had to defend himself in any way he could.

"Here, miss," Molly greeted her as she entered the kitchen. "Sit and have some tea."

Clover smiled faintly as she sat down at the table, in one of the few remaining chairs. "Where are my mother and the twins?"

"Mr. MacGregor sent them off to the shops." Molly served Clover her tea, then sat down to have a cup herself. "He felt it best that they were gone when that rapscallion came a-calling."

"He was probably right. I just hope having people thrashed in my front hall does not become a habit."

"I should not think so, miss. This ought to send that low rascal scurrying back to his hole for good and all."

Although she was not so sure, Clover did not argue. "You need not keep calling me *miss*, Molly. It feels strange for you to do so when you are in fact my teacher."

"I was brought up in service, and 'tis hard to break old habits. But I will try to be less formal. Ah, I just heard the front door shut. I think your man has done his business."

Molly had barely finished speaking when Ballard strode into the kitchen. Clearly, yet again, it had been an unequal fight, for Ballard looked none the worse for wear. Clover noticed, however, that as he sat down to accept Molly's offer of cider, he winced. He might not have gained any new injuries, but he had no doubt aggravated his old ones. When he caught her looking at him, he cocked one eyebrow, and she got the distinct impression that he did not want her to ask about his wounds. She idly wondered how long she would be able to obey that silent command.

"Did you take Thomas over to Sarah's again?" she asked.

"Nay. I tossed him out into the street. He had come in his carriage so his driver picked him up. Last time I had a thought to keep a scandal from brewing, but I didnae care this time. We willnae be here more than a day or two anyway."

"A day or two? But the doctor said—"

"To take it easy. 'Twill be an easy ride down the river and my kin can manage the wagons if need be. The boat will leave soon and there willnae be another for a few days, not one that can carry all of us and our baggage. Do ye have any reason to linger here?"

"None."

Clover was a little surprised at how quickly and firmly she answered him. Although she was somewhat apprehensive about going to Kentucky, she had no qualms about leaving Langleyville. It was no longer home to her. Friends and family had deserted her. It was a little frightening to move to a place most people still considered a wilderness, but there was nothing left for her here.

"No." Clover gave a short, mildly bitter laugh. "It was not easy to get Papa's 'oldest and dearest friend' to let us stay in this house for as long as we have. He will be pleased if we leave early."

Ballard reached out to pat her hand. "Money can turn many folk mean-spirited."

"True enough."

Ballard finished off his drink and stood up. "I dinnae have to meet the barge captain until this afternoon, so I think I will take myself to bed for a wee rest."

"How wise," Clover murmured and met the look he slanted her with a sweet smile.

"Ye could come to tuck me in."

"I think you are quite old enough to do that yourself."

"Weel, ye could check my bandages."

"If they are good enough to fight in, they are good enough to rest in."

"Aye, ye are probably right."

After Ballard left, Clover lingered over her tea. It was a minute or two before she realized that Molly's gaze was fixed on her.

"Is something wrong, Molly? Are we to start lunch already?"

"No. Lunch is cold meat, cheese, and bread. I was thinking that you ought to be looking in on your man."

"Why? He has gone to take a rest. I am sure he does not want me pestering him."

"Miss, I was wed for six years. Injuries or not, if a man like your Mr. MacGregor goes up to bed in the middle of the morning, 'tis because he wants his wife to come up and give him a bit of *attention*."

Clover blushed. "But he is hurt."

Molly shrugged as she collected the teacups and moved to the sink. "I was certain I heard a hint or two. And no man is ever too hurt, not unless he be near death. It won't do any harm to have a peek, will it?"

"No." Clover stood up. "I am sure he will let me know if he wants to be alone."

"He will. That be a plain-speaking man and you will be fair glad of that someday."

A nod was all Clover gave for an answer. Although it made her blush, she was glad of his plain speaking. It would help her grow to trust him.

As she entered her bedroom she found it hard to repress a smile. Ballard was half undressed and sprawled on top of the bed. The slow grin he gave her told her that Molly had been right—the last thing Ballard wanted was a rest. She strolled over to the bed.

"You look very comfortable, sir," she said, and laughed when he tugged her into his arms. "I thought you wanted to rest." She kicked off her shoes and settled more comfortably in his arms.

"Weel, I seem to be having a wee bit of trouble feeling sleepy." He slid his hands beneath her skirts and untied her garters.

"You need tiring out, do you?"

"Before I can have me a lazy sleep in the middle of the morning? Aye." He began to undo the buttons that ran down the back of her mint-green dress. "Now that ye are here, I have an idea or two."

"I just bet you do. What if someone comes looking for us?"

"Now, who would be so all-fired cruel as to disturb a pair of newlyweds?"

"I have no idea, but I locked the door just in case." She laughed along with him.

"Now, lass, I think ye may have to give me some help here, seeing as I am a poor injured soul."

"Since you are injured mayhap you should not be contemplating such a strenuous activity."

"I said I was injured, lass, not dead."

She laughed but then grew serious, placing a light

kiss on his mouth. "I am sorry for all the trouble I have brought you."

"Ye mean Thomas?" When she nodded, he cupped her face in his hands and gave her a slow, gentle kiss. "Ye didnae cause that trouble, lass. 'Tis all that fool Dillingsworth's doing. Now, I can take care of me and mine, so dinnae fret. We have seen the last of that fancy-dressed skunk."

Clover appreciated his effort to comfort her, but she could not share his confidence in their safety. Deep down, she suspected they had not heard the last of Thomas Dillingsworth.

Chapter Seven

Clover grimaced as she leaned on a rope-encircled post on the barge and stared into the muddy waters of the Ohio River. The water smelled as murky as it looked.

Ballard had hired one of the better barges, with cramped but clean quarters for them and their families. The wooden cabin set in the middle of the barge made it look a little more like a proper ship. Nevertheless, this was not the romantic river trip she had envisioned.

Clover watched the crew of a keelboat skillfully navigate the shallow draft freight boat past theirs. She inwardly acknowledged that the rivermen were not, as a whole, the dashing romantic rogues that were often described in local stories. Most of the ones she had seen were weather-hardened and none too clean, men who were struggling to make a living—either honestly or dishonestly. The boats were often precariously crammed with solemn-faced people headed west, many of them desperately poor. What she glimpsed of the houses and towns along the river did not look much better. *New* clearly did not mean *better*. They had been on the river for two days and she had yet to see any real sign of prosperity.

"Dinnae look so sad, lass," Ballard murmured as he stepped up behind her and slipped his arms around her waist. "Kentucky is much prettier."

She leaned back against him. "I am sure it is. I was just thinking of all the grand promises made to people who move west, promises of wealth and the easy life. There are few signs of that here."

"'Twill come. A lot of this land is still rough and new. And many of these folk have come from nothing. To have their own piece of land, to break their backs just for themselves and not for some other men, is prosperity to them. I ken that there are exceptions, but, truth to tell, most folk who have an easy life get their money from the sweat of others. Aye, some of them worked bloody hard to get to where they could work less yet still make an enviable amount of money. But 'tis still the work of others that fills their fancy homes and puts rich food on their tables."

He looked out at the collection of rough cabins they were passing. "This is just the beginning, lass. Just the beginning."

"I know. I am sure that parts of Pennsylvania once looked as rough as this. It just takes some getting used to."

"Where I live it is half settled and half rough. We have passed the raw beginning and started to reach for prosperity. Ye willnae find it as hard a life as some of these folk are living."

"Oh, I am not worried about the life being hard,

Ballard. If I had stayed in Langleyville, my life would
have been very hard indeed. But I do worry whether I
will be able to handle the difficult labor. Molly will not
be with us forever. I have lived a rather spoiled life."

"Aye, but ye are nae spoiled. Ye will do just fine,
lass."

Clover did not share his confidence, but she did
not argue. "Do you live near Daniel Boone?"

"Daniel Boone? Nay, lass. He doesnae live in Kentucky any longer."

"Has he set out to explore someplace else?"

"Nay. I heard that he and his wife are running an
inn somewhere—in Virginia, I think."

"You jest. Why would he leave Kentucky? He opened
the land to settlers. Surely he would have settled there
himself."

"He did. Our government decided Boone's claim
to his land wasnae a proper one and they wouldnae
let him keep it."

"That is appalling. He is fighting them in court, is
he not? He deserves what he claims. After all, he
opened up the route to that land."

"'Tis exactly how a lot of folk feel. I suspect old
Boone will be back in Kentucky someday."

Clover turned and caught sight of Damien playing
tag with Clayton. Both boys were too close to the
edge of the barge and their mother was occupied
helping Molly mend some clothes. Damien stumbled and Clover caught her breath, but then he regained his balance and resumed his reckless course
around the deck.

Clover slipped free of Ballard's light hold. "I had
better go and speak to the boys," she said. "They are
not taking care."

"Do ye want me to speak to them?"

"No, but thank you for offering. You kept them occupied most of the morning."

"They are good lads and no bother, lass."

"Humph. At times. This is not one of them."

She heard him laugh as he left her side and headed toward the captain.

Clover turned her attention back to her brothers, who were still racing heedlessly in all directions. She cursed when she saw Damien running straight for the side of the boat. The boy was so busy looking to see if Clayton was about to tag him, he did not see how near to the edge he was.

"Damien," she yelled, but he just laughed and kept running.

In mere moments he would fly right off the boat. She ran to cut him off, to catch him before he tumbled into the water.

Just as she stepped between him and the edge, he looked around and realized his danger. He yelled and tried to stop, but it was too late. The deck was still slick from an early morning rain and he skidded toward her. Clover grunted as he slammed into her, knocking her backward and sending her out over the side, then down, down. Damien echoed her screech as they hit the water and were swept along by the frigid, swirling current.

Clover tried to grab hold of Damien, but the current quickly dragged him out of her reach. She was being pulled down by the weight of her clothes and could not immediately go after him. Fighting panic, she pulled off her petticoats and skirt. The release of her legs from the tangled wet cloth enabled her to speed back to the surface. She looked for Damien and saw the boy being swept away by the same current that was buffeting her body.

The river was cold and dangerously swift. Clover knew she would never be able to fight against the current and take Damien back to the barge. Her only hope was to get him to shore or to grab hold of some of the rocks or low-hanging branches along the banks.

She spotted a dying tree tipped toward the river on an eroding bank, its branches lapped by the water but apparently sturdy. Clover started to swim with the current, gaining speed as she swiftly approached Damien. She heard Ballard's deep voice as he cursed her and ordered the crew to launch the small rowboat into the water, promising gruesome punishments if the men failed to reach them in time. Confident that Ballard would be setting out after her, she concentrated on getting to Damien.

As she closed in on the boy, she tried to slow down. When he saw her, his movements grew more frantic. She knew he thought she would save him and prayed she proved worthy of his faith in her.

Once she was near enough to be heard, she yelled, "Head toward that tree branch near the bank."

"I cannot."

"Yes, you can, Damien. I will be there to grab you."

"The water's taking me!"

"You do not have to fight it much, just enough to get nearer the shore. Keep your head above the water and try to swim toward the bank."

He began to struggle in the direction she indicated. He would never reach it on his own, she knew, but she hoped he could gain a few feet. Again using the current to give her speed, she swam toward the drooping branch. As she neared it, she began to fear that she would not get close enough to grab it. The fight against the current was swiftly sapping her strength. But suddenly the branch loomed up in front of her, and she grasped it with a sigh of relief.

The branch gave an ominous crack under her weight, but she had no time to worry about that. She edged along the branch until she could go no farther, looped her arm around the rough bark, and watched for Damien. He was weakening fast and it did not look as if he was close enough for her to reach him.

"Just a little more, Damien," she called to him. "Just a little more."

"I am too tired."

"I know, darling, but just a little closer and you will be safe."

She could still hear Ballard shouting, but could not understand what he was saying. All she could do was pray that she could get hold of Damien and keep hold of him until someone could pull them both from the water. As her young brother thrashed past her, she grabbed his outstretched hand. He had the wit to grab her arm immediately with his other hand as well. The force of his current-pulled weight on her arm nearly made her lose her grip on the branch.

"Pull yourself up my arm, Damien," she said as she tried to get a firmer grip on the branch.

Her brother did as he was told and soon had a hold on the branch as well. She steadied her own grasp and wrapped her arm around his waist. Her legs ached from the cold and the strain of keeping them both above water.

"What do we do now, Clover?" Damien asked, his teeth chattering, his body trembling.

"We have two choices. We can try to make our way back along this branch until we can climb onto the bank, or we can wait right here until the barge comes by and rescues us."

"Maybe we should try to get on land."

"It would certainly be easier than hanging here, but I see no place for the barge to dock."

"They can send the little boat for us."

Clover nodded and edged her arm along the branch, tugging Damien with her. The branch gave another ominous crack, and she moved more cautiously. Then her feet touched bottom. To her horror, her feet sank into the mud. It was as if the mud were alive and sucking her down into it. She yanked her foot free and edged back toward the river, nudging a reluctant Damien to do the same.

"What's wrong?" he said.

"Between us and the bank is mud that seems inclined to have me for dinner. I think it would be as dangerous for us to try and get around it as to just hang here until we are rescued."

"Look, Clover! Here comes the rowboat!"

"And none too soon," she muttered as the branch cracked again, dipping a little lower into the water.

"Clover," Ballard yelled as he caught sight of her from the narrow bow of the small boat and directed the barge captain to row toward her. "Are ye all right?"

"Yes, but this branch is beginning to give way."

"We will be there in just a minute, love."

Ballard cursed the caution needed to maneuver the small boat close to her. He had been in a state of panic since Clover had plunged into the river after her brother. Although Agnes and Clayton had assured him that Clover and Damien could swim like fish, it had not eased his fear for them. All he could see was their diminutive forms being swept along by the swift, murky waters of the Ohio.

Ballard steadied himself in the narrow bow as the captain inched the boat closer. "Now, laddie," he said to Damien, extending his hand, "grab hold and I will pull ye in."

"What if you drop me? Clover says the mud here will eat you."

"Quicksand," muttered the burly, gray-haired captain.

"I willnae drop ye, laddie," Ballard assured the boy. "Just reach out and take my hand."

"Go on, Damien," Clover said. "Ballard can hang on to you easily. I will still have hold of you as well."

Damien tentatively reached out toward Ballard. He grabbed the boy by the wrist, but Damien was hesitant to release his grip on the branch. Clover gave Damien a gentle push toward the boat. When Damien finally let go, Ballard quickly yanked the child into the boat. He heard an ominous crack and watched Clover sink a little deeper into the water.

"Hang on, Clover," he yelled as the captain readjusted the position of the boat.

"I am hanging on. 'Tis the branch that is letting go."

"All right, lass, reach your hand out to me."

Clover briefly debated letting go and paddling over to the boat, but knew she did not have enough strength. Her legs were numb and her shoulders ached. The instant Ballard grabbed her wrist, she released the branch. She sank under the water, but felt

Ballard yanking her toward the surface. A grunt of pain escaped her when she was roughly dragged into the boat. She tried to pull away as Ballard tugged her into his arms.

"You will get all wet." She wondered if he could understand her, for her chattering teeth were distorting her words.

"I am pretty wet already, lass. Just rest easy. We will talk when ye are dry and tucked into bed."

Since she did not feel much like talking anyway, Clover did not argue. She huddled closer to Ballard and gave Damien a weak smile. The captain had thrown his heavy woolen coat around the boy, but Damien still looked cold. She was glad to see how quickly they were closing in on the barge.

The minute the rowboat was secured to the side of the barge, Agnes was reaching for Damien. "Clover, dear, are you all right?"

"I will live," she replied as Ballard set her on the deck.

"If ye are lucky," muttered Ballard as he scrambled onto the deck and scooped her into his arms. He marched through their surrounding family and headed for their tiny cabin. He was acting angry, yet why should he be angry with her? It was not her fault that Damien had fallen into the river.

She voiced a complaint when he set her on the bed and started to take off her clothes, but he ignored her. Her temper rose as he rubbed her dry, muttering to himself. It only added to her annoyance that she could not understand a word he was saying. He shoved her into her nightdress and gently but forcefully tucked her into bed.

"Are you quite finished?" she snapped after he secured the blanket around her neck.

"Nay. Ye need a hot drink to take the chill from your bones."

He gave her no chance to say yea or nay, shutting the rough plank door behind him. Clover cursed and loosened the covers he had so snugly wrapped around her. That Ballard should want to care for her after her ordeal was very nice, but his methods were highly exasperating. He was treating her like a child. His sullen attitude puzzled her. She was determined to find out what was ailing the man.

As she waited for Ballard to return and gathered her courage to confront him, she thought about what she had done and shivered. Now that she had the luxury to consider her actions, she realized she could have died alongside Damien instead of rescuing him. Her aching body told her very clearly how great a demand she had placed on her strength. Although she was no longer shivering so badly that her teeth clicked together, she still felt a chill that went clear to the bone. Although she had had no choice but to act as she had, she was glad she had not had time to examine the consequences. Self-preservation might have held her back.

Ballard returned, scowling at the sight of the loosened bedcovers. He sat beside her, a cup of hot tea in his hands. She sat up to drink it and earned another scowl from him. When he just sat there staring at her, Clover decided she had had enough.

"Is something wrong?" she demanded.

"Aside from ye trying to kill yourself—nay," he replied as he leaped to his feet and started to pace about their tiny room. "Ye should have gotten back onto the boat. Ye could have been swept away."

"As Damien could have been."

He stopped by the side of the bed and sighed. "I ken it." He grimaced and ran his fingers through his still damp hair. "What troubles me is that *ye* risked your life by staying in that cold water for so long. I wasted time getting the boat because I cannae swim."

"A lot of people cannot swim, Ballard."

"I ken it, but to tell the truth, I would have wagered that ye would have been one of them."

"Papa taught me. You see, I fell into a creek when I was little and nearly drowned. He knew how to swim and decided that I should know as well. I, in turn, taught the boys." She took another sip of tea.

"It was bloody unsettling to watch ye being swept away. I thought those laggards would ne'er get the boat into the river in time."

"Then I shall teach you how to swim too so that the next time someone falls into a river, I can hold your coat while you hie to the rescue." She smiled faintly.

Ballard grinned back as he sat down on the edge of the bed again. "Ye shouldnae make light of a mon's vanity, lass." More seriously he added, "Aye, I will admit 'twas a wound to my vanity to be so slow to set after ye. Mostly, though, 'twas bloody frustrating to watch first Damien then ye go hurtling down the river and ken that I couldnae help ye."

"You came and got us in the rowboat."

"Aye, but if ye hadnae grabbed on to that tree branch, the rowboat would have been useless. Ye both could have drowned ere I could reach ye." He smiled as he took her empty cup and set it aside. "Dinnae frown, lass. I but grumble o'er my uselessness. No mon likes to accept that he cannae fully protect his family under any and all circumstances. I will eventually recover from this blow to my pride. Ye did fine today and I am fair proud of ye for it. Just allow me to sulk a wee bit."

"Perhaps you can take comfort in the fact that none of the other men were there to stop our fall either."

"Oh, I do, lass. I do. 'Tis bad enough not being able to protect ye meself, but 'twould be far worse to have to listen to some other mon boasting of how he rescued my wife." He winked at her when she giggled. "Now ye must rest. I ken weel that ye took a chill. Aye, and I could tell when I pulled ye out that ye had sapped all your strength. We will be landing at Tullyville by close of day tomorrow and I want ye to rest until then, to be sure that ye have nae caught the ague and have regained your strength for the rest of the journey."

Clover briefly considered arguing, then decided she would be wise to do as he told her. She would take time to pamper herself and prepare for the more arduous part of their journey. As she smiled at Ballard, she prayed that her final destination did not look as destitute as some of the places she had seen so far along the river.

"This is Tullyville?" Clover asked Ballard as they stood on the muddy bank and watched the barge being unloaded. "I had rather thought that the *ville* on the end of *Tully* meant a settlement."

"It *is* a settlement. 'Twas settled by Mike Tully and

his friends." Ballard laughed at her wry look. "'Tis a new town, lass. 'Twill grow."

If it did, Clover hoped it would also improve. Five rough cabins and an assortment of ramshackle sheds lined a muddy, narrow, and badly rutted road. A light breeze wended down the street, carrying the acrid scent of farm animals. She saw only two women, slovenly dressed and leaning on a rail before one of the larger log buildings. Nudging Ballard, she pointed toward it.

"Is that the inn?" she asked uncertainly.

"Aye, but we willnae be staying there. 'Tis little more than a tavern and brothel. We will take the wagons outside of town a ways and make camp. I dinnae want ye ladies anywhere near these men when they start to tippling."

Long before the wagons were loaded and the oxen hitched up, Clover was eager to get out of town. The noise from the inn indicated that the men were already getting rowdy. It sounded jovial at the moment, but she knew that that could change quickly. She helped Molly, Agnes, and the boys into the back of a heavy wagon, then joined Ballard on the driver's seat. Lambert and Shelton each drove another wagon and followed Ballard as he led them out of town.

After only an hour's journey, they reached the place where Ballard wanted to camp. Despite the short ride, Clover's backside ached something fierce. Checking to be sure Ballard could not see, she rubbed her sore bottom as she moved to help Molly unpack what they would need to make a meal. She was going to have to put some padding between herself and the hard seat if she wanted to be able to stand when she got to Ballard's home.

"Now, miss, I want you to make the biscuits tonight," Molly said as they sat near the fire Shelton had made.

Clover grimaced as she started to mix the biscuit batter. "Are you sure this is wise?"

"You have to start sometime." Molly hung a heavy kettle over the fire and began to make a venison stew.

"I know. I am just not sure the men will appreciate being tested after such a hard day."

Molly laughed. "True. We have enough flour, so I will make a small batch too. If yours be cooking up fine, as I am sure they will, 'twill make no matter. You can never have too many biscuits."

Cooking over an open fire instead of in an oven made Clover nervous. By the time everyone sat down to eat, she was reluctant to offer her biscuits. They looked fine, but that did not mean they would taste good. She stifled an urge to hide as Ballard tasted one.

"There, lass, I told ye ye would learn how to cook," Ballard said as he chewed.

Clover sighed with relief and smiled at him, but as the meal continued she began to doubt his word. He drank a lot of water from his canteen and even let a biscuit soak in his stew until it was dripping with gravy. Shelton and Lambert watched him for a moment before each choosing Molly's biscuits instead. Clover tasted one of her own. It was edible but just barely—dry and far too salty.

She felt a sharp pang of disappointment and embarrassment. Before they had married, she had told Ballard that she was no cook. Mistakes were common when learning a new skill. As Ballard doggedly took another of her biscuits, she almost smiled. He was being such a gentleman, trying to salve her pride and her feelings, but she could not let him suffer any longer.

"Ballard," she said, and almost laughed when he coughed a little and took a few hearty swigs of water to wash the dry biscuit from his mouth. "Are my biscuits really all right?"

"Oh, aye, lassie. Just fine."

"You do know that, if I believe you, I will stop practicing." She had to bite her lip to keep from laughing at the arrested look on his face. "I will think that I now know how to make good biscuits, and I will go on to master something else. So you should be very careful about giving such a good opinion so quickly. It could mean that you eat biscuits that taste like that for the rest of your life."

"The rest of my life?" he murmured as he stared at the half-eaten biscuit in his hand.

"Yes. After all, why should I try to improve upon perfection?"

Ballard finally caught the light of laughter in her eyes. "Wretch," he said, and grinned when everyone laughed. "Weel, they are a wee bit dry and I think ye used a touch too much salt."

She tossed the rest of her biscuit into the fire, and laughed when he did the same. "I thought so too." She leaned over and kissed his cheek. "Thank you for being so kind, but I think it would be best for all of us if you were truthful. Now Molly and I can see where I erred and, I pray, fix the problem."

Molly took a small bite of Clover's biscuit, nodded, and tossed it into the fire. "You were that close, miss."

"Good," Clover said. "We cannot have Ballard drinking the well dry every time I cook something." She laughed again.

Once the meal was over, Clover helped Molly clean up. Shelton was to take first watch, so Ballard led her to where they would sleep. He had arranged their bed under one of the wagons. Clover smiled faintly when she saw how he had tacked up blankets to give them some privacy. After indulging in a small toilette with a pan of cold water, she stripped to her chemise and slid beneath the blankets Ballard had spread on the ground. Even as Ballard tugged her into his arms, she yawned.

"Tired, lass?" He smoothed his hand over her hair.

"Yes, although I have not done all that much today."

"Just being out of doors for a long time can make ye sleepy if ye are nae used to it. Ye are probably still suffering a wee bit from your adventure in the river."

"Probably. At least, I hope that is it. I have never considered myself a weak or delicate person." She moved her hand over his broad, warm chest.

"Nay, ye are nae weak or delicate. This is all new to ye, loving. Ye just need time to get accustomed, 'tis all." He grinned and kissed the top of her head. "Dinnae fret. I dinnae expect ye to become a tobacco-spitting pioneer woman who can chop wood with one hand and skin a bear with the other. Leastwise, not right away." He laughed when she gave him a light tap on the arm.

"I should hope not." She peeked up at him and was only able to discern the outline of his face in the shadows. "Do you know many women who spit to-bacco?"

Ballard laughed. "Only old Mabel Clemmons. She sets in a rocker in front of the general store her son owns. She cusses like a sailor and can beat most men in a spitting contest, but once ye get past the shock of it, ye realize she is a clever old woman and worth listening to."

"I had an aunt much like that. She dressed just as she pleased, which was usually quite oddly, said anything that popped into her head, and smoked cigars. I once asked her why she liked to upset and shock people, and she told me she had done everything she was told to do for fifty-odd years and now she insisted on being herself. And she believed that people need to be shocked once in a while." Clover smiled when Ballard chuckled softly.

"Old Mabel started to be herself as soon as she reached Kentucky," he said.

He recalled the look on Clover's face as they had passed some of the rougher places along the river. Clearly she had been alarmed by a lot of what she saw. He had never looked closely at places like Tullyville, just accepted them, but he could understand how she might feel.

"Clover, ye willnae be living in some rough hut. Ye ken that, dinnae ye?"

"Of course, Ballard." She suddenly realized that she had revealed her occasional dismay a little too clearly. "I am sorry if I have led you to believe that I was, well, regretting this move. To be honest, it was not so much the newness or roughness of the places that distressed me, but the filth. I think even Tullyville will improve when a few families settle there. Women do not long tolerate the sort of things that make Tullyville so unsavory."

"Nay, they dinnae, and Pottersville has families. It even has a church."

"Pottersville?"

"That is what they are calling our town now. Truth is, that must be the fifth or sixth name it has had. They cannae seem to settle on what to call it, so most times I dinnae give it a name. They are hankering to be incorporated as a town though, so I suspicion they will make up their minds soon. How did Langleyville get its name?"

"A Langley family owns most of the riverfront."

Ballard nodded. "We are called Pottersville now because Jedediah Potter got the church built. I swear to ye, lass, ye willnae find a squalid mudhole like Tully's place. I live in the sort of town that draws families. It has good farming land, good stock-breeding land."

She gently caressed his cheek, smiling faintly when he kissed her palm. "I will be fine, Ballard. I promise you, I am not one to pout because I do not have some fine brick mansion to live in. I entered this marriage with my eyes open, and I will accept whatever you have to offer."

He held her a little closer, wanting to believe her, but finding his doubts hard to conquer. She would never complain or disparage his efforts, but he still feared disappointing her. Once they were out of Langleyville, away from all she had known, he had thought that his self-doubts would begin to ease. He had naively thought that he only needed to get to Kentucky, to return to the places he knew, to regain his confidence. Instead he was growing more and more aware of the disparities between what he could offer her and what she had known. He dreaded seeing disappointment in her fine blue eyes and knowing that he had failed her.

"Weel now, my wee wife, there is something I

would like to offer ye now, but we will have to wait until we get home," he murmured as he slid his hand down her side to her hip. "There isnae much privacy here."

"None at all," she whispered as she heard Shelton walk past the wagon.

Needing to reassure himself that they still had something in common, he kissed her, slowly and deeply. He felt her breathing quicken and the tips of her breasts harden against his chest. Their passion was still well-matched, he thought, and breathed a silent sigh of relief as he settled them more comfortably on their hard bed. All he had to do was keep that passion alive until it matured into a deeper, richer emotion which would bind her to him for the rest of their lives.

Chapter Eight

"Hey, you long-legged Scot, you running home already?" called a burly man from the front porch of a large wooden building.

"Clemmons, ye rogue," Ballard called back as he pulled the wagon to a stop.

Clover sighed as Ballard leaped off the wagon seat, loped up the three steps, and exchanged a bear hug with the man. Shelton and Lambert were quick to follow. She eased herself to the ground and rubbed her aching backside. Ballard had grinned when she had put a folded blanket on the seat, but she had ignored his amusement. She knew the padding had helped her endure the rough journey.

Just as Agnes, Molly, and the twins joined Clover, Ballard looked their way. "Here, lass," he said as he started toward her, "ye should have waited. I would have helped ye down."

"Right about now, Ballard," she said in a quiet voice as he reached her side, "I would have leaped back into the Ohio River rather than sit on that torturous seat for one moment longer."

Ballard grinned and kissed her cheek, then grimaced. "Dinnae try to smooth over my error. A gentleman would have helped ye and the other women down first, then introduced them all to Jonathan. Weel, ye are here to teach me those pretty manners."

Jonathan Clemmons stepped to the edge of the veranda. "You came back with more than you left with, Ballard m'boy."

Clover smiled faintly at the big man, then noticed that he was looking at Molly, who was staring right back. Molly smoothed the skirts of her plain gray gown and tucked a stray wisp of hair back under her crisp white mobcap. Clover decided to take a closer look at the man as they were all introduced to him.

Clemmons was a big man, almost as tall as Ballard but of a burlier build. His face was square, plain, and weathered. He had hazel eyes with fine lines at each corner that deepened when he smiled. There was no hint of gray in his long, roughly cut brown hair, so Clover guessed that he was under forty years of age. He had a strong, deep voice and when he suddenly bellowed in surprise, she was abruptly drawn out of her thoughts.

"Married?" Jonathan stared at Ballard in open-mouthed surprise. "You got *married*?"

"I told ye I was looking for a wife," Ballard answered as he draped his arm around Clover's shoulders. "Me and Clover have been wed for a fortnight now."

"I know what you told me, you lanky fool. I just did not expect you to be so successful so quick, or"—he smiled at Clover—"to get yourself such a pretty one."

"You are very kind, sir," she said.

"Call me Jon."

"I knew you would do just as you claimed you would, boy," said a deep, raspy voice.

Clover looked at the person who had spoken and struggled to hide her surprise as Ballard introduced them all to Jon's mother, Mabel Clemmons. The woman looked too dainty and slender to produce such a manly voice. She wore a simple blue gingham gown, and her gray-flecked brown hair was neatly pinned up. There was such life in her hazel eyes, it gave her plain, slightly angular face a hint of beauty. There was a bump in one of her freckled cheeks and Clover realized the woman was chewing tobacco. She noticed several spitoons placed strategically around the porch. When the woman suddenly spat into one, Clover was a little startled by the speed, accuracy, and tidiness of the act. She idly wondered if anyone had tried to get Mabel to take up pipe smoking instead.

"Warned her about me, didn't ya, boy," Mabel said, fixing her gaze on Ballard.

"Weel, there are nae many like ye, Mabel," Ballard drawled.

"Damned right. I ain't inclined to become staid and common in my old age." Mabel turned her sharp gaze on Molly. "A maid, eh? Are you getting high and mighty on us, Ballard?"

"Molly was hired for my sake, Mrs. Clemmons," Clover said. "I fear I lack a few housewifely skills."

Mabel nodded and looked at Molly again. "So you are here only for a short spell."

"Maybe. Maybe not. I am of a mind to find me a husband," Molly said, meeting Mabel's keen gaze squarely. "I am fair tired of being a widow."

A faint smile briefly curved Mabel's thin lips

before she turned to Agnes. "You here to find a man too?"

Agnes blushed. "Heavens, no. I am but a month widowed and much too old for such nonsense."

"You're still breathing, ain't you? That's 'bout all it takes to get a man sniffing 'round your skirts in these parts." She winked at Ballard. "And it seems marrying is in the air." She spat again and frowned down the road. "Course, there be one or two what might be displeased about your getting hitched up, Ballard."

Clover felt Ballard tense as he followed Mabel's gaze down the road. She peeked around him. And almost cursed. Loping toward them was a woman, her skirts hitched up to reveal well-shaped black-stockinged legs and red petticoats. Thick raven hair billowed around her head as she ran, and her full breasts seemed in danger of bouncing free of her low-necked gown. Ballard turned to greet the woman, only to grunt in surprise as she flung herself into his arms. Clover muttered a curse. Mabel chuckled.

"Elizabeth, enough," Ballard snapped as he wrenched free of the woman's grasp and held her at arm's length.

"Come now, Ballard, I know we did not part on the best of terms, but—forgive and forget, I always say." Elizabeth glanced at Clover and her family. "I see you have brought some new people to town. Do you mean to settle here or move on?" she asked Clover as she wriggled closer to Ballard.

"I rather thought I would linger in the area," Clover replied wryly.

"Elizabeth Brown, there are some people I would like you to meet," Ballard said, pushing her away as he introduced Clover's family and Molly. He quickly put his arm around Clover's shoulders. "And this is

Clover—my wife." Clover watched with interest as Elizabeth's eyes grew wide and her cheeks flushed with anger.

"You *married* this child?" she snapped.

"I told ye I was going to find me a wife."

"I thought those were just words, said to spite me."

"I dinnae play those kind of games, Elizabeth. Ye have kenned me long enough to realize that."

Clover was tempted to ask for how long and how well, but bit the inside of her cheek to stem the words. Ballard did not look very welcoming. It would be unfair to assume immediately he had lied when he had said there was no one for him in Kentucky. She just wished that this particular "no one" did not look so fulsome and sultry. She wondered crossly if Ballard knew any slender, small-breasted women besides herself.

"I certainly did not think you would be fool enough to up and wed some scrawny chit from back east. You were gone barely more than a fortnight," Elizabeth exclaimed.

"I told nearly the whole town what I planned to do and I did it."

"Well, this pale child will never survive out here. You made a very poor choice, Ballard MacGregor."

"I dinnae happen to think so. And if ye cannae welcome her and her kin, there isnae any reason for ye to linger here."

"No? You owe me—"

"I owe ye nothing, lass. I never made ye a promise or even hinted that I would. 'Tis all in your head, a product of your own vanity. Now, either wish us weel or leave and let that be the end of it."

"The end of it? I think not." She glared at Clover, then marched away.

Ballard sighed. "Sorry about that, lass."

"You said you had no one in Kentucky," Clover murmured.

"I didnae lie. That fool lass thinks every mon in the state is fairly pining away for her."

Clover watched the woman disappear down the road, invitation in every swish of her skirt, and suspected that Elizabeth Brown had some sound reasons for that vanity. A part of Clover wanted to know every detail of Ballard's past relationship with her, no matter how sordid, but a larger part of her desperately wanted to brush the matter aside. She could not stop thinking that Elizabeth Brown was probably an excellent cook too.

"She seemed very sure that you would be one of those pining men," Clover said.

"Aye, but as I said, 'tis all in her head. There was a wee tryst atween us after the harvest frolic, but I ne'er even hinted it would be more than that. I took a quick taste of what she offers half the men in the area, and she decided I was the one who wanted to marry her. I spent nearly all winter trying to make her understand she was mistaken. I thought I had been successful. Weel, she must see the truth now. 'Tis the last we will see of her, lass," he said. "She has plenty of beaus ready and willing to soothe her bruised vanity."

Ballard winced when Clover gave him a look that clearly said he was being either naively optimistic or extraordinarily stupid. "Shall we go into the store?" He took her hand in his.

"Do we need to buy anything?" she asked as he led

her inside, noticing from the corner of her eye that Jonathan Clemmons fell into step next to Molly.

"Some seed. I didnae think I would return in time to plant a full crop, but I have, so I need a wee bit more seed. I thought there might be a few items ye need. Mayhap some cooking supplies. Have a look about, lass, while I talk with Jonathan."

As soon as Ballard tugged Jonathan away from Molly's side, Clover told her, "I get the distinct impression you have already selected your next husband."

"He certainly is a promising prospect." Molly winked at Clover. "Do not be fretting, miss. I will not be leaving you till you know all you need to know about housewifery. If Jonathan Clemmons be the one for me, he will be standing by when I am done." She took Clover's arm and glanced toward Mabel, who was sitting in a rocker next to a cast-iron stove, talking to Agnes. "His mother saw that I be considering her boy and said not a word against it, so that be the first step taken."

"We ain't got no Papist church 'round here," Mabel called over to Molly.

"That be fine, ma'am, as I am of a Protestant bent meself."

As Molly led her around the store, explaining some of the less obvious items for sale, Clover listened carefully. She had shopped before, but now realized her ignorance with painful clarity. She had always taken a list and let the shopkeeper fill her order, or left the shopping to the housekeeper. There was clearly a great deal she had to learn about making selections according to quantity, quality, and price.

When they passed a table stacked with bolts of material, Clover paused and looked down at the gown she was wearing, a green brocade with a lace fichu at the neck. The day's journey had been hard on the lace trim as well as on the delicate material. She knew the work she would have to do as Ballard's wife would be even harder on her gowns. She needed sturdier ones made of kersey, wool, and even homespun. If she had a few more serviceable gowns, she could keep her silks and brocades for any festive occasions, at least until they were so out of fashion that no amount of clever reworking would salvage them.

Molly helped her pick out material that would hold up well yet not be uncomfortable. After a quick glance at her mother's attire, she selected enough fabric to make her mother two gowns as well. She was not sure she would get much assistance from her mother in the more menial chores, but did not want the lack of a sturdy gown to be the reason.

Clover was just walking over to Ballard to make sure that she was not spending too much when a man, two youths, and a boy entered the store. Ballard, Jonathan, Lambert, and Shelton barely acknowledged the group, who were dressed in stained buckskins. Mabel glared at the big man and spat into a spitoon. The way the man and two youths eyed Clover made her hold the bolts of cloth a little tighter against her chest. Although they were at least a yard away, she could smell the acrid scent of long-unwashed bodies. With his bushy black and silver beard, the man reminded her uncomfortably of Big Jim, and she edged toward Ballard.

"What can I do for you, Morrisey?" Jonathan asked the man.

"You can start by getting me some whiskey. Me and my boys done drained our last jug last night." He pushed one of the youths toward the counter. "Sam here knows what else that fool woman of mine thinks she needs."

"A new husband," said Mabel loudly.

Morrisey glared at her. "Enough out of you, old woman. My Bess does fine. Ain't I given her ten strapping boys?"

Mabel snorted. "One right after another till the poor thing looks as old and dried up as I do."

Clover was fascinated by the way Mabel snapped at the huge, ill-tempered man. A slight movement at her skirts distracted her and she looked down into the huge brown eyes of the smallest boy who had entered with Morrisey. He was staring at her as if he had never seen anyone like her before. As she tried to think of something to say, she realized that dirt was not the sole reason for his darker skin tone. Some of the darker patches were actually large bruises and his small nose had a kink in it as if it had been broken and had healed crookedly. As she leaned down to take a closer look, the boy slowly reached out with one bone-thin dirty hand and touched her cheek. Before she could say anything, he was pushed aside so hard that he fell to the floor. Clover looked up to see Morrisey grab the child by the front of his ragged shirt and lift him up.

"Stupid brat, I told you, you ain't to be touching white women."

Clover watched in openmouthed shock as the man hit the small boy with a closed fist, threw him to the floor, and kicked him viciously. Without a second's hesitation, she dropped the bolts of cloth save for one and, as Morrisey bent to grab the boy again, she slammed the heavy bolt of cloth against his head. He bellowed a curse, staggered back a few steps and glared at her, raising his meaty fists. Clover dropped the cloth, grabbed the little boy by the hand as he stumbled to his feet, and tugged him behind her. Out of the corner of her eye she saw Ballard move so that he stood next to Morrisey.

"Give me back that little half-breed, woman. This ain't none of your concern."

"I will not stand here and let you brutalize this child, Mr. Morrisey," she said.

"He ain't your brat; he be mine—bought and paid for."

"Bought? You *bought* this boy?"

"Cost me two silver dollars, he did. His ma was raped by some Shawnee buck and wanted to be rid of him. A man can't be having too many strong backs to work his fields, and he came cheaper than those black ones."

"This boy will never have a strong back if you beat him like that or starve him as you obviously have been."

Morrisey stuck out one big, filthy hand. "That be my business. Now give him back." When Clover did not move, he snapped, "You best do it, woman, or I'll be setting the law on you."

"Clover," Ballard said, stepping over to her, "ye have to give the laddie back to him."

"But, Ballard—"

"Ye have to, loving. 'Tis the law. There isnae a cursed thing we can do about it."

Before she could argue, the boy slipped away from her. To her astonishment, he flashed her a tiny smile, skipped around Morrisey, and headed for the door. As the child passed Mabel, she tossed him a chunk of bread. He was eating it even as he ran out the door.

"I am telling ye, Morrisey," Ballard said, his words spat out from between clenched teeth, "folk are getting weary of ye and your brutish ways."

"Well, you know how to stop it. The judge done told you last summer. Buy the boy."

"No one here has sixty dollars, Morrisey, and weel ye ken it."

"Ain't that just too bad. Reckon I keep the breed then."

"Get out," said Jonathan. "Sam has taken care of your business. There's no need for you to linger here."

As soon as Morrisey and his sons left, Clover looked at Ballard, who had picked up the bolts of cloth she had dropped. "Is that the end of it? There really is nothing we can do?"

"I fear not, lass. We have tried everything. Me and Jon tried to beat some humanity into Morrisey last spring, but it only made it harder on the boy. We even got a circuit judge to listen to us, but it didnae make no difference. The boy is half Shawnee. His own ma doesnae want him and no one kens where his people are even if they would take him in. The judge said that the only thing we can do is buy the boy back, but Morrisey is demanding sixty dollars. Ye ken weel how little coin there is about, and he will-nae take anything but silver." He shrugged. "All we can do is slip the laddie some food now and then, and let Morrisey ken that if he hurts the boy too grievously, he will pay for it. I am sorry, Clover."

"'Tis not your fault." No one said any more about

the boy, but Clover knew that she would not be able to shake him from her thoughts.

Ballard bought every piece of material she requested. He readily agreed that she needed sturdy everyday gowns. She and Molly were discussing what dresses she would make even as they left the store. The Clemmonses followed to say good-bye. It took a while for Ballard to get them all back into the wagons. As soon as they were seated he started them on their way.

As they traveled to Ballard's home, Clover carefully studied the land through which they passed. She grew uneasy as she saw how empty of people the area was. She had spent her whole life in a town house, side by side with other families, in an increasingly busy river town. It did not look as if Ballard had many neighbors at all, and certainly none within calling distance.

"Ye will be seeing my place as soon as we round the next bend in the road," Ballard said after almost an hour.

Clover steadied herself. If she was disappointed with her new home, she did not want to reveal that to Ballard. As they turned the corner, she nearly gasped with relief. It was not the sort of architecture she was accustomed to, but it was no rough cabin either. A sizable two-story plank house sat in a small hollow. It had a large wraparound veranda and Ballard had obviously taken care to leave shade trees standing nearby. A huge stone chimney rose on either side and a smaller one poked up over the roof from the back. Stables and a tidy corral lay just beyond, as well as several smaller outbuildings. She could also see that

Ballard was in the process of building more paddocks for his horses.

As they drew up in front of the house, a man stepped onto the porch. He was reed-thin with a head of thick, snow-white hair. Ballard introduced them all to Adam Dunstan, his hired man. Clover could see that Adam was intensely curious about Ballard's early return with a new wife and added family in tow, but he just murmured a greeting and began to help Shelton and Lambert unload the wagons.

Ballard took Clover's hand and led her into the house, signaling her mother, brothers, and Molly to follow. Clover noticed that the women kept her brothers a few steps behind them, staying close enough to hear what Ballard was saying, yet far enough away to allow her and Ballard to exchange a few soft confidences.

"We can start upstairs, lass, so we will be out of the way when the lads bring your things up," Ballard said, leading her toward the stairs that rose from the front hall.

The second story was unfinished. She saw only two doors. The other rooms were marked out by finished walls and tacked-up blankets. As Ballard dragged her toward a door, Clover counted six blocked-out bedrooms.

"This is to be our room," he said as he opened the door and tugged her inside.

A fireplace dominated the outer wall and a large, roughly hewn bed dominated another. Two bear rugs covered most of the floor. Clover did not want to consider how Ballard had obtained them. The wardrobe, clothes chest, and bedside tables were all handmade. Although the furniture had none of the fancy decorations she was used to, the pieces were beautiful in their heavy, solid simplicity.

As he dragged her through the other rooms, she realized that Ballard, Lambert, and Shelton were adept at making what they needed. There were only a few pieces of store-bought furniture. Clearly Ballard had planned his house carefully, with a keen eye to upgrading it as his fortunes improved.

Molly enthused over the kitchen, set in a side wing that extended out from the rear of the house. Ballard showed Clover the other four downstairs rooms, each with corner fireplaces, then hurried her outside. She found it hard to keep up with him as he showed her the stables, the barn, the smokehouse, the chicken coops, the privy, the springhouse, the icehouse, and even the small log cabin he had built as his first home, which now served as Adam's quarters. There was even a summer kitchen which he said he would eventually attach to the main house. Clover began to wonder when the man had time to raise horses. He had barely indicated the outlying fields, recently planted apple orchard, and kitchen garden when they returned to the house to unpack all their things and cook a meal.

By the time Clover crawled into bed that night she was exhausted. She smiled faintly as Ballard slipped in beside her and tugged her into his arms. As he ran his hand up and down her sides, her fatigue faded. Her passion for him flared to life and she snuggled closer.

"Ye have nae said much since we arrived," he murmured as he encircled her neck with soft, nibbling kisses.

She smoothed her hands over his strong, warm

back. "There has not been much chance to talk. Actually, I did wonder when you found time to plant your fields and raise your horses."

"I didnae build the house all on my own, or the stables and the barn. We had one of those fine, neighborly parties where nearly everyone for miles around comes to lend a hand. Although I have plenty of other work to do, there are times when I can work on the house. I built most of the furniture in the evenings and over the winter."

"Ah. That explains the lumber and tools down-stairs."

"I can move them, clear it all out, if ye want." He undid her nightgown, carefully kissing each newly exposed patch of skin.

"Keep it as it is for as long as you like. There is plenty of room here." She murmured her pleasure when he cupped her breast in his hand. "It does seem as if you can do most anything you set your mind to. I hope I can learn to be half as self-sufficient. A great deal of what you do for yourselves, others did for us."

"Ye will learn, lass." He tugged off her nightgown and tossed it aside. "I had to. This place has been my dream for a very long time. Sometimes I think I was born dreaming of it. Even as a lad I was always seek-ing to learn things that would help me build this place. I pestered carpenters and made a nuisance of myself at farms, always trying to see how things were done. Every job I did taught me another skill. 'Twas all work with my hands, though—building, farming, and tending the animals. Now that I am that much closer to fulfilling my dream, I see that I should have taken the time to learn to read, to write, to figure more than a length of board or the exact amount of seed needed to bring in a good crop, and to act as the gentry act."

"And I am sure you will learn those skills as well. Probably a great deal faster than I learn to cook." She smiled when he laughed. "I hope you continue to be amused by my mistakes."

Ballard kissed her, softly growling his appreciation when she responded to his hunger with equal intensity. As he moved his hands over her slim body and she responded with eager passion, he knew she had missed their lovemaking during the journey as much as he had. She trailed her fingers up the inside of his thigh and lightly touched his erection. He shuddered, hoarsely whispering his approval. His lovemaking grew fiercer as she caressed him, but she offered no complaint. When he finally joined their bodies, she met him stroke for stroke, curling her lithe form around him in eager welcome. His release came but a heartbeat after hers and then he collapsed in her arms. It was several minutes before he had the breath to speak.

"It appears ye are a quick learner after all, lass." When she giggled, he briefly grinned against her skin and prayed he could keep this part of their marriage alive, no matter what difficulties lay ahead.

Chapter Nine

"Go to Kentucky? Are you completely mad?" Sarah frowned at Thomas as he paced their front parlor.

"That cursed Scotsman must pay for what he did to me. When he left a month ago, he no doubt thought he had escaped my wrath, but he will soon see how wrong he was." Thomas gingerly touched his nose, which had healed crookedly after his last fight with Ballard. His nose ached all the time and he blamed his increasingly frequent, fierce headaches on it. It was a constant glaring reminder of how Ballard Mac-Gregor had defeated him time and time again.

"He is gone. Let it be," Sarah told him. "We have been married only a week. How will it look if you race off to the wilderness now?"

"They cannot laugh any harder or louder than they do already," Thomas replied, and poured himself a brandy. "They have seen me fail at the hands of that lout from the frontier. He has done what those cowards in town could not do, and they savor my defeat."

"You imagine that the laughter is a great deal

louder than it is. It will all be forgotten soon anyway.
You have the people here so afraid of you, they will
quickly cease to chuckle now that he has left."

"*I* will never forget it. Every time I look into a
mirror, with every throb inside my head, I remember
it. That bastard took Clover away from me. He stole
my stallion, and interfered with my revenge on Grendall, and he beat me—twice. No one makes a fool of
me like that. No one. That bastard will pay and so will
Clover. I will make her dearly sorry that she scorned
me for that lout."

"Well, you can damned well do it on your own."

Thomas looked at Sarah. "What? My dear wife refuses to help me?"

"Yes, she refuses. I will not go to that wilderness just
so you can have revenge. If you want it so badly, go
get it yourself."

He went to the settee where she lounged and
touched her cheek. "He refused your favors. Do you
not want to make him pay for that?"

"If he was right at hand, I might, but he is not. He
is hundreds of miles away. And he was most insulting
that day. I see no wisdom in traveling hundreds of
miles to offer him a second chance to slight me."

"Fine." Thomas finished off his brandy and set the
glass on a side table with a snap. "Stay here. But do
try to act with some discretion while I am gone."

Sarah shook her head as he strode from the room.
When Thomas had realized he had failed to kill the
horse or murder Ballard, he had behaved like a
madman. Still she had thought that once Ballard was
gone, Thomas's ravings would cease. When Thomas
discovered that his nose would never be straight
again, his fervent need to make Ballard pay dearly

for each and every defeat had only increased. He even blamed his sick headaches on his broken nose and Ballard, conveniently forgetting that he had had them long before Ballard MacGregor had arrived in Langleyville. Sarah considered Thomas's obsession with Ballard not only mad but also stupid. She did not think Thomas would survive a third confrontation between the men, especially if he did anything to hurt Clover.

As Sarah stood up to pour herself a brandy, she heard the front door slam. She moved to the window, saw hulking Big Jim Wallis get into the carriage with Thomas, and grimaced. They were united in stupidity, she mused as she took a sip of brandy. She cursed the day Thomas had met Big Jim at the Sly Dog and discovered that they shared a common bond of hate for Ballard MacGregor. As the carriage pulled away, Big Jim's three dirty friends riding behind it, she felt certain that she would never see Thomas Dillingsworth alive again.

She wondered if widows really had the freedom they were rumored to have.

Clover set the basket of eggs on the kitchen table and frowned at her hands. The chickens were as reluctant to give up their eggs as the cows to relinquish their milk. She moved to the sink, poured some water into a bowl, and washed her badly pecked hands. Although she did everything just as Molly told her to, there always seemed to be one chicken who was ready and waiting to make her pay dearly for the eggs.

She dried her hands, shaking her head. For one month she had been in Kentucky struggling to learn, but she seemed to be making little progress. Her first attempt to churn the butter had produced cheese. Her second attempt had been better, but, as with so much of the other food she made, it was too salty. When she had tried to milk the cows, not one of the obstinate beasts would give up a drop. Clayton had shown a real knack at the chore, and even liked to do it, so she had gladly relinquished it to him, but she knew she would have to learn sometime. About the only thing she had done right was to add plants to the kitchen garden, or at least she thought so. She could not be sure until the garden began to yield something. And she had made some new gowns for herself and her mother, she mused as she looked down at her simple blue gingham dress. She could not consider that a big achievement, however, since she had already known how to sew.

She sighed and moved to the pile of dirty laundry. This was the first time she would do the washing without Molly's supervision. She carried the laundry onto the back veranda, hefted the washing tub down from the pegs on the wall, set it on a sturdy table, and filled it with hot water.

As she began to scrub the clothes, she looked out over the land Ballard was so proud of. The delicate blooms of the bluegrasses were fading now. A few of the trees that ringed Ballard's property and shaded the house still held lingering blooms while the others were filling with leaves. It was a beautiful place and she could easily understand Ballard's love for it. Everyone was out in the field, working hard to see that the crop was planted in time. The corn was in and they were planting the other crops. They were nearly finished and the constant work would soon ease a little, at least until it was time for the harvest.

A deep-throated yowl startled her and she turned to see a large yellow tomcat sitting on the veranda railing. She had discovered that Ballard had a soft spot for the many farm cats. He did not spoil them so badly that they grew lax in containing the vermin which attacked the grain, crops, or food stores, but he did treat them well.

"And he treats you best of all, right, Muskrat?" She smiled faintly as the cat meowed. "You are such a clever cat, maybe I can teach you how to clean clothes."

The cat stared at her for a moment, then started to wash himself. Clover laughed, shook her head, and began to scrub at a stain on one of Damien's shirts. She suspected Molly had some clever way of getting it out, but she did not want to go and ask her. It seemed to Clover as if she was forever asking Molly how to do things. It must make Ballard all too aware of how ignorant she was.

Neither was her mother learning very much, simply keeping an eye on the twins and occasionally assisting in simple tasks, but Clover found little comfort in that. No one expected or needed Agnes to do much, for she had spent every day of her forty years being cared for. And her mother had not offered to be Ballard's partner for life.

After setting the scrub brush aside, Clover held up the shirt she had been diligently working on and groaned. She had certainly gotten the stain out. Now there was a shredded hole where the stain had been. Clover was not sure she could even mend it. A good hard scrubbing was clearly not the way to get a stain out of a fine linen shirt. She muttered a few well-chosen curses under her breath and gave a soft screech of surprise when she heard an all-too-familiar masculine chuckle.

"Hello, Ballard," she muttered.

Feeling a deep blush heat her cheeks, and not wanting to add to his amusement, she did not turn to look at him. It never failed, she thought crossly. Whenever she did something foolish, Ballard appeared to witness it. When he reached around her and poked his finger through the hole in Damien's shirt, she had to bite her lip to keep from cursing again.

"Ye have a wee bit more strength than ye kenned, lass." He slipped his arms around her waist and kissed her neck. "Dinnae frown so, loving. It takes time. I mangled a few clothes meself when I first took up doing the washing."

"Yes, but you are a man."

"I dinnae believe lasses are born kenning how to wash clothes or scrub floors."

"Or how to cook," she muttered as she wrung out Damien's shirt and set it aside, hoping that when she calmed down a little, she would see a way to mend it. "Is the planting done already?"

"Most of it. The others can finish what little is left, and I have come in for my reading lesson."

"Oh, Lord, is it that time already? It seems I am behind in my work—as always. Just let me rinse these and put them on the line to dry."

She did not refuse Ballard's help when he offered to empty out the soapy water and get her some clean, for she had begun to doubt she would be able to heft the tub. As he dumped the dirty water on the kitchen garden and refilled the tub, Clover tried to decide what to do for his lessons. She was no teacher, but he was a fast learner. Clover began to fear that she would fail Ballard there as well.

He noticed her frown as she rinsed the clothes and wrung them out. "If ye have too much to do now, Clover, I can come later for my lesson." He leaned against the rail and scratched Muskrat under the chin, eliciting the tomcat's deep purr.

"I have no more work than you have, Ballard. I can do that," she protested when he began to hang the clothes on the line.

"So can I. No sense in me just standing about watching ye. The quicker the job is done, the quicker we can get to the lesson."

When they were finished, he tipped the rinse water onto the kitchen garden as well, hung the tub back on the wall, and escorted her into the house. She hurried up to her mother's room for a copy of *Poor Richard's Almanack*. It was a lot harder than the twins' readers, but Ballard had already mastered those little books and she had no secondary readers. As she set the almanac on the table between them, she watched his eyes widen slightly.

"I fear I have nothing between the boys' little books and this. 'Tis not as difficult as it looks," she assured him.

He moved to sit on the bench next to her. "I am just not sure I agree that I have gone beyond those wee readers." He frowned as he thumbed through the almanac.

"You certainly have. In fact, I think you know those little books by heart now."

"Weel, let us set to it then. We only have an hour. I

dinnae want the others to catch me stuttering over these new words."

Clover sat quietly, gently advising him when he stumbled over a word. Ballard needed little more than supervision, for he had quickly learned his letters and how to sound out the words. As he read through a dry piece on crops, her thoughts drifted to everything she still had to learn and how little she had really mastered.

She still lacked the ability and confidence to prepare a meal completely on her own. It was not difficult to scrub the floors and tables, but her muscles still protested such hard work. The boys were doing a great deal better than she was, adapting to their new life with an ease and enjoyment she dearly wished she could share. Everyone assured her that she was improving a little more each day, but she was not sure she believed them. Although she truly liked Molly and deeply appreciated the woman's patient instruction, there were days when she almost resented Molly's skills, for they made her look even more incompetent.

Ballard slipped his arms around her waist and lifted her onto his lap, abruptly yanking her from her thoughts. "I do not believe this position will facilitate your reading," she said even as she draped her arms around his neck.

He grinned and kissed the tip of her nose. "Ye can talk like a wee princess, cannae ye? And ye were nae listening."

"Oh, I am so sorry. You need so little help, I am afraid my thoughts wandered. From now on, I think we can just have a short practice reading and then move on to something else—like your writing. The time you are able to steal from your work is too precious to waste on things you have already learned." She murmured her pleasure when he kissed her, slowly and gently until her passion began to stir to life.

"Aye, I do need to improve my writing." He started to unbutton the bodice of her gown. "But I dinnae feel inclined to be tutored just now, leastwise not in reading and writing."

Clover gasped and covered his hand with hers. "Ballard, we are in the kitchen. Anyone could come in and see us."

"Then we had best go somewhere private," he said as he stood up, keeping her in his arms.

"Ballard," she cried in a halfhearted protest. "'Tis the middle of the day and we have work to do."

"Newlyweds are expected to be, er, distracted." He started up the stairs.

"Distracted, is it? I call this shirking."

"Weel, lass, I intend to have a verra enjoyable shirk afore the noon meal."

She blushed, but also laughed, infected by his passion and good humor. Suddenly she too relished the thought of stealing away from work to enjoy the desire that flared so hotly between them. She traced the shape of his ear with her tongue and kissed the hollow behind it, laughing when he hastened his strides, nearly running the last few feet to their room. He kicked the door shut, gently tossed her onto the bed, and sprawled on top of her. She laughed again.

But at the realization of how light it was in the room, a hint of embarrassment crept over her. "Ballard, 'tis very bright in here."

"Are ye feeling shy before your husband?"

"Less and less," she admitted with a faint smile. "But could you draw the curtains?"

"Then I willnae be able to see ye," he said, but he got up and pulled the curtains together just enough to lessen the sun's glare.

Ballard returned to her side and kissed her. The slight change in lighting was clearly enough to ease her embarrassment and he found it a comfortable compromise. He distracted her with his kisses as he eased off her simple gown. Her increasingly responsive movements against him told him that she had discarded the last of her modesty. He stripped her to her thin chemise, then shed his own clothes, smiling faintly when he saw that she had already begun to unfasten his shirt.

He respected Clover's modesty but was glad to see her relinquish it. Soon he would try something more daring, perhaps making love in some place other than their bed. He ached to look at her without the constraints of clothing or shadows.

He slid his hands along her legs, catching the hem of her chemise and slowly easing it up her body. He smiled as he slipped it over her slim hips and paused to kiss her taut stomach. Clover had insisted earlier that there was no red in her hair, but the curls at the juncture of her thighs were a bright coppery color. One day soon, when she was not so easily flustered by his blunt talk, he would point that out to her.

Clover trembled as Ballard tugged off her chemise, tossed it aside, and finally pressed his body against hers. The feel of their skin touching never failed to ignite her desire. She ran her hands down his side and caressed his taut, smooth hips. She savored his warmth, the texture of his skin, and the feel of his muscles beneath her fingers. When she slid her hand between their bodies and began to stroke him, he kissed her with a barely restrained ferocity. She liked the way his whole body expressed his appreciation of her intimate touch and the way his control rapidly began to fray. He always worried that he was too rough when his desire grew fierce, but she was determined to show him that she was not made of glass. She reveled in the full strength of his passion.

She tried to continue her caresses, but he soon moved out of her reach. As he peppered her breasts with kisses, she threaded her fingers in his thick hair. A soft cry of delight escaped her when he drew the aching tip of her breast into his mouth. He slid his hand down her stomach and she opened to him, craving the feelings his intimate caresses brought. Clover lost all sense of time and place, giving herself over completely to the desire thundering through her veins, until Ballard shifted his kisses upward along her inner thighs. For one brief moment her shock over such an intimate act checked her passion, but that shock had no chance to take root. It was banished with one slow stroke of his tongue.

With a soft groan born of both passion and a willing surrender, she opened herself to his intimate kiss. A part of her responded eagerly to his hoarse compliments and encouragement. The exquisite sensations built and built until suddenly she felt near her release. She called his name, but even as she started to recover from the semiconscious state into which her climax had hurled her, she felt her passion rising again, kept alive by his caressing hands and tongue.

Suddenly he was in her arms, holding her close as

he turned onto his back. Clover began to wonder what he would do next when he neatly joined their bodies. She gasped, shuddering with the sensations inspired by this new position. Ballard tugged her face down to his. He kissed her, grasped her hips, and silently showed her what to do. Clover needed little instruction. She wanted to test herself in this new method of lovemaking, but their desire was too hot, too greedy. Ballard gave a hoarse shout as his release tore through him. He held her firmly against him, spilling his seed deep within her. Clover quickly followed him, collapsing in his arms as the culmination of her passions raced through her, leaving her weak and trembling.

It was a long time before Ballard eased the intimacy of their embrace. He wanted to stay where he was, their bodies entwined, but there was too much work to do. As he turned on his side to look at Clover, he noticed the color tinting her cheeks and the tension in her lovely body. He began to fear that he had pushed her too far too fast. When he kissed her cheek, she barely glanced at him, blushing even more.

"Lass, there is naught to be embarrassed about in a man and a wife taking their pleasure of each other," he said. "I told ye I had a little experience. We have nae done anything odd or unseemly."

"Are you quite sure?" she asked, timidity stealing the strength from her voice.

"Quite sure. Ye and I will be sharing a bed for many a year to come, lass—God willing—and it doesnae hurt to have a wee bit of variety." He took her hand in his, kissed the palm, and then frowned when he noticed all the little wounds on the back of her hand. "Have ye been dragging your hands through the brambles, loving?"

Clover took one brief look at her hands and grimaced. "No, merely collecting eggs."

"Ah, so The Bitch has been at ye." He cursed, distressed to see how hard work was stealing the softness from her delicate hands.

"The Bitch? That is not really that hen's name, is it?"

"Aye. Do ye have a better one?"

She laughed. "No. 'Tis a terrible name, but it suits her. You could have warned me about her."

"Sorry, loving, I should have thought. I would have roasted the cursed beastie by now, but she is the best egg-layer I have. I will be letting her hatch a clutch soon so ye can have a respite. Have ye tried tossing the food down right in front of her, then grabbing the eggs when she isnae looking?"

"It does not work. She either stays on her eggs or comes right back to fight me for them."

"Weel, mayhap it is time to put that ill-tempered fowl on the spit," he said as he sat up and stretched.

"Oh no, at least not until I win one battle with the wretched thing." She sat up, clutching the sheet to her chest, and picked her chemise up off the floor. "I will not allow her to get the best of me." While Ballard busied himself getting dressed, she quickly slipped into her chemise. "It must be time to begin the noon meal."

"Aye, 'tis time we both returned to our chores."

"You look very pleased with yourself, considering you are about to go back to work."

At the door, he winked at her. "Ah, weel, nothing

can improve a mon's mood more than a morning's roll in the clover."

Clover blushed, gasped, and looked for something to throw at him. By the time she picked up a candlestick, the door was shutting behind him and his soft laughter was fading as he hurried downstairs. She finished getting dressed and tidied her hair. He was a rogue, rough but charming. He made such remarks just to see her blush. She intended to learn to control that. One day she would surprise him and not bat an eyelash when he made one of his outrageous remarks. Perhaps she would even reply with something equally outrageous. Her modesty was slowly being banished and she was confident she would soon be as bawdy as Ballard sometimes was. But first, she thought with a sigh as she hurried down to the kitchen, she had to learn to care for the house.

She grimaced when she found Molly already in the kitchen. "Sorry, Molly," she murmured as she moved to check the bread, which she had left to rise in breadpans on the counter.

"No need to apologize. I was a newlywed once too." She winked and grinned. "You blush so well."

"'Tis a curse. Ballard finds it far too amusing for my liking." She eased the cloth off the bread and gave a cry of delight. "Look, Molly, I think I got it right this time." She waited tensely as her friend inspected her efforts.

"It certainly looks so. Put it in the oven, girl, and then you can be giving me a hand in cutting up this ham."

After sending up a brief, silent prayer that her bread would turn out well, Clover put it in the oven. She had made bread a few times in Langleyville, but always with help from the cook and the housekeeper.

Her first attempts here had been dismal failures, good for nothing more than chicken feed or hogs' slops. She needed one success to bolster her badly sagging confidence, some sign that, with perseverance, she could be the partner to Ballard that she so badly wanted to be.

"Well?" she pressed as Molly carefully tasted the first slice of bread.

Molly took another bite and finally nodded. "It be nearly as good as mine,"

Clover caught the glint of laughter in Molly's eyes and grinned. "At last," she cried, clapping her hands together and doing a brief jig around the kitchen.

"Best not do too much of that, or your man will be thinking you are tippling."

"You cannot know how badly I needed a success." She hugged Molly, laughing at the woman's wary expression. "I was beginning to fear I would never get it right," she said as she put her bread on the cutting board.

"I do not think I have ever seen anyone be so delighted over one bleeding loaf of bread—well, save for them what be starving."

"'Tis not the bread really, 'tis the success. I have been here a month and it seemed I would never get anything right. Oh, I have gotten close, but never from start to finish all on my own. This shows me that if I stick with it, I can succeed."

"I understand," Molly said as she started to set lunch out on the table. "Still, you expect too much too fast. You were not raised to this life—I was. Truth is, I have been surprised that you are learning as fast as you are." She looked at Clover. "Or that you keep at it when most women of your class would have given up."

"But I am no longer of that class."

"True, but most folk cling to old ways. If you stop fretting so, I wager it will come easier. Sweet Lord, girl, do you really think I never make a mistake?"

"I have not seen one yet."

"Well, I be trying too hard to be perfect." She grinned when Clover laughed. "No, 'tis just luck. Once you learn the basics, I will be showing you the tricks I have learned to hide mistakes. Things like how to patch that shirt you done scrubbed a hole in."

"Oh, you saw that, did you? It was silly, but I was reluctant to ask you how to get that stain out. I am forever asking you how to do things."

"Good thing you did not waste your time. I saw that stain and knew there would be no getting it out. The shirt can be mended, and I know I will not have to be showing you how to do that. Now go and ring that dinner bell."

Clover stepped out on the front veranda and clanged the bell. She smiled faintly as she watched everyone gather. She had only a brief sight of her mother, for the woman always went in the kitchen door and straight up to her room to prepare herself for the meal. The twins went to the pump to wash up just like the men. She watched Lambert and Shelton exchange splashes with the twins and Ballard genially scolded all four of them. Ballard was good with the twins, patient yet firm, and the boys had clearly made him their hero.

"Do not run in the house," she reminded her brothers as they dashed past her. She had to bite back a smile when she saw Lambert and Shelton immediately slow their pace.

Ballard draped an arm around her shoulders and pulled her into the house, regarding her in a way that made her blush. Without words he told her he was recalling their earlier lovemaking. He grinned at the fleeting embarrassment she could not hide and she slipped free, hurrying to help Molly finish setting out the dishes.

She watched carefully as everyone ate. Her bread disappeared quickly and she savored a secret sense of accomplishment. Clover knew the quality of her cooking would never become the be-all and end-all of her life, but this first success was important.

"One of the local lads stopped 'round this morning," Ballard announced between mouthfuls of Molly's apple cake. "The spring get-together is planned for a fortnight from this Saturday. There will be dancing and drinking and a fine table of food."

"And some fighting," murmured Shelton.

"Ye shouldnae give the ladies such ideas, lad." Ballard smiled faintly at a frowning Agnes. "There may be a set-to, but 'tis usually a small fracas, quickly subdued. Folk come to enjoy themselves and dinnae want trouble."

"Can we go, Ballard?" asked Damien.

"'Tis up to your mother, laddie."

Agnes briefly dabbed at her mouth with her napkin. "Are children allowed?"

"We are not children," protested Damien.

"Here now, laddie, ye shouldnae speak to your mother that way. 'Tisnae respectful, or kind either."

Damien flushed. "I am sorry, Mama."

"Much better. And aye, Agnes, they allow children,"

Ballard said. "Most folk out here must take their bairns or leave them home alone."

"Well then, the twins shall go," Agnes said, smiling when the boys cheered.

"Is it not a rather busy time of year to have a celebration?" Clover asked.

"Verra busy, but 'tis one reason we started having this revel. By then most folk have done all their planting and have earned a wee bit of fun. Aye, and we like to visit after the winter."

"Of course. I forgot how far apart people are out here. 'Tis not like in town where you sometimes see far more of a person than you care to. Where is the get-together held?"

"This year it will be in the upstairs hall of our new church." Ballard fixed his gaze on Clover. "I accepted for all of us but after the lad rode away, I recalled that I cannae answer for all of ye. Ye dinnae have to go."

"And why should we refuse? It sounds lovely."

"Weel, it willnae be like the balls or fancy teas ye went to in Langleyville."

"I am sure it will be great fun."

"Good." Ballard stood up. "Everyone is expected to bring some food. Clemmons always supplies the drink and we take up a collection to compensate him, although I am certain he never gets the full cost back. Weel, laddies, back to work."

As soon as everyone was gone, Clover helped Molly clean up. She wanted to go to the spring revel, but could not stop worrying about meeting more of Ballard's friends. Her mother had told Mabel Clemmons their whole sad tale, and Clover knew the story would have spread far and wide. She prayed she would not face the same kind of ostracism she had in

Langleyville—the looks of pity, the abrupt dismissals. Although she would never ask her mother to lie, she did wish Agnes would be a little less forthright. They had come to Kentucky to leave the painful past behind them, to start a new life. Clover prayed she was not about to discover that one could never really start afresh.

Muttering curses, Clover hefted the pile of wood. Ballard had told her to call Shelton, Lambert, or him when she needed the woodbox filled, but she had not wanted to interrupt their field work. She decided she would not be so reticent next time. The wood was dirty, heavy, and awkward to carry. At the rate she was toting wood from the woodshed to the woodbox near the house, it would take her the rest of the day to finish. She had not yet gained the strength for such a chore and her hands were riddled with splinters.

She dumped the wood into the box, moved to brush off her skirts, and screamed. Squatting on her skirt was a huge spider, bigger than her hand. Just as she told herself not to panic, Ballard loped up to her side.

"Get it off," she whispered pointing at the spider, afraid of speaking too loudly and causing it to move up her dress.

Ballard picked up a piece of wood, brushed the spider from her skirts, and crushed it. He watched her closely as she sat down on the back steps. Although she was pale and shaking, she looked unhurt.

"Ye gave me a fright, lass," he murmured as he sat down next to her. "I feared the bears had returned to the area and wandered up to the house. They used to do that at this time of the year. They are powerful hungry after the winter."

"I believe I would have been less upset by a bear."

He laughed and kissed her cheek. "That *was* a big spider, although I have seen bigger."

"You must be joking. Spiders are supposed to be small, things you can brush away and step on. That thing covered the whole front of my apron. What kind of spider was it?"

"No idea. We call them wood spiders, as we only seen them 'round the wood."

Clover sighed, a little embarrassed now that her shock had passed. "I am sorry. I am not usually such a hysterical—"

He stopped her words with a quick kiss. "Dinnae apologize, lass. No one likes spiders that big. The first time I saw one, I ran inside, got the musket, and shot it. Put a hole in the woodhouse. 'Tis why I told ye to tell the boys when ye need wood."

"Have you ever found one in the woodbox?"

"Nay, never. 'Tis built a mite tighter than the woodshed. Are ye all right now?" She nodded and he stood up. "Need any more wood?"

"I have enough for now, but the box does need to be refilled."

"I will get the lads to do it afore supper."

She watched him walk back to the stables and sighed. A glance at the dead spider assured her that it was as big as she recalled, but that did not make her feel much better. Pioneer women were supposed to be a hardy lot. They were not supposed to scream loud enough to raise the dead just because a spider climbed onto their aprons, even if it did look big enough to eat her for dinner. Ballard must think her a complete fool. She was glad the others were too far away from the house to have heard her.

After rinsing off her hands, she went to bring the laundry in. All the confidence she had gained from her success at breadmaking had vanished. Ballard needed a strong wife, not one who trembled at the sight of an overfed insect.

Chapter Ten

"Are ye sure ye willnae come into town with us, lass?" Ballard asked as he stepped out onto the veranda, Clover following.

"Quite sure." She smiled faintly as she watched Shelton and Lambert lift her lively brothers into the back of the wagon. Molly scolded them for their rambunctiousness as she climbed onto the wagon seat. "Molly knows what we need from Clemmons's store, and I should stay with Mama."

"Agnes said it was just a wee headache."

"She always says that and sometimes it is. It could also be a sick headache that ties her to her bed. She has had a few since Papa died, although this is the first one since we arrived five weeks ago. It does worry me a little that they might have returned."

"'Tis probably just something in the wind or she but needs a wee rest. Our taking the twins with us for a few hours might be all the cure she requires." He put his arm around her shoulders and kissed her cheek. "Are ye sure she doesnae just wish to be left alone?"

"I think she might be a little frightened if she was left here all by herself."

"Weel, she wouldnae be alone for long. Adam should be back from his hunt in a few hours."

"I fear Mama would be quite hysterical by then and poor Adam would be at his wit's end." She smiled when Ballard chuckled and nodded. "Go on. I will be fine."

He frowned up at the sky. "We willnae be gone long. I dinnae want to get caught in the storm."

Clover saw only blue sky with shapely if swiftly moving clouds. Before she could ask him why he thought the weather would turn poorly, however, he was on the wagon and heading toward town. She waved until the wagon was out of sight, then returned to the house.

A quick peek in on her mother revealed she was sleeping, a cool compress balanced precariously on her forehead. Clover went back down to the kitchen and began to make bread. She was just taking the last loaf out of the oven, enjoying the sight and smell of her accomplishment, when her mother descended the stairs. Clover prepared some tea and sat down at the kitchen table to enjoy a cup with her mother.

"Has your headache gone then?" she asked after they had savored a few sips.

"Yes. It was just a little one. Perhaps it was caused by the weather," Agnes replied.

"It is still clear outside, but there could be something looming. Ballard seemed to think so."

"Have they returned from town yet?"

"No, but I am not worried. Ballard had a lot of things to do there. He wanted to judge the work of the blacksmith's son, who has taken on the chores of his late father. If his work is as good as his father's, Ballard will hire him for some tasks. Then he spoke of doing a little horse trading with Mr. Potter. For a moment, I was concerned that Molly would be sitting around twiddling her thumbs, waiting for the others, for she did not have much shopping to do. Then I recalled that she has set her sights on Jonathan Clemmons." She shared a brief smile with her mother. "I am sure our Molly will make excellent use of any idle moments."

"Unquestionably. I must say, I am not accustomed to being here alone. 'Tis such an isolated place."

"It does make me a little uneasy when all the men have gone, but I tell myself that Ballard would never leave us if he thought there was any real danger."

"Of course not. He would be sure to have someone stay behind to watch out for us." Agnes took her empty teacup to the sink and washed it out. "And that man of his should be returning soon."

"He should be, although he has been gone longer than he was supposed to be. He either is having a good hunt or is still trying to find something to bring home." Clover also rose and washed out her teacup.

"Yes, a man would hate to come back empty-handed from a hunt." Agnes leaned against the kitchen sink and watched Clover scrub down the kitchen table. "Now that I have had such a long rest, lying about in bed for half the morning, I have the inclination to do something."

"There is certainly an unlimited supply of work you can put your hand to."

Clover laughed at the expression on her mother's face. She knew what her mother meant. Sometimes one suffered a restlessness that could not be satisfied by hard work.

"Perhaps we could explore Ballard's lands," Agnes suggested.

"As the twins have done? Somehow I think we ought to choose something with a little more purpose." Clover shrugged. "I have never liked aimless strolls. I like to be going somewhere or looking at something, such as a pretty garden."

"We can look for something. I was asking your husband about what sort of berries and nuts or natural herbs grow around here, and he did not really know. All he mentioned was a patch of wild strawberries in the orchard. We can search for berries and the like."

"They will not be ready so early in the year," Clover protested, although she liked the idea of exploring Ballard's lands for useful plants.

"True, but we can still locate the bushes so that we know where to go when the season approaches. Our knowledge of plants, both medicinal and edible, could be really useful. 'Tis a woman's job to know about tisanes, poultices, and such, after all. I doubt Ballard has any knowledge about it at all. I recall some of my acquaintances thinking it was rather common for us to go berry-picking or even to go out looking for herbs and medicinal plants, rather than just buying them from the apothecary and plucking them from the garden the maids had planted."

"And Alice truly loathed those trips to the forest. Do you know, I have been so intent on learning how to cook and clean and tend the barnyard beasts, I completely forgot about woodland plants. It *would* be helpful to know what is around for us to use. It would also be nice to have some fresh berries this summer.

Of course, I do not know how to make jam or the like. We just picked the berries, then handed them over to the cook."

"Molly will teach you. Go on, get your cloak and bonnet and we shall go exploring," Agnes said even as she hurried away to get her own garments.

Clover wrote a note to say where she and her mother had gone. She propped it up against the cooling bread, knowing that fresh bread would quickly draw at least one member of the family, or Molly would see the note when she brought the new supplies into the kitchen. Even as Clover draped her light summer cape over her shoulders and tied on her simple bonnet, she wondered if she needed to wear so much. It was a very warm day and the air was growing heavy. Then she shrugged. Her mother would insist that she be properly dressed even if they were just going into the woods.

"I have brought a little basket in case we find anything that might be useful," Agnes said as she headed outside.

"Perhaps we ought to wait and take one of the men with us," suggested Clover, hurrying after her mother.

"Nonsense, dear. Ballard allows the boys to roam his lands freely with no more than a caution. Why should we be treated any differently? We will just walk straight ahead and search that particular section of the forest first," Agnes said as she stepped off the veranda. "We can explore another part on some other day."

"It might be a good idea not to wander too far afield," Clover said as they entered the woods. "We could get lost, and Ballard seemed to think that the weather is going to turn today."

"Well, it does not look stormy," Agnes murmured as she glanced briefly at the sky.

"I do not think so either, but I assume Ballard knows about such things."

"At the first sign of a dark cloud we will head back. As for getting lost, I have brought some scraps of twine. We will tie a little on the branches of the trees along the path we take."

"This little stroll is not a recent idea, is it?" Clover murmured and smiled at her mother's brief, guilty look.

"Well, no, I have been thinking about it for a while, but I did not want to go alone."

"And I have been very busy."

Clover set her mind to helping her mother search for plants. It was a little difficult to put aside all her uneasiness about being in the forest. This was no small patch of wood such as she and her mother had meandered through in Pennsylvania. There were no farms within easy walking distance in any direction. She was also a little nervous about what else might be roaming about. She tensed at every rustle of the leaves or snap of a twig and was a bit envious of her mother's blissful ignorance of the trouble into which they might stumble.

When they discovered a patch of blackberry bushes, Clover lost some of her wariness and became more engrossed in the search. She and her mother exchanged only a few soft words on what they hoped to find and occasionally tried to figure out what something was. It was as if the forest itself urged them to be quiet.

A dramatic increase in the wind finally drew Clover

out of her absorption. Grabbing hold of her bonnet before it was whisked off her head, she frowned up at the sky. The clouds spinning into view were ominously dark. She nudged her mother, who was intently studying a clump of moss, and pointed at the sky.

"That one dark cloud is bringing its whole family with it," Clover said.

"It certainly does look stormy now. We had better hurry back then."

As she nodded her agreement, Clover turned to start toward home and gasped. Meandering down the path they intended to take was a huge bear. She frantically tried to think of what to do next, but before a plan formed in her mind, the bear saw her and her mother. It slowly stood up on its hind legs and its loud, deep growl caused them to cry out in fright. Agnes grabbed her hand and they started to run. Clover cursed when she heard the bear thundering after them.

"I am not sure this is what we should be doing," Clover yelled as she kept pace with her mother.

"What would you do? Stop and have a chat with the beast? Somehow I do not believe he can be reasoned with."

Clover looked over her shoulder and cursed again. "I think he is gaining on us."

"I cannot run any faster."

Clover could tell from the way her mother was panting that she could not go much farther. Since they were running in blind panic, weaving among the trees and constantly changing direction to follow the easiest path, in the vain hope of eluding the bear, they were getting hopelessly lost. Their best hope was to find a safe spot out of the bear's reach.

Just ahead she saw a thick-trunked, twisted old tree that should prove easy to climb even for them.

"Mama, go up that tree just ahead of us," she yelled.

"Climb a tree? I cannot climb a tree."

"Can you keep running fast enough to tire out or lose that bear?"

"No, but cannot bears climb trees?"

"I have no idea, but his size should prevent him from climbing as high as we can. Get up there, Mama."

Her mother scrambled up onto the lowest branch and Clover quickly followed. She urged her mother to continue on up. The bear stopped a yard or so away, then ambled up to the base of the tree. It stood up and fell against the trunk, shaking the tree so powerfully that Clover and her mother had to hang on to keep from falling. When it stretched one huge paw toward her, Clover knew that they had to go higher still. She pushed her mother up another branch and was just following when the bear took a swipe at her. Clover screeched as its claws tore through her skirts. She hastily finished her climb.

She and her mother clung to the branch and looked down at the bear, trying to catch their breath. It stared up at them for a long moment. It tried climbing and Clover and her mother quickly scrambled up just a little higher. The bear was too heavy and the tree too old. The first branch on which it put its considerable weight broke, sending it tumbling to the ground. It satisfied itself by banging up against the tree as if to shake them loose like ripe fruit, and Clover joined her mother in hanging on for dear life.

"How long do you think he can keep this up?" asked Agnes.

"I have no idea," replied Clover. "All I know about bears is that they are very big and one should not get too close. This is far closer than I care to be."

"I wish we knew how to shoo the beast away."

"A bear is not an animal you can shoo, Mama. Chances are good that he will seek shelter when the storm hits, just like any other animal would."

"Yes, but then we shall be caught out in the storm." Agnes frowned up at the nearly black sky. "And it looks as if it will be a severe storm."

Clover shivered. She had been too busy trying to escape the bear to notice the increasingly threatening weather. The wind was very strong and the sky was a swirling mass of black clouds. She looked down at the bear again.

"I think I would rather take my chances with the storm, Mama," she said. "Let us hope that he leaves soon."

Ballard strode into the house calling Clover's name. He frowned when no one answered. The others were just coming in when Adam walked out of the kitchen and handed him a piece of paper. *We have gone exploring in the woods. Be back soon. Clover.*

Ballard cursed and looked at Adam.

"Ye let them go out into the woods alone?"

"Nope. I ain't been here but a few minutes meself," Adam replied.

"Something wrong, Ballard?" asked Shelton as he and Lambert joined him.

"My wife and her mother have gone exploring in the woods." Ballard crumpled the note in his hand.

"But a storm is coming," mumbled Lambert. "They must have seen that. 'Tis dark as night out there."

"They might not understand the danger such a storm can pose," Ballard replied.

"They would understand that it brings rain, Ballard, and I cannot believe they would wish to be caught out in the wet."

"Nay, they wouldnae. Something has gone wrong."

"Perhaps they have gotten lost."

Ballard took the musket down from over the fireplace. "Shelton, ye come with me. Lambert, ye stay here and help Adam secure everything and get everyone in the storm shelter if need be."

"Why must we leave the house?" asked Molly. "'Tis a good sturdy place. A little wind and rain should not be hurting a house like this."

The fact that Molly did not understand the threat of such a storm confirmed Ballard's suspicion that Clover and Agnes would not either. "Have ye e'er heard of a tornado, Molly?"

"No. What is that?"

"A verra large whirlwind. A storm like this at this time of year can spawn one of those hellish things. I have seen only one, soon after I came here, and I thank God for each year that passes without another. It can pull trees right out of the ground and toss cows about like they were child's toys. If Lambert tells ye to, ye are to get into the storm shelter."

"There is no storm shelter in the woods," Molly said in a quiet voice.

"If they are nae too far away, I will get them back here in time."

"Godspeed," Molly called as Shelton and Ballard hurried off.

Shelton pointed at the ground just beyond the veranda. "Until the rains come we can at least follow their trail."

"Aye. Let us move as fast as we can, brother. That rain isnae going to wait on us."

Ballard fought to remain calm. He would need all his wits to find Clover and her mother. When he noticed little twine bows on the trees, he was at first relieved. At least the women were not foolishly ambling through the woods without giving a thought to getting back home. Then he realized that if they had so carefully marked their path, they should have returned by now. His fears doubled. When they could find no more markers, Ballard had to fight the urge to start running and yelling Clover's name. He gritted his teeth and joined Shelton in searching for some other sign to follow, then cursed when the first drops of rain began to fall.

"Over here, Ballard," Shelton called, waving.

"Have ye found their trail then?"

"Nay, and I dinnae think ye are going to like this."

One look at the tracks Shelton pointed to confirmed Ballard's worst fears. "A bear."

"Aye. I thought we had driven them out of the area. It has been a long time since we have seen any sign of them."

"He couldnae have just plucked them up and run off, so there must be some sign of their tracks around here. We just have to look harder."

What with the wind and increasing heavy rain, it took Ballard several minutes before he picked up Clover's trail. It was clear from the tracks that the women had run off with the bear close on their heels. Ballard did not have to say a word to get Shelton to follow with speed. They both knew that the rain could swiftly wash away the trail and leave them with no clear way to find Clover and her mother.

Clover felt the first fat drops of rain and almost cheered. The bear shook the tree once more and then lumbered away. Her mother started to climb down, but Clover grabbed her arm, stopping her.

"But the bear has left," Agnes protested.

"I want to be sure he is far, far away before I get back down. I have no idea of a bear's capabilities. Let us wait just a few minutes so that we are sure he can neither hear us nor see us get down."

Agnes frowned up at the sky. "We shall be very wet before we get home."

"Better wet than dinner for that bear. Ah . . . we may have another problem—getting back home."

"Not that much trouble, surely."

"We are not woodsmen, Mama, and the moment we saw that bear we stopped marking the trail."

"And we took a very crooked path." Agnes shook her head. "I am sorry, dear. It was a silly idea to go into the woods."

"No, we just should have waited until someone who knows this forest could come with us. We acted a little rashly."

"Ballard will keep us locked in the house after this," muttered Agnes.

"I am sure the idea will occur to him. I just hope he does not worry too much when he finds us gone." Clover started to climb down the tree. "Come along,

Mama. That bear must be far away by now. We had better see if we can find our way back to our marked trail."

"And pray that this wind has not ripped our markers off the trees."

Clover silently cursed as she continued to climb down the tree, pausing to help her mother from time to time. Once on the ground, she sagged against the gnarled trunk and looked around, trying to remember how they had approached the tree. To her dismay everything looked the same to her. She could see nothing that urged her to go one way or another. She shook her head and stared at the ground, desperately trying to concoct some plan. Just as she was about to admit defeat, she noticed something on the ground.

"Mama, look there. Those are our footprints. And the bear's too. Can you see them?"

Agnes frowned and nodded. "Very nice, dear."

"Mama! We can follow our own footprints back to where we met the bear."

"They will not all be as clear as these are."

"True, but there may well be other signs to follow. Two women and a bear racing through the woods without a thought have to leave some marks." She grabbed her mother's hand and tugged her through the woods. "We had better hurry, for this rain will most certainly wash away any marks we made."

"So we follow this just as some trapper or hunter would."

"Only a great deal more slowly. And we pray that our running steps left nice, deep, clear prints. A footprint is something anyone can follow—even us. If they fade or wash away, we will be right back where we started—hopelessly lost."

Hand in hand they walked with their gazes fixed upon the ground. Clover felt the growing strength of the rain on her back and could only hope that their ignorance did not cost them dearly.

"The rain is getting heavy," Shelton said as Ballard paused to study more closely the signs they followed.

"I ken it. The women were running hard and fast, leaving deep prints, but they are already being washed away. They ran a lot farther than I expected them to." He started walking again.

"A bear on your tail can make ye strong and swift." Shelton followed Ballard for a few yards before stopping. "Do ye hear that?"

Ballard listened carefully, struggling to hear over the wind and rain. Finally he realized what had alerted Shelton—voices. Someone was coming their way. Ballard tried to keep his hopes from rising too high as he hurried on.

Suddenly he saw Clover coming through the trees. Despite his worry, and the anger that always comes with such concern, he had to smile. Clover and her mother were oblivious to everything save the tracks on the ground. They walked along hand in hand, water dripping off their bonnets, bent slightly forward. He was sure that if he did not speak up soon, they would walk right into him.

"Clover," he called, and laughed when she and her mother screeched in surprise.

Clover was so pleased to see Ballard, she sprinted across the last yards that separated them and flung herself into his arms. Her mother quickly followed, grasping Ballard's arm as if it were a lifeline. The trail they had been following had been growing dimmer with each drop of rain and Clover had begun to fear that she and her mother would be lost again.

"We are so glad to see you," said Agnes. "We can go home now."

"Aye, and when we get there, we can have us a wee talk about what possessed ye to go for a stroll alone in the woods."

"We were doing just fine," Clover protested as Ballard took her hand and started to drag her along. "Unfortunately, a bear came and we forgot to mark our trail. Of course, that would have been a little difficult while we were running for our lives."

"So ye did meet the bear." Ballard could see no outward signs of injury on either woman.

"Oh yes, we met the bear. We were just headed back home when he ambled up to us."

"Ye were bloody lucky, lass."

"I was surprised that we outran him."

"He *let* ye outrun him. Ye were lucky in that ye met a bear who wasnae hungry or in a bad temper. He was just playing with ye."

"Playing?" Clover stumbled over a rain-slick root, but Ballard gave her very little time to regain her feet before dragging her along.

"Aye—playing. A bear intent on catching ye can do so with ease. They dinnae always want to, though. We are nae their first choice of a meal." He nodded grimly at the women's wide-eyed expressions.

"Thank God he had a full belly then," Clover murmured.

"Now we must get to some shelter."

Even as he spoke, thunder crashed and both women screeched at the deafening sound. They barely had time to recover when a tree only yards in front of them was split by lightning. Ballard got Agnes and Clover out of the way just before the smoldering tree crashed to the ground. He spared only a moment to assure himself of their safety before joining Shelton in throwing mud on the fire that was struggling to life in the stump.

"Does that happen often?" Clover asked as he returned to her side.

"More often than I like," Ballard answered as he resumed tugging her along.

Clover tried harder to keep up with Ballard. They had suffered some harsh storms in Pennsylvania, but she could recall none as fierce as the one raging around them now. The house was just coming into view when she heard another crash. Ballard cursed.

"Did ye hear where that came from, Shelton?" Ballard asked, looking around.

"It hit near here again?" Clover asked, sure that it had, yet hoping Ballard could assure her that it had been far away.

"Aye. Over there," Ballard cried, pointing to a knot of trees right behind his barn. "It caught. Ye can see the smoke."

Within minutes Shelton had urged everyone from the house and they had established a bucket brigade. The rain was easing already and Clover knew they could not count on it to douse the flames in those trees. Her arms ached as she pumped water from the well near the stables and passed bucket after bucket to her mother, who handed them swiftly down the line to Ballard who threw the water on the flames.

By the time Ballard declared the fire out, Clover was trembling with weariness. It took her a moment to realize that the rain had stopped and the dampness she felt on her face was sweat. She pumped a little water into her hands and splashed it on her cheeks and forehead. When Ballard reached her side, she shivered and stood a little closer to him.

"Are you sure the fire is out?" she asked.

"Aye, but Shelton, Lambert, Adam and I will keep a close watch all through the night. Ye did weel, lass."

"We have bucket brigades in Langleyville too, you know, although I have never manned one."

"I hope ye dinnae get much more practice here either."

"I wholeheartedly share that hope. You live in a very exciting place, Ballard MacGregor."

"It does keep a mon alert." He kissed her on the tip of her nose. "I think we need to have us a wee talk about what ye can and cannae do—for your own safety of course."

She smiled up at him. "Of course. Shall we have this talk over a good meal? I am absolutely famished."

Ballard laughed and escorted her into the house, the rest of the family trailing wearily behind them.

Chapter Eleven

"Well? What do you think?" Clover carefully spun around in front of Ballard.

She had altered one of her better gowns, removing some of the expensive lace and silk ribbons for a simpler style. The last thing she wanted was to attend the revel dressed better than anyone else. The men would probably not notice, but the women might resent her if she arrived decked from head to toe in her best finery. It would be the surest way to start her relationship with her neighbors on the wrong foot. After a little over six weeks in Kentucky, she had no intention of ruining her first real chance to make some new friends.

But Ballard, studying her, was suddenly not sure he wanted to take her to the spring revel. Every man there would be after her. Her blue-green gown complemented both her fair coloring and her slim figure, and her breasts swelled gently above the low neckline. Her thick golden hair hung loose down her back, the sides tied with ribbons that matched her gown. She looked beautiful. So beautiful that he had to fight an urge to keep her hidden away at home.

"Ye look lovely, Clover." He kissed her palm and led her out of the room. "I will be beating the lads off ye all night."

Clover laughed and grabbed her cloak from the wall hook. "I was thinking much the same about you in your fine courting clothes."

"That ye will have to beat the lads off me?"

"Wretch." She gently punched his arm. "The lasses, of course. You will draw them like bees to honey."

Everyone was waiting on the veranda for them. Even Adam Dunstan was freshly shaved and dressed in his best homespun shirt and pants. Clover realized that such occasions for socializing were probably rare and thus were attended by everyone who could walk, ride, or crawl.

She sat beside Ballard on the wagon seat, with everyone else in back, except for Shelton, who rode his horse beside them. "Are you sure 'twill be safe to return in the dark?" she asked.

"Aye. 'Tis a full moon," Ballard replied. "The road will be lit enough for us. Some folk will spend the night, but the accommodations are rough. Shelton will ride in front of us to lead the way." He patted her knee, grinning when she blushed and carefully removed his hand. "Dinnae fret over it, lass. Just have a good time."

"I intend to."

When Ballard pulled their wagon up in front of the church and Clover saw all the people who had already arrived, she hoped she could stick to her resolve to enjoy herself. Whole families made their way into the church, each dressed in different degrees of finery, from clean homespun to calico with lace trim. Clover was heartily glad she had not worn her finest gown. Her silks and brocades would have been glaringly out of place.

Inside the hall, Clover helped Molly and her mother set out the food they had brought on the large table placed at one end. Molly had made apple cake and scones. Clover had baked two loaves of bread and made a small pot of blackberry jam, the last with Molly's help.

Agnes sought out Mabel Clemmons in a corner, immediately starting a conversation. Clover was glad her mother had found a companion, but she was a little surprised it was Mabel, whose rough, outspoken ways were so different from Agnes's refined manners.

The fiddlers struck up a tune and Ballard tugged Clover onto the floor for a rowdy country dance. She was quickly caught up in a dizzying round of lively dancing and unending introductions. She doubted she would ever remember all the names and faces paraded before her. When Ballard became immersed in a discussion on horse breeding with a balding man named Chester Tuttle, Clover slipped away to fill a plate with food and, seeing that Mabel was now alone, went to join the woman. Before she could begin a conversation, however, her mother returned and sat down next to her.

"Where were you?" she asked her mother.

"I needed a moment of privacy," Agnes replied, blushing faintly.

"Oh. And where can that be found? I might need a little privacy myself before the evening is ended."

"Out back."

"Well, I be damned," said Mabel, looking across the room. "There be Colin Doogan and his brood."

Clover was just looking toward the group Mabel had pointed out when she heard a thud. She turned to see her mother lying sprawled on the floor. Just as Clover hurried to see what ailed her, several women rushed over to help. Molly pushed her way through the women and knelt on the other side of Agnes. A moment later Ballard, Lambert, Shelton, and the twins huddled around them as well.

"Does she do this often?" asked Mabel, staring down at the unconscious Agnes. "She will be causing herself an injury."

"I have seen her swoon only once," said Lambert, "and I have known her for nearly two months. She collapsed when Clover said she was marrying Ballard and they were all coming to Kentucky."

Mabel laughed and Clover shot her a brief look of mild annoyance. She cushioned her mother's head in her lap as she and Molly tried to rouse her. Just as Agnes began to stir, a shadow crossed over them, and Clover looked up to see the man whom Mabel had identified as Colin Doogan staring down at them, his face pale and his gaze fixed firmly on Agnes.

Clover saw at once that Colin Doogan was a dangerously attractive man. She heard Molly whisper "Black Irish" and nodded in agreement. His hair was glossy black with a touch of white at the temples, and he had the bluest eyes she had ever seen.

"Agnes McGillicuddy?" he said, his voice soft and hoarse.

"McGillicuddy?" Molly looked at Clover. "You are Irish?"

"Mama's father was. He died before I was born." She frowned at Colin Doogan. "Do you know my mother, sir?" Clover's heart pounded faster as she suddenly recalled the story her mother had told her on the day before her wedding, of a certain man named Colin whom she had known before she married Clayton Sherwood.

"I knew her many years ago when she was newly engaged to some young lad named Sherwood," Colin Doogan replied.

"My father," Clover whispered and looked down at her mother, whose eyes fluttered open.

"Oh, heavens above, child," Agnes muttered, and rubbed her temples. "I thought I saw a ghost."

"The ghost of Colin Doogan perhaps?" Clover suggested. She glanced at Colin's three sons and murmured, "You neglected to tell me that the man was married. Or was he still a single gentleman when you knew him?" Looking at the brood of grown Doogans clustered around Colin, Clover knew the man must have been married even then.

Agnes slowly looked up until she met the gaze of the man leaning over her. For a moment she came close to fainting again and felt Molly and Clover each slip an arm around her in support.

"Lord above, Colin, what are *you* doing *here?*" Agnes demanded.

"I told you I wanted to move west," he said as he took her by the hand and helped her to her feet.

"Many men spoke of going into the frontier in those days. 'Twas a common dream."

"Well, I acted upon it. I came here fifteen years back, brought my family three years later. You do not look any different than you did the night we shared a dance at the Langleys' May ball."

"Nonsense." Agnes blushed. "I have grown quite plump."

"No, you have just matured into the fine woman I saw promised in the young girl you were then."

Clover caught Molly rolling her eyes and had to bite back a chuckle. She stood up and moved to Ballard's side as the other onlookers gradually drifted away. For a moment they let Colin and Agnes exchange information, each sympathizing with the other's loss of a spouse. Ballard finally interrupted to perform the introductions, presenting to Clover and Agnes Colin's eldest sons—Patrick, Michael, and David—who all carried the strong stamp of their father. The other seven children stood still long enough to be introduced as well, and Clover knew she would be hard-pressed to recall their names. When Colin excused himself for a moment, promising to return as soon as he was sure his younger children were all being looked after, Clover turned to her mother, who appeared hale but flushed and a little dazed.

"Well, Mama, I must say I never realized you were such a flirtatious girl in your youth." Clover winked at a chuckling Ballard. Since almost everyone had drifted away, Clover could not resist the chance to tease her mother just a little bit. "A married man? Tsk, tsk."

"Oh, hush." Agnes giggled. "Imagine finding him here. He is right. He did talk of moving west, as many young gentlemen did back then. We ladies all oohed and aahed and declared them such daring heroes. Of course most of them never went anywhere and we ladies politely forgot their boasts."

Ballard shook his head. "More games."

"I am afraid so. Flirtation and courtship do contain such mild deceptions and vanities. Oh, and Colin Doogan was a master player." She grinned when Ballard laughed. "In his defense, I must say that I never heard a whisper that Colin had been unfaithful to his wife." She frowned. "He had four children even then."

"Has ten now, ma'am." Ballard said. "His wife was ready to have some more, but he said enough was enough. He wanted to be able to give the ones he had a good life and enjoy some time with his wife without a bairn at her breast." He glanced around and caught all three women blushing while Mabel cackled. "Did I say one of those words I shouldnae say?"

"Well, I suspect such indelicacy is acceptable around family and such, but never in the company of others," Clover replied. She suddenly thought of how long it would take a woman to produce ten children, especially if there had been long separations here and there. "Colin Doogan never got to spend that time with his wife, did he," she guessed.

"Nay. She got a fever and died. Been dead for three years now."

"How sad," murmured Agnes.

Clover nodded and refrained from teasing her mother anymore. The fiddlers struck up a waltz and she gasped with delight. "Oh, Ballard, they know the waltz."

"Colin taught them," he murmured, frowning at the small knot of dancers. "Only a few of us have learned it."

She grasped his hands. "Shall we dance?"

"I fear I am one of those many who have nae learned yet."

"I shall teach you. Please come along."

His reluctance was clear as she dragged him out onto the dance floor. At first their movements were stiff and awkward, but Ballard was a quick learner with natural grace. She laughed when he lost the last of his resistance and began to whirl her confidently around the floor. By the time the dance was over she was breathless and giddy and gladly released him to go and talk to friends. She got a glass of punch and one of Molly's scones and returned to her seat next to Mabel, only to notice that her mother had disappeared again.

"Where is Mama now?" she asked Mabel as she took a sip of the tart punch and set her cup down on the bench.

"Out there swirling about with that rogue Colin."

"Oh."

Clover ate the scone as she watched her mother dancing with the tall, handsome Irishman. Agnes was smiling and clearly enjoying herself. Suddenly, all Clover could think about was that her father had been dead for only a few months.

"You ain't sure you approve of our Colin, are you?" said Mabel.

"I am sure Mr. Doogan is a very nice man." Clover could see from the look on Mabel's weathered face that her polite response did not satisfy. "All I want is for my mother to be happy. As my father made her happy."

"Ah, I see." Mabel spat, hitting the spitoon with her

usual accuracy. "Child, ain't nothing wrong with your ma wanting to cure her loneliness."

"Loneliness? How can she be lonely living in a household of nine people?"

"I reckon you know demmed well what kind of loneliness I be talking of. If you don't, then Ballard MacGregor ain't the man I think he is." She cackled when Clover blushed deep red. "Your ma loved your pa. I hear it clear when she talks of him. But your pa done took himself away from her. I suspect she is still grieving, but she has the sense to know that life goes on. So does Colin. Now, those two flirting and laughing like they are might raise a few eyebrows back where you come from, but out here we ain't bothered by such petty and useless niceties. Agnes and Colin know they are in the autumn of their lives, and neither of them wants to spend those years with just memories."

"Of course. Then again, they could be acting just like any two friends who have not seen each other in years."

Mabel snorted. "That sure as hell was no 'let us be friends' gleam I saw in old Colin's eyes."

Clover caught sight of Molly and Jonathan Clemmons sitting close on a bench, their heads together as they talked. She smiled at Mabel. "And what kind of gleam do you see in your son's eyes?"

"I demmed well hope it's a marrying sort of gleam. The fool ain't getting any younger, and I have a hankering to see a grandchild or two before I die."

Clover restrained a laugh. "Well, Molly *is* determined to find a husband."

"Good. I reckon Jon needs a determined woman to get his backside afore a preacher." Mabel looked

Clover over carefully. "Just when are you and that long-legged Scotsman gonna start a family?"

"You are a rude woman, Mabel Clemmons," Clover said genially.

"Demmed right, and proud of it. It is one of the few good things about getting old. You can speak your mind and be crotchety and nobody troubles you about it." She winked at Clover. "I got a soft spot for that Scot of yours, but don't you go saying nothing to him about it."

"Of course not. We would not want him to get too puffed up."

"Exactly. Now, that's why I'm asking you about starting his family. I know he wants one."

"Yes. He was very clear on that matter. So do I. If God is willing, there will be a babe started before too long."

Mabel nodded. "Reckon that boy is doing his best."

"Definitely his best," Clover drawled, and they shared grins that turned into hearty laughter.

Mabel had an odd effect on her, Clover mused, then frowned when the old woman scowled at the dancers. Clover looked to see what had caused Mabel's dark expression, then grunted when she jabbed her in the side with a bony elbow.

"What is wrong? I see nothing but people dancing."

"Then you ain't looking hard enough. That hussy, Elizabeth Brown, has dragged your man onto the dance floor."

Clover could see Ballard's head, but it was not until the crowd parted a little that she caught sight of Elizabeth. The woman was dressed in a red gown, tight and low-cut, and she was pressing herself scandalously close to Ballard. Clover fought a swell of fury at seeing

Elizabeth reap the benefits of the dancing lesson she had just given Ballard. After taking a deep breath to steady herself, Clover tried to see how Ballard felt about Elizabeth's actions, but there was little expression on his face.

"Well, what are you waiting for? Go after your man, child," said Mabel.

"He is only dancing," she murmured, silently cursing the fact that she even cared who was in his arms.

"That slut is clinging to him like a limpet. Go and tear her off him."

"Perhaps he likes dancing with her."

"Balderdash! I know that boy. He don't get that cursed stone face on him when he's having fun." She frowned at Clover. "Don't you care that she's trying to steal your man right afore your eyes?"

"Mrs. Clemmons, it is not a matter of caring. It is a matter of dignity. I do not wish to act the jealous, interfering wife."

"Maybe where you come from you sit back and let such nonsense go on, but 'round here we do something about it. Ain't you seen how the other women are looking at you to stop the hussy?"

Clover did notice, but that did not change her mind. All her life she had been trained to be dignified, not to cause scenes. Such matters, if mentioned at all, were to be dealt with in the strictest privacy. She ached to go and yank Elizabeth away from her husband and throw the woman to the floor, but everything she had been taught told her not to succumb to that raw emotion.

"Lookee here, girl," Mabel continued, grasping Clover's arm and giving her a little shake. "Elizabeth wants your man and you know it. Hellfire, the whole cursed county knows it. That hussy got into his breeches once and liked what she found. Ballard had the wits to button himself up tight after that, but it ain't stopped her. 'Tis clear his marriage ain't gonna deter her neither, especially not if his wife just sits by twiddling her thumbs. Do you think that Scot would sit idly by if some man was lifting your petticoats?"

Clover stood and calmly brushed down her skirts. "No, Ballard would not just sit by. However, Mrs. Clemmons, if I discover that you have advised me poorly in this, I shall find some way to make you regret it."

"I ain't got no doubt about that. You be a sprightly one." She gave Clover a light push toward the dancers. "Go and set that hussy straight, girl. Old Mabel will be watching."

"I am sure you will."

As Clover wended her way through the dancers, she thought she saw looks of approval on the women's faces, but she could not be certain. When she failed to find Ballard and Elizabeth among the dancers, she grew unsure. A woman nudged her and pointed toward open doors leading to the stairs. Clover could think of only one reason that Ballard and Elizabeth would escape the crowd. The last thing she wanted was to catch the pair in a heated rendezvous, but she took a deep breath and started after them. It was best to know the truth, she decided, no matter how painful it might be.

Once outside, she walked around to the rear of the church. She wanted to trust Ballard, but she had to wonder why he would take a moonlight stroll with a woman he claimed he did not want. As she rounded the corner she came upon Elizabeth in Ballard's arms, and winced at the painful sight.

"Curse it, woman," Ballard snapped as he yanked Elizabeth's arms from around his neck and held her at a distance. "I didnae come out here for that."

"Well, that is a relief," Clover drawled.

Ballard cursed, pushed Elizabeth away, and stepped closer to Clover. He had allowed Elizabeth to drag him outside because he thought it would be kinder to rebuff her in private. Before he could say a word, however, she had clung to his neck and covered his face with kisses while rubbing her fulsome body against his in blatant invitation. He did not have to see the cold anger in Clover's expression to know how the scene had looked to her. He heartily cursed his attempt to be considerate of Elizabeth's feelings. The woman did not deserve such courtesy.

"Lass, I didnae come out here for an adulterous tussle. I swear it," he told his wife.

"Everyone believes you did. After that tasteless display on the dance floor, most people think you slipped outside to continue your rutting in private. Now you tell me this moonlight stroll was not inspired by a sudden desire for decorum?"

For a moment, Ballard just stared at Clover, somewhat impressed at how she could say such biting, angry words in such a cool, polite voice. Most women he knew would be screaming at him and trying to do him and Elizabeth bodily harm. Since the look in Clover's eyes told him she longed to do just that he had to admire her restraint.

Elizabeth stepped closer to Ballard and took hold

of his arm. "It should be clear, even to you, that Ballard has finally come to his senses," she told Clover.

"Aye, I have." He yanked free of her hold. "I have been trying too hard to play the gentlemon and spare your feelings. 'Tis clear ye misunderstood my kindness. I didnae want to marry ye before I left for Pennsylvania and I sure as hell dinnae want to leave my wife for ye now. Just let me be, woman, before ye make an even greater fool of yourself."

Elizabeth glared at Clover. "He wasn't being so coy before you arrived."

"Was he not? I would have thought you would have more pride than to keep hurling yourself at a man who says he does not want you."

"He wanted me once—badly."

"That *once* is now past." Clover stepped closer to Elizabeth and said softly, "This had better be the last I see of you, Elizabeth Brown."

"I live here too!"

"I know, but whether you do so comfortably or not will be up to you."

Clover was a little surprised when Elizabeth glared at her and strode away. It was clear that the woman blamed her for Ballard's rebuff. There had been a flash of fear in her eyes, which Clover had rather enjoyed. She hoped that Elizabeth believed her threats and stayed away.

She turned her attention to her husband, who was regarding her as if she were aiming a loaded musket at his head. It amused her that such a strong man could look so afraid of her. That hint of amusement told her that her anger was already fading. She prayed common sense was prompting her trust in him, and not blind loyalty.

"I swear to ye, lass, I wasnae out here to have meself a wee bit on the side."

"What a crude expression." She sighed. "I really want to believe you."

"Good." He quickly closed the distance between them and tugged her into his arms.

She looked up at him. If he was just not so heart-breakingly handsome, it might be easier to cast aside her doubts and fears. But she still found it a little hard to believe that such a man could be fully satisfied with her as his wife.

"I am not sure you have solved the problem of Elizabeth yet," she murmured.

"She has to ken that her pursuit of me is already a joke around here."

"That might make her all the more determined to win you."

"Then she is an even bigger fool than I thought." He touched a finger to Clover's lips when she started to reply. "Someone is coming."

"It sounds like Mama and someone else." She gave a little cry of surprise when Ballard dragged her behind a thick tangle of lilacs. "Why are we hiding?"

"I would like a minute or two alone with ye, just to make sure ye dinnae still doubt me."

Before she could reply, she glimpsed her mother through the foliage, arm in arm with Colin Doogan.

"I was sure Clover and Ballard would be here," Agnes said. "Elizabeth looked furious when she came back inside."

Colin took both of Agnes's hands in his. "They have probably slipped away to make amends. I think we should use this moment of privacy to our own advantage."

"What do you mean?"

"There is something I have wanted to ask you since I set eyes on you tonight. I want to court you, Agnes."

"Colin, my husband has been dead for only a few months."

"And you loved him. I know that. I knew it all those years ago. I loved my wife too, then and until the day she died. But that does not change the fact that there was something special between us, Agnes. It is still there."

"I should be draped in mourning, but I did not have the money for mourning clothes."

Colin kissed her forehead. "You will not have a great deal of money if you hitch up with me either, but I can keep you in some comfort."

"Colin, it is too soon."

"I do not expect you to stand before the preacher with me tomorrow. I just want to start courting you."

"I would feel disloyal."

"Why? I do not ask you to forget him, just as I could never forget my Anne. Hell, I have ten children as living reminders of her. I also do not expect you to set aside that part of you that still loves him and probably always will. But that does not mean we cannot care for someone else. Our loved ones would not expect us to pine for them forever and live alone for the rest of our days."

"No, of course not."

"Then why wait for some arbitrary mourning period to pass? The worst of your grief is over. Now is the time to pick up the threads of your life. All those years ago we could have loved each other if we had not already given our hearts and our promises to others. Not many people are fortunate enough to have a second chance. I do not want to spend the rest of my life alone, Agnes."

"Neither do I, Colin. I am just not sure everyone will understand that."

"Hey, I was listening," Clover protested when Ballard started to tug her even farther away from the couple, deep into the thick wood behind the church.

"Would ye eavesdrop on your own mother?" he demanded.

"Yes." She frowned when, once out of earshot and sight of her mother and Colin Doogan, Ballard pulled her into his arms. "I thought we were going back inside."

"I want to be sure ye dinnae still think poorly of me."

"No." She sighed, then smiled faintly when he gave her a quick, exuberant kiss. "If there is a next time, however, do you think you could give Elizabeth her setdown in a public place? Unfortunately, the first thought that enters people's heads when a couple tiptoes off into the moonlight is *not* that the man is going to explain a few moral truths to the lady."

Ballard laughed, then grew serious. "I was feeling a mite alarmed for a moment. You looked prepared to shoot me."

"The thought crossed my mind." When he backed her up against a tree and began to spread soft kisses along the neckline of her gown, she made no effort to push him away. "Should we not be getting back to the revel?" she finally asked.

"In a wee bit. I need reassurance that ye have really forgiven me."

She welcomed his slow, hungry kiss and returned it in full measure. When he ended the kiss she realized he had reached up under her skirt and untied her drawers, letting them fall to the ground. After a brief hesitation she stepped out of them. She ought to be scandalized by what he planned, but instead she felt a growing excitement. The dark wood sheltered them, and rays of moonlight gave their trysting place an exciting secrecy. Only one thing checked her sudden urge to be daring.

"I cannot return to the revel in a rumpled, grass-stained gown," she murmured, shivering with delight when he loosened her gown just enough to free her breasts for his kisses.

"Then we shall have to be verra careful that ye dinnae fall on the ground," he replied, as he freed himself from his breeches.

She gasped in soft surprise when he lifted her up in his arms. Without thinking, she wrapped her legs around his waist. He slowly joined their bodies. She shuddered with delight. Her desire had been strongly stirred by his caresses and the thought of making love outdoors in the primitive privacy of the tall trees, but now it totally engulfed her. As her release swept over her, his mouth on hers smothered their cries of ecstatic fulfillment. He sank to his knees, their bodies still united, and they clung to each other as they tried to regain their senses.

Later, back inside the hall, Clover left Ballard talking with Jonathan and hurried over to Molly, who was perusing the remaining food on the table. "Do I look presentable?" Clover asked.

"Except for this piece of bark in your hair." Molly fished it out and surreptitiously brushed off the back of Clover's gown. "Apparently you and Mr. Mac-Gregor sorted out your differences. Although I guessed that when that hussy came stomping back in here alone, looking like she had been sucking on lemons."

"Did my mother and Mr. Doogan return?" Clover asked, nibbling on a piece of cake.

"Yes, they are sitting over there talking quietly." Molly frowned. "Here is something interesting. It looks to me as if those men who just walked in are not welcome."

Clover looked toward the door and nearly gasped. Everyone in the room was falling silent and keeping a close eye on the four men. Big Jim Wallis and his three friends were clearly disliked by nearly everyone. She wished that had been enough to make the man stay away, but realized it had been foolish to hope they would never cross paths in Kentucky. When he fixed his dark gaze on her and started toward her, she resisted an urge to look for Ballard, and struggled to meet Big Jim's glower calmly.

"I'da thought you'd be hightailing it back to Pennsylvania by now," he said as he stopped in front of her.

"This is my new home. Why should I leave?" She heartily wished there was more than the food table separating them.

"'Cause you ain't built for this life and there ain't gonna be a husband here for you much longer."

"Is that a threat, Big Jim?" Ballard asked, stepping up to the man's side.

Big Jim glared at him. "We got some unfinished business, you and me."

"I dinnae think so. I believe we settled everything that day at the riverfront in Langleyville. We have no quarrel between us, unless ye are thinking of starting one." He glanced around. "It would appear that ye and yours are nae exactly welcome here. People have long memories, Big Jim, and 'tis hard to forget that ye nearly killed William Sutter at last year's spring revel. Maybe it would be better if ye left. A lot of his kin and friends are here." He nodded toward a large group of men edging toward Big Jim, their fists clenched and their expressions hard and angry. They outnumbered him and his friends nearly three to one.

Big Jim spat on the floor. "I ain't here to have fun anyhow. Just came to warn you."

"Warn me?"

"Enjoy her while you can, MacGregor. The day is coming fast when the enemies you done made are gonna get you. You ain't gonna be standing so tall and cocky then." He glared at everyone in the room. "And these fools ain't always gonna be at hand to save your hide. Or hers."

Ballard frowned as Big Jim and his friends turned and swaggered out the church door. It would be foolish to ignore the man's threats, but he did not know what to make of them. Briefly he considered gathering up a few men and going after Big Jim to beat a few facts out of him, but he decided against it. It would not be wise to stumble around in the dark after a man who would have no qualms about stabbing someone in the back.

"What the hell was that all about?" demanded Lambert as he and Shelton hurried over.

"I dinnae ken, but I think it would be wise if we keep a close watch out for trouble," Ballard answered.

"Big Jim wants revenge for that day at the river-front?" asked Shelton.

"That is certainly some of it, but there seems to be more." Ballard shrugged. "I cannae figure it all out yet." He looked at Clover. "Are ye all right, dearling?"

"Fine. It was just a bit of a shock to see him here. Do you have many enemies, Ballard?"

"A few. I dinnae set out to make them, but that doesnae stop me from collecting them. Dinnae fret over it, lass. We will keep a close watch. I have dealt with tougher foes than that oaf."

As she watched Ballard walk away, Clover knew he was not making an idle boast. Ballard MacGregor would be a hard man to bring down, but he was not invincible, and that knowledge stirred her fears. She could not shake the feeling that she was the cause of the trouble he now faced, and not simply because he had rescued her from Big Jim that day on the waterfront. But the only person who might want to hurt her was Thomas Dillingsworth, and she could not believe he would come all the way to Kentucky to satisfy some twisted need for revenge. He enjoyed his creature comforts too much, for one thing.

"Heed your man," Molly advised as she handed Clover a cup of punch. "He can take care of himself."

"I know." Clover took a bracing sip of the alcoholic brew. "I feel very confident of Ballard's ability to protect me. What troubles me is that although we know some threat hangs over us, we do not know when the danger will come or why. Our enemies know a great deal more about us than we do about them, and that is never good."

"Well, if I be judging it right, those men now talking to Mr. MacGregor are offering their help."

"That is certainly some comfort."

"Pssst."

Clover frowned and looked at Molly. "Yes?"

"I made no noise. Sounded like it came from under the table." She glanced down and signaled Clover to do the same.

When she looked down, Clover found herself staring into a pair of familiar brown eyes. The little boy's face was marked by several bruises. He had obviously suffered even more of Morrisey's brutality since their brief meeting in Clemmons's store on her first day in Kentucky. Such behavior was beyond her comprehension.

"Hello again," she said.

"How do, ma'am. Could I be troubling you to hand me down a bit of cake?"

Although she cautiously slipped the child a piece of apple cake, she asked, "Why not just fill up a plate like everyone else?"

"I been bad and they told me I ain't to have none of this fine food. That be my punishment." His words were a little garbled as he tried to eat and talk at the same time.

She slipped him a chicken leg, at the same time looking around for his family. The Morriseys were bunched together in a far corner of the hall. A few women stopped to talk to a bone-thin gray-haired woman whom Clover knew must be the beleaguered Bess, but only one man was talking to the brutish Morrisey. Everyone in the family held heavily laden plates of food, which they were wolfing down. Clover suspected the food was what they had mainly come for. There was a gentle tug on her skirts and she slipped the boy some bread, wishing she could do more for him.

"I think that pig Morrisey must be looking for the lad," Molly whispered as she sneaked a cup of sweet apple cider down to him.

The boy cursed, causing Molly and Clover to exchange amused smiles. "I was hoping they be too busy eating to see that I done crept away," the boy muttered, then downed the cider and returned the cup to Molly. "Reckon I best creep back."

"Make sure you brush all those crumbs off," Clover advised, then looked down to see that he was already gone. "I hope he heeded me. 'Tis bad enough to know I cannot help him, but 'tis worse to think I might cause him more pain simply because I gave him some food."

"A boy kept that hungry does not fret over a beating. He will endure it if it means he can fill his empty belly."

"That is so sad."

Molly shrugged. "I fear the world ain't always a pretty place, Clover MacGregor."

Clover watched the Morriseys until the boy appeared back in the group. Morrisey swung a fist at the boy but he neatly ducked the blow. The second time Morrisey struck out, the child tumbled to the ground. As he tried to scramble out of reach, Morrisey kicked him in the ribs. Not one sound escaped the child, which further troubled Clover.

The Morriseys had finished what Big Jim had

begun. They had taken away the last shred of her enjoyment of the evening.

"Ballard?" Clover leaned against her husband as he drove their wagon home. The rest of their family dozed in the back while Shelton kept a close watch on the road ahead of them. "Are you very certain we can do nothing about that boy of Mr. Morrisey's?"

"Aye, lass. Sorry. The whole demmed town has been trying to come up with the money Morrisey wants, but I have a strong suspicion that if we ever get it together, he would just demand more and we would be back where we started."

"You are probably right. And I suppose there is nothing we can do about Big Jim's threats until he acts on them."

"Not unless I want to face the circuit judge next time he meanders this way."

She curled her arm around his and snuggled closer to his warmth. "That is not exactly the news I want to hear. Ballard, do you think the other enemy Big Jim referred to is Thomas?" She yawned and closed her eyes, nuzzling her cheek against his strong arm.

"It could be, lass, but I would be surprised if Thomas bothered to chase us down here. He considers Kentucky uncivilized, the end of the world. I cannae see him inconveniencing himself. I reckon we will just have to wait and see."

"Wait and see and do nothing. You know, I never would have thought that those two things would be so hard."

Ballard smiled faintly when Clover barely finished her sentence before falling asleep. He tightened his arm around her shoulders, holding her more securely against him. She was right. It would be hard to wait and watch. Ballard ached to prevent any danger before it got within miles of her, but he had no choice. He must wait until Big Jim, and whatever ally he had, made the first move. And pray that he would be able to thwart them.

Chapter Twelve

Clover waved as the carriage carrying Molly, Agnes, Jonathan Clemmons, and Colin Doogan drove away. It had been only a week since the spring revel, but Jonathan and Colin were clearly eager to get down to the business of courting, without further delay. Clover was pleased that Molly and her mother were going to have a leisurely day of relaxation, but she heartily wished she could go with them. Their absence also meant that she would be completely responsible for doing the chores and preparing supper. Clover was not sure she was ready for such independence.

She was just about to return to the house when Ballard emerged from the barn and reached her side in several long strides. His dark expression made her tense with concern.

"Lass, your ma and Molly just left, didnae they?"

"Yes. Do you need them back? I am sure you can catch them if we have to."

He shook his head. "Nay, 'twould only be so someone could stay with ye for an hour or so, mayhap more. One of my mares is missing. One of the fence rails got knocked down and she slipped out of her paddock. She is one of my best breeders. I will need every pair of eyes I have at hand to find her."

"Do you want me to come too?"

"Nay, ye stay here, lass. Just keep to the house and dinnae let anyone in."

"Ballard, do you think someone let her out on purpose?"

He grimaced and ran a hand through his hair. "I cannae say, love. If the mare is only roaming free, 'tis just a petty revenge, but if she is gone or hurt, it could prove to be a costly one." He kissed her cheek. "I dinnae think ye are in danger. I can leave Adam or your brothers here, if it will make ye feel better."

"No. You need Adam, and the boys are only eight. They could hardly protect me if something should happen. Are you sure they will be much help to you?"

"Aye. They can look about as well as I can. Last week they found that lost pig, if ye recall."

"Yes, of course. Go. We must not let that oaf Big Jim rule our lives with his threats. I will be fine. To tell the truth, I do not think Big Jim Wallis is clever enough to plan my deliberate abduction. He would just charge in blindly."

Ballard laughed and nodded. "Aye, I think ye judge the mon right." He gave her a quick kiss. "Stay in the house and I will be back as soon as I can."

"Good luck," she called as he loped off.

Clover watched the men ride away, her brothers sharing the horse Ballard had given them. Just as she headed back into the house, she heard an odd creaking sound, as if someone was trying to approach her unseen and unheard along the veranda. She stood still and listened hard, every muscle tensed. Even as she was thinking that she ought to run into the house, the Morrisey boy scrambled nimbly up and over the veranda railing.

"Oh, you gave me a fright. What are you doing here?"

"I just come to visit. Is that all right?" He edged closer and gave her a tentative smile.

"Well, 'tis fine with me, but will you get into trouble?"

"I already be in trouble today. Thought to meself, well, you gonna get a beating anyway so why not later instead of sooner. So I decided to come a-calling."

"Pleased to have you." She pointed to the washing bowl set on a table near the door. "Just wash your face and hands and then you can come inside." While he did as she asked, she studied him. "What is your name?"

"Brat," he mumbled as he rubbed his face dry with the cloth hanging on a peg by the bowl.

"That is a horrible name. You must have another."

"Nope. Weren't never given no proper name and Brat's one of the nicer ones the Morriseys call me."

She shook her head as she ushered him inside. "I simply cannot call you by that name. Do you have another name you might like, one you might give yourself if you had a choice?"

He sat at the kitchen table, watching Clover with wide eyes as she filled a plate of food for him, and considered her suggestion. Finally he said, "Willie."

"Willie? Why did you choose that name?" She sat down opposite him as he wolfed down the food and cider she served him. The child was fed barely enough to keep him alive.

"I just always liked it. Sorry," he said as he tried to wipe up the crumbs that had sprayed from his mouth.

Clover smiled. "You are forgiven—this time. But if you intend to visit me often, I will have to teach you some table manners. How old are you, Willie?"

"Near as I can figure, I be about eleven, maybe twelve."

It was not easy for Clover to hide her shock. She would not have guessed he was any older than the twins, probably younger, for he was so small and thin. Lack of nourishment had clearly stunted his growth.

"Morrisey says I be a runt. He says all Indians are runts—little, bandy-legged, and stupid."

"If that were true, then the settlers would not have had so much trouble taking their land from them, would they?"

Willie nodded and smiled his thanks when she re-filled his cup with sweet cider. "I figured that much for meself. I know all the folk 'round here ain't poor fighters either."

"Have you ever thought of running away to join your father's people, the Shawnee?"

"Once or twice, but they'd be hating my white half and I ain't been brought up Indian." He tensed, listening. "Rider coming."

Clover heard the rider approaching a moment after Willie spoke. She quickly got the musket down from over the fireplace. Ballard had not taught her how to fire the thing yet. She did not even know if it was loaded. But she hoped that whoever was now banging on her door would not guess that.

"Open this door, woman. I know you got that brat in there."

"Morrisey," Willie whispered, and stuffed his mouth with the last of his food.

"Calm down, Willie," Clover said, hoping she could follow her own advice as she opened the door and aimed the musket at the red-faced man standing there. "What do you want, Mr. Morrisey?"

He took a step back. "I want that boy. He is mine and I have a judge's word on that, so don't you be trying to steal him."

"He will be home when he has finished sharing a meal with me."

"He ain't got time to be socializing like some demmed gentleman." He took a step toward her but quickly retreated when she steadied her aim. "He is mine, woman, and the law says you gotta give him back."

"As much as I hate to, I will obey the law. But he is a visitor in my house and I refuse to let you drag him off. He will come home when our visit is over and not before." She frowned when Morrisey glared at the boy.

"It'd be right smart of you to come home with me now, brat, or you will be paying dearly for this game. You know how I treat disobedience."

"'Tis that child's misfortune to know exactly how you treat anything and anyone smaller and weaker than you," said Clover. "I believe it would be a grave error in judgment on your part if you made this child suffer for visiting me."

"Oh, it would, huh? And just what will you be doing about it?"

"Let me suggest"—she aimed her musket at his crotch—"that you consider what life would be like if you no longer had anything dangling between your legs." When he flinched and covered his privates, she flashed him a cold smile.

"That be agin the law."

"If I claimed I did it in self-defense, I suspect it would be difficult to find anyone who would dispute my story."

Morrisey glared at her and the boy for another full minute before he strode from the house, mounted, and rode off. She kept her musket aimed at him until he was out of sight. After shutting the door and replacing the musket over the fireplace, she returned to the kitchen table. Willie was staring at her, his brown eyes wide.

"That were a right fine thing you done for me, ma'am. Right fine. It won't be making no nevermind though. He might be too scared to whup me for this, but he will whup me good for something else."

"I am afraid you are right. Then again, my interference has allowed you to stay here until you decide to leave. And you might even be able to come back another time if you feel inclined to."

"I would like that real fine, ma'am."

Clover noticed the boy was now playing with his food and peeking at her through his surprisingly long black lashes. It was clear that he had something on his mind, but was reluctant to speak.

"You want to ask me something, am I right?" He nodded. "Just ask me, Willie. The worst that can happen is that I will have no answer or will say no."

Willie nodded, took a deep breath, and asked, "Will you teach me what you be teaching the Mac-Gregors?"

"You mean how to read and write?"

"And figure and act proper and speak good like

you do. See, I figure I will get free of Morrisey someday, but he ain't raising me to be any more than a big dumb brute like him. Now, I know being half-Shawnee's gonna be trouble, but maybe if I got me some learning and fine manners I could still be more than dirt-poor. I ain't gonna get nowhere if I be nothing but a half-breed what acts and thinks like Morrisey."

"I will be pleased to teach you anything you want to know. What would you like to try first?"

"Well, I reckon I best learn my letters."

"We can start that now. Are you finished eating?" He nodded and she started to clear the table. "Upstairs in the third bedroom on your right you will find a slate and chalk on the table by the bed. Bring them down and we can get started." She smiled and shook her head as he bounded up the stairs.

Clover was just wiping off the table when the kitchen door slammed open. She screeched, whirled around, and came face to face with Big Jim, a wide leer on his face. Two of his disreputable friends blocked the door behind him.

"What are you doing here?" she demanded.

"Why, sweet thing, I done come to take you to your man," Big Jim answered.

"Ballard would never send you after me."

"Not that bastard. Your fine, pretty man from back home. Come along now, he be waiting on you."

She tried to run but he reached for her, grabbed her, and tossed her over his shoulder. Her struggles had no effect on him as he carried her out the door. Through the curtain of her tousled hair she caught a glimpse of Willie and prayed the boy would have the sense to go alert Ballard and the others.

Big Jim tossed her across his saddle, and before she could scramble free, one of his cohorts bound her wrists and stuffed a filthy gag in her mouth. She felt someone tightly bind her ankles and knew she could not escape now. Big Jim mounted up behind her and, to her disgust, rested his beefy hand on her backside as he rode. She tried to see where they were going, but her hair obscured her vision. All she could do was try not to be sick to her stomach and pray that Ballard would find her before it was too late.

Clover could not restrain a groan as she was dragged off the horse. Her whole body ached and she was nauseated and dizzy. Big Jim picked her up and carried her under one arm like a sack of grain, took her inside a foul-smelling cabin, and roughly tossed her onto a filthy cot.

It took her several moments to recover from her ordeal. She cautiously opened her eyes and looked around. She could hear the men talking just outside the door. She grimaced as she studied the cabin; the place was little more than a hovel. If she was not rescued soon, she could contract some very unpleasant, if not fatal, disease here.

Big Jim entered the cabin, strode over to her, and yanked off the gag. "So you are awake, huh?"

"Might I ask what you think you are doing?" she snapped.

He untied her wrists and ankles. Before she could massage some feeling back into her feet and hands, he looped a thick rope snugly around her neck several times. For a brief moment she was terrified, certain that he meant to strangle her. She struggled to calm her fears when he stood on the cot and tied the other end of the rope to a hook in the ceiling. Even if she stood on the bed, she would never be able to reach the knot. The rope around her neck was wrapped too tightly for her to try to work it off over her head. If she tried to move too far or too fast, she could easily hang herself. She was trapped.

Clover wished she had regained the feeling in her hands and feet so that she could inflict some hurt on Big Jim before he stepped out of reach.

"There, that ought to hold you." He jumped off the bed and grinned at her. "You can just sit there and think on what's to come."

"And what *is* to come? Is there some reason for this madness, or have you just completely lost what little mind you have?" She gritted her teeth against a hiss of pain as her hands and feet tingled painfully back to life.

Big Jim's two friends, who had entered the cabin in time to hear her tart remark, chuckled. "Shut up, Poonley. You too, Toombs," Big Jim snarled at them. "Has Ben gone?"

"Yup," answered the shorter of the two men. "He and that feller ought to be here before nightfall."

"And then the fun begins." Big Jim poked Clover in the ribs. "You and us are gonna have a fine old time, and that big dumb Scot ain't gonna be around to help you this time."

"I thought we was supposed to tell MacGregor we got her," said the short man.

"Shut your mouth, Poonley. We'll be telling that fool when we feel demmed good and ready." Big Jim reached out to stroke Clover's hair. She jerked away from his touch. "You ain't gonna be so demmed high and mighty soon," he said. "Once that feller what's paying us gets here, we'll work that haughtiness right outta you."

"Ballard will make you pay dearly for this," Clover warned. "He will hunt you down."

"That be just what we want him to do. You are the bait in a trap, woman. You will bring that bastard right to our door, and this time we will have the advantage. He ain't gonna be so tall and cocky when we get done with him. Not so pretty either. I aim to enjoy taking him down a peg or two, and I know our new friend will too. He be right eager to see you too."

"And who is this new friend of yours?" she asked, a cold knot forming in her stomach.

"That fancy man of yours from back in Pennsylvania. Me and him met in a tavern in Langleyville and found out we had a lot in common. We both owe your man."

"Thomas Dillingsworth is in Kentucky? I find that very hard to believe."

"I ain't no liar!" Big Jim yelled, and shook his fist at her.

"You ain't supposed to touch her till Dillingsworth gets here," Poonley reminded him. "That man was real firm about that."

"All right. Ain't no need to ride me so close, Poonley." Big Jim glared at Clover, then moved to the table where the other two men were sitting. "You hear me, woman? That fancy man of yours is on our side now. Hell, he be paying us good money. Now, you be a cute little thing and I be looking forward to having my turn at you, but truth to tell, I ain't sure why that man be going to so much trouble to get his hands on you."

"Do not look to me to end your confusion. I have never understood madmen." Clover edged along the bed until she was able to rest her back against the rough log wall.

"You saying that Dillingsworth ain't right in the head?" Big Jim demanded as he poured some home-brew into a battered cup.

"Does his behavior seem to be that of a sane man to you?"

Big Jim shrugged. "The man hankers after you so he takes you." His companions nodded in agreement.

"You are a master of simplicity, Mr. Wallis." She watched him frown and eye her narrowly, not certain if he was being insulted. "I believe what you are planning is a hanging offense," she warned, "and I do not believe that a completely sane man plans to do something that will get him hanged."

"They gotta prove we did it before they can try and hang us, and there ain't gonna be anyone left to say that it was us."

Clover slumped against the wall and closed her eyes. She knew of only one witness Big Jim and his cohorts did not know about—Willie. Although it was hard to say if anyone would believe the boy, even if he was able to tell what he saw.

She was tired and afraid, and she could see no way from the trap she was in, or from the trap she had inadvertently helped them set for Ballard. He would do exactly what he was told in the vain hope that he could save her. If there was no safe way to bring help, he would come alone. He would be one man against five. Formidable odds.

"That's it, woman. You get some sleep. We want you well-rested when our friend gets here 'cause we'll be keeping you real busy."

As she listened to their crude guffaws, Clover wished she had Mabel's ability to spit. It seemed the perfect response to their taunts. A night of pure horror, perhaps many nights of such horror, was being planned for her, and they laughed. Anger twisted her roiling stomach, but she was too tired to act on it. Besides, railing at her thickheaded captors would gain her nothing. It seemed strange to go to sleep when she was in such danger, but sleep would at least clear her head and give her a respite from her fear and worry. It would also give her the strength to get away if, by some miracle, a chance for escape presented itself.

Thomas sipped from a tankard of ale and stared at the man called Ben. He was a hulking, filthy brute, and Thomas was a little embarrassed to be seen with him. He needed a strong man whom he could easily control, however. Besides, he doubted he would meet anyone he knew in the dirty little inn, the only one in this squalid town a few miles south of Pottersville.

"Why are you staying here?" grumbled Ben as he scratched his straggly gray beard. "Coulda set yourself closer."

"I am here because I would rather not alert Ballard MacGregor to my presence." Thomas glanced around the small, dark common room of the inn with ill-disguised disdain. "'Tis a poor place for a man of my stature, but I suspect Pottersville is an even more wretched place."

"It ain't a bad town." Ben took a long swallow of ale and wiped his mouth on the stained sleeve of his buckskin coat. "We got the girl. Did just what you told us to and it worked real good. We got her trussed up back at Big Jim's place."

"Ye-es. I wish I had taken the time to find someplace other than that flea-infested hovel to hold her in." Thomas finished off his ale and stood up. "Shall we go?" He started out of the inn.

Ben cursed, gulped down the rest of his ale, and hurried after Thomas. "Ain't no need to hurry. She ain't going nowheres."

"True, but MacGregor may stumble upon his loose mare sooner than we planned. I do not want him to know what has happened to Clover until I choose to tell him."

"Are you sure MacGregor will do just what you tell him to do? He ain't never struck me as the sort of man to just walk into a trap, like a lamb to the slaughter. He be a fighting man and a good one too."

"I have his little wife. He will do exactly what I tell him." Thomas ran a finger down his crooked nose. "I have that bastard now and he will soon be wishing he never set foot in Langleyville."

Ballard frowned as he rode up to his house. He had felt uneasy for an hour or more, unable to shake the conviction that something was dreadfully wrong. Finally he had ordered the others to continue their search for the mare and had spurred his horse into a gallop for home. He dismounted and leaped up the steps, into the house.

"Clover!" he bellowed and grew even more concerned when there was no answer.

Fighting his burgeoning panic, he bounded up the staircase. He searched every room twice, then ran back downstairs and inspected the rooms again to be sure she had not fallen asleep somewhere, which he had caught her doing a time or two. As he went back outside to check the outer buildings, he began to move faster. Soon he was running from place to place. His calls for Clover grew more frantic. Back inside the house, he slumped against the kitchen table and tried to gather his wits.

Suddenly he noticed that the outside kitchen door was wide open. He was certain he had not opened it and moved to take a closer look. When he saw the splintered door frame and broken latch, he realized someone had forced his way into the house and taken Clover. He was sure of it.

Cursing, he took his musket down from over the fireplace and loaded it. What was he to do? He did not know who had taken Clover, although he had a strong suspicion, and he did not know where they had gone. He was alone with no idea of how many men he would face if he did find her. Without some answers to his questions, it would be foolhardy to plan his next move.

He sank into the heavy rocker in front of the fireplace and tried to think. Big Jim and Thomas had to be behind Clover's disappearance. Ballard could almost hear Big Jim's threats at the spring revel. He thoroughly berated himself for not taking those threats more seriously. Instead of keeping close to

Clover, instead of guarding and protecting her, he had run off to find his mare, leaving her completely alone and defenseless. Yet again he had failed to protect her from danger,

Muskrat rubbed against his legs and he scratched the animal's battle-scarred ears. "I failed her, Muskrat. It seems I am always failing her."

The cat stretched up on his hind legs, placed his big front paws on Ballard's knees, and hoarsely meowed. Ballard recalled how he was always catching Clover slipping the big tomcat treats and shook his head. The cat had begun to leave his catches at the kitchen door to impress her. Several times Ballard had come home to find a dead mouse or other small creature covered by a linen napkin, awaiting the proper burial that Clover insisted upon.

"I cannae just sit here and moon over her, Muskrat." Ballard gently pushed the cat away and stood up. "There must be something I can do. Maybe there is a trail I can follow," he muttered as he walked to the door, Muskrat ambling behind him.

Outside, he found the hoofprints of several horses. No effort had been made to hide their trail. Clover's abductors had known he would not be there. They led around the house and into the forest. Ballard was puzzled by the small human footprints that blended with the other prints and disappeared into the forest. Someone was already following Clover and her abductors. A small someone. Since Damien and Clayton were still with Shelton, Lambert, and Adam, Ballard had no idea who that small someone could be.

He stared into the woods for a long moment before returning to the house. He was going to follow that trail. It was probably not the safest or wisest thing to do, but he could not just sit and wait for some word from her kidnappers.

Ballard began to collect a few supplies. If his family did not return before he was ready, he would try to write a note for them.

A bellow startled Clover out of her doze. She fell forward and felt the sharp jerk of the rope around her neck. As she tried to rub her chafed neck between the thick coils of the rope, she quickly returned to an upright position against the wall.

"Damnation, Big Jim, your barn is on fire," cried Poonley as he squinted out one of the cabin's tiny begrimed windows.

Clover could not recall having seen anything worthy of being called a barn as she was dragged into the cabin. Poonley must be referring to the large lean-to she had briefly glimpsed. She watched the three men stagger outside, cursing each step of the way. It was evident that they had spent the evening drinking.

A familiar small figure appeared in the doorway a moment later. Clover blinked several times before she trusted what she was seeing. "Willie?"

He hurried over to the cot, hopped up onto the bed next to her, and pulled an impressively sharp knife from inside his ragged coat. Clover recognized it as the big hunting knife Ballard kept over the fireplace in their bedroom. An intent look came over his face as he sawed away at the rope leading from her neck.

"You be real still, ma'am," he said. "I might cut you if you move too sudden-like."

"How did you get here?"

"I followed you."

"But, Willie, we must be miles from Ballard's house."

"Ten miles as I figure it. I woulda helped you sooner, but I needed to take a rest once I got here."

"I am not surprised," she murmured. "You are obviously a great deal stronger than you look."

"They ain't hurt you yet, have they? I fear I was just too weary to think on what they might be doing to you while I was having a rest. Then I had to think of a plan to get them outta this cabin."

She stared at him in admiration. "You set the barn on fire."

"That ain't no barn. Just a rickety bunch of sticks and branches. I let the animals out first. They ain't done nobody no harm." He finished cutting through the rope and put his knife away. "We best hurry outta here, ma'am. That shed was burning up fast. Those drunken fools ain't gonna waste much time trying to save it, especially when they figure that the animals ain't in it."

Clover stood up, swaying slightly. As Willie grabbed her hand, she took several deep breaths to steady herself. She refused to let her weakness ruin her one chance to escape.

"Do you know how to get back to Ballard's?" she asked as they hurried to the door.

"Yup. I can take us straight there or, if these fools try hunting us down, I can get us there by a real crooked route." He glanced at Clover's skirts. "I reckon it ain't something ladies oughta do, but could you hook them skirts up, ma'am? 'Twill make it a sight easier for us to run through the woods."

Although she found it a little odd to be taking orders from a child, Clover did as she was told. She brought the back of her skirts through her legs and hooked it under the waistband. Clover just prayed she was not putting too much faith in a boy's bravado.

Willie peered out the door. "Them fools be standing there with their backs to us just gawking at the fire. Come on, ma'am. We gotta run as fast as we can into the forest. We can slow down a mite sometime later if we make it into them trees without them seeing us."

He bolted out the door and Clover followed. His speed astounded her. If Morrisey would treat the boy with just a little kindness, he would have a strong worker.

As they ran she waited tensely for a bellow to indicate that they had been spotted and the pursuit had begun, but none came. Even once they reached the shelter of the trees, Willie kept running and she tried her best to keep up. By the time he slowed up a little, Clover was gasping for breath and feeling weak in the knees.

"I think I need a moment or two to catch my breath," she called as she sagged against a tree trunk.

"I reckon you can, but only for a minute or two," he said as he walked back to her and sat down. "Once we get to the house, ma'am, I gotta be getting home."

"You should rest first."

"I shoulda been back home to milk the cows. If luck be with me, it will be dark by the time I get home and I can sneak in. Morrisey has usually got his fat head stuck in a bottle of homebrew by sunset. If he don't see me, he don't hit me, and come the morning he might forget he was a-wanting to."

"Perhaps if I went with you and explained—"

"That ain't gonna do no good. I know how to take care of myself, ma'am, and now I know where to get something to eat." He grinned at her, then stood up and brushed himself off. "Best we be going now, ma'am. We can run easy for a ways. Leastwise till we hear those fools coming after us."

Clover straightened up and followed him as he led her deeper into the forest. "Are there many wild animals here?"

"Some, but most of them ain't of a mind to get near us. If one does come sniffing 'round, we just have to scramble up the nearest tree and wait him out. Can you climb trees, ma'am?"

"I climbed one not long ago. A bear convinced me to try my hand at it."

He nodded. "I reckon climbing trees ain't something ladies are supposed to do."

"No. After all, it might allow a gentleman to peek up your skirts." She smiled when he giggled. "Willie, if Big Jim and his men get too close, I want you to take care of yourself and not worry about me."

"But I came to save you."

"And you might yet succeed. You will do me a greater service by not allowing yourself to get captured if Big Jim starts to run us down. If you remain free, you can tell Ballard what has happened, who has me, and where I am."

Willie nodded. "That be sound thinking, ma'am."

"Thank you." She exchanged another brief grin

with him, then tensed when he went still, listening. "Big Jim?"

"Reckon so. Come on, ma'am. Time for us to be taking that crooked trail."

As they ran, Clover heard, and occasionally caught sight of, Big Jim and his two men searching for them. The trees and thick underbrush impeded the men's progress, for they were inebriated and on horseback. Slowly dusk settled over the forest. It became harder and harder to follow Willie's twisting journey through the wood. She knew the lengthening shadows aided their escape, however, and struggled to keep pace with the boy. Some time later, badly winded, she stumbled over a root and landed hard on her backside, the breath knocked out of her.

"You all right, ma'am?" Willie asked as he crouched by her and helped her up.

"I will be in a moment. Do you think I can take a small rest again? I do not hear Big Jim."

Willie sat down next to her. "Reckon he ain't wanting to get too much closer to your man's land. It ain't fully dark yet and if Big Jim rides after us much further, he could get himself seen by MacGregor."

"Are we that close?" Clover could not believe they had covered so much ground. "I do not see the house."

"Too many trees. We ain't *that* close, but close enough so Big Jim might stumble into the open if he keeps after us."

"Oh, thank God. I feared I was slowing you down and putting us both at risk."

"You ain't done too bad, ma'am. Fact is, you kept up real good. I reckon ladies don't do much running through the woods."

Clover smiled and shook her head. "None at all."
She struggled to her feet. "Well, if we are that close
to home, let us continue. I can rest when I get there."

"You got spine, ma'am, you surely do," Willie said
as he led the way.

"Thank you—I think."

The trees thinned, and at last Ballard's house came
into view. Clover wished she had enough energy left
to run. She hoped Ballard was home. He might be
able to catch up with Big Jim and put an end to their
troubles before they got any worse.

"It just ain't smart to go any closer," Poonley said,
shaking his head when Big Jim let out a stream of
curses. "Fact is, I think we be close enough to Mac-
Gregor's place that you ought to be thinking on
being a mite quieter."

"We had her, curse it all to hell! How the hell did
the demmed bitch get loose?" Big Jim tried to turn
his panting horse and slapped it on the head when it
failed to move quickly enough to suit him.

"I reckon someone cut her loose," Poonley said,
and nodded.

"Think it was MacGregor?" asked the other man.

"You just ain't got no brain in that head, do you,
Toombs," snapped Big Jim. "If MacGregor had come
after us, he would never have left us standing there
scratching our arses. Whoever helped her just cut
her loose and ran."

"I reckon Dillingsworth ain't gonna care much
how she got away, just that we ain't got her no more,"
said Poonley.

Big Jim cursed again and headed his horse back

to his cabin, Poonley and Toombs falling in behind him. "And since we ain't got her no more, Dillingsworth ain't gonna give us our money. Well, if he thinks he's so blasted clever, he can just come up with a new plan. We got her once. We can get her again."

Chapter Thirteen

As Clover ran across the clearing to Ballard's house, she briefly considered falling to her knees and giving thanks. The horse tied up in front told her that someone had returned home. She prayed it was Ballard. She wanted to tell him about her ordeal first, without the others clamoring for answers. She would let him know exactly what threat they faced. And then she would go to bed.

"Are you sure you will not stay, Willie?" she asked the boy as she opened the door.

"No more'n a minute or two, just to be sure Mac-Gregor knows where to look for that scum."

As Clover stepped into the house, she nearly walked into Ballard, who was on his way out. He stood with a small sack in one hand and his musket in the other, and he had never looked so good to her.

As the realization that she was indeed safe at home at last struck her full force, one thing became blindingly clear. She loved the big man standing before her, staring at her as if she were a specter risen from the grave.

When he did not immediately drop everything and take her into his arms, her heart broke. She desperately wanted a hug, wanted to sink into his embrace, safe again. Instead, Ballard remained as if turned to stone.

"Ballard," she said, and reached up to touch his arm, grimacing when she saw how filthy her hand was. "I have had a rather distressing afternoon."

"Oh? A distressing afternoon, was it?"

He almost laughed, then wondered why. It really was the last thing he felt like doing. His insides were twisted with conflicting emotions. He was overjoyed that she was safe back home, yet devastated because again, she had been forced to take care of herself. Her presence seemed glaring proof that he could not protect her. He had dragged her from the safety of her tidy brick home in Langleyville to the wilds of Kentucky and plunged her into one trouble after another.

She looked terrible. Her dress was torn, stained, and bundled up above her knees. Her stockings were shredded and stuck with leaves and small twigs. Her hair hung down her back in a thick, tangled mass.

Finally he noticed the boy.

"What are ye doing here, laddie?" he asked, then wondered why he was talking to the boy when his recently kidnapped wife was standing there looking as if she had been dragged through the brambles backward and would dearly love to collapse onto something soft.

"I done brought your missus back to you," Willie answered.

Ballard looked at Clover again. "Who did it?"

"Big Jim and his cohorts. They dragged me right out of my kitchen."

"Why did they take you?" He ached to pull her into his arms and hold her close until he was completely reassured that she was safe, but he felt he had no right to offer such comfort.

"To give me to Thomas and to draw you into a trap." She sank into a chair by the fireplace. It was clear that Ballard was not going to give her the exuberant, loving welcome she craved. Suddenly she was exhausted.

"And ye followed her?" he asked Willie as he put his bag down by the fireplace and replaced the musket on the rack over it.

"I did," Willie replied. "Got her free of them bastards too."

Clover told Willie, "You must not use such bad language, and I thought you were in a hurry to get home."

"I be due for a beating no matter when I get home. I wanna stay for a while and be sure MacGregor knows everything he needs to so's he can make that scum pay good and proper for what they done."

"So Willie helped ye get free and ye made your way back here?" Ballard was dismayed that a small, barefoot boy had offered the protection he had failed to provide.

"More like she done *run* back," said Willie. "Nearly got caught a time or two, but we proved too quick for them."

Ballard sat down opposite Clover, unable to take his eyes off her. She was safe but through no help from him. He saw no condemnation in her tired eyes, but he was sure there was a hint of disappointment in them. He painfully accepted it as well-deserved.

"Perhaps, between the two of ye, ye can tell me all that happened."

Clover carefully related everything that had occurred from the moment Big Jim had burst into the kitchen. Willie added his own colorful details from time to time. All the while she wondered why Ballard looked sad, hurt, and a little angry. Anger she could understand, but not the others. And she had the strangest feeling that the anger was not directed at her kidnappers.

Ballard shook his head when they were done. "I never thought Thomas would pursue us here. Aye, I could see his madness, but I truly thought that, once we were in Kentucky, he would direct that madness elsewhere."

"Out of sight, out of mind," Clover murmured.

"Something like that. 'Tis my shortsightedness that has put your life in danger."

"What nonsense. No one can anticipate the actions of a madman."

"I left ye here alone, didnae I? Despite Big Jim's threats. That was a mistake. I shallnae make it again."

"Do you think someone'll be trying to grab her again?" asked Willie.

"They were mad enough to try it once. Aye, they might well try it again. I cannae ignore that possibility just because I see no sense in it."

Clover tensed when he reached out to cover her hand with his. She longed for him to pull her into his arms, but he still made no move to do so. Her ordeal seemed to have put a wide gulf between them, yet she did not understand why. It should be bringing them closer together.

"Did they hurt ye, Clover?" he asked.

"No, save for a few bruises. The hurting was to come later."

"When Thomas arrived."

"Yes. Thomas has hired Big Jim and his friends to do the brutish work for him."

"Here come your brother and the others, MacGregor, and some folk in a carriage," said Willie, looking out the window. "Now you got some help to chase that varmint Big Jim."

The riders and the carriage halted in front of the house. Clover suddenly realized that everyone would see her in her bedraggled state and stood with the intention of fleeing up to her room. But before she could accomplish that, her mother stepped inside the house, caught sight of her, and cried out in alarm. Agnes broke free of Colin's guiding hand and rushed over to Clover. Molly was quick to follow. Clover sighed. She was not sure she was strong enough to endure another round of questions and explanations.

Ballard saw how pale Clover was, and the moment Agnes and Molly reached her side, he ordered, "Ye women take Clover upstairs. She can tell ye what has happened as ye tend to her. The boy can tell us anything else we need to know."

"His name is Willie," Clover murmured as she was led away.

"Willie, is it?" Ballard asked the boy.

He nodded. "The missus said she hated the name Morrisey done gave me so we decided on another."

"We found the mare, Ballard," Shelton said. "Now what the devil has been going on here?"

"Can you use some help?" Colin asked, Jonathan at his side.

"If ye are nae too tired to go riding after some vermin—aye." Both men nodded and Ballard looked at the twins. "Fetch some water and take it up to your sister." When they hesitated, he added, "Dinnae fret. Ye will get the whole story before the night is over." As soon as they were gone, he turned to Willie. "Weel, laddie, tell us again what happened. Tell us everything ye ken."

As Willie spoke, Ballard grew angrier and angrier. A lot of that anger was directed at himself. He had played the fool from the start. He should have seen that the missing mare was a lure to draw him away from Clover. He should never have left her alone.

"I should have seen the trap for what it was," he muttered when Willie finished his tale.

"You cannot hold yourself responsible, Ballard," said Jonathan.

"Nay? I should have listened to Big Jim's threats more closely. I should never have left Clover alone. Shelton, Lambert, get us some fresh horses. Tell Adam what we are about and ask him to stay here to guard the women and the twins. I dinnae think we have much chance of catching the bastards, but I have to try." He turned back to Willie. "Are ye staying the night?"

"Nope." He grasped Ballard's shirtsleeve and tugged him closer. "Can I be asking you something, sir?"

"If ye are quick." Ballard saw Jonathan and Colin move away, giving them some privacy.

"Why didn't you give your missus a hug when she come back? I thought folk like you did that sorta thing."

"Because I am an idiot." He sighed when the boy ignored that and waited for a better answer. "Weel, maybe because Clover is a fine, learned, and pretty lass and I am an illiterate Scotsman with grand ideas and no money. Maybe because I failed her."

"Nah, you ain't failed her. She don't think so neither. I be that sure of it. And you being what you are? Why should that matter? Hellfire, if your missus was one of them what care about money and fancy ideas, why would she be so nice to me?" He shook his head. "I be thinking that marriage mighta addled your wits."

"There is a verra good chance ye are right. Are ye sure ye willnae spend the night here?"

"Real sure." Willie held out the hunting knife. "You'll be wanting this back, I reckon."

"Aye. I see ye went after her weel armed. Clever lad. 'Twill be dark soon. Do ye need someone to take ye home?"

"Nope. I can find my way. I will just go and say goodbye to your missus."

"I owe ye her life, Willie, and from all that ye have told me, probably mine as weel."

"I just helped a friend, MacGregor. You gotta help your friends," he said, and dashed off up the stairs.

"Somehow I have to get that boy away from Morrisey," Ballard said.

His brother and cousin led fresh horses up to the door and without another word, the five men mounted and rode off toward Big Jim's cabin, carefully following Willie's surprisingly precise directions. Ballard had little hope of catching up with his wife's kidnappers, but he had to try. If he could get his hands on

just one of them, he might be able to find Thomas.
And eventually he had to get to Thomas.

This time Ballard knew he would have to kill
Thomas Dillingsworth. The man had left him no
choice.

The sound of the horses riding off distracted
Clover from her muttered complaints about Bal-
lard's lack of welcome. "Is that the men leaving?"
Clover asked as her mother tucked her into bed.

"Yes," Molly answered, moving away from the
window, shooing the twins out of her way. "The Mac-
Gregors, Lambert, Jonathan, and Colin have all
ridden after those madmen who kidnapped you. I
just wish I had faith that they will find them."

"We must find Thomas."

"What we need now is to get you a hot cup of tea
and some bread and cheese," Molly said as she
opened the door, only to find Willie standing there.
"Your hero is here. Go on in, lad." She paused to
add, "Before you leave, Willie, m'lad, you be sure to
pick up the sack on the kitchen table." She winked at
the boy. "I suspect you are a clever lad and know how
to keep your treasures safe from those what haven't
earned them."

"Real safe, ma'am." As soon as Molly left, Willie
edged up to Clover's bedside. The twins stepped
back to give him room. "I just wanted to see if you
was still all right. You were looking a mite sickly there
for a bit."

"I will be fine. I just need to rest. I suppose you are
headed home now."

He nodded. "It only makes trouble for folk if I try

to stay away. You ain't got to worry about me, ma'am. I'll be back for my lessons."

"Be sure that you are. And be sure to pick up that sack. Molly is a very fine cook." She touched his cheek. "If it gets to be more than you can bear, or you begin to fear for your life, do not hesitate to come here. Be careful on your way home."

"I will, ma'am."

"We will go with you for a ways," said Damien as he and Clayton moved to his side.

"Oh, I am not so sure you ought to," murmured Agnes. "You do not know your way around as well as Willie does."

"We will go only as far as we know, Mama," Damien said. "And we will be back before it gets really dark."

"All right. Off you go then, but be careful."

As soon as the boys left, Clover looked at her mother. "Do you still have the money from the sale of the furniture?"

Smiling, Agnes sat down on the edge of the bed. "I do, but 'tis barely forty dollars, and that beast Morrisey wants sixty for the boy."

"I know, but it would be a very good start. I will understand if you do not want to give it to me. 'Tis all you have."

"I have all I need because of you. The money is yours, Clover. And if you can think of a way to make it grow to sixty dollars, just let me know. Ballard has some coin. Together it might be enough."

"If Ballard has much coin, he will need it to buy supplies and such. He has a lot of mouths to feed."

"You do realize that Morrisey could raise the boy's price again."

"He could, but I have to try."

"I know. Clover, about Ballard—"

Clover grimaced and wished she had not been so vocal about her hurt and confusion over Ballard's lack of warmth. "I really do not want to talk about that, Mama. 'Tis something Ballard and I will have to sort out ourselves. All I can say is that I really want to make this marriage work."

"Because you love the man."

"Yes, I do, curse him. I love him, but I will not play the fool for him."

"Well, let us hope that he returns safely so that you two can sort out your differences."

"She got away?" Thomas rubbed his temples. His head throbbed so badly he could barely see straight.

"Someone set the barn on fire and cut her loose while we was trying to fight the fire," Big Jim explained.

"Fools!" Thomas hissed. "Now we must start all over again."

"Ballard will be keeping a close watch on her now." Big Jim looked around the cabin. "And we ain't gonna be able to stay here no more. Fact is, we better get riding. MacGregor will be out looking for us and he ain't gonna be alone."

Thomas strode from the cabin, cursing when he heard the four men stumble after him. "We will go back to the inn tonight. You can bed down in the stables there. Perhaps by morning the four of you will have gathered together what few wits you possess and thought of a place where we can keep a close watch on Ballard MacGregor without drawing his notice."

"Maybe we oughta just give it up," Poonley said,

and hastily backed away when Thomas whirled
to glare at him. "Just for a little while," he added
meekly.

"Never! I have not traveled to this godforsaken
wilderness just to give up. Now ride. I hope you know
more about eluding capture than you do about
holding on to one small female," he snapped as he
mounted his horse and roughly spurred it to a gallop.

Ballard picked up the thick coil of rope left on the
filthy cot and stared up at the piece still dangling
from the ceiling. It looked so much like a gallows
rope that he shuddered. He was not surprised to find
that his prey had eluded him, but he cursed his poor
luck anyway.

"You are dealing with a madman," Colin said as he
stepped next to Ballard and looked at the rope.

"I ken it. I guessed that he wasnae sane when we
were in Pennsylvania. Still, I hadnae really believed
that he would go this far. I cannae judge how a mon
like him thinks, and that puts me at a disadvantage."

"You are going to have to kill him."

"I ken that too." He threw the rope down on the
bed. "First I have to find the bastard."

"We will help you in any way we can."

"Thank ye." He turned to Shelton. "Find anything?"

"Nay, not a cursed thing. They hid their trail weel.
Maybe we will find something in the morning."

Ballard nodded. "We can try. Dillingsworth is
clever, though. He will move again by daybreak. I had
hoped to end this here, tonight, but it looks like it
will be a long summer."

* * *

Clover heard the door of her room open and watched Ballard enter. For a brief moment she considered feigning sleep, but decided that would be cowardly. No matter what lay unresolved between them, Thomas was a threat to both of them and they had to fight him together. She sat up and lit the candle by the bed. Ballard looked tired and she felt a bit of sympathy for him.

"You did not find him, did you?"

"Nay." Ballard took off his shirt, moved to the stand that held the china bowl and pitcher, and started to wash up. "We couldnae find his trail either, but we will go back in the morning. The shadows may have hidden something."

"And if you do find a clue or a trail to follow, Thomas will probably still elude you." She slumped against the pillows. "He is quite mad and that makes him unpredictable, which only makes him more dangerous."

"I will find him, lass. On the morrow I will send Adam into town to put out the word about those bastards. Nearly everyone in the county will be looking for them." He walked over to the bed, sat down, and yanked off his boots. "I will have to kill Dillingsworth."

"I know, and I am sorry for that. 'Tis because of me you had to tangle with Thomas at all, so 'tis because of me that you will have blood on your hands."

"'Tisnae your fault, loving. Ye did nothing to the mon except refuse to be his whore." He took a deep breath and looked at her. "I failed ye, lass. I failed ye badly."

"What are you talking about?"

"I left ye here alone and unprotected, easy prey for those traitorous hirelings. I should have been here with ye. Instead ye had to depend on a wee laddie."

Clover suddenly understood what was troubling Ballard, why he had been acting so oddly. The man was sunk in self-chastisement. He truly believed he was at fault in some way. She reached out and smoothed her hand down his arm.

"You can be such an idiot." She smiled when he regarded her in openmouthed surprise. "You really believe some blame for this rests on your shoulders."

"And where else does it belong?" Ballard asked.

"On Thomas and Thomas alone."

"Lass, Thomas didnae leave ye here alone. I did. I discounted Thomas as a real danger because he was far away and I didnae give Big Jim's threats the weight they deserved."

"Neither did I, but I do not blame myself. Neither should you. For mercy's sake, Ballard, we are dealing with a madman. Our only error was in not realizing just how mad Thomas is, or how doggedly he would pursue us. Now we can see that in his madness, he has centered all his efforts on us. He is convinced that he must defeat you. Lord knows why. 'Tis impossible to follow such twisted reasoning. You have become his personal demon and he will not stop tormenting us until he has vanquished you. You cannot be blamed or faulted for not anticipating that."

Ballard lightly traced a scratch on her cheek. "I saw ye come back looking so bedraggled, knew ye had been through a harsh ordeal, and was ashamed that yet again ye had had to face such danger alone. I didnae feel worthy of touching you."

"Yes, you did seem to be acting in a particularly thickheaded way." She met his sharp glance with a sweet smile.

"I was riddled with guilt. It can cloud a mon's thoughts."

"You have nothing to feel guilty about. You were coming after me; I could see that. What else could you do?"

He shook his head. "God help me, I have made your life a real misery."

"What *are* you muttering about?"

"Ye turned to me for help. 'Tis why ye proposed. And what have ye got? Ye nearly drown on the way here, ye get chased by a bear, nearly struck by lightning, and now my enemies are after ye."

"They are my enemies too," she said, but she could see that he was too caught up in his own thoughts to listen.

"And I have forced ye to put away your pretty gowns and wear calico." He took her hands in his. "And look at your wee hands. 'Tis a wonder ye can abide speaking to me."

"Ballard, do you think me so shallow that I have naught to do but fret over the condition of my gowns and hands?"

"Nay, lass. But everything is different for ye now."

"Ballard, I have no complaints and you are to stop wallowing in self-pity and blame. Right now."

He smiled faintly. "Are ye giving your husband an order?"

"I am, and I was sorely tempted to give you one or two when I arrived."

"Oh, aye? Such as?"

"Such as please hold me," she whispered and then grimaced. "I wanted a hug. I wanted a big welcome."

"And I just looked at ye."

She nodded. "It sounds a bit weak, but I wanted to hide in you for just a little while because I was afraid and tired and sore."

"It doesnae sound weak, lass. I wish I hadnae acted like such an idiot. Is it too late now?"

"Well, with a little effort you could make amends." She patted the mattress next to her. "Come to bed, Ballard." She almost laughed at how quickly he acted upon her invitation.

He gently pulled her into his arms. "Are ye hurt badly, loving?"

"Sore, but that could be as much from the rescue as the capture."

"I dinnae seem to be doing much rescuing meself," he murmured, stung again by his inability to keep her safe.

"Poor Ballard," she teased, then grew serious. "'Tis all up to you now, though."

"I ken it. I will get him, Clover. I will put a stop to this."

For a while they just held each other. Clover knew it would be some time before she completely recovered from her ordeal. Now she was deeply afraid— for herself and for Ballard. Even being in Ballard's strong arms could not completely dispel that fear. She was pleased that he was no longer holding himself apart from her, however. They needed to be together now. It was the only way they would have a chance of beating Thomas Dillingsworth.

"Clover?" Ballard kissed her cheek. "What is in the box on the dressing chest?"

She smiled. Several times in the last few minutes he had glanced at the box her mother had brought in to her. It held the money from the sale of their belongings in Langleyville. Ballard had been curious, but he had restrained himself from peeking. She wondered how he would react when she told him what she planned to do with the money. She knew he wanted Willie to be free of Morrisey as badly as she did, but money was hard to come by.

"'Tis the money from the sale of our furniture. I am going to use it to get Willie away from Morrisey. Mother freely gave it to me for that purpose."

"How much do ye have?"

"Not quite forty dollars." She frowned when he slipped out of bed, went over to the wardrobe, and lifted a small sack down from a top shelf. He tossed the sack onto her lap. "This will help."

Clover opened it and gasped. She tipped it out and carefully counted fifteen dollars.

"Ballard, I cannot take all of your money too," she protested.

"'Tisnae all mine. I hold it for all of us who are collecting money to free the boy. Little by little, penny by penny, we have managed to collect this much toward buying Willie's freedom. Although I dinnae like to use the word *buying*."

"Neither do I." She put the money back into the pouch and set it on the bedside table. "This means that he will be free soon." She kissed him. "Thank you, Ballard."

"Dinnae get your hopes up too high, lass. Morrisey still might refuse ye."

"Then I shall have to use all of my powers of persuasion." She smiled sweetly. "I *will* free that boy."

"I almost pity Morrisey. He doesnae ken the power of a foster mother defending her cub."

Chapter Fourteen

"Are you sure about this, dear?" Agnes asked, regarding the ramshackle Morrisey house with distaste, then looking wistfully at Adam, who waited with the wagon.

"Very sure, Mama." Clover rapped on the door again, wishing she had come sooner instead of allowing her mother and Ballard to coddle her. She had not been seriously injured in her ordeal, and it had been selfish to leave Willie in Morrisey's brutal hands for four more days.

"You do not have the full sixty dollars," her mother reminded her.

"I know." She smiled at Bess when the timid woman eased open the door. "Mrs. Morrisey? You may not remember me, but I am Ballard MacGregor's wife, Clover. This is my mother, Agnes Sherwood."

"What do you want?"

"I would like to talk to you."

"'Bout what?"

"The boy. The one who is half-Shawnee?"

"My husband ain't wanting to talk about him. He ain't giving that boy up for nothing."

Clover took the bag of coins from a pocket inside the folds of her cloak and hefted it in her hand so that Bess Morrisey could hear the distinctive chink of money. "I am here to do more than talk."

Bess opened the door wider. "I will send one of the boys after my husband."

As she entered the house, her mother following on her heels, Clover saw three young girls standing in the doorway of the kitchen, watching her closely. When Morrisey had mentioned his family that day in the Clemmons store, he had talked only of sons. She suspected the girls were treated almost as badly as Willie.

Bess tugged a small boy out of a dark corner of the room and sent him to get her husband. She then signaled Clover and her mother to sit at the long plank table.

"You got all sixty dollars?" Bess asked as she sat down across from Clover and Agnes.

"Not quite," Clover replied, noticing how hard Bess stared at the sack of money she had set on the table in front of her.

"Then he ain't gonna be agreeing with you."

"There is no harm in trying, is there?"

"Reckon not. Still, if my man said sixty, then he means sixty. He can be stubborn." Bess tentatively reached toward the sack of money, but did not touch it. "How much do you have?"

"Forty-two dollars." She saw Bess's tired eyes grow wide and knew she had guessed correctly in thinking that the Morriseys rarely saw any coin at all. She had held back some of the money and began to think she would be able to keep it. "I realize it is short of the fee your husband has been demanding, but 'tis far, far more than he paid for the boy, and I suspect far more than anyone else has ever offered. After all, he is quite small and ill-fed. Judging from how often your husband feels it is necessary to discipline the boy, I would say that he must be a very difficult child." She met Bess's sardonic look and knew the woman was not fooled by her carefully chosen words. Clover also sensed that Bess would say nothing, however.

"Ma, we ain't never seed that kind of money before," said the tallest of the three girls.

"This ain't none of your business, Lottie," Bess said. "Your pa won't want to be hearing from you. You three get back to the cooking." She looked at Clover. "Why do you want the boy so bad?" she asked in a soft voice, glancing at the door as she spoke.

Clover realized that Bess was trying to find out something before her husband arrived. She wished she knew what it was. For a moment she hesitated, then decided to tell the truth. Since Bess clearly did not want her husband to hear the conversation, Clover felt certain that whatever she said would not reach Morrisey's ears, to be used against her later.

"What I want, Mrs. Morrisey, is to get that child away from your husband before he kills him," she replied in an equally soft voice. "I owe that boy my life. Four days ago he saved me from Big Jim."

"Four days back, huh? That was the day my man came back spitting poison about you. He don't like you much."

"I suspect my threat to shoot off his manhood rather

soured his opinion of me." To Clover's astonishment Bess briefly, timidly smiled.

"You did that?" When Clover nodded, Bess quickly grew solemn again. "That ain't gonna put him in a humor to bargain with you."

"I am hoping this will put him into a more reasonable state of mind," Clover said, lightly touching the money bag. "Fifteen dollars was collected from the townsfolk. The rest is mine. I am not the only one who wants that child taken from your husband's hands."

Bess nodded. "It mighta been better if you shot him when you had the chance. He will be holding that agin you."

"To be honest, I have never handled a gun in my life. I was lucky I aimed the right end of the musket at him. I will get the boy free of him. If not today, then another day. I will not give up. As I said, I owe the boy my life. I owe him my husband's life as well, for our enemies meant to use me to draw Ballard to his death."

"I ain't gonna be able to help you."

"I do not ask or expect you to."

"I ain't even sure you will be safe in my house right now. My man purely hates you. I reckon he figures you shamed him. Scared him too, and he ain't gonna forgive that. I ain't gonna be able to help you if he sets on you."

"You do not have to worry about us. As you saw, Adam Dunstan brought us here. At the first hint of trouble he will enter, gun in hand, and *he* knows how to use it."

At that moment Morrisey slammed into the house, stopping just inside the front door to glare at Clover. "What the hell are you doing here, woman?" He glowered at his wife. "Why'd you let her in after all I been saying 'bout her?"

"She done come to buy the boy." Bess pointed to the sack on the table.

Morrisey strode over and reached for the sack, but Clover snatched it away. She did not flinch under his hard glare, not even when he raised his fists. He had come in the front door, so she knew he had seen Adam and understood what would happen if he touched her. Clover was not sure how long the threat of Adam would restrain Morrisey, however, so she hurried to get down to business.

"You do not get this money until I get the boy," she said.

"Then show me your money."

Clover tipped the coins out on the table. Morrisey stood there for a long time, staring at it and not saying a word. When she caught a glimpse of his lips moving, she realized he was struggling to count it.

"There ain't sixty there," he accused.

"I know."

"I said his price is sixty."

"And do you really think someone will pay that much for the boy? He is underfed, battered, and obviously troublesome. We both know a lot of people want that boy free. They have been trying to raise the ridiculous price you are asking for a year, and they still do not have enough."

"They got this much together. They can get the rest."

"That money does not come from your neighbors," said Agnes, speaking for the first time. "It is my money. I sold nearly everything I had just before I left Pennsylvania, and this is all I could raise. The pot will not grow any bigger. Yes, a few dollars did come from others, but only a few and, as Clover said, it has taken them nearly a year to gather even that small amount. I doubt they will ever get a full sixty dollars together. You have overpriced the child, Mr. Morrisey, and that means no one here will ever pay your blood money."

"Then I can sell him someplace else," Morrisey grumbled, but his gaze remained fixed on the silver coins.

"I sincerely doubt that Mr. Morrisey. He is a skinny, dirty little boy and half-Indian. You know most people do not believe Indians can work hard. A number of people would not want him near them because of their dreadful fear and loathing of Indians. And, for sixty dollars, a person can get a good strong black man, perhaps even more than one black slave. I detest the business of buying and selling people, as does my daughter. Nevertheless, if we must stoop to meet your despicable demand in order to free that child, we will. We will not, however, pay a price you could get nowhere in this country. What my daughter is offering is more than generous. I suggest you think twice before you refuse."

While her mother spoke, Clover carefully returned the coins to the pouch, determined not to reveal her astonishment at her mother's boldness. The usually timid woman was talking in a firm voice, calmly facing the large, glowering Morrisey. She had also lied about how much of the money had come from the townsfolk. It was a clever lie intended to convince Morrisey he would never get his asking price, and Agnes Sherwood never lied.

Clover looked up at Morrisey as she dropped the last coin into the pouch and closed it. He really wanted the money. Just as she had hoped, showing him the coins had aroused his greed. She still had thirteen dollars in her pocket for bargaining, but it began to look as if she would not need it.

"Take the money, Jake," urged Bess, tensing when he glared at her.

"This is my business, woman," he snapped.

Bess flinched, but pressed on. "Folk 'round here just ain't got much money. They ain't never gonna get sixty dollars together, not for no half-breed boy. The only reason this money is here is because these ladies done brought it with them to Kentucky. We got plenty of workers, Jake, but we ain't got no coin."

Morrisey scowled, then held out his hand. "Fine, then. Buy the brat. Give me the money and you can take him away."

"I want to see the boy first," said Clover. "Until he is in my hands, you do not get a penny."

"Get the brat, Bess."

Bess's expression as she moved to do her husband's bidding made Clover uneasy. When Bess pushed aside a thin rag rug on the floor and Clover saw the tiny trap door, she understood Bess's shame. Clover struggled hard to control her rage as Bess helped a filthy, unsteady Willie up through the hatchway. He shielded his eyes against the light. Clover suspected he had been in that hole since he had returned home after helping her. She looked at Morrisey and knew that he could see the fury in her eyes.

"You already done agreed to the price," he said.

"Come here, Willie." Clover frowned when Bess had to help the boy over to her. "You are coming home with me. Is there anything you want to take with you?"

"The brat don't own nothing," Morrisey said even as Willie shook his head.

"I need your mark on this piece of paper, Mr. Morrisey," Clover said, and pulled a small bill of sale she had written up out of a pocket inside her cloak. "It simply says that, for the sum of forty-two dollars, you will relinquish all claim to the child." She pointed to the bottom of the paper. "I want you to make your mark here and make a thumbprint right next to it."

Even as she pulled from her bag the ink, quill, and paper Morrisey needed, Clover asked Willie, "Are you hurt?"

"Just some bruises. Ain't nothing broken. I just be a mite stiff 'cause that punishment hole ain't too big." He looked at her in awe. "Am I free then?" His eyes widened when she nodded. "I could hug you, ma'am, but I'm powerful dirty."

"You can hug me after you have had a bath." She smiled when he grimaced at the word *bath*, revealing that, despite his sad condition, his spirit was undaunted.

"Where am I going now that I be free?"

"Well, you can come and live with us, but since you *are* free, it must be your own decision." When she saw that Morrisey had finished putting his marks on the paper, she held the man's belligerent gaze and asked Willie, "Were you being punished for spending time with me?" Morrisey lowered his hand to his loins and Clover smiled coldly. He had not forgotten her threat that day at Ballard's.

"Nope. I forgot to do the milking."

Clover suspected that the milking had not been done because the boy had been with her and his punishment was for that visit as well, but Morrisey had had enough wit to claim another reason. Since she had no weapon and probably lacked the backbone needed to shoot a man anyway, she decided to let well enough alone. The important thing was Willie's freedom.

Morrisey thrust the paper at her. Clover took it, studied his mark, and put it back in her pocket. She signaled her mother to take Willie out to the wagon and then tossed the money onto the table. Morrisey snatched it up so quickly she was not sure it even touched the surface of the table.

"I have found this transaction extremely distasteful, Mr. Morrisey," Clover said. "The child is no longer yours. If you ever touch him again, I will see that you pay dearly for it." She nodded at Bess. "Good afternoon, Mrs. Morrisey." She hurried out of the house, briefly wishing there was something she could do to help Bess and her children and knowing there was nothing.

As she climbed onto the wagon seat next to Adam, waving aside his offer of assistance, she looked at her mother and Willie seated in the back. Willie was eating a scone Molly had packed for him, struggling valiantly to obey her mother's gentle commands to eat slowly. Clover almost dreaded cleaning him up, for she knew that once the dirt was washed away, she would see the results of Morrisey's brutal hand all too clearly.

"Lord above, did he crawl out of a mudhole?" cried Molly as she gingerly helped Willie from the wagon.

"Actually, Molly, you are almost right," Clover said

as she hopped down from the seat and went to help her mother out of the wagon. "He has been in a punishment hole since the day he rescued me. He needs a good scrubbing."

"He does that."

"I should go and thank MacGregor." Willie tried to squirm free of Molly's grip on his arm.

"Mr. MacGregor be doing some business. He will not be wanting a dirty little boy rushing over and interrupting." Molly towed him toward the house. "You can thank him when you are clean, though I be thinking he might not recognize you." She looked back at Clover. "Your man said to come and join him when you get back. He be in the stables with a Mr. Potsdam, talking horses."

"I think some of the twins' clothes will fit Willie," said Agnes as she followed Molly into the house. "We will burn those rags of his."

Clover laughed softly as she watched Molly drag a reluctant Willie into the house. She then looked toward the stables. It was not going to be easy to meet Ballard's best customer when she was still feeling somewhat shaken from her dealings with Morrisey. She would much prefer to have a long hot bath, but Ballard was eager for her to meet Mr. Potsdam, a member of the area's small society.

"Adam?" she called, halting the farmhand as he started to drive the wagon back to the barn. "What is Mr. Potsdam like?"

"Good man. Money. Pretty manners. A gentleman," he replied before continuing on to the barn.

"Succinct," she murmured and, taking a deep breath, headed for the stables.

Although Adam's reply had been terse, Clover

felt she knew the sort of man she was about to meet. It was to feel equal to and comfortable with men like Mr. Potsdam that Ballard had been seeking a wife with her particular qualifications. She wished she had thought to ask Ballard just how much of a proper lady he wanted her to be.

It took a moment for her eyes to adjust to the dim light of the stables. She spotted Ballard at the far end, discussing the merits of a yearling whose stall they leaned against with a slender, silver-haired gentleman. She was just nearing Ballard's side when he turned toward her.

"Clover, did everything go weel?" he asked, taking her hand and drawing her close.

"A complete success. Much better than I expected."

"Good. There is someone here I would like ye to meet. Clover, may I introduce Cyril Potsdam. Cyril, my wife, Clover." He grinned and winked at her. "How was that?"

"Very proper." She smiled and shook Cyril's hand. "I am pleased to meet you, sir."

"I have been eager to meet you." He kissed her hand and smiled when she blushed. "I am pleased to see that you have recovered from your ordeal."

"Thank you. I am very resilient and my kidnappers were not the most intelligent men."

Cyril laughed, then grew serious again. "We are all looking for the rogues. Rest assured, we will find them."

"I hope so, although there must be a lot of places for them to hide around here."

"Not as many as there used to be, loving," Ballard said. "I ken it might look wild and empty to ye since ye have always lived in a town, but there are nae so many free and open places as there were in the beginning. Those men will eventually chance being seen. We just have to wait until they are and hope they are seen by the right folk, ones who will come and tell us."

"Your husband is correct, Mrs. MacGregor," said Cyril. "It will not be long before we put an end to this threat."

Clover smiled and thanked him, but did not share his confidence. She had grown somewhat fatalistic about Thomas Dillingsworth and whatever twisted plans he had concerning her and Ballard. Nothing they had done so far had stopped Thomas, and she did not believe they would suddenly get lucky.

After a few moments of pleasant conversation, she left the men to dicker over the yearling. She smiled to herself as she walked back to the house. Mr. Potsdam was a pleasant gentleman, refined and well-mannered, and he did not care a jot about Ballard's lack of bloodlines or education. One thing she had learned while a part of society was how to see the person behind the fine manners and social niceties. Cyril Potsdam held none of the prejudices that often cursed the upper classes. He liked Ballard Mac-Gregor for the man he was.

She briefly considered telling Ballard he did not have to learn fine manners to be accepted as an equal by men like Cyril Potsdam, then decided it would not make any difference. Ballard was learning everything he could to please himself. Mr. Potsdam did not care if Ballard knew one wine from another, but Ballard wanted to be able to stand toe to toe with any man as an equal. He sought to avoid those painfully awkward moments that so often occurred when one entered an unfamiliar world.

Clover's musings came to an abrupt halt when she entered the house and found Willie sitting at the table. Molly and her mother had wasted no time in scrubbing him from head to toe and dressing him in clean clothes. Clover doubted she would have recognized him, except that he was eating with his distinctive lack of restraint.

She sat down opposite him and studied him carefully. His skin had a faint coppery tone. His hair, a thick rich black, fell past his shoulders to ragged ends. Several faint scars marred his body from past beatings, and more vivid bruises recalled his recent ordeal. She could also see that, with a little care and plenty of food, Willie would grow into an extraordinarily attractive man.

"You are very handsome," she said, and smiled when a hint of color bloomed in his high-boned cheeks.

"I ain't never been so clean. Molly and your ma sure do know how to scrub a feller till he fair squeaks." He took a drink of cider, then asked in a small voice, "I am really free of Morrisey?"

"Yes, you really are free of him."

"You ain't gone and paid him the whole sixty dollars he asked for, has you?"

"No. I suspected that if he saw a goodly pile of silver coins, he would agree to a lesser amount just to get his hands on them. He did. I put forty-two dollars on the table and let him stare at it until he was tempted into agreeing to my offer."

"So now I belong to you and MacGregor."

It was flattering to see how pleased he was with his

new situation, but clearly he did not understand the concept of freedom. Either he had not listened to her back at Morrisey's or he simply did not understand. She put the paper Morrisey had signed on the table between them.

"You belong to no one, Willie. I recalled that you cannot read and took the chance that Morrisey cannot read either. Yes, I paid Morrisey some money, but I did *not* buy you. This paper says Morrisey accepted money to release you of all obligations. It is rather like the manumission papers some slaves get from their masters when they are made freemen. You belong to no one, Willie. You owe no one. You are your own man. You can go or stay as you please."

"I ain't rightly sure I understand this. Can I stay here?"

"Of course you can and for as long as you like. You are welcome to be a part of this family. I just want you to know that you do not *have* to do anything unless you want to."

He nodded. "I will pay you back, ma'am."

"I do not expect you to."

"I know that, but I will."

He turned as the twins burst into the house. In a moment he was off and running with them. Clover hoped that was how it would be from now on. Willie would have to do his share of the chores, as the twins did, but he would also get to be just a child.

"Ballard?" Clover called, frowning as she sought a glimpse of him among the apple trees.

She stopped and, with her hands on her hips, looked around. Someone was playing tricks on her.

Damien had told her that Ballard wanted to see her in the orchard, dragging her away from a discussion of Willie's future with her mother. Yet now there was no sign of Ballard. She was about to go find her mischievous little brother, and give him a scolding that would leave his ears ringing for the rest of the afternoon, when she whirled around, took a step back toward the house . . . and walked right into a grinning Ballard's arms.

"You wretch!" she cried, and swatted at him. "You scared me half to death."

"Is your heart pounding?" he asked, pulling her tighter against him.

"Of course it is. It always pounds when some great fool terrifies me." She slipped her arms around his neck as he lifted her up in his arms so that their faces were level.

"And is your blood running swiftly through your veins?" He slowly dotted kisses over her face.

"I should say so."

"Feeling a wee bit light-headed?" he asked as he steered them toward a thick knot of trees.

"A touch." She squeaked with surprise when he stepped behind a clump of birches at the far end of the orchard and set her abruptly down, so abruptly that she stumbled and landed with a thump on the blanket spread out at their feet.

It was hard to hide her amusement when Ballard yanked off his boots, gracefully sat beside her, and then tumbled her onto the blanket. There was a certain gleam in his eye that told her exactly why he had lured her there.

She looked around and saw nothing but trees: the neatly set out orchard in front of them, and the encroaching forest on the other three sides. It was a beautiful sunny day, warm but not hot, and a perfect place to make love, as Ballard so clearly wanted to. She did not feel even the smallest tickle of shyness or embarrassment over the thought of indulging in such intimacies in the bright glare of day. Instead, a swift, heady rush of excitement made her head spin.

Clover smoothed her hand over the blanket they were sharing and gave Ballard a look of sweet, wide-eyed admiration. "I did not realize what a skilled farmer you are, husband. 'Tis not every man who can grow blankets, ones already woven and seamed."

Ballard gave her a disgusted look before he kissed her. After his meeting with Potsdam, he had been wandering through the orchard, checking the apple trees, enjoying the peacefulness and fine weather, and suddenly he had wanted Clover—badly. It had been easy to draw her out to the orchard, but he wondered if she would want to celebrate the beauty of their surroundings the same way he did. She was responding to his kiss with all her usual passion, but he was not sure if that meant what he hoped it meant. Although she rarely allowed modesty to disrupt their passion anymore, making love under a tree in the middle of the day was very daring, even for him.

He finished kissing her and rolled onto his back, tugging her up against his side.

"Potsdam invited us to his home for dinner a fortnight from this Saturday," he said.

"That will be nice," Clover murmured, a little confused. She had been so sure Ballard wanted to make love, but now he acted as if he just wanted to sit with her privately for a while and talk.

"Ye did a fine job of getting Willie out of Morrisey's clutches. I was worried ye would come away empty-handed. I ken weel how that would have upset ye." He rubbed his hand up and down her arm and wondered how long he should spend putting her at her ease before he let her know what he really wanted.

Clover caught him looking at her. That gleam was still there. He *did* want to make love to her, but was holding back for some reason. She shifted slightly so that her body was partly sprawled on top of his and kicked off her shoes.

Ballard talked about how young Willie would fit neatly into their lives. She replied in all the appropriate places, but her focus was on how to turn his thoughts to more passionate subjects.

Ballard had never before been reticent when it came to lovemaking. In fact, he had freed her of the restraints of her own well-taught modesty, and she knew she had learned the lesson well. It was amusing now to realize that she was eager to make love in such a beautiful place while Ballard was hesitating.

She was just going to have to show him, she thought with an inner grin. Part of her was shocked at how daring she felt, but it was a good feeling and she wanted to revel in it. The only word she could think of to describe the mood she was in was *wicked*. She was not sure she had the skill to do so, but suddenly she wanted to put Ballard into such a state of passionate confusion that he did not know which way was up. All he would know was that he was thoroughly enjoying himself. Clover smiled faintly as she slowly began to unbutton his shirt.

Ballard tensed, not sure of Clover's intention. He wanted to be sure. For once he wanted her to initiate the lovemaking, with the same passion and eagerness with which he made love to her. He did not want to have to seduce her, cajole her, or even ask her. She had grown deliciously free in her lovemaking and now he wanted her to take that final step, to have the courage to ask him to share her desire.

"Did ye think I was feeling a wee bit warm?" he asked, a little surprised when she tugged off his shirt.

"I was rather hoping you were," she murmured as she ran her hands over his chest.

"Actually, lass, it does seem to be getting a wee bit hot."

As she touched her lips to his, she whispered, "Hot is very good, is it not?"

He had no chance to respond before she began to kiss him. Her kiss was deep and hungry, and Ballard wrapped his arms around her to hold her close. She was acting very boldly, far more boldly than he had imagined she would, but he had no inclination to stop her. Although it was what he wanted, it was a little confusing, for it was as if she had become someone else, and he could not be sure what she would do next. Her daring behavior had his passion running hot, but he struggled to restrain himself and see just how far she would take them. However, he could not resist undoing her bodice so that he could feel her silken skin beneath his hands.

She ended the kiss and sat up, straddling him. As she held his gaze, she unpinned her hair and shook it free until it tumbled around her shoulders. His hungry, surprised expression encouraged her. She slipped out of her bodice and tossed it aside. As she stood up, she untied her skirt and petticoats and let them fall, kicking them away. She rested her foot on his chest, untied her garter, and slowly rolled her stocking down. Ballard's breathing visibly increased as she did the same with the other stocking. After shimmying out of her underdrawers, and laughing softly at Ballard's groan, she sprawled on top of him again. It felt good to see that hot desire on his handsome face and know that she had caused it. She wondered when she should take off her chemise, trying to decide what would be the sultriest way to go about it.

Clover kissed Ballard, but when he tried to put his arms around her, she grasped his wrists and pinned his hands to the blanket. He could break her hold easily, but he did not try. Often when he stared at her as intently as he was now, she began to grow uncertain, wondering if she was doing something wrong. This time his look only inspired her. She slowly began to kiss her way down his lean body.

He shifted restlessly beneath her soft, warm kisses and caresses. He groaned and tried to speak his pleasure when she drew idle designs on his stomach with her tongue. She began to undo his breeches, and when she started to tug them off, he shifted his body to help her. As she slid her hands up and down his legs, then placed shy kisses on his inner thighs, Ballard feared he would soon lose the ability to lie calmly and enjoy her every touch and kiss. He ached to touch her.

When she placed her warm lips on his erection, he gave a hoarse cry and reached down to thread his fingers through her thick hair. He lost control rapidly as she caressed him with her lips and tongue. The last thread of that control snapped completely when she took him into her mouth. His body bucked from the force of the pleasure that ripped through him. Clover hesitated, but cupping her small face in his hands, he silently urged her to continue. He had the strength to savor that delight for only a moment before he grasped her under the arms and tugged her up his body.

To his surprise, Clover still kept control of their lovemaking. She eased their bodies together and then grew still. Ballard was breathing hard and fast as he watched her seductively shed her thin linen chemise. With her delicate hands on his chest, she began to move. He tried to keep some rein on his needs, but his body wanted no more of his self-imposed restraints. As his release tore through him, he gripped her slim hips and held her tightly against him as he tried to bury his body as deeply within hers as he could. Her cry of satisfaction quickly followed his, and he held her close when she sagged against him.

For a long while Ballard just held Clover, staring up at the sky, listening to their breathing slow to a normal rhythm and feeling the lingering tremors of their sated bodies begin to fade. When she eased the intimacy of their embrace, he allowed her enough leeway to shift into a comfortable position, still keeping her close. He suddenly wished he had some skill with pretty words so that he could tell her how much pleasure she had given him.

Clover peeked up at Ballard and caught him watching her. She expected to suffer at least some embarrassment over her wantonness, but she did not. Today she had wanted to be bold and daring, and she had heartily enjoyed herself. Making love to Ballard had soothed something else inside her.

From the moment she had recognized how much she loved him, the words to tell him so had sat on the tip of her tongue. Every time she talked to him, she was afraid she would say those words. Theirs was a marriage of mutual convenience, with the welcome addition of a strong passion. He had not spoken of love, however, and she could not bare her heart and soul to the man until she had some clue that he wanted or even sought such an emotion. But in their lovemaking, she could show him how much she loved him. She did not need to keep her feelings locked away.

"Weel, loving," Ballard murmured, "'tis clear ye can be powerfully inspired by a fine, sunny day."

She laughed. He appeared extraordinarily content.

Her desire for brazen lovemaking might not come upon her often, she mused, kissing Ballard again, but when it did, she could be sure he would eagerly accommodate her.

Chapter Fifteen

"Betrothed?"

Staring at her mother, Clover sank onto the bed. Her mother calmly nudged her off the dress Clover had laid out to wear to dinner with Cyril Potsdam. She numbly inched aside.

Although she had accepted her mother's romance with Colin Doogan, she had never fully considered what it might lead to. And so soon! It was only a month since the spring revel and, while Colin and Jonathan had come around nearly every day, she was still surprised at the short duration of her mother's courtship.

"Did you think Colin and I were just playing some idle game?" Agnes asked.

"No," Clover answered. "I never really gave it much thought, I guess."

"One does not work so arduously at something, as arduously as Colin has worked at courting me, without a set purpose in mind."

"No, of course not. I began to wonder if he and Jonathan ever got any work done because they were over here so often. Thank you," she murmured to Molly, who handed her a cup of tea.

"The same can be said for Jonathan Clemmons," Agnes said with a quick glance at Molly.

"Surely you are not surprised by that," Molly said. "I thought you had guessed my plans for the man the day we all first met. Although Jonathan *was* quicker to fall in with my intention than even I hoped he would be! I suspect Jonathan was inspired to propose when Colin made up his mind to ask your mama for her hand. It certainly did not hurt our cause that Colin's family and Jonathan's mother were eager for the matches and willingly freed them of work whenever possible."

"Are you to be married in a shared ceremony?" Clover almost laughed when her mother and Molly nodded, but her shock was still too strong to allow more than a hint of amusement.

Agnes sat down next to Clover. "You are thinking that I am being disloyal to your father."

Clover shook her head. "No, not really. To be honest, Mama, I am not sure what I am thinking." She looked at Molly. "I know you wanted a husband, Molly. I am just a little surprised at how quickly you got one. Do not mistake me, I am pleased for you, but are you sure Jonathan is the one you want?"

"Very sure," Molly answered. "I was sure the first time I set eyes on the man. I took one look at that big plain face of his and said to meself, That be the one, girl. Decided not to let any grass grow under my feet."

"You certainly did not. I am glad for you, Molly. I hope this marriage brings you happiness."

"It will. Now I will leave you and your mother alone so you can talk."

Molly left. Clover took another sip of tea. She did not really want to talk about Colin and her mother's impending marriage. Her feelings were too unclear and she knew her mother would want to know exactly how she felt. Clover was afraid her uncertainty would hurt her mother, that Agnes would interpret it as disapproval.

Agnes touched her arm and sighed. "I am sorry this has upset you, dear," she said.

"Mama, I do not know if it has *upset* me or not. When you told me you were planning to marry Colin, I was plunged into confusion. I simply have no idea what I am feeling or thinking."

"Are you scandalized perhaps?"

"Maybe just a little, but that has already begun to pass. For one brief moment I thought, Oh, God, what will people say? Then I realized I do not care."

"There, you just clarified one of the things you are feeling." Agnes stood up. "We can discuss your other feelings while I help you prepare for your dinner at Mr. Potsdam's." She took Clover's hand.

Even as she allowed her mother to pull her to her feet, Clover protested, "I really would prefer not to talk about it. I do not want to inadvertently hurt your feelings in some way."

Agnes began to help Clover into her blue brocade gown. "I am not so fragile, dear. And we can only settle what troubles you if we can figure out what it is. The wedding is to take place in one month's time, when the preacher will be stopping in town. I do not want to spend one day of that time wondering if my daughter approves of what I am doing. In truth, I will settle for acceptance if you cannot bring yourself to wholly approve."

"You really want to marry him," Clover murmured, smoothing down her skirts while her mother fastened her gown. "Do you love him so much then?" She let her mother lead her to a stool and begin to put up her hair.

"I *do* love him. I loved him all those years ago. Later, I convinced myself it was just passion. How could I love two such different men? Well, now I can accept that I did. In a way, it was a blessing that he was married and I was betrothed. It saved us both the agony of trying to choose between two people we loved. Our decision had already been made for us. We just suffered that bittersweet knowledge that there could be nothing between us and went our separate ways."

"And now you have been given a second chance."

"Exactly, and I have decided to take it. I loved your father dearly, child, and if any other man was trying to court me, I could probably follow all the rules. 'Tis Colin, however, and I do not want to wait. In a way, I feel fate has thrust us together again, that this has always been my destiny. You must admit 'twas an unusual sequence of events that led us to Kentucky. Fate has always intended that Colin and I should be a comfort to each other at this time in our lives."

Clover smiled. She had always believed in fate to some degree. Now that she loved the man she had so impulsively married, her faith in fate had grown. How else could she explain her luck in simply plucking a man off the street yet still getting the perfect partner?

"How have the twins taken the news?" she asked as

she studied the way her mother had arranged her hair, with fat sausage curls draped artfully over one shoulder.

"They are young, dear. They just accept such things. They were a little concerned that they would have to call Colin Papa right away, which they do not, and they are not sure they like the idea of living elsewhere, for they have come to love Ballard and this farm. As you can see, children only concern themselves with basic matters."

For a moment Clover stared at her hands. Talking had helped. Her shock and surprise had faded. She did accept her mother's forthcoming marriage, even her mother's love for Colin Doogan. She stood up and hugged Agnes.

"I hope you will be very happy. He is a good man."

"Are you sure, dear? You seem to have settled your confusion rather quickly."

"It was mostly shock, Mama. Once that faded, I found nothing to upset me about the marriage." She grimaced. "There was only one troubling emotion."

"And what is that?"

"Jealousy." She gave her mother a crooked smile. "You and Molly were courted and you fell in love."

Agnes hugged her daughter, holding her close for a full minute. "I know. I realized that myself, was ashamed of myself for enjoying such frivolities while you have never had them with Ballard. One cannot count that betrothal to Thomas, for he was clearly insincere in his emotions." She held Clover at a slight distance. "But then I recalled that you have fallen in love with Ballard. Perhaps you two were also fated to be together."

"I was just wondering that myself. Well, I suppose I am ready to go now."

"You look lovely. Now, dear, there is one more thing I must tell you. I am going to Colin's for dinner with his family, where I will try and get to know his many children. Since that may take until very late at night, I will be staying there in his housekeeper's rooms. I am afraid Molly will not be here either. She is to have a celebratory meal with Jonathan and Mabel, and will spend the night in town."

Clover groaned. "That means I must get the morning meal all on my own."

"You will do just fine. Now I hear your husband coming to collect you. Have a nice time tonight, dear."

"You too, Mama. And wish Molly the same."

"Are you certain about this?" Thomas demanded of the man standing before him. "I am a hunted man, as are my cohorts. It seems that bastard Mac-Gregor has every man, woman, and child in Kentucky beating the bushes for us. We cannot afford to go off on any wild goose chases." He shot a condemning glare at Poonley and Big Jim, who were lounging in a dark corner.

"This ain't gonna be a wild goose chase," promised the stranger. "Ain't no one who could know where Ballard MacGregor will be tonight better'n me. I be Cyril Potsdam's top stablehand," said Corey Winston. "I know everything what goes on at that demmed mansion of his."

Thomas took a slow swallow of bitter ale and tried to think what to do next. The constant pounding in

his head made that difficult. Since Clover's escape
from his dim-witted associates, he had been forced to
hide in the tiny, squalid cabin belonging to Poonley's
lover Helen. With each miserable day he spent in the
filthy confines, he had grown to hate Ballard Mac-
Gregor all the more, but his efforts to hurt the man
were thwarted by the large number of people searching for them. A few times they had nearly been caught
at Helen's. Now the chance for revenge was being
handed to him on a silver salver. He was not sure he
ought to trust in such a stroke of luck.

"Why are you doing this?" he asked Corey. "Since
you are one of the very few men who knows that
Poonley sometimes comes here, why help us instead
of turning us in to our enemies?"

"'Cause the fool is sweet on Elizabeth Brown," revealed Big Jim. "You want the little whore all to yourself, ain't that right, Corey? But she just ain't gonna
stop panting after MacGregor." He laughed when
Corey lunged at him. Poonley knocked the man to
the floor.

"You ain't got no call to talk about Elizabeth that
way," Corey protested as he staggered to his feet and
wiped the blood from his lip. He turned back to
Thomas. "I ain't doing this just because Elizabeth
wants to make an ass out of herself over that cursed
Scot. His prissy wife done threatened Elizabeth and
put the fear of God into her. Elizabeth be too scared
to come outta her house now."

"And so you ain't getting no honey," said Big Jim.

"Shut up, Jim." Thomas studied Corey for a moment, then nodded, wincing as a shaft of pain ripped
through his head. "I find it hard to believe little Clover
could scare anyone, but perhaps her time with Ballard

MacGregor has already made her somewhat of a barbarian. Anyway, I believe your reasons for helping us, stupid though they are. A few facts would help us now. When will he arrive, when will he leave, what road will he travel, and will he have extra men with him for protection ?"

"Well, I ain't sure I can answer all them questions. Potsdam told them to come by eight, but there ain't no telling when MacGregor will decide to leave and go back home. I do know he told Potsdam he wouldn't be spending the night. There is only one road MacGregor can go on to get to Potsdam's house since he be driving a wagon. Big Jim knows where it is as well as I do."

Big Jim nodded. "I know a good spot where we can jump the fool. About a mile or two of that road goes through some thick wood. We can hide there till MacGregor ambles by."

"And how many men will he have with him?" Thomas asked Corey.

"I told you, I ain't got no idea. MacGregor ain't let his wife go nowhere alone since you tried dragging her off. He might have a guard or two riding with him, but who can say? He might think he is protection enough."

"Can you get one of these fools close enough to see for himself without being spotted?"

"Reckon I can."

"Poonley, you go with him." Thomas gave Corey a small pouch of coins. "You had better not be leading us into a trap. Just keep in mind that if even one of us survives a surprise attack you will pay dearly for any treachery. Poonley, as soon as you know how well MacGregor is protected, ride back here."

Poonley nodded. "Wouldn't you be better placed setting in them woods?"

"Not just yet. The MacGregors will be at Potsdam's for several hours at least. That leaves us plenty of time for you to come back here, tell us what we face, and allow us to set the trap."

"You sure they will be there for so long? They ain't doing nothing but having a meal."

"'Tis a formal dinner at a rich man's house. They will be there for hours, and Potsdam's place is but a few miles south of here. Go on, and be sure you get your facts straight before you return." As soon as Poonley left with Corey, Thomas looked at Big Jim. "Do we have him now?"

"Sure do sound that way." Big Jim took a long drink of ale and belched. "Are you planning on taking him and the woman, or just the woman? If it were me, I would just kill her demmed husband. He ain't gonna be easy to hold while you be playing some fancy games with his wife."

"I may yet settle for just killing him. We will see how things play out tonight. I *do* want him alive long enough to know that I have taken his little wife, and maybe even a few of my plans for her. And I want Clover Sherwood to know the full price for refusing me."

Once again Ballard glanced over at Clover as he drove to Potsdam's house. She was beautiful. She also looked elegant, wealthy, and well-bred. Just like the ladies he had watched as a child in Edinburgh.

It caused him some dismay that Clover looked so much like the women in those fancy carriages. He was painfully aware that he owned no carriage and was taking her to dinner in a farm wagon. He felt uncomfortably like that raw boy again, the dreamy child who was sharply refused when he tried to touch something he could never have. Ballard wanted to stop and make love to Clover, to reassure himself that she was his wife, not some stranger's elegant lady. But, of course, making love to her now was impractical.

"Did your mother tell ye her news then?" he asked Clover, hoping that a little conversation would pull him out of his dark musings.

"Yes." Clover smiled at him. "It did take me aback a little and I needed some time to get over the shock, but I *am* happy for her. Now I just hope others do not judge her too harshly for remarrying so soon after my father's death."

"There will be little of that nonsense around here. It will help that Colin Doogan has few enemies. 'Tis sad that it should matter, but the fact that your father killed himself will help them to accept the hasty union. Fair or not, folks around here call that abandonment."

"I do sometimes think of it that way. It is probably not fair, for I have no knowledge of the depth of the despair he must have been suffering that day. The more I think on those last months with Papa, the more I realize that he and Mama were not happy. Papa had distanced himself from us. He was completely engrossed in his financial troubles.

"Ballard, I must ask—is this journey wise?" She looked around, distrusting the shadowy depths of the forest.

"Since your kidnapping, no one has seen hide nor

hair of Big Jim, his three friends, or Thomas. That doesnae mean that there is no longer any danger, but it suggests that they are in hiding."

"That makes sense. They would plan to stay hidden too, at least until people cease to look for them as diligently as they are now. It just makes me a little nervous to go out without two or three people." She grinned when he laughed.

"I was a little overcautious, for a while there," Ballard said. "I admit it. As ye once said, we cannae let these threats rule our lives." He patted the musket on the seat between them. "We are nae completely unprotected. And, lass, if we have nae seen the rogues about, then how could they learn where we will be tonight? That takes some spying, and I am sure the bastards have nae been close enough to do that."

"Of course." She relaxed. "I shall cease worrying about them and just enjoy the evening."

Ballard inwardly winced as he drew the wagon to a halt before the elegant brick two-story house. A liveried hand came to take the wagon and another servant stood by the front door. Clean white pillars framed the brick steps to the wide veranda. He glanced at Clover and watched her gracefully mount the steps, nodding elegantly to the servant as he opened the door for them. She looked perfectly suited to the grandeur that had always intimidated him.

Ballard smiled at Cyril Potsdam and his eldest son, Theodore, as the men welcomed him and Clover. Potsdam had had money when he had come to Kentucky, a hefty sum from his father to start anew, away from Virginia and a scandal concerning a married lady with whom he had become entangled in the latter years of the Revolution, when he was a new widower. He had the only brick house in the area and, Ballard noted as he followed Cyril, Theodore, and Clover into the parlor, all of the elegant trappings of the gentry, from gilt-framed mirrors to multi-branched pewter sconces and silver candelabras.

Here were all the things Clover had had to give up. Ballard knew that had not been his fault, but he could not help her regain all of her losses either. There would probably never be matching portraits of him and Clover hanging over the fireplace as there was of Cyril Potsdam and his late wife Emily. Ballard did not think he would ever reach the point where he could enjoy the elegance and comfort Cyril did, an elegance and comfort Clover had, until recently, taken for granted. Ballard heartily wished he had not brought Clover to Potsdam's, for she must be realizing all she had lost and knowing that he could never get it for her.

"Your boys should be home soon, shouldnae they?" he asked Cyril as he sat next to Clover on an elegant silk brocade upholstered settee. A tall, silent man served them drinks before slipping noiselessly from the room. "He has two more sons—Joshua and Kenneth. They are at two of those fine schools back east," he told Clover.

"They should be back before too much longer," Cyril replied as he sat in a chair facing them. "It seems Joshua has become engaged and he will be bringing his young lady here to visit."

"So ye ought to be enjoying some grandchildren soon," Ballard said.

"Well, I am sure Joshua will have children, but I

do not believe they will live here. From his letters I
get the feeling he will be joining a rather prestigious
banking firm in Boston. A good opportunity, but I
had hoped all of my sons would return to Kentucky
to live. Kenneth has not made any choices yet so
there is still time."

"There does appear to be a great deal of opportunity right here," said Clover.

Cyril and Theodore heartily agreed and began to
tell her of the various ways people were finding prosperity. She began to see that Ballard clearly had the
same keen eye for opportunity yet with the caution
that came from having limited funds. Ballard would
prosper. Education would be important, however,
and Clover promised herself that the children she
and Ballard would be blessed with would have as
much schooling as they could afford.

Later, as they ate dinner in the extravagantly can-
dlelit dining room, Ballard listened to Clover, Cyril,
and Theodore talk. He knew he was foolish for feeling ignored. Though he was kept involved in every
conversation, he began to feel set apart from his wife
and his host. They touched upon similar pasts that
he had no knowledge of—of balls, teas, books they
had read, the theater, and various social rules that
often resulted in some amusing situations. Not knowing what the rules were, Ballard often did not understand what they found so funny.

The dinner itself was an ordeal for Ballard. He had
to keep a close eye on what Clover, Theodore, and
Cyril did for, despite all of the lessons Clover had
given him in the last three days to prepare for the
dinner, he was intimidated by the elegant setting.
The candlelight gleamed off the heavy silver and

pewter serving dishes lined up along the center of the huge table. He warily eyed the delicately embroidered tablecloth, wondering how easily it would stain. As he took a sip of wine, he feared breaking the etched glass he held. It made him a little uncomfortable to be waited upon by Cyril's man, the tall, silent, and stone-faced Carter. Ballard was relieved when the meal was over and they returned to the parlor for a brandy, but it was short-lived.

Cyril stood by his massive fireplace, a brandy in his hand and his arm resting on the marble mantelpiece. Ballard almost smiled. Cyril Potsdam looked every inch the aristocrat, a comparison he knew the ex-Continental Army officer would not appreciate.

His amusement fled, however, when he looked at Clover and Theodore. The young, fair-haired Theodore had taken a seat right next to Clover on the elegant settee. There was room for him too, but the pair was so immersed in a lively discussion he knew he would feel as if he were intruding.

They discussed the theater some more, talking knowledgably about the plays they had seen. It did not soothe Ballard's growing sense of estrangement to hear that Clover had not been to the theater very often, for he himself had never been. Since he had just begun to read, he had read none of the plays and books they spoke of. He smiled and responded politely when they drew him into their conversation, but despite his strenuous attempts not to, he began to count the ways he and Clover were unalike.

Clover had seen a live performance on stage while he had once begged for pennies outside of a theater. Clover had heard an opera singer. He was not even sure what that was. Clover knew of the latest in

French fashion while he knew who made the best homespun for the least money. The list of their differences grew and grew until his head ached. He began to wonder how soon he could get Clover out of there without offending his host.

It was almost midnight when Ballard decided it was time to leave. Cyril sent his man to order Ballard's wagon brought round and they waited on the veranda for the stablehand to hitch it up and drive it over. It was a warm, moonlit night and Ballard wondered if he would be able to convince Clover to stop along the way and make love under the stars. After a long evening in her world, feeling increasingly estranged from her, he had a strong need to feel her wrapped around him, her passion warming them both.

Cyril leaned against a wide column at the top of the veranda steps. "I was wondering if you both would come back for a visit when my other two sons return."

Ballard glanced at Clover, who nodded, and replied, "We would like that very much, sir."

"I will confess to having ulterior motives." Cyril smiled at Clover. "Certain things Joshua has said in his letters make me think he has become caught up in the social whirl in Boston. His fiancée is from a prominent family."

"He has become an intolerable snob," Theodore muttered.

Ignoring his son's sour interruption, Cyril continued, "When Joshua left for school, there was little one could call society around here. I have always considered that a good thing myself. But if that is what Joshua thinks he wants, or what his fiancée requires . . ."

"Showing him that there is some society here might make it easier for you to convince him to stay," Clover finished.

"Yes. Selfish of me, perhaps, but I want *all* my sons near me. Kentucky is growing fast and I believe each of them could make a good life here. Sending them back east to school may not have been a good idea. I was looking for them to gain the skills needed to help build this land, but it appears they may have been seduced away from it." He smiled briefly at Theodore. "Well, some of them anyway."

"Then we shall have to show them that they can have the best of all worlds right here," Clover said.

"I certainly intend to try. Here is your wagon."

Ballard tensed with jealousy when Theodore kissed Clover's hand. It required an effort to give the young man a friendly smile and agree that they ought to get together again soon. It would be both impossible and somewhat childish, but he had a strong urge to keep Clover far away from Theodore Potsdam.

Corey Winston, who had brought the wagon to a halt, hopped down from the seat. Clover was startled by the venomous look the man gave her before he strode away. Ballard's frown told her that he had seen it too. She thanked Cyril and Theodore again for a pleasant evening and let Ballard help her into the wagon seat.

"Ballard, have you done anything to that stablehand?" she asked as the wagon pulled away.

"Nay, not that I recollect. I have nae even met the mon more than a few times. I got the feeling that glare was aimed at ye as weel, which makes no sense at all."

"No, it does not, for this is the first time I have ever set eyes on him."

"There is obviously something stuck in his craw, but I cannae be bothered about it now."

She nodded. "We have more than our share of villains already. And although it is a lovely night, I shall be glad to get home."

They rode for a while in silence. Clover's obvious contentment after a pleasant evening only added to Ballard's tense restlessness. There was just no way around it. Tonight he had been forced to face the inescapable truth—he would never be able to give Clover the kind of life she deserved. And now that her mother was about to marry Colin Doogan and the twins would go live with them, Clover was free to seek a better life elsewhere—with the man of her choice.

He loved her too much to try to stop her.

Yes, he loved her, he realized with sudden conviction. What had begun as a marriage of convenience had been fed by passion and nurtured by growing understanding and respect, and had blossomed into a deep and abiding love. A love that had become the very foundation of his life.

Yet *because* he loved her, he must let her go, if that was what she wanted.

At last he could keep silent no longer. "Clover, we need to talk."

She turned to him in surprise, her alarm growing at the sight of the dark scowl on his face, visible despite the deepening shadows as they traveled through a particularly dense stretch of woods.

"You sound so grave," she said.

"'Tis a grave subject I wish to discuss."

Ballard swallowed hard and wondered why he was having such difficulty spitting out the words. For a moment he considered allowing himself just a little more time with her, but he quickly dismissed the thought before he could give in to temptation. If he kept her any longer, it would only make their eventual separation more painful, and they would risk making a child. Then she would be truly trapped.

"Did ye like Cyril's home?" he asked, and inwardly grimaced at that foolish start.

Clover frowned at him. "Yes. It is a very elegant home. It reminded me of some of the estates back east."

"I thought it might have reminded ye a little of your home in Langleyville before your fortunes soured."

"Just a little. Mr. Potsdam has a larger purse than my father ever did. It was dreams of being like the Mr. Potsdams of the world that drove my father to gamble what money we did have on such chancy investments."

"Aye. It can make a mon do some foolish things."

"Ballard, is something wrong?"

"Why do ye ask?"

"Oh, perhaps the way you keep going so quiet, glowering at the road. I am having some difficulty resisting the urge to smack you on the back to try to force you just to spit out whatever is making your mood so sour."

"Are ye now."

"I am. The evening was very pleasant and 'tis somewhat annoying that you would try to ruin the nice feelings a good meal and good company have left me with."

"Sorry, lass."

"Do not apologize. Just tell me what is wrong."
Ballard took another deep breath and decided to
try again.

Thomas listened to Poonley's report and smiled,
causing Poonley, Ben, Toombs, and Big Jim to relax.
MacGregor was traveling without outriders, just him
and Clover on a wagon. Apparently Thomas and his
men had kept out of sight long enough for Mac-
Gregor to let down his guard, to think Thomas had
given up his search for vengeance. Thomas felt
victory almost within his grasp.

"I followed their wagon to Potsdam's stable and
looked inside. He only has the one musket," Poonley
finished as he sat down at the table. Helen hastily
poured him an ale. "Thankee, woman," he murmured, and patted her plump backside as she walked
away.

"Did you unload the musket?" Thomas cursed
when he saw the arrested look on Poonley's homely
face. Obviously the thought had never occurred to
the dolt. "Very good, Poonley," Thomas said sarcas-
tically. "And when MacGregor starts shooting at us, I
hope he hits you!"

"We'll grab him afore he can reload," said Big Jim.

Thomas fixed his attention on him. "You said there
is a good place to hide along the road Ballard must
take?"

"Yup. It be thick with trees. Even better, it slopes
down on the sides so 'tis powerful easy to hide. We can
tuck up on either side of the road, wait until the bastard's right in the midst of us, and slaughter the pig."

"You sound as if you mean to go after him with guns blazing."

"You can't be too careful around a man like Mac-Gregor."

"And just what is so special about this cursed Scot?" Thomas snapped.

Big Jim shrugged. "He be a demmed good fighter."

"Well, his fighting days are over. But I *do not* want you leaping up and emptying all your guns at him. I want him to die slowly. And I want Clover alive." Thomas rubbed his temples, though it did little to ease the pain in his head. "I want him alive long enough to know that I have Clover, and to realize what I am going to do to her."

"Why do you want that girl so bad?" demanded Ben. "She ain't got no flesh on her bones. And she been sharing MacGregor's bed for weeks. That Mac-Gregor done looks a good randy sort of gent. I bet he done had that little girl more times than you can count. You got coin. Why not just kill 'em both and go home? You made it clear you ain't liking it here."

Thomas had to take several deep breaths, then a long swallow of the poor ale Helen served, before he felt calm enough to reply. He wanted to shoot the man for reminding him that Clover was no longer innocent. The thought of her lying with MacGregor, of giving him her lithe body, had eaten away at him since her wedding day. All the time he had courted her, he had treated her with the utmost care to ensure that her total innocence would be preserved for their wedding night. Her father's insistence that they never be left alone for a moment had helped him stick to his plan. When his intentions changed because of her poverty, he had eagerly anticipated tasting her innocence on their first night as lovers. Now he would make her pay dearly for giving her passion to another man.

"I want the girl," he said, his words forced out between clenched teeth. "I do not care if you fail to understand why."

Ben shrugged. "'Tis your coin."

"Exactly. Now, shall we go so you can earn it?"

Thomas swore almost constantly as they saddled their horses and set out for the ambush. The four men he had hired were utter idiots. He was astounded that they had not been killed or captured already, and he was half afraid that in their utter incompetence they would allow MacGregor and Clover to slip through their fingers once again. He had no doubt that, somehow, Big Jim and his friends would find a way to foil his perfect plan.

As they rode to the spot where they would lay the trap for Ballard, Thomas imagined what he would do to Clover. She had made a complete fool of him. When she became his whore she would compensate him for that humiliation. He would regain his reputation in Langleyville as a man to be wary of. Everyone would see that he had gotten her back, and they would know that Ballard MacGregor had paid dearly for thwarting Thomas's will.

In private he would make Clover suffer for the times she had allowed MacGregor to touch her. By giving herself to MacGregor, she had forfeited all rights to being handsomely paid for her favors in gifts and comforts. If she was willing to give herself to some illiterate backwoodsman for nothing, then she could service him for nothing as well. And he would no longer ensure that she was taken care of when he tired of her. He would make Clover regret her rejection of him every day that he kept her with him, and for however long she survived after he cast her out on the street.

When they arrived at the place of ambush, Thomas dismounted. He sagged heavily against his horse for a moment. His headache was much worse. There was no respite from the pounding pain. Ballard Mac-Gregor would pay for crippling him and taking what was rightfully his, he swore as he staggered into the wood and hunkered down next to Big Jim to await their prey.

Sometime later, a nudge in his side made him curse and he realized he had dozed off. He caught the rumble of a wagon coming down the road. Any moment now he would have his revenge.

The wagon came into view. Thomas easily recognized Clover's fair hair. But as his men raised their muskets to fire he realized with a pang that he had forgotten to remind them again that he wanted Clover alive.

Ballard's mind was so cluttered with thoughts of how to tell Clover she was free, and what the hell he would do with himself when she left, that at first he did not realize why the sight of something glinting in the bushes should alarm him. At that moment a breeze parted the thick canopy of leaves and moonlight briefly brightened the road, and all at once he saw the long barrel of a musket protruding from the thick growth. In seconds the wagon team would pull him and Clover directly into the line of fire.

He shouted a warning and hurled himself toward Clover, but he was an instant too late. Something slammed into him, throwing him backward. He gave a loud bellow of pain and frustration as he felt himself fall from the wagon. He could hear other shots being fired, a man's voice screaming for them to stop, and Clover calling his name as she reached out to him. Then he hit the ground hard and lost consciousness.

Clover was only faintly aware that the shooting had stopped. She leaped off the wagon and knelt beside Ballard who lay sprawled on his back in the road. Blood covered his crisp white shirt all along his midriff. He appeared to be dead and her heart pounded in fear, but then he groaned.

"Gut shot," muttered Big Jim as he stepped into her line of vision.

"Bastard," she cried and lunged for him, but Thomas and Poonley were too quick for her. Emerging from the bushes, they grabbed her firmly as Big Jim secured her wrists with a thick rope. Even after they set her back on her feet, Thomas kept hold of the rope they had also wound around her waist.

"To be gut shot is to suffer a very long and agonizing death, correct?" murmured Thomas as he looked down at Ballard.

"That be right," answered Big Jim. "I hear tell that most men who get gut shot end up screaming for someone to kill them."

"I am sorry I will miss that," Thomas said, "but I cannot linger here." He kicked Ballard and smiled coldly when his adversary cried out in agony and opened pain-glazed eyes, staring at him. "I thought you might like to know that I have reclaimed what is mine."

"Clover was never yours," Ballard denied, and Thomas kicked him again.

"Here now," said Big Jim. "If you be wanting him to die slow-like, best you stop that. That could kill him right now."

"Well, we cannot have that. You have lost, Ballard MacGregor. You will never see your wife again, and by the time I have taught her a lesson or two, you would never want to either. No doubt you will soon be wishing for a few wild animals to come and finish you off. I can think of few better ways to make you pay for taking what I wanted, for thwarting me and making me look weak before all of Langleyville. And for maiming me." He touched his crooked nose.

"Maiming ye? What the devil are ye babbling about?"

Thomas bent closer to Ballard and pointed to his nose. "Look!" he screeched. "Look what you did to my face."

"Ye are mad."

"I should have known a barbarian like you would never understand. So lie there and rot. You might even stay alive long enough for someone to find you, but I doubt anyone will be able to understand your ramblings. Clover and I should have a comfortable ride back to Langleyville."

"Thomas, you cannot leave him here like this!" Clover protested hysterically. "At least allow me to bandage him and leave him some water."

It was the last thing Ballard wanted her to do. He was not really gut shot. The bullet that had knocked him from the wagon seat had grazed him, ripping a piece from his side. It was bloody but not a fatal wound. In the dim light all Thomas and his hirelings could see was the blood soaking his crisp white shirt-front. He had clasped his hands over his stomach just to make them believe the worst. If Clover tried to help him, his deception would be discovered. The only chance they had was to make Thomas believe he was being left to die in terrifying agony and, sadly, that meant he had to keep Clover believing it too.

"There is nothing ye can do for me, Clover."

"I can try to make your last hours bearable."

"Not with this kind of a wound, ye cannae."

"How touching," drawled Thomas. "You play the concerned wife well, Clover. Perhaps he will recall that tenderness as he screams his life away."

"Ye willnae get away with this, Dillingsworth."

Ballard found it easy to keep his voice low and hoarse. The fury pounding through his body gave it just the right tone. He fought to keep that rage under tight control. Not by the flicker of an eyelid did he want to appear to be any more than a fatally wounded man, his only concern that his wife did not suffer.

"And just who is going to stop me? I believe you will be dead," Thomas said.

"She has other family and friends. They will not let ye get away with it," Ballard replied.

"Once I make her my whore, no one will want her back."

"Dinnae ye ever believe that, Clover," he said. "Dinnae let the bastard weaken ye by making ye believe it."

Thomas kicked Ballard in the ribs and Clover screamed. With all her strength she pulled back on the rope Thomas held, partially succeeding in unbalancing him. Finally she flung herself backward as hard as she could, nearly tumbling both her and Thomas to the ground. He whirled and struck her, and there was a cry of rage from Ballard.

"Concerned about her treatment?" Thomas asked, giving Ballard a malicious smile. "So you should be. I am not taking her back to be my pampered mistress, not after what she has done. No, now she will be my whore. I have even promised Big Jim and his friends a quick turn with her before I take her out of this wretched backwater. And when I grow weary of her, I will toss her to the dockside scum."

"Ye will pay for this, Thomas. Mark my words."

Thomas just laughed, kicked him once more, and dragged Clover to his horse. "Secure that wagon so that the horses cannot drag it home and alert someone there. I want to be sure MacGregor lies out here alone for a very long time."

"Maybe we oughta check and make sure he be gut shot," said Poonley.

"You wanna open that shirt and see which parts of him are tumbling out?" Big Jim laughed at the sickly expression on Poonley's face.

Clover struggled to look back at Ballard, but Thomas roughly forced her to face forward. By the time he threw her up onto his saddle, her wrists were rubbed raw and bleeding.

"How did ye find us?" Ballard called, his voice weak and raspy. "I want to ken what bastard betrayed us."

Thomas mounted behind Clover. "It seems a certain Corey Winston is tired of having you as a rival for Miss Elizabeth's affections. You do appear to have bad luck with women, MacGregor." Thomas chuckled and spurred his horse into a trot.

Ballard watched them ride away. He did not move for several minutes after all the riders were out of sight. There was always the chance that someone might think to take one last look at him to be sure he was dying.

Then he rose cautiously to his feet, for he knew he had lost a lot of blood. Once he was steady, he took off his shirt, ripped it into strips, and tied them around his waist to try to stem the flow of blood. Fighting the urge to race off to rescue Clover, he walked to the horses still hitched to the wagon and freed the mare. He took the musket from the wagon, shaking his head at the ineptitude of the fools who had left it behind. If he had really been gut shot, he could have used it on himself. Wincing with pain, he mounted, then turned the horse back toward Potsdam's home. He had to get his hands on Corey Winston. The man would know where Thomas had taken Clover.

The ride to Potsdam's proved more of an ordeal than he had expected. He headed straight for the stables, determined to get Corey before the man could be warned and before he lost his remaining strength.

Ballard kicked in the door of Corey's little room located at the far end of the stables, pointing the musket at him. Corey stumbled to his feet, fear twisting his features, and thrust up his hands. Without a word Ballard signaled him to go to the main house, keeping the musket aimed squarely at his back as they walked. He was glad of the dim light, for he knew one sight of his face would reveal the full extent of his weakness. He doubted he would be able to hold the man if he had tried to bolt. Until he had a moment to catch his breath and have his wound seen to properly, Ballard doubted he could hit the man if he did shoot at him.

At the front door of Cyril's fine brick house, Ballard supported himself against one of the sturdy columns and hollered for Cyril. It was a moment or two before the butler opened the door. Behind him, Ballard saw Cyril hurrying down the stairs, tucking in his shirt as he went, and Theodore coming out of the parlor. The expressions on Cyril's and Theodore's faces revealed that the men immediately understood the significance of Ballard's reappearance.

"Where did they attack?" Cyril asked.

"About halfway between here and my place." With the musket barrel Ballard nudged Corey toward Cyril. "Can you secure this bastard for me? It seems he told Dillingsworth where we would be. I am also going to need some bandages, maybe even some wrappings for my ribs."

Ballard gratefully relinquished control to Cyril, Theodore, and the butler, Carter. Cyril and Theodore tied Corey to a chair in the front parlor and left him to sweat as Carter tended to Ballard's wounds. Not until after he had had a bracing sip of the brandy Theodore poured him was Ballard able to give them a succinct version of the attack.

"Are you sure it was Corey who told them how to find you?" asked Cyril.

"Aye," answered Ballard with a hard glare at the stablehand. "It seems he considers me a rival for Elizabeth's affections. He is under the same delusion Elizabeth is in thinking that I want her. Only where Elizabeth just tries to make everyone's life miserable, this fellow works to get us both killed."

"Carter, send young Henry to the MacGregors' to bring Shelton and Lambert here as fast as possible." Once Carter left, Cyril turned to Corey. "I cannot believe you have betrayed my trust in this fashion. You had better pray that everyone comes out of this alive or you shall hang right alongside Big Jim, his three reptilian friends, and that madman Thomas Dillingsworth."

"What I want to ken is where they will take Clover," Ballard said. When Corey refused to answer, Ballard rose threateningly to his feet his fists clenched.

"Sit down, Ballard, and take this chance to regain your strength," Cyril advised. "I know you intend to go after your wife." To Corey, he said, "I suggest you rethink your silence. You have been well and truly caught and helping us now may benefit you. Keeping silent will gain you nothing."

"They done gone to Helen Lewis's house. She be Poonley's new woman. I was one of the few what knew he had taken up with the wench. That's how I found them."

"And there are only the four of them plus Dillingsworth?"

"And Helen, of course, though she's bound to run to the hills the minute something starts happening. She generally stays in the kitchens. They'll put Ballard's woman up in the hayloft of Helen's barn. Poonley was showing me that Dillingsworth done made her a little nest up there. So's he can have her, I reckon. There ain't gonna be room for that in Helen's tiny place."

"Ah, Carter," Cyril said as his man returned to the parlor. "Please secure this fool in a safe place. We want to keep a tight grip on him until we know the

extent of the tragedy he has helped to bring about."
As soon as Carter dragged Corey from the room,
Cyril asked Ballard, "How did you escape? I cannot
believe they purposely left you alive."

"It seems they thought I was gut shot. It delighted
Thomas to leave me there to rot. I hated having to
leave Clover thinking I was dying."

"Then she shall be very glad to see you when you
walk in alive," Theodore said. "Just keep still now and
rest, and you will soon regain enough strength to
rescue her."

"We cannae leave her with that mad dog for long,
Theodore. He means to rape her and then hand her
around to the curs who ride with him. He wants to
humiliate her as he believes she humiliated him. He
wants to make her pay for God knows what imagined insults. He cannae stomach the fact that she
turned to me. Do ye ken, one of the many reasons he
wanted me dead was because I broke his nose and
it healed with a wee bump in it?"

"Sweet mercy, he really is mad," murmured Cyril.

"Aye, and he keeps rubbing his head, like he is in
constant pain. Clover is in real danger with that mon."

Cyril clasped Ballard's shoulder. "I realize I am
asking the impossible, but try to calm yourself. Acting
hastily will not help Clover now. The wisest thing is to
get some strength back. Rest until your brother and
cousin arrive here and then we will kill that mad dog."

It was one of the hardest things he had ever done,
but Ballard struggled to do as Cyril suggested, for he
knew the man was right. His wound was not serious,
but he had lost a lot of blood. It would be a hard ride
to Helen Lewis's house and he would need every

ounce of strength he could muster to fight Thomas and his cohorts.

By the time his kin arrived Ballard had rested and then grown agitated again. Too much time had passed. He was all too aware of what could be happening to Clover. When Shelton and Lambert entered the room, Ballard leaped to his feet and was immediately assailed by dizziness. His brother hurried over to support him, but Ballard waved him off.

"I will be fine. I just got to my feet too fast," he grumbled.

"Weel, ye are going to have to stand on your feet if ye mean to fight these bastards," said Shelton.

"I hope ye are nae suggesting I stay here like some hand-wringing maiden while ye hie off to the rescue?" he snapped.

"Hellfire, Ballard, ye have been shot and kicked about. 'Tis no weakness to stay put in the circumstances and let others do it for ye."

"Your brother is right," said Theodore, urging Ballard to sit down, but again Ballard shook him off.

"I willnae stay here. Curse it, the first time Clover needed rescuing, she saved herself and her brother Damien. The second time, it was young Willie who got her out. I willnae sit by and let ye do my work for me this time."

"You mean to risk your health for the sake of your pride?" Theodore asked.

"Aye, 'tis pride talking as much as anything else, but I will go even if I can only sit on the ground and tell ye which ones to hit. I owe this bastard Dillingsworth dearly, verra dearly. 'Tis time I made up for not killing him back in Langleyville."

Cyril handed Ballard a brace of pistols. "I think

these will prove easier to handle than a musket, with the wounds you are sporting."

"Thank ye, Cyril."

"I was wondering when you would get around to calling me by my Christian name. All that calling me *sir* made me feel rather old. Come on, I have a stable full of fresh, fast horses. At least they had better be fast," he said as he led them from the room. "The man who sold them to me swore they were." He winked at Ballard, who managed a weak smile.

"'Tis not your fight, Cyril. Nor yours, Theodore," Ballard said as he watched Cyril saddle two horses. "Ye dinnae have to risk your life. I would ne'er ask it of ye."

"I know, but 'tis a fight any man would rush to join in," Cyril assured him.

"Even Carter wanted to come," said Theodore, "but someone has to stay here to be sure that weasel Corey does not slip loose."

"Ye ken that I dinnae hold ye accountable for what he did," Ballard said as he mounted the gelding whose reins Cyril handed him.

"Nevertheless I do hold myself partly accountable," Cyril replied. "Ready, lads?" he called to Shelton and Lambert.

"Aye, sir," answered Shelton. "I was just wondering which one of us is supposed to ken how to get to this Helen Lewis's place?"

"I know where her cabin is," said Theodore. "I spent some time with her last fall. Just watch closely for my signal to halt. We do not want to go in at a gallop."

"Aye," agreed Ballard. "We must use stealth. Of course, since they think I am dead or dying, and are convinced no one kens where they are, we have the element of surprise in our favor."

It was not a long ride, but it took a toll on Ballard.

At Theodore's signal, he and the others immediately reined in and dismounted.

"We walk from here, lads," Cyril announced in a soft voice as he lifted his gun from his saddle. "The cabin is mere yards from here. Smell that chimney smoke?" He waited until all four of his companions nodded. "It is essential that we move through the woods without making a sound."

"We should scatter ourselves around and try to make them believe they are surrounded," Ballard suggested.

"Good idea," Cyril agreed. "One of us will have to go after Clover. I figure that might as well be you, Ballard. I doubt you will be much help to us if we send anyone else."

"I fear ye are right."

"The rest of us will space ourselves around the cabin in the cover of the trees."

"So we shouldnae all be firing at the same time," said Shelton.

"You would make a good soldier, son. Well, let us hope they are not expecting anybody. I have no doubt we can outfight these mongrels, but I much prefer catching them by surprise. So hold your fire as long as possible."

"Should we try to take any of them alive?" asked Theodore as he checked his musket and then his pistol.

"Only if they surrender with their hands up and crying for mercy," answered Cyril.

"I think they will fight to the end," said Ballard as

he followed Cyril's careful advance through the woods. "If they are caught, they all face hanging."

Cyril nodded. "That might make them desperate. And treacherous." He glanced back at Theodore, Lambert, and Shelton. "You lads be careful." He looked around. "I was a little worried because the moon is so bright, but we should be all right as long as we stay in the woods."

In a few minutes they were near enough to see the cabin and barn. All five crouched in the underbrush and watched as one of the men wandered out of the cabin, relieved himself off the end of the veranda, and strolled back inside. The barn was located on the far side of the house, surrounded by several yards of open land. There were no guards posted, and Ballard was sure he could make it to the barn unseen by anyone in the house.

"We will hold off shooting as long as we can, Ballard," Cyril told him.

"I will give one sharp whistle as soon as I have gotten into the barn and made sure Clover is there," Ballard said. "One sharp whistle and then ye can start shooting and making all the noise ye like."

"Good luck. We will wait for your whistle unless they see us and open fire. Then it will be every man for himself."

Ballard nodded and started to creep forward. He heard Cyril whisper orders to Theodore, Shelton, and Lambert, then heard soft rustles as they made their way to their chosen positions.

Keeping to the shadows of the trees and undergrowth, Ballard made his way toward the barn. Voices drifted from the hayloft. He listened carefully. One sharp comment was Clover's. An instant later there was the sound of a slap and a soft cry quickly muffled. It took every ounce of his willpower not to rush to her aid. But he knew any rash action on his part could endanger them all. He could not bolt straight to the barn door. He had to creep up on it from the wooded side, or he could easily be seen by someone in the house. He breathed a sigh of relief when he reached the place where he had chosen to leave the cover of the trees.

A quick dash across the narrow open space between the forest and the barn brought him to the side of the rough plank building. He rested against the wall for a moment, waiting for any sound indicating that he had been discovered. He drew both pistols from the waistband of his breeches and crept to the corner. He peeked around the side and immediately stilled. A mangy dog, tense and bristling, stood there watching him.

Ballard silently cursed. If he moved, the dog would probably bark and warn everyone of his presence. If he shot the dog, which he was loath to do, the noise would alert the men in the cabin, and, worse, the man now with Clover. He slowly crouched down until he was almost eye level with the animal.

"Easy, laddie," he murmured as he cautiously extended his hand, palm up.

The dog growled softly and hunkered down. Ballard cursed silently, afraid the dog would sense his tension and react to it.

"Soft now, laddie. I willnae hurt ye. No need to be giving an alarm, eh?"

He kept speaking quietly, hoping the man in the barn could not hear, offering his open hand to the dog. Finally, the dog eased its guard. Still Ballard hesitated, taking more time to assure the animal that he meant it no harm. When the dog finally allowed him to pat it, Ballard knew from its thin frame and half-healed wounds that it had been badly abused. That such a sadly treated animal would accept any friendly approach was pure luck, and Ballard prayed that such luck would stay with him.

As he slipped into the barn, the dog followed. Ballard wished the animal would go away for it might still inadvertently cause an alarm to be raised. Then he turned his full attention to climbing the ladder to the hayloft without making a sound.

Chapter Sixteen

Clover fought the urge to flinch as Thomas slowly stroked her hair. He had brought her to the hayloft the moment they had arrived. Still in shock over Ballard's mortal wound, Clover had not been able to hide her horror when Thomas had secured her wrists to two metal rings in the wall. He had then left her there for an hour or so, her feet barely brushing the floor, before he returned to her.

Gradually she had begun to fight the slide into hysteria. She had even faced down a dark moment when she wondered why she should try to stay alive now that Ballard was dead. Three thoughts kept her clinging to a hard-won strength. Dillingsworth wanted her to cower, to be wholly submissive to him, and she refused to give him what he wanted. And if by some miracle Ballard survived, he would come for her. She must hold herself together in case he did. Finally, if he died, she would live to make Dillingsworth pay.

At first, her loathing for Thomas shocked her. Then she realized the strength it gave her. It also angered Dillingsworth. Dangerous though the game might be, she enjoyed that small victory over him.

"You really are mad, Thomas, if you believe you can get away with this," she told him.

"I have simply taken back what is mine."

"You cast me aside, Thomas. I still have that polite letter you sent telling me so."

"I could not marry you, but that did not mean I had cast you aside. You should have understood that."

Clover laughed, a short, bitter sound, and shook her head. "I guess I am sadly ignorant then."

"After all the time we spent together, how could you believe I would let you go completely? I needed money. That is the only reason I married that whore Sarah, but I would still take care of you."

"By making *me* a whore. Your kindness knows no bounds, does it, Thomas?"

"I would have given you a good life. Instead, you married that barbaric Scotsman and came to this wretched backwoods."

"Ballard is not a barbarian, Thomas. You are." She could not restrain a cry of pain when he slapped her across the face.

"You will learn to train that sharp tongue of yours." He ran a finger over the palm of her hand. "Look what he has done to you. When I courted you, you had the softest, prettiest hands I had ever seen. Now you have the hands of a kitchen maid."

"I earned these calluses in the honorable state of marriage to a good man. Far better to have hands as hard as a blacksmith's than those kept soft in the service of a madman who would make me his whore. *I* cannot understand how *you* could believe I would accept the life you offered me."

"Because it was a good life. I even would have taken in your wretched family just to keep you happy. Instead you ran off to the wilderness with that swine. You let him touch you."

"And I quite enjoyed it too."

Uncontrolled fury twisted Thomas's face as he grabbed her by the throat. Her body clenched with fear. What a fool she had been to anger him to the point where he might kill her in a mindless fit of rage. When he slowly eased his choking grip on her throat, she breathed a sigh of relief.

"You will pay for letting him touch you. I was so careful with you," he murmured as he lightly stroked her face. "I worked so hard to preserve your innocence. I even tolerated your stupid father's interference, for it helped me keep you pure. That purity was to be mine to enjoy. Once we were together I was going to train you to please me, and only me. I knew that no other man had taught you anything, not even how to kiss. Then you stole that from me. You and that Scot."

Clover was stunned by his words. "No one stole it. You threw it away."

"I will not be as gentle with you as I planned to be," Thomas continued, ignoring her words. "Now I must try to erase the stain of another man's touch. And the touch of such a peasant." He shook his head.

"And your wife Sarah approves, does she? I find it hard to believe she would blithely allow her husband to carry on with another. She is a very proud woman."

"She is a whore. She needed me, a husband of some standing in the community, to salvage some scraps of her tattered reputation." Thoughtfully he added, "She will probably be sorry that I have killed the Scot, for she did fancy him."

"You cannot be sure you *have* killed Ballard," she said, tensing when he began to undo her bodice.

"Of course he is dead. The man had a gut wound. Although right at the moment, he may still be screaming from the pain of it."

The evident joy Thomas took in that thought made Clover ill. "He might also be coming after you."

Thomas laughed. "The man is dead or within a breath of being so. You cling to a false hope, Clover. Your barbarian will not be rushing to your rescue."

"I wouldnae lay a wager on that, ye bastard."

Clover was sure she looked as stunned as Thomas to see Ballard standing there, only feet away from them, pistols held in each hand, both aimed at Thomas. Although a little pale and bloodied, he looked far from mortally wounded. Her surprise grew when Ballard suddenly gave one sharp whistle. An instant later the sound of gunfire split the night air.

"You were gut shot," Thomas muttered. "Curse you to hell, how did you get here?"

"I had help, as ye can hear. And I wasnae gut shot. Ye really shouldnae count so much on the opinion of those fools ye have working for ye."

Thomas bellowed and rushed toward Ballard. Just before Ballard fired a pistol, Thomas suddenly moved, so that the bullet skimmed his shoulder. An instant later, he slammed into Ballard. They hit the floor hard and Ballard cried out in pain. Both pistols skittered across the hay-strewn floor.

Clover watched the two men fight in growing alarm. Ballard had beaten Thomas neatly and swiftly twice before, yet he was clearly struggling for his life now. He might not be suffering from the fatal wound Thomas had thought, but he was seriously injured and had apparently lost a lot of blood. Thomas also had the added strength born of madness. When a knife appeared in Thomas's hand, she feared she was about to witness Ballard's murder only moments after knowing the joy of seeing him alive.

Over the sound of a furious gun battle going on outside, Clover could hear a dog barking. She struggled fruitlessly to free herself of her bonds even as her gaze remained fixed upon the two men. Then a mangy dog scrambled into the hayloft and began to run in circles around the thrashing men, jumping up and down. Clover knew it was Poonley's mistress's dog, for she had briefly glimpsed it snarling at everyone before she was dragged off to the barn.

Then, suddenly, Thomas was on top of Ballard, his knife aimed directly at Ballard's heart. Clover could see the tremor in Ballard's arm as he clasped Thomas's wrist and tried to halt the knife's descent. In desperation she pulled against her bonds until blood slickened her wrists, yet still she watched the knife point draw nearer and nearer to Ballard's chest.

"You *will* die this time, MacGregor," Thomas said, jubilation in his voice. "You will not be able to rise after I cut out your heart."

"Killing me willnae win this game for ye, Dillingsworth. My friends will see that ye never leave this place alive."

"Neither will Clover."

"Curse ye!"

Ballard tried to muster up the one swift burst of strength he needed to stop the deadly advance of

Thomas's blade, but he had none left. He could not stop the death strike. Just as he tensed anticipating the touch of the knife against his flesh, he heard a low, feral growl. An instant later Thomas screamed as his wrist was completely lost in the jaws of the dog.

Thomas rolled off Ballard as he tried to shake free of the dog. Ballard staggered to his feet. He watched the man and the animal roll about on the hayloft floor, waiting for a chance to grab the knife to which Thomas still miraculously clung. Then he saw the glint of his pistol in the hay and lunged for it. Was it the one he had already fired? Even as he aimed at Thomas, Ballard espied his other pistol. Just as his hand closed on it, he heard a sharp yelp from the dog.

Thomas punched the dog in the head a second time and the animal fell from him. Ballard was stunned to see that, despite the blood pouring from his mangled wrist, Thomas still held the knife. As he staggered to his feet and stepped forward, Ballard aimed both pistols at Thomas and fired. Thomas screamed as a bullet tore through his chest, throwing him backward onto the hay where he lay still. Ballard cautiously approached to be sure he was dead. It took only one look at the flat, lifeless eyes to tell him that Thomas would never be a threat again.

"Is he dead?" Clover whispered.

"Aye, lass."

She briefly closed her eyes and shuddered. "I was so afraid I was about to watch you die."

"It isnae easy to kill a MacGregor," he said as he stumbled to her side.

Clover studied his face as he untied her and they both sank to the ground. He was bruised, dirty, and bleeding, but he had never looked so beautiful to her. She slumped against him as he put his arm around her.

"I thought you were dead," she murmured.

"I needed ye to believe it. It helped convince Thomas and the others."

"I understand. If they had taken a good look at you, they would have seen that you were not dying. It is a bad wound though. I can see that it pains you."

"Aye. Here, lass, the shooting has stopped. I had better reload these pistols just in case it is not a friend who comes looking for us."

She sat back a little as he reloaded his guns, and looked toward the dog. "Do you think Thomas killed that poor animal?"

"I hope not, but I cannae take the time to examine the wretched creature now."

He heard someone enter the barn and quickly moved in front of her. With a pistol in each hand he waited to see what the outcome of the battle had been.

"Ballard?" called Shelton from the bottom of the ladder leading to the hayloft. "Are ye up there?"

"Aye, I won my fight," Ballard replied as he relaxed and put down his pistols. "With a wee bit of help." He glanced at the dog and was relieved to see it tremble. "Careful as ye come up, lad. There is a dog up here who isnae too sure who is friend and who is foe."

Shelton cautiously climbed into the hayloft. Although still unable to stand, the dog growled and Ballard murmured a word to soothe it. Shelton glanced at Thomas's body, then moved to Clover and Ballard.

"I hope it wasnae ye who nearly chewed the mon's hand off," he said as he crouched before them.

"Nay, the dog came to my rescue." Ballard held his

hand out as the animal crept warily closer. "Thomas was about to stick a knife in me and this ragged beastie stopped him. I think we will take him home."

"That old tomcat Muskrat willnae be too pleased. How are ye two?"

"We will live," Ballard replied. "What about the others?"

"All fine. It wasnae a fair fight really. Those oafs hadnae the wit to give us a real battle. None of them surrendered. Cyril offered them the chance, but ye were right. They chose to go down fighting rather than face a rope. We cannae find the woman. I suspect she ran off and will return when we are gone. Theodore, Cyril, and Lambert are burying the bodies."

"So it is finally over," Clover said, not sure she dared believe it.

"Aye." Ballard caught sight of her wrists and cursed. "Those need to be seen to."

"I think ye both need some doctoring," said Shelton. "We will tend to that before we leave." He glanced at the dog lying next to Ballard's leg. "Do ye think he can climb down as weel as he climbed up?"

"I dinnae think so. Thomas hit him pretty hard. Can ye pick him up? He doesnae weigh much."

It took a little coaxing, but the dog finally allowed Shelton to carry it down the ladder. Ballard was glad Shelton went down first for he was feeling weak and might need some help himself. He let Clover precede him, feeling her pain as she winced over her own bruises and badly chafed wrists. When it was his turn, he descended the steps slowly. At the bottom he swayed and took a moment to recover, waving away Shelton and Clover's attempts to help him as they left the barn.

"I will be fine," he said, and draped his arm around Clover's shoulders.

"So you finally succeeded in a rescue," teased Lambert as he stepped forward. "You do not look as if it was an easy one."

"Nay, it wasnae. My side needs to be re-bandaged and Clover's wrists need tending to."

Cyril arrived and took over. In no time he had Ballard patched up again. It annoyed Ballard that Theodore was the one to see to Clover's injuries. Shelton found some ale in the house. Although it was of a poor quality they all had a drink.

"I suppose this must all be reported to the authorities," said Clover.

"Weel, aye, but ye need not worry that it will cause us any more trouble," Ballard assured her.

"Five men are dead. Although they deserved it, it must raise some questions."

"None we cannae answer. Fact is, we willnae have to answer any." Ballard smiled at Cyril.

"You see, m'dear," said Cyril, "the circuit judge gave me the power to act as magistrate. He will take my word for what happened without question or repercussions. It is over, Clover. You can put it all from your mind now."

"That is a relief." She smiled at Ballard. "Now perhaps we can begin to live a normal life."

Ballard briefly returned her smile, then said, "I suppose we ought to put Thomas in the ground as weel."

"He does not deserve a proper burial, but, yes, we will bury him." Cyril looked at Theodore, Lambert, and Shelton. "I should not be too particular as we ought to be getting back."

As soon as the men left to carry out the grisly chore of disposing of Thomas's body, Cyril asked Clover, "Is there anyone back in Langleyville we should notify?"

"His wife, Sarah Marsten. I can give you her address."

"Do you think she will cause any trouble?"

Clover considered for a moment before shaking her head. "No. I suspect she will relish her new role as wealthy widow to the fullest."

"Good. That will ensure that we will hear no more of it."

An hour later, they all mounted and set out for Cyril Potsdam's home.

Molly, Jonathan, Agnes, and Colin all burst out of the house as they rode up. Clover found herself even more wearied by the constant rounds of questions and explanations. Finally Ballard politely ordered everyone to be quiet. He told them the whole story clearly and succinctly, then asked that they be taken home.

Clover found herself in the back of the wagon, securely wrapped in a blanket and Ballard's arms. As the murmur of conversation drifted around her, she savored the feel of Ballard, warm and alive. Finally she was able to put the last of her fears to rest.

"Did he hurt ye, lass?" Ballard asked in a near whisper so that the others could not hear.

"Thomas did not have a chance to do all he threatened. He was still talking about it and trying to frighten me."

"I am verra glad to hear it, lass," he muttered, tightening his arms around her.

"And I cannot tell you how glad I was to see you

standing in that hayloft, alive and ready to fight. I really did think you were out on this road dying a horrible, slow death."

Ballard kissed her cheek. "Ye should ken by now that it isnae easy to kill a MacGregor. We have had people trying for years and still we go on."

She tentatively reached out to pat the dog's head in Ballard's lap. "Do you think this poor fellow will recover from his hard life?"

"Aye. The fact that he takes to a touch of kindness so weel shows that they hadnae turned him mean yet."

"What will you name him?"

"The Bruce."

"The Bruce? That is an odd name for a dog."

"'Tis the name of one of Scotland's greatest kings. The beastie saved our lives. 'Tis right that he have a grand name."

Clover smiled faintly when the dog shyly licked her hand.

When they arrived home, Clover found herself again caught up in a confusion of greetings from friends and relatives. The twins and Willie had to be reassured that she was all right before her mother and Molly could get her up to bed. They gave her a hot bath and tucked her in as if she were a small child again. When Ballard finally came to bed, his hair still damp, she realized that the men had done the same for him.

"We have rather a lot of people looking after us," she murmured as he slid beside her and pulled her into his arms.

"Aye. It can occasionally be irritating, but at times

like this, ye can see the worth of such good friends and family."

She snuggled closer to him. "We shall have to keep that in mind when we grow annoyed over their mothering in the next few days."

Ballard laughed softly. "Aye. We shall try to remind each other."

He held her close as she drifted off to sleep. A few days was all he could wait before he confronted the need to give her her freedom, if that was what she wanted. He would let her fully recover first, enjoying the chance to take care of her. It hurt to think of her leaving him, but he knew he would have to hide his feelings. Clover was so loyal, she might stay with him if she thought he cared for her. The thought of her remaining his wife because she did not want to hurt his feelings, because she felt duty-bound to him, was appalling. He would release Clover to go back to the life she deserved, but without letting her know how deeply it hurt him.

Chapter Seventeen

Something was wrong. It had been over a fortnight since her rescue from Thomas, and Ballard had been acting strangely every one of those sixteen days.

At times he was almost desperately attentive. The first night they had been well enough to make love, and every night since then, there had been a ferocity to his lovemaking. Although it thrilled her, its cause worried her. At other times he seemed to be drawing away from her, trying to put some distance between them. His words had a rough edge; his behavior was sometimes surly. He had never been a moody man before and she was at a loss to explain what was ailing him now.

In addition, he seemed to be encouraging her to spend time alone with Theodore Potsdam. The young man had called on them a couple of times right after the rescue, to see how they were mending. Clover appreciated his concern and enjoyed his company, but she was baffled by her husband's refusal to stay and socialize. Instead, he always left them alone together on one pretext or another, and even urged

Theodore to stay longer and return again soon. Ballard had never been a particularly possessive man, but he seemed to be encouraging a relationship that might once have aroused his jealousy. It was almost as if he wanted Clover to develop an emotional attachment to Theodore!

Now, as she stood on the front veranda and waved good-bye to her family, who were all headed off in various directions, she decided to confront Ballard.

Molly was with Jonathan. Agnes and the twins would be spending the day with the Doogans. Shelton, Lambert, and Willie were on the way to Cyril's to deliver the yearling the man had bought. Even Adam was gone, off to court the blacksmith's widow. For once she and Ballard were completely alone.

For a while she busied herself in the kitchen, hoping Ballard would seek her out. He had always done so before when they had been blessed with a rare moment of privacy. But when there was no sign of him after an hour, Clover knew she would have to take the first step.

She was just putting her apron away, intending to go and look for him, when Theodore Potsdam knocked on the open door and strolled into the house. "Hello, Theodore," she greeted him. "Where is Ballard? Did you see him outside?"

"He told me to come on in and keep you company. He has a lot of work to do."

"Does he."

Clover absently waved him toward a seat at the kitchen table and put the kettle on the fire. She leaned against the sink and studied Theodore. He was a handsome young man with thick fair hair and a pleasing face. Again it struck her as odd that her husband was allowing such a man to run free in his home.

"Have I grown a wart?" asked Theodore.

She smiled and shook her head. "No. I was just thinking that something very odd is going on with Ballard. Do you feel that something is—well—not quite right with him?" She set the teapot on the table, spooned tea leaves into it, and filled it with boiling water.

"Odd? How so?" Theodore's eyes twinkled with amusement and understanding. "I thought every husband allowed his wife to spend hours alone with another man."

She set his teacup in front of him with a clink and gave him a mildly reproving look. "How droll. I think I may have a real problem here, Theo."

"Pour us the tea and sit yourself down. I began to think you would never mention it or, worse, would play the martyr and bear all of Ballard's recent slights in tortured silence. 'Tis one reason I have been visiting with such annoying regularity. I thought you might need someone to talk to."

She poured the tea and sat opposite him. "I have plenty of people to talk to."

"True, but they have not noticed anything *odd*, have they? And I suspect you do not wish to intrude on Molly's or your mother's happiness just now. So that leaves me—your newest and dearest friend."

"You can be very irritating when you try."

He grinned. "And often when I make no effort at all." He grew serious and reached across the table to pat her hand. "We may not have known each other for very long, but I consider you and that big Scot my friends. I do not like to see this trouble between you."

She sighed. "I do not like to see it either. What is worse, I do not know its cause. It started after I was rescued yet again." She started to sip her tea and abruptly stopped. "No, Ballard began to act oddly right after the dinner at your father's home. Yet that does not make sense. It was a lovely evening."

"Did he say anything?"

"Not much. He kept asking me if I liked your house, wanted to know if it reminded me of my old home in Langleyville. Why are you smiling?"

"Just amused that a man as smart as Ballard can be such an idiot."

"You are not being very helpful."

He took a scone from a plate on the table. "Since I first began to notice that there was a problem between the two of you, I have given the matter a great deal of thought. Clover, you and Ballard come from very different backgrounds."

"That does not matter."

"No, it does not matter to *you* at all. It is one of the things that makes you so endearing. But such things can matter a great deal to a man. All men like to think they can give their wives everything they need or want. It is possible that the evening you spent at my home reminded Ballard of all that you used to have. I suspect I did not help much by talking about the theater and the opera and such. Right now I suspect Ballard is doing the noble thing—he means to set you free. In fact, I believe he is trying to match us up."

"You may leave now."

Theodore choked on the last bite of his scone and quickly washed it down with a large gulp of tea. "Pardon?"

"You are right in everything you said. I just think you had better go home. After all, it would not do for the son of the magistrate to witness a wife murdering her husband."

He laughed, stood up, leaned over the table, and kissed her cheek. "Do not be too hard on the boy."

"Of course not. I fully intend to have a reasonable discussion with him—right after I strangle him."

A few moments after Theodore departed, Ballard entered the kitchen. Clover was sure Theo had said something to Ballard to get him to come after her. He had that dark, solemn look on his face again. She was heartily sick of it.

"Ballard, we have to talk," she said, and sat down at the kitchen table, motioning for him to join her.

"Aye, we do." He poured himself a large tankard of ale, as if he needed a bracing sip or two to get through the discussion.

Clover was not sure she liked his ready agreement. What if the trouble between them was completely different from what she suspected? What if he truly no longer wanted to be married to her and did not know how to tell her? Nevertheless, she knew she would not rest easy until she knew the truth.

"You have been acting very strangely the last two weeks," she said, silently cursing her trembling voice.

"I have?"

Ballard tried not to show his surprise. He had been working hard at hiding his feelings and he thought he had succeeded. Each time Theodore had visited he had done his best to leave Clover and the man alone. He thought he had executed his machinations with great subtlety. It was unsettling to realize that he had somehow given himself away.

"Yes, you have been acting strange. Ballard, what is wrong? I am sure something is troubling you. You are not a moody man, yet you have certainly behaved like one since we were rescued. I realize that I have brought you a lot of trouble. My Lord, I nearly got you killed and I put your kinsmen and friends in great danger. Yet, now that Thomas is dead—"

Ballard stopped her rambling with a finger against her lips. "The trouble wasnae of your making. Dinnae be blaming yourself for my moods, loving."

"'Tis easy to do when no other reasonable explanation comes to mind. And I have spent over a fortnight trying to understand your behavior."

"I was but wrestling with a decision."

His tone of voice alarmed Clover. He sounded so sad and regretful. Her whole body tensed in readiness for his next words. "A decision?"

"Aye. A decision about ye and it was hard-wrought I can tell ye." Ballard took a long drink of ale to steady himself. "Lass, I ken that ye were nae intended to live in the wilderness, that it isnae your world. So I have decided that it would be kinder to let ye return to the life I dragged ye away from."

Clover stared at him for one full moment as his words throbbed in her mind. It was just as she and Theodore had suspected, but she was still shocked to hear Ballard say it. After all they had been through together, she could not believe he was telling her to go away. It did not make sense. It was certainly the last thing she wanted to hear.

"What do you mean?" she asked, her voice hoarse and unsteady.

"Ye are a lady born and bred, loving. This isnae the life for ye. I am giving ye your freedom."

Stunned, she continued to stare at him. There was no way to ignore or deny what he was saying. He had made it painfully clear.

As pain swept over her, Clover clasped her hand to her mouth to keep from crying out loud. She did not think anything could hurt as badly as his rejection, even though she had thought herself prepared to hear it. Ballard reached toward her and she flinched away. If his words could cut her so deeply, she could not risk his touch.

Then fury began to push through the knots of hurt and sorrow inside her. She would not allow him to hurt her so badly. If Ballard thought that he could discard her so callously, that she would just slink away quietly into the night, he was due for a rude awakening.

"*You* have decided, have you?" she asked in a near hiss of anger as she rose to her feet.

"Now, lass, we both ken that this is for the best."

Ballard watched her warily. For a brief moment he thought he had seen hurt in her eyes, a deep hurt that broke his heart, but he had even less idea how to deal with the intense anger Clover was now displaying.

"The best for whom? The best for you, Mr. Mac-Gregor? And why would being rid of me be good for you? Is there some other woman you prefer to have? Elizabeth perhaps? Am I to be set aside so that you can join up with that whore? Is that why you have been playing the matchmaker? You need not feel so guilty if you can just hand me over to another man, is that it?"

"How can ye think I would be so fickle, so heartless?" he demanded, his fists clenched at his sides.

"Me? *Me?* I am not the one who has just calmly announced he wishes to end our marriage, to cast aside vows spoken before God. I have not been pushing you into another woman's arms in the hope that you would run off with her. There has to be a good reason for your behavior. Since you have not seen fit to give me one, I have supplied it."

"I told ye my reasons. This isnae the life for ye, Clover. Since ye came to Kentucky, the circumstances that made ye marry me have changed. Your mother and brothers will soon be living with Colin Doogan. Ye have no dependents to worry about now. Without them clinging to your skirts, ye are free to return to your old life."

Clover trembled with outrage. Words failed her. Without hesitation she picked up his tankard and poured the ale over his head.

He yelped and glared through the dripping liquid, then slowly, carefully took a linen napkin from the table and wiped his face.

Clover threw the empty tankard against the wall, but her small act of defiance did little to ease her pain and anger. "Have I been such an inadequate wife that you wish to toss me aside like rotted hay?"

Throwing down the napkin, Ballard scrambled to face her as she circled the table. "Nay, ye have done verra weel. But a lass like ye shouldnae have to be working like ye are now. Ye should have servants to wait on ye."

"Have I complained?"

"Nay. Not once. And I have no complaints about how ye are doing as my wife. None at all."

"I see. You are casting me aside because you are

so pleased with me. 'Tis a strange way to thank a person, I must say."

He grasped her by the shoulders and gave her a little shake. "I am doing what is best for ye. Cannae ye see that, loving? Ye deserve so much better than this. I saw that the evening we dined at Cyril Potsdam's. I heard it in every word ye and Theodore exchanged about places and people I ken nothing about. Ye fit into his life so weel that there was no denying the truth to meself any longer. That is the sort of life ye deserve. That is the comfort and elegance ye were born to.

"When ye asked me to be your husband," he went on, "ye had three other people to care for and little chance that ye would ever regain what your father's suicide had taken from ye. Now that Doogan will be caring for your family, ye can return to that fine life, back to the silks and satins and carriages. Ye no longer have to settle for gingham, callused hands, and riding to fetes in a hay wagon. I am certain that Cyril will help you all he can. Theodore certainly will. He likes you and he kens that ye were born to a better life than this."

Clover could not believe what she was hearing. After all she had done, after all she had struggled to learn, Ballard still thought she wanted a pampered life. He really believed that she would welcome a chance to walk away from their marriage, from all that they had together, simply because he could not give her pretty dresses or silver servingware. With a vicious curse, she hit him square in the stomach. She rather savored his grunt of pain.

"Ballard MacGregor, you have got to be the dumbest man I have ever had the misfortune to know! I cannot decide whether to cry or punch you again. Well, Mr. MacGregor, you will not escape this marriage so easily. It is not some horse deal you can slink out of. We are bound by words before God, and bound we will stay."

Ballard straightened painfully and looked at her. Matters were not progressing in the way he had imagined as he had pondered his decision over the last sixteen torturous days. Clover should be a little sad, a little reluctant, but glad of the opportunity to try for the life she had once known. She should be ready to pack up and run to Theodore. Instead she looked as if she wanted to kill him. Ballard was not sure what to do next. He had convinced himself that she could not possibly want the little he could offer, but her reaction was swiftly undermining that conclusion.

"I was just trying to give ye what ye wanted," he said, his voice softened by his increasing uncertainty.

"I begin to think you have no idea what I want, or even who I am, Ballard MacGregor. I am no longer so sure of that myself. I had believed myself married to an intelligent man, but 'tis clear that I was wrong." She shook her head, suddenly overcome by the force of her feelings. "I do not know how on earth I could have fallen in love with such an idiot." Clover gasped and clasped a hand over her mouth. With a cry of frustration, she bolted for their bedroom.

Ballard stared after her, the light of understanding slowly dawning in his brain and then he set out after her.

Clover was wrong to think she could hide away after what she had just said. He had seen her astonishment, knew she had not intended to reveal herself in that way. It only added weight to her impetuous words. Ballard forgot his plans to send her back to her old way of life, to sacrifice his own happiness so that she could be with Theodore. If she loved him, he would never let her go.

He caught up with her just as she was trying to shut the door to their room. He easily held it open, pushed his way inside, and caught her arm. Ignoring her strenuous efforts to escape, he dragged her over to the bed and pinned her down on it.

"Now, mayhap we can have a reasonable talk," he said, trying to catch his breath after their vigorous struggle, to ignore the enticing way her breasts rose and fell.

"There is no being reasonable with you. Get off me," Clover cried, trying to buck him off her. But that only brought her into more intimate contact with his long, lean frame.

"Not until I try and explain what I was doing. Or what I was *trying* to do."

She glared at him. "You were trying to throw your wife away. Worse than that, you had already chosen the man you intended to give her to."

"Nay, lass, never that. Now, cease glaring daggers at me and just listen while I explain." He sighed as he struggled to say the right words. "I want ye, lass, never doubt that. I also want ye to have the very best life ye can possibly have. I saw ye in Cyril's home, saw how weel ye fit, and kenned I could never give ye that."

Clover was slowly beginning to understand. She had struggled with her own doubts about being the wife he needed. Those doubts and fears had rushed to the fore with every meal she had burned and every cow she had failed to milk properly. Ballard had obviously struggled with his own doubts and fears—particularly the doubt that he could ever give her the things he believed she needed and deserved. It was almost laughable. They had both been struggling to do what they thought the other wanted, but never thought to just ask. If they had only indulged in a little honest talking, they might have eased each other's concerns. She could understand how difficult such an honest conversation would have been, however.

"I can live without those things, Ballard," she said in a soft voice, her anger slipping away. "I thought I had succeeded in showing you that."

"But that isnae the point. I can see it so clearly, 'tis hard to understand why ye cannae. Ye shouldnae have to struggle to show me what ye can and cannae live without. Your husband should be able to give ye everything ye could possibly want or need. It was when we dined at Potsdam's that I kenned I would never be able to."

"There you go again—thinking you know exactly what I want and need." Clover felt so frustrated by his obstinacy, she wanted to strike him, but he still had her firmly pinned to the bed. She had to settle for an unsatisfactory scowl.

"Lass, ye wed me because ye needed someone to help ye take care of your family. Ye dinnae need that anymore."

"And so naturally you assume I want to leave." She shook her head. "I am trying so hard to understand how you could come to such a wrongheaded conclusion, but 'tis a little difficult to get beyond the insult of it all."

"I dinnae mean to insult ye. I just want to do what is best."

"And I just want to be your wife. I love you, Ballard, and I want to be with you."

Finally her words seemed to penetrate. His hands relaxed on her. "Lord, lass, I have wanted ye to love me for longer than I ken," he whispered. "Truth to tell, I think I wanted that from the verra beginning. It would certainly explain a lot of the odd emotions that have beset me since the moment I met ye."

"You never gave me any indication that you wanted my love." She hastily thought over everything he had said about marriage and she knew she was right. He had discussed only the practical aspects of their union.

"I didnae want to force ye into something ye were nae ready for or didnae truly feel. 'Tis always easier and safer to deal with the day-to-day aspects of a marriage like ours. Ye needed a provider and I needed a bedmate. True, we didnae look at it that coldly, but I dinnae think we looked too much further either. And, to be honest, I wasnae sure what I truly felt until I came to this decision."

"I see. You decide that you care for me and then decide to send me away. It still makes no sense, Ballard."

He grimaced. "Nay, it doesnae. When ye say it that way, it makes me sound nearly as mad as Dillingsworth. Hellfire, mayhap I am. Since the day I met ye, I have certainly felt a wee bit mad from time to time." He pressed his forehead against hers, further easing his grip on her. "I dinnae ken what to do now, loving. It took every scrap of will I have to let ye go, but ye have cast that all asunder in about ten minutes. I do love ye, Clover, and I can never tell ye what it means to have ye love me."

The words Clover had so longed to hear dropped so easily from his lips that it took her a moment to realize he had said them. Then she curled her arms around his neck and gave him a light kiss. Concentrating on how they felt about each other might well be the way to convince him that his grand plan was in error. "You could try to show me."

"I would like to, but we still have nae sorted this out. I dinnae think I will ever be as rich as Potsdam." He grunted when she hit him lightly.

"Stop that this instant," she ordered. "I was just feeling very pleasant and you ruined the mood with more idiocy. I am *not* such a spoiled, selfish child that I cannot be happy without a pile of things scattered around me. I love you, Ballard MacGregor. Try to use the wit I know you have and think on the answer to these questions. Would I love a man I did not have complete faith in? Would I love a man I thought was a failure? Would I love a man who did not make me happy?"

Ballard stared at her. He could see the truth of her emotions in her eyes, which had turned a rich, enticing blue. It both elated and stunned him. Clover did love him, rough manners and all. And she would not love him if she was not completely satisfied with him and what he could offer her.

Since he did not know what to say next, he kissed her hoping to relay through touch all the things he could find no words to express. Her response was immediate and passionate. His own desire, already stirred by the knowledge that she loved him, flared to full life. Ballard did not think he could get her clothes off fast enough, and the way Clover tugged at his shirt and breeches told him that she felt the same.

Once they were both naked, he eased his body over hers, savoring the sensation of their flesh pressing together. He wanted to make love slowly, to show her how much he cherished her, but then she moved her hands down his sides and he knew that it would be impossible to go slowly. His emotions were too fierce, his passion too intensely urgent.

Clover reveled in his frantic lovemaking. It soothed many of her hurt feelings. She had wanted to hold him in that intimate embrace since he had confessed to loving her. It was the best way she knew of showing him how much his love meant to her.

She left no part of his lean frame untouched or untasted, and he did the same to her. Knowing that he returned her love made Clover's desire so intense, she grew as fierce in her passion as Ballard was in his, fighting him to return kiss for kiss, stroke for stroke. One moment she was on top, the next he was, until they were a blissfully heated tangle of flesh and linen.

Their releases shook them both simultaneously. Ballard collapsed in her arms. She held him close and hoped he would never again talk of her leaving him. After the passion they had just shared, he must know that there was no place else she wanted to be. Such intense lovemaking must have burned away his doubts and fears, just as it had hers.

"Ah, loving," he murmured when he finally eased the intimacy of their embrace and rubbed his wounded side. "I think we had best keep a tighter rein on that fire until we are completely healed." He kissed her wrist, then pulled her back into his arms.

"So you have decided I can stay?" she murmured, and grinned when he cursed against her neck.

"How do ye make my good intentions sound so idiotic?" he muttered.

"Perhaps because they are." She smiled at him when he lifted his head to give her a cross look. "Ah, Ballard, you are such a good man." She kissed him briefly. "With a little work I will yet cure you of these bouts of stupidity." She giggled when he tickled her in retribution.

"I didnae ken that ye loved me, Clover," he said quietly when they relaxed again.

"Would that have made a difference?"

"All the difference in the world. When did ye ken that ye loved me?" He idly drew designs on her taut stomach as he waited for her answer.

"When I came back that day after Big Jim had grabbed me and I wanted you to hold me so badly, to show how pleased you were that I was safe." She almost laughed at the look of dismay on her husband's face.

"And I stood there like a dumb oaf. I am sorry. That must have added to the turmoil ye suffered that day."

"To put it mildly. You were clearly feeling in some turmoil as well, so 'tis easily forgotten."

"Why didnae ye tell me? Ye forgave me for that, believed in me when I told ye what had happened, and we were close again. Why didnae ye tell me then that ye love me?"

"Because we had never discussed love as part of this marriage." She smiled at his startled look. "We talked of sharing work, of building a life together, and even of children, but we had never mentioned love."

"And I never did get around to courting ye," he said, mildly disgusted with himself.

"I should not worry about that. I did not miss it." Clover lightly traced his face with her fingertips and knew she would never tire of looking at it. "We had a great deal to resolve and Thomas's attacks gave us little time for such frivolity."

"Weel, maybe now that the danger has passed we can go away somewhere together—alone—as newly-wed folk are supposed to do. We can steal a few moments of privacy, something we dinnae get enough of. Then I can practice a wee bit of courting."

"I would like that." She murmured her appreciation when he gave her a slow, deep kiss. "Perhaps we should invite Theodore." She laughed, then grew serious. "When did you decide that you loved me?" she asked softly.

"When we were coming home from Potsdam's and I thought of how I had to let you go."

"Well, perhaps you have paid enough of a price for such idiocy."

"Oh, aye, lass. I have paid ten times over since devising that mad plan."

She cupped his face in her hands. "And we will never have such foolishness again?"

Ballard smiled at her. "Not if ye keep reminding me that ye dinnae want to leave."

"Oh, I shall have no trouble making you believe that right here in your arms is exactly where I want to stay. All you have to do is remind me that here is where you want me."

He touched his lips to hers. "That will be the most pleasurable chore any woman has ever asked of a mon."

An enchanting new novel from New York Times *bestselling author Hannah Howell that will make you believe in the power of destiny—and desire—all over again . . .*

SHE SEES HIS FACE EVERYWHERE . . .

Lady Alethea Vaughn Channing is haunted by a vision of a man in danger—the same man who she has seen in dreams time and time again. She doesn't even know his name, and yet she feels the connection between them, knows she is the only one standing between him and disaster . . .

. . . YET THEY HAVE NEVER MET

But rakish Lord Hartley Greville is capable of protecting himself, as he has proven more than once in his perilous work as a spy for the crown. If he's to carry out his duty, he'll need to put aside the achingly beautiful woman with the strange gift. And yet, when Alethea's visions reveal a plot that could endanger children, Hartley will not be able to ignore the destiny that binds them together—or resist the passion burning between them . . .

Please turn the page for an exciting sneak peek of

IF HE'S WILD,
coming in June 2010!

Alethea Vaughn Channing looked up from the book she was trying to read to stare into the colorful flames in the massive fireplace and immediately tensed. That man was there again, taking shape within the dancing flames and curling smoke. She tried to tear her gaze away, to ignore him and return her attention to her book, but the vision drew her, ignoring her wants and stealing her choices.

He was almost family for there was no denying that they had grown up together. She had been seeing glimpses of the man since she was but five years old, although he had been still a boy then. Fifteen long years of catching the occasional peek into his life had made her somewhat proprietary about the man, even though she had no idea who he was. She had seen him as a gangly, somewhat clumsy youth, and as a man. She had seen him in dreams, in visions, and had even sensed him at her side. An unwilling witness, she had seen him in pain, watched him weep, known his grief and his joy and so much more. She had even seen him on her wedding night, which had been oddly comforting since her late husband had been noticeably absent. At times, the strange connection was painfully intense; at others it was only the whisper of emotion. She did not like invading his privacy yet nothing she had ever done had been able to banish him.

This was a strong vision, she thought, as the images before her grew so clear it was as if the people were right in the room with her. Alethea set her book down and moved to kneel before the fire, as a tickle of unease grew stronger within her. Suddenly she knew this was not just another fleeting intrusion into the man's life, but a warning. Perhaps, she mused as she concentrated, this was what it had all been leading to. She knew, without even a hint of doubt, that what she was seeing now was not what *was* or what *had been*, but what was to come.

He was standing on the steps of a very fine house idly adjusting his clothes. She could smell roses and then grimaced with disgust. The rogue had obviously just come from the arms of some woman. If she judged his expression right, he wore that smirk her maid Kate claimed men wore after they had just fed their manly hungers. Alethea had the suspicion her vision man fed those hungers a lot.

A large black carriage pulled up. She almost stuck her hand in the fire as a sudden fierce urge to pull him back when he stepped into it swept over her. Then, abruptly and without warning, her vision became a dizzying array of brief, terrifying images, one after another slamming into her mind. She cried out as she suffered his pain along with him, horrible continuous pain. They wanted his secrets but he would not release them. A scream tore from her throat and she collapsed, clutching her throat as a sharp, excruciating pain ripped across it. Her vision man died from that pain. It did not matter that she had not actually seen his death, that the fireplace held only flame and wispy smoke again. She had suffered it, suffered the cold inside his body as his blood flowed out of him. For one terrifying moment, she had suffered a deep, utter desolation over that loss.

The sound of her servants hurrying into the room broke through Alethea's shock as she crawled toward the table where she kept her sketchbooks and drawing materials. "Help me to my seat, Kate," she ordered her buxom young maid as the woman reached for her.

"Oh, m'lady, you have had yourself a powerful seeing this time, I be thinking," said Kate as she steadied Alethea in her seat. "You should have a cup of hot, sweet tea, you should, and some rest. Alfred, get some tea," she ordered the tall, too thin butler who no longer even attempted to explain the hierarchy of servants to Kate.

"Not yet. I must get this all down ere I forget."

Alethea was still very weak by the time she had sketched out all she had seen and written down all she could recall. She sipped at the tea a worried Alfred served her and studied what she had done. Although she dreaded what she had to do now, she knew she had no choice.

"We leave for London in three days," she announced, and almost smiled at the look of shock on her servants' faces.

"But, why?" asked Kate.

"I must."

"Where will we stay? Your uncle is at the town-house."

"It is quite big enough to house us while I do what this vision is compelling me to do."

"And what does it compel you to do, milady?" asked Alfred.

"To stop a murder."

"You *cannot* meet with Lord Hartley Greville."

Alethea frowned at her uncle who was only seven years older than she was. She had been too weary to speak much with him when she had arrived in London yesterday after three days on the road. Then she had slept too late to breakfast with him. It had pleased her to share a noon meal with him and she had quickly told him about her vision. He had been intrigued and eager to help until she had shown him the sketch she had made of the man she sought. Her uncle's handsome face had immediately darkened with a scowl.

"Why not?" she asked as she cut a piece of ham and popped it in her mouth.

"He is a rake. If he was not so wealthy, titled, and of such an impressive lineage, I doubt he would be included on many lists of invitations. If the man notches his bedpost for each of his conquests, he is probably on his third bed by now."

"Oh my. Is he married?"

"Ah, no. Considered to be a prime marriage candidate, however. All that money and good blood, you see. Daughters would not complain as he is also young and handsome."

"Then he cannot be quite so bad, can he? I mean,

if mothers view him as a possible match for their daughters—"

Iago Vaughn shook his head, his thick black hair tumbling onto his forehead. "He is still a seasoned rake. Hard, cold, dangerous, and the subject of a cartload of dark rumor. He has just not crossed that fine line which would make him completely unacceptable." He frowned. "Although, I sometimes wonder if that line is a little, well, fluid as concerns men like him. I would certainly hesitate to nudge my daughter in his direction if I had one. And, I certainly do not wish to bring his attention your way. Introduce a pretty young widow to Greville? People would think I was utterly mad."

"Uncle, if you will not introduce me, I *will* find someone else who will."

"Allie—"

"Do you think he has done anything that warrants his murder?"

"I suspect there are many husbands who think so," muttered Iago as he turned his attention back to his meal, frowning even more when he realized he had already finished it.

Alethea smiled her thanks to the footman who took her plate away and set several bowls of fruit between her and Iago. The moment Iago silently waved the footman out of the room, she relaxed, resting her arms on the table and picking out some blackberries to put into her small bowl. As she covered the fruit with clotted cream, she thought carefully over what she should say next. She had to do whatever she could to stop her vision from becoming a true prophecy, but she did not wish to anger her uncle in doing so.

"If wives are breaking their marriage vows, I believe it is for more reason than a pretty face," she said. "A man should not trespass so yet I doubt he is solely to blame for the sin." She glanced at her uncle and smiled faintly. "Can you say that you have not committed such a trespass?"

Iago scowled at her as he pushed aside his plate, grabbed an apple and began to neatly slice and core it. "That is not the point here and well you know it. The point here is whether or not I will introduce my niece to a known seducer, especially when she is a widow and thus considered fair game. A rogue like him would chew you up and spit you out before you even knew what had happened to you. They say he can seduce a rock."

"That would be an intriguing coupling," she murmured and savored a spoonful of her dessert.

"Brat." He grinned briefly, and then quickly grew serious again. "You have never dealt with a man like him."

"I have never dealt with any man really, save for Edward, and considering how little he had to do with me, I suppose dealing with my late husband for a year does not really count for much."

"Ah, no, not truly. Poor sod."

"Me or him?" She smiled when he chuckled. "I understand your concerns, Uncle, but they do not matter. No," she hastily said when he started to protest. "None of them matter. We are speaking of a matter of life and death. As you say, I am a young widow. If he seduces me, then so be it. That is my business and my problem. Once this difficulty is swept aside, I can return to Coulthurst. In truth, if the man has anywhere near the number of conquests rumor claims, I will just disappear into the horde with barely any notice taken of my passing."

"Why are you being so persistent? You may have misinterpreted this vision."

Alethea shook her head. "No. 'Tis difficult to describe, but I *felt* his pain, felt his struggle not to weaken and tell them what they wanted to know, and felt his death. There is something you need to know. This is not the first time I have had visions of this man. The first was when I was just five years old. This man has been visiting me for fifteen years."

"Good God. Constantly?"

"No, but at least once a year in some form, occasionally more than that. Little peeks at his life, fleeting visions mostly, some clearer than others. There were several rather unsettling ones, when he was in danger, but I was seeing what was or what had been. Occasional dreams, too. Even, well, feelings, as if we had suddenly touched in some way."

"How can you be so sure that this vision was not also what was happened or had already happened?"

"Because amongst the nauseating barrage of images was one of a newspaper dated a moth from that day. And, of course, the fact that the man is still alive." Alethea could tell by the look upon her uncle's face that he would help her, but that he dearly wished he could think of another way than by introducing her to the man. "I even saw him on my wedding night," she added softly.

Iago's eyes widened. "Dare I ask what he was doing?"

"Staring into a fireplace, just as I was, although at least he had a drink in his hand. For a brief moment, I felt as if we were sharing a moment of contemplation, of loneliness, of disappointment, even a sadness.

Not an inspiring vision, yet, odd as it was, I did feel somewhat comforted by it." She shrugged away the thought. "I truly believe all that has gone before was leading up to this moment."

"Fifteen years of preparation seems a bit excessive," Iago drawled.

Alethea laughed but her humor was fleeting and she soon sighed. "It was all I could think of to explain why I have had such a long connection to this man, to a man I have never met. I just wish I knew why someone would wish to hold him captive and torture him before killing him. Why do these people want his secrets?"

"We—ell, there have been a few rumors that he might be working for the home Office, or the military, against the French."

"Of course! That makes much more sense than it being some fit of revenge by some cuckolded husband or jealous lover."

"That also means that a great deal more than your virtue could be in danger."

"True, but it also makes it far more important to rescue him."

"Damn. I suppose it does."

"So, will you help me?"

Iago nodded. "You do realize it will be difficult to explain things to him. People do not understand ones like us, do not believe in our gifts or are frightened by them. Imagine the reaction if, next time I was playing cards with some of my friends, I told one of them that his aunt, who had been dead for ten years, was peering over his shoulder?" He smiled when Alethea giggled.

Although his example was amusing, the hard, cold

fact it illustrated was not. People did fear the gifts so many of her family had. She knew her dreams and visions would cause some people to think she had gone mad. It was one reason she shunned society. Sometimes, merely touching something could bring on a vision. Iago saw all too clearly those who had died and not yet traveled to their final destination. He could often tell when, or why, a person had died simply by touching something or being in the place where it had happened. The only thing she found unsettling about Iago's gift was that, on occasion, he could tell when someone was soon to die. She suspected that, in many ways, he was as alone, as lonely, as she was.

"It does make life more difficult," she murmured. "I occasionally comfort myself with the thought that it could be worse."

"How?"

"We could have cousin Modred's gift." She nodded when Iago winced. "He has become a hermit, afraid to touch anyone, to even draw close to people for fear of what he will feel, hear, or see. To see so clearly into everyone's mind and heart? I think that would soon drive me mad."

"I often wonder if poor Modred is, at least just a little."

"Have you seen him recently?"

"About a month ago. He has found a few more servants, ones he cannot read, with Aunt Dob's help." Iago frowned. "He thinks he might be gaining those shields he needs, but needs to gather the courage to test himself. But, then, how are we any better off that he? You hide at Coulthurst and I hide here."

"True." Alethea looked around the elegant dining

room as she sipped her wine. "I am still surprised Aunt Leona left this place to me and not to you. She had to know you would be comfortable here."

"She was angry that I would not marry her husband's niece."

"Oh dear."

"Quite. I fear she changed her will when she was still angry and then died before the breach between us could be mended."

"You should let me give it to you."

"No. It suits me to rent it from you. I keep a watch out for another place and, if this arrangement ever becomes inconvenient, we can discuss the matter then. Now, let us plan how we can meet up with Lord Greville and make him understand the danger he is in without getting the both of us carted off to Bedlam."

Two nights later, as she and Iago entered a crowded ballroom, Alethea still lacked a sound plan and her uncle had none to offer, either. Alethea clung to his arm as they strolled around the edges of the large room. Glancing around at all the elegant people, she felt a little like a small blackbird stuck in the midst of a flock of peacocks. There was such a vast array of beautiful, elegant women; she had to wonder why her uncle would ever think she had to worry about her virtue. A hardened rake like Lord Hartley Greville would never even consider her worth his time and effort when there was such a bounty to choose from.

"Are you nervous?" asked Iago.

"Terrified," she replied. "Is it always like this?"

"Most of the time. Lady Barnelby's affairs are always well attended."

"And you think Lord Greville will be one of the crowd?"

Iago nodded. "She is his cousin, one of the few family members left to him. We must keep a sharp watch for him, however. He will come, but he will not stay long. Too many of the young women here are hunting a husband."

"I am surprised that you would venture forth if it is that dangerous."

"Ah, but I am only a lowly baron. Greville is a marquis."

Alethea shook her head. "You make it all sound like some sordid marketplace."

"In many ways, it is. Oh, good, I see Aldus and Gifford."

"Friends of yours?" Iago started to lead her toward the far corner of the ballroom, but she was unable to see the men he spoke of around the crowd they weaved through.

"No, friends of the marquis. He will be sure to join them when he arrives."

"Misery loves company?"

"Something like that. Oh damn."

Before Alethea could ask what had caused her uncle to grow so tense, a lovely, fulsome redhead appeared at his side. If she judged her uncle's expression correctly, he was not pleased to see this woman and that piqued Alethea's interest. Looking more closely at the woman's classically beautiful face, Alethea saw the hint of lines about the eyes and mouth and suspected the woman was older than Iago. The look the woman gave her was a hard and assessing one. A moment later something about the woman's demeanor told Alethea that she had not measured up well in the woman's eyes, that she had just been judged as inconsequential.

"Where have you been, Iago, darling?" the woman asked. "I have not seen you for a fortnight."

"I have been very busy, Margarite," Iago replied in a cool, distant tone.

"You work too hard, my dear. And who is your little companion?"

"This is my niece, Lady Alethea Channing," Iago said, his reluctance to make the introduction a little too clear in his tone. "Alethea, this is Mrs. Margarite Dellingforth."

Alethea curtsied slightly. The one Mrs. Dellingforth gave her in return was so faint she doubted the woman even bent her knees at all. She was glad Iago had glanced away at that precise moment so that he did not see the insult to his kinswoman. The tension roused by this increasingly awkward confrontation began to wear upon Alethea's already taut nerves. Any other time she knew she would have been fascinated by the subtle, and not so subtle, nuances of the conversation between her uncle and Mrs. Dellingforth, but now she just wanted to cold-eyed woman to leave. She leaned against Iago and began to fan her face.

"Uncle, I am feeling uncomfortably warm," she said in what she hoped was an appropriately weak, sickly tone of voice.

"Would you like to sit down, m'dear?" he asked.

"You should not have brought her here if she is ill," said Mrs. Dellingforth.

"Oh, I am not ill," said Alethea. "Simply a little overwhelmed."

"If you will excuse us, Margarite, I must tend to my niece," said Iago even as he began to lead Alethea toward some chairs set against the wall.

"Not a very subtle retreat, Uncle," murmured Alethea, quickening her step to keep pace with his long stride.

"I do not particularly care."

"The romance has died, has it?"

"Thoroughly, but she refuses to leave it decently buried."

"She is quite beautiful." Alethea sat down in the chair he led her to and smoothed down her skirts.

"I know, that is how I became ensnared to begin with." He collected two glasses of wine from the tray a footman paused to offer them, and handed Alethea one. "It was an extremely short affair. To be blunt, my lust was quickly satisfied and, once it eased, I found something almost repellent about the woman."

Seeing how troubled thoughts had darkened his hazel green eyes, Alethea lightly patted his hand. "If it is any consolation, I, too, felt uneasy around her. I think there is a coldness inside her."

"Exactly what I felt." He frowned and sipped his drink. "I felt some of the same things I do when I am near someone who will soon die, yet I know that is not true of her."

"What sort of feelings?"

He grimaced. "It is hard to explain, but it is as if some piece of them is missing, has clearly left or been taken."

"The soul?"

"A bit fanciful, but, perhaps, as good an explanation as any other. Once my blind lust faded, I could not abide to even touch her for I could sense that chilling emptiness. I muttered some pathetic excuse and fled her side. She appears unable to believe that I want no more to do with her. I think she is accustomed to being adored."

"How nice for her." Alethea sipped her drink as she watched Mrs. Dellingforth talk to a beautiful fair-haired woman. "Who is that with her now?"

"Her sister Madame Claudette desRouches."

"They are French?"

"Émigrés. Claudette's husband was killed for being on the wrong side in yet another struggle for power and Margarite married an Englishman shortly after arriving."

"For shame, you rogue. A married lady? Tsk, tsk."

"A widow, you brat. Her husband died six months after the wedding."

"How convenient. Ah, well, at least Margarite did not stink of roses. If she had, I might have been forced to deal with her again."

Iago scratched his cheek as he frowned in thought. "No, Margarite does not use a rose scent. Claudette does."

Alethea stared at the two women and briefly wished she had a little of her cousin Modred's gift. It would make solving this trouble she had been plunged into so much easier if she could just pluck the truth from the minds of the enemy. She suspected she would quickly be anxious to be rid of such a gift, however. If she and Iago both got unsettling feelings from the two women, she hated to think what poor Modred would suffer with his acute sensitivity. Although she would prefer to avoid both women, she knew she would have to at least approach the sister who favored roses at some point. There was a chance she could gain some insight, perhaps even have a vision. Since a man's life was at stake, she could not allow fear over what unsavory truths she might uncover hold her back.

"I believe we should investigate them a little," she said.

"Because they are French and Claudette smells of roses?"

"As good a reason as any. It is also one way to help solve this problem without revealing ourselves too much."

Iago nodded. "Very true. Simple investigation. I even know a few people who can help me do it." His eyes widened slightly. "Considering some of the lovers those two women have had, I am surprised they have not already been investigated. Now that I think on it, they seem overly fond of men who would know things useful to the enemy."

"And no one has seen them as a threat because they are beautiful women."

"It galls me to say so, but you may be right about that. Of course, this is still all mere speculation. Nevertheless, they should be investigated and kept a watch on simply because they are French and have known, intimately, a number of important men."

Alethea suddenly tensed, but, for a moment, she was not sure why she was so abruptly and fiercely alert. Sipping her champagne, she forced herself to be calm and concentrate on exactly what she was feeling. To her astonishment, she realized she was feeling *him*. He was irritated, yet there was a small flicker of pleasure. She suspected that hint of pleasure came from seeing his cousin.

"Allie!"

She blinked slowly, fixing her gaze on her uncle. "Sorry. You were saying?"

"I was just wondering if you had a vision," he replied in a soft voice. "You were miles away."

"Ah, no. No vision. Just a feeling."

"A feeling?"

"Yes. He is here."

ABOUT THE AUTHOR

Hannah Howell is an award-winning author who lives with her family in Massachusetts. She is the author of thirty-two Zebra historical romances and is currently working on a new historical romance, IF HE'S WILD, coming in June 2010! Hannah loves hearing from readers and you may visit her website: www.hannahhowell.com.

More by Bestselling Author
Hannah Howell

Romantic Suspense from
Lisa Jackson

See How She Dies	0-8217-7605-3	$6.99US/$9.99CAN
Final Scream	0-8217-7712-2	$7.99US/$10.99CAN
Wishes	0-8217-6309-1	$5.99US/$7.99CAN
Whispers	0-8217-7603-7	$6.99US/$9.99CAN
Twice Kissed	0-8217-6038-6	$5.99US/$7.99CAN
Unspoken	0-8217-6402-0	$6.50US/$8.50CAN
If She Only Knew	0-8217-6708-9	$6.50US/$8.50CAN
Hot Blooded	0-8217-6841-7	$6.99US/$9.99CAN
Cold Blooded	0-8217-6934-0	$6.99US/$9.99CAN
The Night Before	0-8217-6936-7	$6.99US/$9.99CAN
The Morning After	0-8217-7295-3	$6.99US/$9.99CAN
Deep Freeze	0-8217-7296-1	$7.99US/$10.99CAN
Fatal Burn	0-8217-7577-4	$7.99US/$10.99CAN
Shiver	0-8217-7578-2	$7.99US/$10.99CAN
Most Likely to Die	0-8217-7576-6	$7.99US/$10.99CAN
Absolute Fear	0-8217-7936-2	$7.99US/$9.49CAN
Almost Dead	0-8217-7579-0	$7.99US/$10.99CAN
Lost Souls	0-8217-7938-9	$7.99US/$10.99CAN
Left to Die	1-4201-0276-1	$7.99US/$10.99CAN
Wicked Game	1-4201-0338-5	$7.99US/$9.99CAN
Malice	0-8217-7940-0	$7.99US/$9.49CAN

Available Wherever Books Are Sold!
Visit our website at **www.kensingtonbooks.com**